MW00963803

As much as she tried not to think about what had happened between them that night, for the life of her she couldn't figure out why Lovell didn't understand that he was Barbara Jean's man. Barbara Jean's man! And it was high time he started acting like it. Or was it that he was so bold and full of himself that he thought he could be with the both of them? As far as she was concerned, what they had almost done by allowing passion to take control that night while her mother was out somewhere being robbed had been wrong. And in no way, none, was it happening again...

OCT 1 2002

3 1116 01618 2682

Genesis Press, Inc.
315 Third Avenue North
Columbus, MS 39701
www.genesis-press.com

Copyright © 1999 by Debra Phillips

Kiss or Keep

ISBN   1-885478-96-8

All rights reserved. No part of this publication may be repro-
duced or transmitted in any form or by any means, electronic
or mechanical, including photocopy, recording, or any information storage and retrieval system, without permission in
writing from the publisher.

Manufactured in the United States of America

FIRST EDITION

Book design by Susan R. Simpson

Kiss or Keep

by

Debra Phillips

INDIGO

Dedication

To my husband Reginald.
Without his love and
patience, this dream would
not have been possible.

Kiss or Keep

by

Debra Phillips

Chapter One

Lovell Joyner felt it the moment he steered his shiny white Cadillac Seville onto the oil stained driveway. There was no denying it. The feeling was deep, like a cool shiver running down to his core. Something was wrong.

His newly manicured nails clutched the steering wheel tighter, then released it. He loved when his nails shone and glistened in the sunlight. Nothing that he could think of compared to the feel of having his nails freshly done. Well, almost nothing. Actually, it was the same way with his hair. After coming from Bloodshaww's Barber Shop with his nice hip-hop modern hair trim that left a little at the sides and more at the top, he had been feeling something good. A seeped-in good like he could conquer the world.

He loved days like these—clear, sun-drenched Saturdays with happy birds chirping in the distance, and more sun than he could ever wish for. More of what he called picnicking at the park kind of weather. For once, man talk at Bloodshaww's had been tantalizing and somewhat stimulating. Even though the subject, true to the nature of most males, had been mostly fabricated tales about women and the constant pursuit of more money, he had made it a point to put more than his two cents worth in. He felt good and proud just being a man. Good feelings were still trying to cling to him, at least they should have been. But something was wrong.

It wasn't something that he could actually put his finger on, or give a solitary name to. But unmistakably, a strong foreboding tugged at his insides as he climbed from the overly warm car and stood with a hand hooding his eyes from the late September sunlight.

Pride smiled across his thirty-two-year-old face as he gazed affectionately at his blooms. The house he shared with Rita, a two-bedroom rental, was really perking up with the fresh new coat of sky blue paint and royal blue trim he'd added. But his blooms were the icing on the cake.

Rich orange and yellow marigolds lined the short walkway leading up to the new oaken door while magnificent yellow, red, and blue ribbon gladiolus hugged each side of the modest structure. Red and yellow roses at the front beneath the French style window. Though he wasn't one to brag about it, he secretly reveled in the fact that if it came in a seed, he could grow it.

For he had selected each plant and bulb with the same intensity of a man selecting the sex of his own offspring. He had actually gotten down on his hands and knees, low to the earth, and planted every seed, bulb, and starter plant one by one. Sometimes he felt like the rich soil itself was his second home. Even from his early childhood, digging down deep into the cool earth had been a regular ritual to him, a calling. If all went okay, next weekend he would plant some Carolina Jasmine, too. Maybe even throw in some yellow Day Lilies, his favorite.

Not ashamed to admit it, Lovell considered himself a man who loved flowers—everything about them. The mere idea of life rising out from the earth like tender green people with multi-hued souls was a fascination that never left him. But now, as he stood looking over his created splendor, the September heat was like a hostile enemy, waiting. The very air around him didn't feel in sync with nature.

The air felt too thick, like clear blue walls slowly easing in for the kill. The sensation tensed his muscles. Even his wonderful blooms somehow seemed different to gaze upon. They looked sinister, like muted yellow and red aliens trying to warn him. But warn him of what?

Shrugging the feeling off, Lovell closed up his car, flung his beige Members Only jacket casually over his shoulder, and headed for the door.

For the most part, the heat of the day had gotten the best of him. The steam and ickyness under his arms alone was enough to drive him crazy. A tall glass of lemonade and a nice cool shower before dinner would do him justice after having a shave and haircut. His hair was looking good, which made it all the better for him to be feeling the same. Passing his roses, he reached over and carefully broke off a red stem bud barely opening. He sniffed the heavenly fragrance and smiled inward. For his Rita. Something pretty for the pretty. And good Lord, he thought, it sure would be nice if Rita-girl had fried up some of her southern style chicken. Lord, that woman can cook some chicken, he mused. She didn't do too bad on some butter-whipped potatoes either.

Inserting his key into the lock, he could almost smell and actually taste Rita's chicken in his mouth, each spice and herbal seasoning like magic specks along his tongue and dancing with his taste buds. But the thought dropped away like stones from a hilltop, quickly replaced by the realization that his key wasn't turning in the lock. "Say what now?"

He took his key out to examine it. The thing looked okay. He turned it sideways and looked at it. Nope. No dents or bending along the cuts. He tried it again. The shiny metal slid in easily, a perfect fit into the slot, but when he turned the key, nothing happened. No pins clicked to signal his right to enter.

"Darn kids," he chided softly to himself. Lovell knew that he shouldn't be so critical and ready to blame Rita's two kids, but what else could it be? It had to have been one of Rita's boys breaking something off in the lock.

He'd been with Rita a good ten months already, and he had to admit it himself—Rita was a good catch. The sister had it going on. The woman had a good paying job as an Engineer for a major aircraft company in Long Beach. She kept herself smelling and looking good. Her nails, her hair, the works. This alone was worth a good eight points on his mental scale to ten. She kept a clean house, and when it came to cooking up a good meal, hell, even Julia Child herself didn't have nothing on Rita. But those two young boys of hers were another story. Twice last month he'd found broken off pieces of wood stuck in his car door. Little good it did to tell Rita about their constant pranks. In her eyes they were earth-walking angels. Six and seven year-old, budding hoodlums, if anybody asked him. Always off somewhere doing something stupid, like sticking something in a door lock to keep him constantly doing some work around the place.

"Damn," he muttered under his breath.

Taking in a deep, agitated breath, he rang the doorbell. It was Saturday, a little after three in the afternoon, which meant that Rita was probably doing her exercise routine in front of the living room television while those boys of hers scouted the neighborhood on their daily mission of destruction.

Yep, he smiled to himself at the thought of Rita doing her exercise. His baby was built like a Texas brick house. He had to give that another three points. Not too big and not too small. Just the right size for a man like himself.

What was taking her so long to answer? Lovell pushed the white button again. After ten or more seconds, he got a mental flash to just go around to the rear entrance. For her boys, who constantly ran in and out of the house, it was a habit for Rita to leave the back door unlatched. He frowned at the thought. More than once he'd tried to explain to Rita the risk of keeping a door unlocked in a dangerous city like Los Angeles. But little good it did. Besides, he figured, there wasn't much he could do about it. Just to make sure, he tried the door bell one last time, counting down from ten. Maybe the woman was asleep or taking a shower. Nine, eight, seven, six.

With a sudden whoosh, the door flung open with a force so hard Lovell's long dark eyelashes fluttered. His eyes grew wide as he gasped and sucked air back into his throat. His sight was trying to deceive him—too much sunlight was in his eyes.

Everything that had ever felt like it was wrong in his heart, his consciousness, his life even, was now standing right before him: a large man. A large and shiny black man he'd never seen before. Standing right in the very door of his house. Well, almost his house. *For all the work I do around this place*, he thought, allowing indignance to slip over him, *it's my house too*.

The big man didn't blink or crack a smile or look nothing like friendly. "Can I help you?"

"Say what?" Lovell leaned slightly back and gazed up like any fool at a sudden loss for words. He sized the man up, then quickly found himself wondering if he could take him if things got out of hand. The single rose dropped from his hand, forgotten.

"I said, can I help you?"

"Who the heck are you?" Lovell could feel beads of sweat gathering strength, an army, in the pits of his arms as he stepped back to get a better look.

The dark man blocking his way stood an impressive height, a good six feet two compared to his own five feet and eleven inches. The man's head was shaved clean, giving the comical appearance of a black "Mr. Clean" figure. Lovell thought for sure that he could detect the pleasing aroma of Cool Water Cologne radiating from the man's persona. The thought, for the moment, seemed as humorous as it was absurd. Not only that, but the man was wearing brown silk boxer shorts in his house. Two big, strong-looking mahogany arms sprouted like thick tree trunks from a flimsy white t-shirt, which was something else to consider. He angled his head back and sniffed the air twice. A play on his imagination, perhaps. Lovell thought the man even smelled threatening. A hot red vibe seemed to radiate up and out from him.

Summoning up some courage, Lovell stood his ground. Even the tone of his voice, which at first had been ready and willing to crouch somewhere in the darkness of his throat, took on a different timbre, came out more macho.

"Who the hell are you?"

"I heard you the first time."

It didn't seem possible, but the outside air was suddenly hotter. Outside heat, like invisible hands, pushed at his backside. Chirping birds he'd heard earlier ceased their rampant songs while the air took on a hush. The man was holding the door in a way suggestive of allowing him no passage. Lovell swallowed hard as the big hunk of flesh freed his hands from the door and moved to stand completely in the doorway of his home. The ultimate blockade.

"Anybody should be asking the questions here, should be me. You the one come ringing my door bell."

"What?! Man, I live here." Lovell grimaced and hoped his words sounded braver than he felt. Sizing the man up again, push come to shove, he'd be needing more than just his bare fist for the tackle.

"Oh," chuckled the man, almost cracking a real smile. "You must be Lovell. Well, well now. Guess my baby, Rita, didn't tell you yet, huh?"

"Rita?" Lovell blinked too fast and snorted, as if he was hearing her name, foreign, for the very first time. "Nah, man. Guess she didn't. Tell me what?"

"That you don't live here no more. You've been replaced, evicted, turned away, put out. I'm the new man of the house now. I'm Rita's new man." A menacing smirk tugged at the corners of his mouth as he said this. A weird glint was in the corner of his right eye.

"Is that right?"

"Yeah, that's right."

"Rita's new man?"

"What? Somethin' wrong with your hearing?"

"I wanna speak to Rita then."

From the back of the room Rita's sugary sweet voice cried over, "Baby, who's that you talking to?"

Big or not, Lovell gathered up his strength and aimed his shoulders as he forced his way through the door. "Rita?"

"Hey, man! Watch it!"

Words flying over his head, Lovell shouted back, "Man, I live here!"

Once in the plush living room with its new cream-hued carpet he'd picked out, cream-colored drapes that he'd special ordered, glass and oak coffee table, and antique-white walls that his own hands had lovingly painted, he spied Rita. His Rita. She was looking as fly as always, the picture of perfection as she splayed sensually across the length of the white leather sofa. Her long and flawless cinnamon-touched thighs carelessly showed from under a sinful red Spandex dress.

Moving up closer, Lovell had the sensation of not trusting his own eyes. The woman he'd held so tenderly in his arms the night before, smothered against his masculine chest, and declared his undying love for while cocooned between those very cinnamon thighs was now showing herself boldly for some other man. His Rita!

The big man came up right behind him and stood breathing a warm path down his neck. Standing so close, Lovell could hear the rhythmic beat of the man's heart speeding up to a faster tempo.

Regarding Rita with a questioning look, "Well?" he prompted. Lovell braced himself, standing like a man that should be ready to go off, ready to explode, but held enough sense to know better. "I go out for a few hours for a shave and haircut and I come back to this. Rita, tell me what's up."

Lovell noticed the coffee table where a tall bottle of expensive pale pink wine stood half-empty. That wasn't so bad. It wasn't any secret that occasionally his woman took a drink in mid-day. Usually nothing too strong. No big deal. But next to that he spotted a clear cigarette shaped glass pipe lying next to a magazine. A black coating of smoke was at one end of the pipe, and on the magazine itself, in full view for all the world to see, was the white chunk. The stuff. Not a huge piece, but surely enough for him to be concerned about. According to his Rita, she'd given up smoking crack a good two years ago.

Following his gaze, Rita put her hand down along her luscious thigh and looked at him like a bored spectator at some game show. His head jerked back as if he'd been punched in the face. "Lovell, Lovell. Such a kind-hearted lover. Such a Mr. Goody-two-shoes. Such a lazy live-off-a-woman bum."

"Oh please stop," Lovell smirked, keeping his cool about it. "Just tell me what's up."

Enjoying every slurpy word from her mouth, the big man anxiously threw in, "Want me to kick his butt, baby, huh? Want Big Daddy to fix 'im up for you?" He moved to the side of Lovell to make eye contact.

Calmly, Lovell stared off in his big meaty face, right off into those homicidal looking brown and bloodshot eyes that had to be a tad too close together in a wide face, a face filled with battle scars. Lovell didn't like what he was seeing. That look, a hungry look for violence, made his knees want to buckle.

Smiling, Rita cooed back, "No, sugar. Good ole Lovell here is not the violent type. He'll leave as quiet as he came. Right, Lovell?"

Lovell could feel sweat tickle along his scalp. What had he really expected from a woman he'd met at a club on a Sunday night? Undying love? A lifetime of loyalty? "But baby girl," he tried to reason and tried to put the sweet back in his voice, "help me understand this now. Why you wanna do a brother this way?"

"Man," quipped the big man, "she ain't your baby no more."

"This ain't right, Rita. I don't get it." Clearly angered, Lovell paced up one side of the room and came back to stand, jingling the coins in his pocket. "I just don't get it."

"No?" Rita perked up at his words. "Well, perhaps I should explain it to you, Lovell." She waved a frivolous hand over in the big man's direction. "Meet Maurice, my new man. He lives here now. Sorry, no more free ride."

Be cool, Lovell told himself as his stomach twisted in knots. Stay calm. He clenched his fist, unclenched it. He could feel the muscles in his stomach tightened up. Nervousness sometimes did this to him. Hadn't he read somewhere that ninety percent of all domestic violence cases revolved around love relationships gone bad? He could see how such a thing was possible. No matter how much he tried to live right and stay away from trouble, inevitably, trouble always sought him. Lovell wondered what kind of trouble Rita was trying to cook up now.

"Thought we had something special?"

"Negro, pah-leez. You must be talking about the special thing you had going with my credit card and my wallet. Oh, yes. It was special alright."

"Sure thing," Maurice said and had the nerve to grin ear to ear at her words. Loosening up, he sniffed the air and moved over to the sofa, sat down, and patted Rita's exposed thigh, looking up at Lovell for his reaction. Getting no where with angering Lovell, he went back to the matter of his chunk, breaking off a small piece of the white stuff and placing it at the open end of the glass pipe. Swooping up a butane lighter from the coffee table, Maurice flicked the wheel until yellow-red flame popped up to greet him. After taking a few pulls, he leaned over and offered the pipe to Rita. "Here, baby."

Lovell could feel his own heart speed up. "Ahh, no, Rita. Don't. Don't start back with that again. You don't need that."

"Oh, hell, Lovell," Rita cried, exhaling at the same time. "You think you the right person to be telling me what I need in my life? What I need is a BMW, which for me is a 'black man working'. Thank you."

"Rita, I can get a job."

"Too late for that, Lovell. You no longer live here."

"I'll get a job, Rita. Just give me a chance."

As if her words marked his cue Maurice shot him an impatient look. "Man, you best to get your tired butt outta here and get on the further before I change my mind 'bout you leaving quietly. You don't live here no more. So get with the program."

But Lovell couldn't just let it go. Not this way. "Rita, if this is about a job, I'll get one. You know I can. I'll get one."

She was holding the stuff in her lungs as long as she could. A wonderful rush of lightness seemed to swoop down from some great place and lift her up with careful lovingness, rocking her gently back and forth like a baby being lulled.

Rita exhaled slowly and leaned over reaching for the pipe for another hit, another flight to her own heaven. But too late. Maurice had the glass to his lips pulling hard on the fumes, pulling every bit of the poison deep into his own waiting lungs.

"Ten whole months," Rita yelled over in Lovell's direction. "Count 'em, Lovell. Ten months of feeding you, clothing you, and keeping a roof over your pretty little head. Hmph. I bet you thought that those pretty green eyes of yours would keep me spellbound forever, huh?"

"I'll get a job, Rita. Watch me."

"Yeah. Claim you been looking for one for ten whole months. Why get serious 'bout one now?"

Angrily, Lovell felt a mean chill run up his back. He tossed his jacket to a nearby chair and missed it entirely. It came to rest in a heap along the floor. "So just kick a brother out and go back to crack, huh? All because I don't have a job!"

Maurice hastily lifted one of his bushy black eyebrows. "Hey, man, don't be hollering at my woman in my house."

"Man, this ain't your house either!"

Fingering her straight-edge bangs made shiny and glossed to black, Rita pulled herself up straight. "Yes it is. It's his house now 'cause he can pay the bills. And yes, it's because you don't work. Maurice may be a security guard where I work, but at least he believes in working. You see, Lovell, it's not Christmas right now, and it's certainly not my birthday. I guess that means that those dreaming looking bedroom eyes of yours, that curly black hair and that great body ain't the gift anymore. I'm the gift now. Right, Maurice?" To punctuate her words she leaned over and planted a kiss gently to his lips.

"That's right," Maurice confirmed. "You the gift, baby, and I'm the receiver."

The gift and her new man. Lovell thought they both sounded crazy, like two candidates for the crazy farm. Her words were slaps to his face, leaving Lovell speechless. And even if he did have something worth saying, what good would it do anyway?

"So be a good boy," Rita went on in a tone that Lovell knew that she often used on her own two boys from time to time, "and box up all your little stuff you brought with you, which wasn't much, and just leave."

"Just like that, huh?"

"That's the lick," Maurice added in his own tone of smugness.

Rita gave him another long frivolous sweep of her hand. "Maybe you can hook back up with that Mexican heifer, Yolanda. You know, the one that keeps calling here every now and then and pretending you have some mail at her house to pick up. Maybe wrap yourself up with a nice shiny red bow and give yourself back to her. Tell her it's a gift from me to her."

Lovell couldn't believe the way she was behaving and talking to him, like they were two people on a bad date for the first time. He fished Chapstick from the pocket of his tan Dockers shorts, opened it and swiped the soothing ointment along his lips. "That's real funny, Rita."

"Here, baby." Maurice passed the pipe and lighter to her.

"Fine. I'll get my grip and leave."

Lovell couldn't think straight. Rita's brazen indifference, brought on suddenly like a fever, agitated him to the core as he stormed into the bedroom and went to the closet looking for a piece of luggage. Anything. The large dark blue Samsonite he spotted belonged to Rita, and the way he was feeling, he didn't want to take one thing of hers with him. Nothing that would give him an excuse to get in touch with her after his departure.

He grabbed the few clothes he owned, all expensive pieces of silk shirts and slacks, a couple of Armani suits—a new one purchased a few months back, one older, and a few pairs of expensive Italian alligator shoes. Lovell threw it all on the queen-sized brass bed. He stopped for a moment to take a sweeping look around at what he'd thought was his home. Such a nice room, too. He'd done most of the painting of it himself, carefully choosing the perfect touch of peach for the walls and carpet. A mid-line wall border of painted peaches ringed the entire room. Even the white bedspread had hand-painted peaches all over its entirety. Of course, that had been Rita's selection. To him, hand painted flowers would have been nicer and added a cozier effect.

A large crystal vase of fresh cut flowers sat on the oaken dresser. He'd bought the yellow and red tulips just the other day from the market. Sweet reflections. What had he been thinking then? That he could kiss and stroke himself through a lifetime of her grace? Beautiful flowers. At least once a week he'd made it a point to bring home fresh cut flowers. Mostly because he felt that all women should be surrounded by fresh flowers at all times. To him, a room without fresh cut flowers was like a room without sufficient oxygen.

A tall potted palm tree sat in one corner of the room, a brass coat rack in the other. He bet that monkey-looking Maurice wouldn't be bringing her flowers every week. *What a trip*, he thought. *Put out just like that*. Why hadn't he seen her discontent with him sooner?

It took five large trash bags and four trips to his car to load all his belongings. The whole time the two fools, Rita and her new man, Maurice, went on with their self-absorbed party, smoking and drinking, laughing as if he were a mere spirit hovering back and forth between the rooms.

On his way out for the last time, Rita stopped what she was doing long enough to look up and over at him with a knowing look playing on her face. Her fire engine red lips looked ready to form an 'O'.

"Oh, Lovell," she chimed in her sweet tone. "Don't forget to leave that nice diamond and onyx ring I bought you last month."

"No problem." Big deal, Lovell felt. He hadn't asked for the damn ring to begin with. He went back over to stand in front of the coffee table while twisting and pulling the gold band from his finger. Once off, he tossed it haphazardly to her lap.

"And my Mastercharge," Rita prompted.

Maurice dropped his head and shook it. "You gave the dude your Mastercharge to keep? Damn, baby. You was too good to his worthless behind."

Rita smiled in affirmation. "You know it too."

Lovell wondered about her two destructive boys. He hadn't seen them since he'd returned, and it really wasn't his business to be asking, at least not now. But what the heck. "Where's Kenny and Tyrone?"

High and tipsy, Rita threw her head back and grinned up at him with amusement playing across her face. "Excuse me?"

"You know," Lovell said boldly. ". . .your two sons. You do recall that you have two kids living here? Won't do 'em no good to see their mama laying up with some strange man hitting a pipe."

From the buttoned pocket of his cotton Dockers, Lovell took out his wallet and found her credit card and tossed the plastic to the coffee table. Already he felt the pain of absence. The stupid diamond ring he could do without, but he would truly miss her card. One of the main things he'd liked about Rita was her generosity. The same day she had received the card in the mail, she'd happily turned it over to him, making it clear that his spending for necessary things wouldn't present a problem. "You don't even know where the boys are, do you?"

Maurice frowned up at him. "It really ain't yo' business no more. Now is it?"

"Negroe man, pah-leez," Rita droned. "Like you care so much. For your information, I dropped the kids off at my sister's for the day. You know, you really got some nerve. You have never been concerned about my boys before, so don't even go there." She held up a hand, a stop sign, then took it down.

"Rita, I care about those boys and you know it."

Lovell knew it was pointless trying to explain. He did

care. Just the thought of trying to convince her only made it more frustrating. If it was one thing about Rita he knew from experience, the woman could be pretty stubborn and hard-headed when she felt like it. As Rita shook her head, large gold hoops dangled at each side of her pony-tailed head. Lovell blew an agitated breath out. He had never cared much for large hoops on a woman. Large hoop earrings or too much makeup. To him, a circle of holes dangling at a woman's ears seemed too close to her brain.

"No, Lovell. Don't even go there. During the whole time you've been here I've never seen you do one single thing with my boys except scold 'em and complain."

In a way she was right and Lovell knew it. Was it his fault that her boys never obeyed him? 'Hell no, he thought defiantly. Most of the time those wonderful boys of hers had treated him as if he were their older stepbrother that they didn't have to listen to when Rita was gone somewhere. More than once he'd had to use outright threats of doing bodily harm to get them to obey him. Of course, he knew better than to lay a hand on them. Rita didn't take no mess when it came to her kids. All the same they were hooligans. It didn't take a psychic to figure it out that true bonding between him and her boys simply hadn't taken place. Still, he refused to accept that it was all his fault.

"And...," Rita was saying, all high and mighty. ". . . with taking care of your jobless behind, I really had three kids."

"I believe I did the best I could," Lovell said tightly before looking away, which made him feel even worse.

"Man, who the hell cares now?" Maurice challenged boldly with his eyes. "Just leave."

Maurice put the pipe and lighter down, stood up and stepped around the coffee table with his face pulled into some kind of twisted mask. He was right in Lovell's face, almost taking his breath away with the sour stench of liquor and smoke. "Just get the hell out!"

Lovell stood his ground. "Man, you might be big and ugly, but you don't scare me." Brave choice of words, but Lovell could feel the fine hairs on his back stir and slowly rise, and the muscles in his anus slowly tighten up. It wasn't that hot in the room, but sweat squeezed out from the tiny pores along his scalp and neck. A thin river was racing down the crease of his back.

Every muscle in Lovell's body was coming to attention. God, he hoped the big fool didn't really want to fight. Fighting was for people who'd lost the knowledge of communication. Fighting was for fools who couldn't harvest their fears and channel their energy into a positive direction. He was a man who loved women, beautiful flowers, and fragrant vines—and a man who enjoyed breathtaking sunsets over a restless ocean. He was a man who pined for love under a moonlit night. He couldn't even recall the last time he was made angry enough to actually strike another human being. Not even those hard-headed boys of Rita's.

"He'll leave, Maurice. Just let 'im leave. 'Sides, I don't want no blood shed up in my house."

"Got that right," quipped Maurice while holding a stare-down with Lovell and loving every minute of it. "I suggest that you get to stepping."

"Man, get your big monkey self outta my face!"

It happened too fast. In one quick flash Maurice pushed him backwards, but not hard enough to steal his balance. Hope surged into Lovell like a switch flipped on. Coming back with full force, he pushed the big man backwards right over Rita's nice new glass coffee table between it and the sofa. Maurice's dark and thick legs were sticking out and over, kicking and struggling in the air.

Her eyes growing big as golf balls, Rita looked scared and shocked as if the thought of a pending battle was too much to bear. "Oh, no. . ."

Lovell swallowed hard, the taste in his mouth suddenly bitter.

"Man," Maurice said coldly as he clambered back up to a stand, "you one dead niggah now."

Looking around for a weapon, an equalizer to aide his defense, Lovell felt like fleeing. Being brave was one thing, but a big man like Maurice tearing after his average-sized frame was nothing to take lightly. He could see the fire in the man's eyes.

Maurice was back on his feet and Lovell still hadn't found anything he could use to swing at the man. Hell, if anything, the place looked intentionally cleared of all objects that could possibly be used as a weapon. Where were all the heavy figurines Rita usually kept scattered about the place? Where were the heavy whatnots and solid marble ashtrays? His breath came in quick gulps. He did spot one thing that he could use, but too late, Maurice picked up the fairly empty wine bottle and broke it over the edge of the coffee table just like something he'd probably seen done in a movie. Pale pink wine rained down in blushing drops onto the carpet.

All the wine suddenly drained from her head, Rita screamed, "Maurice! Are you crazy? Look at my new carpet!"

Maurice flew into Lovell like a hyped-up linebacker with the gleaming shard of broken bottle held firm in his hand and aimed straight for Lovell's stomach. Lovell caught his hand as the force of Maurice's body weight knocked him to the floor.

Rita screamed again and jumped up. "Maurice, stop it! You said no fighting!" Pulling her dress down to a decent length, she sprinted over to the kitchen entrance and stood. When the two men didn't stop at her command, she ran into the kitchen and came back with a large cast iron skillet. Down on the floor, hands and legs were tangled every which way, and somebody, she couldn't really tell which one, somebody was bleeding red onto her new carpet. "Stop it I said!" She felt like killing both of them. "I'm not playing, Maurice! Let go of 'im, now! Just let 'im go!"

A loud voice cried out in agony. Everything was happening too fast. Somebody was hurt bad. Rita jumped quick to do something. Anything. Lifting the heavy black skillet she crowned Maurice's head with it to stop his assault.

Suddenly unconscious, Maurice went slack with his body half on Lovell's. Seeing his chance, Lovell wiggled out from under him.

"Damn!" Lovell shouted. "He tried to kill me! He was really trying to kill me!" He didn't feel any pain but had some specks of blood on his face and a few scratches here and there. But thank God, he thought, he was still breathing.

There was a large spot of blood seeping down deeper into the fibers of the new carpet and two small spots right along the side of that. Lovell looked down and saw blood on his white polo shirt as well.

"I can't believe this!" He tried slowing his breathing down.

Rita looked away. "It wasn't supposed to happen this way." She let the iron skillet drop to the floor. It looked like Maurice was already coming to. "If I were you, Lovell, I'd be smart and leave."

"Rita, please, can't we at least talk about this? Girl, you know I care about you. Why you wanna be this way?"

"Lovell, just get the heck outta here! Now!" Arms folded stubbornly in front, her body language screamed no in big bold letters.

Momentarily hurt, more spiritually than physically, Lovell stood for a few seconds longer to compose himself, then stooped and swept up his jacket along the floor with one hand, clutched his bleeding side with his other, and left.

Chapter Two

Dipping her right hand finger into the cool white cream, Nylah Richardson held her breath a few seconds before slowly letting it out as she gently smeared the cream along the top of her hand before placing the cap back on the tube. 'Darn it', she thought. It was just so irritating. The fact that she couldn't tell if there was a change in her skin rash or not.

Dressed in her crisp white uniform, she was standing at the small window of the drab kitchen while she waited for the heat bubbles to form in the pot of chicken soup along the range top. A large fly caught her attention as it buzzed from one end of the open curtained window to the other. Watching it for a few seconds, she smiled as she reached over and opened the window to shoo it out to freedom. Helping a pesky fly to freedom, she mused, her sister would tease her for days for doing such a deed. But all things deserved a chance at life, even the small. She couldn't help if that was how she felt.

The soup was starting to boil. She had a whole hour to go before her shift started at Park One Memorial. The least she could do was make sure that Mama Jo had a hot meal before she left the house. Not that anybody would appreciate her effort.

Unconsciously, she rubbed the rash along her hand again. Confined to the top of her left wrist, the rash still wasn't too bad, at least not yet. But Nylah had a sneaky feeling that if she didn't nip it in the bud early, it could get worse. Just a quarter size of dry, scaly-looking red bumps. Small and itchy. Four days ago it appeared on her walnut-shell brown skin. The darnedest thing, Nylah thought with agitation, the way it had come up so suddenly.

Girl, she told herself, don't even sweat it. Just keep putting something on it. It'll go away. In fact, one of her doctor friends at Park One Memorial, one of several that were sweet on her at times but clearly not her type, had given her the Cortisone cream trying to help. He had even said that it was probably just a fungus and nothing to be too worried about. So far the rash was no better or worse. Nylah knew that it was mostly a mind thing, the way it sat there on her hand, an ugly patch of skin to remind her that something in her body was protesting or trying to go wrong. One thing she knew for sure, she'd have to do her best to cover the breakout up. Not many sick folks wanted to be touched by a nurse with a mysterious-looking rash on the very hand that had to help them. The best she could do was to keep applying the medicated cream and keep a large sterile Bandaid over it. Maybe she was just being too impatient, always expecting results to manifest instantly.

She focused on the pot of chicken soup. Her mother, Mama Jo, didn't like soup when it was too hot. Hmph. When she really thought about it, Mama Jo didn't like soup when it was too cold either. Soup, like so many other things that were done to please her mother, had to be just right. There could be no in between or compromise. Sometimes her mother's unfocused obsession with constantly having her way was enough to drive her crazy. Sometimes it aroused in her the notion to throw her hands in the air and scream, 'I give up!' But it never happened.

She turned the pot off, walked over and got a cereal bowl from the cabinet and came back over and poured the savory brew into it. From the ancient dull white refrigerator, she took out the loaf of bleached white bread. Frankly, she preferred whole wheat, but not her mother. Her mother couldn't tolerate any other kind of bread, be it wheat, rye, or just plain brown-smelling.

Nylah chuckled to herself, thinking of the time she had tried to fool her mother by making French toast with wheat bread. Purposely, she'd made sure that the egg batter had covered every inch of the bread. She'd even cut off the darker edges and sprinkled powdered white sugar on top. But nothing got past her mother. Taking the French toast up, the woman took one big whiff of it and tossed it back to the plate and ranted, "Can't eat it. Can't eat it cause it smells brown." Just another impossible situation to deal with was all it had been. Her mother drove her crazy that way. If it wasn't bleached white bread, something else had to be wrong. Nylah knew she really couldn't complain. She was happy for her mother to eat anything at all, just to get some serious weight on the woman.

She removed two slices of bread and popped them into the toaster, then added a tall glass of orange juice and a large banana. That much should hold her mother until her sister, Barbara Jean, got home from her shift.

Keeping her gait steady, Nylah carried the tray of food in through the short hallway, which was one of numerous things she disliked about her mother's four bedroom house. Everything was small. The living room, even with its large picture window and sweeping view of the old houses across the street, was simply too small. The two restrooms, one with only a shower stall and toilet, and the kitchen were too small. She didn't even want to think about the bedrooms.

Nylah figured the house had to be at least thirty, maybe forty years old. It was now only one of a slew of multi-colored tract houses. Nothing fancy looking, a single level light brown structure with a half brick facade and outdated windows trimmed in brown. The magnolia tree-lined street it perched on was once considered prime property for Lynwood until too many blacks and Hispanics began moving in. Of course, that was many moons ago. A young girl at the time, Nylah still held a curious recollection of the first time she'd heard the expression 'White Flight'. To her young ears at the time, hearing such a term had conjured up a curtain of pure white birds crossing the sky's blue horizon. Too young to know any better, Black folks moving in and White folks moving out had never occurred to her at the time. Her parents had been the third Black family to move on her street, helping to pave the way for more to come. And come they did. And they kept coming.

It was a lousy job of house designing. Whoever had designed her mother's house didn't have a clue what the word 'spacious' meant. Each of the four bedrooms had to be about the same, a pitiful ten by eleven feet. No more, no less.

Even the hallway leading to each tiny bedroom was too short. And if it wasn't for the lamp she'd bought to sit on the table she kept across from Mama Jo's bedroom door, it would be too dark in the pathway. Somewhat relieved that someone had come up with a way to solve the problem, it had been her sister Barbara Jean's idea for the lamp to burn night and day. Barbara Jean had claimed that it added more cheer to the dreary house and gave the illusion of natural light in a space that was impossible for sunlight to get to. Nylah had managed to keep her opinion to herself, thinking that the idea of burning a light night and day was not only foolish, but also wasteful. But at the same time, it did help.

Setting the tray sideways on the hallway table she took a deep breath to steady herself like always. She hoped that her mother was in a better mood than last night. Just last night after she had helped her mother with a nice hot tub bath, and after she had oiled and massaged Mama Jo's scalp with warmed virgin olive oil, the woman's mood had stirred and rose up like a suddenly freed demon and turned on her.

Mercy Jesus. Her mother could curse up a storm when she really didn't have to. Usually, there was no cause for it, which only confirmed to Nylah how hard it was to get used to constantly being verbally abused while trying to do something good. Nylah got the same kind of behavior from sick patients at the hospital. It came with the kind of work she did. But Mama Jo was another matter entirely. She was blood, and she was family. That fact alone only made the hurt more real.

The key to her mother's security barred room was kept right beneath the lamp base. Knowing that it would be an odd sight to behold inside a house, Nylah herself had put up the money to have the white security door installed. The handyman who'd installed it had scratched his gray-haired head and made a funny looking face in bewilderment and asked, "What in the name of Jesus y'all need with bars on the inside of a house?" And Nylah had bit her tongue lightly to keep from being impolite. She had wanted to tell him that it was none of his "bee's wax." But after carefully explaining to the man that the room would be used to store valuables, the man had accepted that, put up the door, and collected his fifty dollars and handing the keys over to her. It wasn't like she'd told the man a bald faced lie. Behind the locked door was her mother, and to her, if not to another living soul, her mother was something to be considered valuable.

No one else knew where the key was kept except for Barbara Jean and herself, which were all the souls in the house that needed to know. When she wasn't there to see after her mother, Barbara Jean had to kick in. True enough, Nylah saw it as a very demanding and thankless job that required a trove of love, patience and human compassion. Sometimes, she felt as if it drained all the energy and life out of her, like an orange being squeezed too tight by powerful hands. But ultimately, it was something, like eating and sleeping, that had to be done.

The only other person living in the house was Brittany, her five year old niece. And poor Brittany with her allergies and asthma took a lot of looking after too.

Nylah took the key up and stuck it in the lock of the security door, then slowly pushed open the wooden door beyond that. With no locking mechanism on the wooden door, her mother often closed it when she wanted total privacy, which to Nylah seemed like every minute of every day.

Thank God, she thought. The door opened to a peaceful scene. No harsh words to rush up to greet her. Still clad in her white cotton gown, her feet bare on the old and dirty carpet, Mama Jo stood looking out of the barred window at the playful antics of some zealous brown sparrows in a nearby cherry tree. Nylah eased her average-size frame into the room and tried to sound as cheerful as possible.

"Morning, Mama."

She shined her mother's sour mood on. It wasn't the first time her mother greeted her so coldly, not even bothering to turn around and face her with eye to eye contact. Nylah supposed that it certainly wouldn't be the last time either.

In spite of the early Saturday morning heat collecting up strength outside, Nylah felt a mild chill in the room. She hated this room. She hated the floral pattern of the faded pink wallpaper that was tearing and lifting in various places and the old carpet that had once been some strange hue of green, but was now, irreversibly, reduced to a hideous and heavily stained fiber-worn thing that felt strange to walk on. She hated the old fashioned push up windows and the rusted iron security bars that had been installed years back when her father was still living. She hated the strange smell of the room that no amount of scrubbing and disinfectant could seem to take away, like mildewed clothes and hopelessness.

More often than not, the push up windows stuck like mad in the wintertime, but a vicious draft always found its way in. Sometimes, when she really let herself dwell on it, it bothered her that the outside bars on the windows weren't the kind that could be pushed out from the inside in case of a fire. For that reason alone, matches and cigarette lighters were kept away. But thank goodness her mother had given up cigarette smoking about the same time she'd discovered smoking crack cocaine, not that she saw either vice any healthier than the other.

The room was way too small for the full-sized, solid-wood bed and two badly scratched, dark-wood endtables. Mama Jo had insisted that her ancient television set be moved from the living room into her bedroom as well, which only amounted to more walking room being used up by twenty-five inches of dark wood cabinet and an obsolete picture tube. A nineteen inch color television, a gift from Barbara Jean last Christmas, sat on top of it. A large oscillating fan perched next to it. A portable toilet sat isolated in one far corner of the room like a wayward child being punished.

Nylah placed the tray down along the dresser and methodically started picking up pieces of paper, shoes, and clothes strewn carelessly about the floor. She did it as if in a trance, her efforts so mundane and repetitious that she clicked on auto pilot the minute she entered her mother's room. Being a hard working woman herself who loved her mother dearly, she just didn't understand it. The woman could live like a common pig and think nothing of it. It was a puzzling reality—things hadn't been that way when she was coming up. Nylah still remembered when she was growing up, how her mother would sweep the sidewalk in front of their house several times a day just to keep dust from resting too long.

"Warmed you up some soup, Mama. Your favorite, chicken noodle. I even cut up pieces of celery and onions. Just the way you like it." Nylah looked up for some small sign of approval, half a smile or a twinkle in an eye. Anything. Her spirit slumped a little when she didn't find any.

As usual, her mother turned around looking vaguely amused and nowhere near grateful. Her thin arms were folded at the place where her breasts had once been. She tried a brief smile, as if doing so any longer would make her situation even worse. Nylah made an effort not to frown at what she was seeing. She could still see a sick longing in her mother's eyes, almost like flames swallowing up all the brown. But when her mother spoke, her words presented calm.

"You think I'm weak, don't you? You really think you can keep me locked away forever?"

"Try to eat something, Mama."

"Foolish woman. You and yo' sister both. Just plain foolish!"

Nylah's mouth tightened noticeably at her words. She heaved a sigh as she straightened up with a small pile of dirty clothes in her hands. "Mama, let's not do this today. Okay? Can't we just have one good day a week? Just one."

Now her mother was shouting. "I'm not the child here, Nylah!"

"Mama, don't shout. I can hear you."

"Then act like it!"

Looking like a stubborn fifty-three year old child, her mother unfolded her wispy arms and quick-flung herself back down along the rumpled bed, face up. It wasn't much of her tired body left to fling, mostly loose skin and fragile looking brown limbs still clinging to life.

"Hell, Nylah!"

Trying to calm her, Nylah smiled and gestured to the tray of food. "Why don't you eat something. You'll feel better. You'll see."

"Drop dead."

"Mama, you don't mean that and you know it."

Nylah swallowed the lump that rose in her throat. She could feel the tears ready to spring to her eyes, then the rushed feeling of foolishness. She should be used to her mother's insults by now. She should be able to let the words roll right from her consciousness like rain from a slippery leaf. But sometimes, the words still hurt. But words being words, they never hurt as much as looking at what was left of her mother after the crack cocaine had had its way.

As much as she thought about it, tried to figure it out, Nylah still didn't know how something so sneaky, so awful could happen to her mother. Her mother, from as far back as she could remember, had always been a hefty-sized woman with wide and shapely hips that had once turned the heads of many men. Nylah missed her mother's big beefy arms that could grab up an unruly child as if she were a feather turned wild in the wind and squeeze goodness and respect right back into that child without actually saying one harsh word.

Some folks, mostly relatives, had thought that her mother had been too fat in her younger days. But as a child, Nylah had felt that her mother was as big and soft as love could ever get. She had been a woman that loved all people and all people that chanced to meet her couldn't help but love her back. If her mother was down to her last three dimes she'd give up two for someone in need. And her father, Poppa James, had loved her mother with a fierceness that was deep and hard to find. She would never forget how her father used to carry on about her mother's cooking to family and friends, always adding on to the end, "I like a woman with some substance to her bones."

Sometimes she could still hear her father's deep voice vibrating through the small house. "Give me a healthy woman with some meat on her any day, 'cause the only thing that want a bone is a dog." That was the mother she used to know. Not this...this stranger wearing her mother's face.

"It's another beautiful day out, Mama."

Mama Jo was frowning up at the ceiling. "I know I'm sick of being in this room."

"I know, Mama. I know."

"Smells funny too."

"Mama, stop complaining and eat."

Her mother was down to skin and bones. Down from three hundred pounds to ninety-five pounds, give or take a few. Probably more take than give. Darn woman was too stubborn to step on a scale to let anybody see.

Allowing sweetness to slip back into her voice, Nylah tried again, "At least try'n eat, Mama. Do it for me."

"I'm not hungry."

"Well, at least try."

The strength and patience, where did she find it? Sometimes Nylah thought that it had to be something that she had soaked up after six years as a registered nurse at Park One Memorial. Most folks were their worst when they were sick. She understood that much. Of course, it was slightly different dealing with her mother.

On her job people had a real easy-to-see illness, a legitimate reason to be cranky and occasionally ill-mannered. But Nylah felt that with her mother, it was a mental illness. It was her mother's mind that constantly reminded her that she needed a pipe to live one day at a time. With no intervention, her mother would have smoked away the rest of her life on the filthy streets.

Having taken up all the dirty clothes about the floor, Nylah sighed wearily and looked at her mother still reclining along the bed and refusing to eat. There was a scattering of darker spots in her mother's face, which was something she was accustomed to seeing on crack addicted skin. She knew it had resulted from the body trying to rid itself of toxins.

Nylah had a mild sensation of her heart melting at the

sight of the woman before her. Her mother was so thin, drawn, and tired of living. In fact, her mother actually looked to her as if someone had literally taken her up like a thick brown towel and twisted her body to wring all the vital moisture and the fat clean away. Resentment swept through her. It was wrong and she knew it, but Nylah felt the stream of resentment run clean through her over how her mother had ruined her own life and almost destroyed herself in the process.

Mama Jo's once shoulder length black hair was now, sadly, the length of her baby finger, swept backwards and usually covered with a dirty scarf or rag. Her long fingernails were down to dried, bloody stubs. They had been chewed away with a seemingly constant restlessness that came and went like mysterious muscle aches. Not only had her mother's lips thinned out, but they actually looked as if someone had removed them from her face and baked them to a darkened shade before placing them along her skin-slacken face. Once all the fat had been smoked away, her mother's brown eyes seemed to have migrated, moved in closer to one another. If you dared to look hard enough, Mama Jo's eyes took on a look that bordered on being cross-eyed. Nylah found the change in her mother's appearance extremely dramatic. A deep pain rocked her soul every time she looked at the woman.

Moving over to the door, Nylah tossed the pile of dirty clothes down at the entrance to be carried out with her departure.

"Want me to bring you anything special when I get off work? How 'bout some ice cream, Mama? You know how much you like that flavor called Blueberry Waffle Cone. I can stop off and get some."

"And you can let me outta here too."

Nylah tried a weary smile. "You know I have to work. Maybe later."

"Drop dead then."

"Mama, don't say that."

"Drop dead, Nylah. Dead! Dead! Dead!"

Reaching for the rumpled bed covers, Mama Jo pulled them up to her chin, then over her head. "Yeah, you can bring me somethin' special back. Bring me a new life. That's what I need." A sniffle punctuated her request.

Nylah went over and checked the portable toilet. Empty. God she wished they could afford to have another small bathroom attached to her mother's bedroom. Anything to keep her mother from having to go in a portable toilet that had to be checked and cleaned daily. They needed another bathroom the way they needed a larger house.

For years Nylah had been saving her money for the day when she would find the perfect man to marry. The perfect man. She almost laughed every time she thought about such a thing. But as the years kept dwindling by, she found herself more and more tempted to just withdraw her sizable nest egg and add an extra bathroom onto her mother's house. Several times she had almost done it, but with no joint cooperation from Barbara Jean or her mother, the idea always turned sour and slipped away like mist.

"Nothing wrong with the life you have, Mama. You're doing real good." Nylah paused, then as an after thought added, "Look how long it's been now."

"All I know is I'ma die up in this here room. I know that. This is my house, Nylah. I shouldn't have to be locked in my own house by my own damn kids."

Sighing heavily, "I know, Mama." Nylah lowered her eyes and wished that things could be different. Her mother wasn't the only one suffering behind her addiction problem. "I feel the same way. But let's not dwell on it." She went back over to the door and picked up the small pile of dirty clothes. "I'll bring some ice cream home with me."

Opening the door she stopped and looked back over at her

mother still under the bed covers when she heard the front door slam shut. Sounded to her like Barbara Jean had arrived home. Scanning her watch she puzzled over why her sister was home so early. Now what? she mused. Hope she didn't go and get herself fired like her other job. According to Nylah's mental calculations, Barbara Jean's shift wasn't due to be over for another couple of hours.

"Talk to you later, Mama."

Her mother grunted and mumbled something that Nylah paid little attention to as she stepped out of the room and closed the steel framed door. Once back in the hallway she took a deep breath and let the pile of clothes fall to the floor while she secured the door back as Barbara Jean headed in from the living room carrying a wheezing five year old Brittany in her arms.

Her sister was wearing starched white slacks, a pink and white pullover top with a white lab coat on top of it all, which only made Nylah think of how ridiculous her job was being for making nurses stick to a strict dress code of pure white that didn't include other hospital employees. The words "Barbara Jean Richardson" were printed in bold black letters along the name tag pinned at the left side of her sister's lab coat, over her right shoulder were slung the straps of a tattered-looking, brown leather purse surely at the end of its life span, and that same dark blue insulated bag her sister always carried her lunch in. Actually, she didn't see why Barbara Jean just didn't buy lunch at the hospital cafeteria like most of the staff did. It wasn't the best food in town, but it was better than toting that blue bag back and forth.

Nylah smiled at a warm thought that flowed into her mind. In a way, it was kind of nice having her sister working at the same medical facility. Their work schedules molded out fine to accommodate the supervision of their mother. Barbara Jean had the daytime hours of mother-supervision, while she settled for the nights. It didn't leave a whole lot of free time to pursue their own lives, and most of the time Nylah didn't mind it so much. Anyway, it was like her mother used to always say, "Ain't nothing out in the streets to find, but some more trouble." And her mother should know.

Yes sir, Nylah thought fondly as she locked Mama Jo's security door back and picked up the pile of clothes, Barbara Jean's job at Park One Memorial was working out just fine. In a way, oddly soothing to her, she was proud of her little sister. It would be nice if the girl could do a little something better with her hair every now and then besides gel it down to the shape of her head. One week her sister's hair was black and newly permed, the following week it would be dark auburn, two weeks after that it was honey blonde, then back to black again.

Now, damaged and badly broken off, her sister's hair was like the heads of the girls they used to tease in high school—the ones they used to laugh at, tease behind their backs, and call 'chicken heads'. Nylah hated the way she wore it. Not that she considered herself some raving beauty with twenty extra pounds clinging passionately to her five foot five frame, but she did manage to keep her own permed black hair up, usually pulled back and away from her slender face in a neat French roll with a few pin curls at the top. She even took pride in the fact that the natural pink of her lips took the place of having to wear lipstick. Her own walnut-hued face was flawless, and any makeup more than black eyeliner, Nylah simply considered way too much.

Trying not to seem too nosy, Nylah walked over and stood in the doorway of Brittany's room with the bundle of clothes still in her arms. She cocked her head sideways to keep from shaking it in disgust. It was always a surprise and somewhat suspicious to her to see her sister home early from work. Barbara Jean was twenty-eight, a mere three years younger than herself, and had not quite jelled in having to work every day for a living. But after Brittany came along, she had had no other choice. County Welfare was slipping dangerously fast into the clutch of Reform. Even though her younger sister wouldn't admit it, the best thing that the County Welfare System could have done for her was to help her into the job training program that ultimately landed her a job at the same hospital where she worked. Two years into being a trained Lab Technician, as far as Nylah could tell, the mere sight of blood still awed and thrilled her sister.

"Hey now." Trying not to frown, Nylah gave in to mounting curiosity by asking, "What happened? Why are you home so early?" She moved to the side for Barbara Jean to pass from the room.

"Brittany got sick," she called back over her shoulders. "The babysitter called me at work."

Nylah winced at the news. "Her asthma again?"

Barbara Jean strolled back into the room with a clean and cool wet towel to wipe Brittany's face. Nylah watched her maternal nursing with fondness. Anybody could see that her niece was a smaller clone of her mother, even down to Barbara Jean's wide, flat feet.

"Can't you hear her wheezing? God. I'll be so glad when she outgrows it."

"Maybe you should try taking her to a specialist." Nylah took a tired breath. She wasn't sure if Barbara Jean heard her or not. She couldn't recount how many times they had had this same conversation regarding her niece's asthma. Nylah felt that her niece should see a doctor that specialized in respiratory conditions, but Barbara Jean had her own agenda. She kept looking for a miracle that was taking too long to come. Nylah wanted to tell her the cold truth, that true, some kids outgrew their asthma over a course of years, but there were plenty of others that didn't. Every so often, she still witnessed adults dying from complications of the dreadful lung disease. "Barb, I don't know why you keep putting it off, but Brit needs to see a specialist."

"Trust me," Barbara Jean agreed with an air of annoyance. "I plan to if all else fails. I wanna try a few other things first. I think she's getting better."

"Not really. Probably because it's always so stuffy in this room." Her arms still full, Nylah moved to one of two windows of the room and used one hand to push it up. "Let some air in here. There." Pleased, she stood back and looked around with a grin. Brittany's room was one of the most cheerful rooms in the entire house. The room had been lovingly painted lavender and white. Sheer lavender curtains hung at both windows, and above that, white vinyl window treatments. On days when the sun was generous, an abundance of pure, warm sunshine cheered the room up even more.

Nylah couldn't think of what framed picture of a cartoon character was missing from the walls. It seemed to her that Barbara Jean had meticulously found and purchased all of them from Mickey to Porky Pig. She watched her sister carefully pull back the pink and lavender chenille bedspread and undress a quiet Brittany. With air rambling around in constricted lungs lost and unable to find a smooth passage out, every breath the child drew seemed a great effort. Nylah couldn't help feeling sorry for her little niece. Why her mother refused to take the child to a specialist was an irritating mystery to her.

"Did you give her some medicine?"

"No."

Nylah looked slighted alarmed. "And why not?"

"She ran out of it." Barbara Jean sat down at the edge of the bed and gazed dubiously at her constantly ailing child.

"Again, Barbara Jean? Girl, what's wrong with you?" She knew her sister didn't want to hear it, but Nylah didn't care. It just didn't make any sense to be so careless about the health of a young child. "And when was this?"

Her sister drew in a weary breath. It was the sound of a mother who was tired but couldn't find a better way. When she spoke again, there was no denying the annoyance in her voice. "Look, don't start with me, Nylah. I know what I'm doing. I'd rather give her something natural like an herbal tea, rather than some drug that can't make her problem go away for good."

"Maybe that's because you're not the one trying to breathe."

Rolling her eyes, Barbara Jean cleared her throat. "Shouldn't you be on your way to work or somewhere?"

Boldly Nylah walked back to the door. "Barbara Jean, go and get that girl some more medicine for her asthma or I'll bring some home from the hospital pharmacy and give it to her myself."

Her jaw freezing stiff, Barbara Jean tossed her an irritated look and mumbled quietly under her breath before speaking up. "Hmph. You do best to get your own kids and do all that. Brittany's mama's name is Barbara." Lines of annoyance tugged at the corner of her mouth as she all but wrestled Brittany into a clean undershirt and helped her into bed. "Like I said, big sister, the herbal tea is working fine and I know what I'm doing. Okay?"

Nylah felt like she'd just been slapped twice in the face. Darn you, Barb, she thought with a muted tongue. The woman could be more stubborn than two mules on Sunday.

"Okay," Nylah said mildly. "Okay." She shook her head and held her opinion as feelings of anger and defeat passed over her. Maybe she should just stay out of it. Maybe Barbara Jean did know what she was doing and knew what was best for her own child. Poor Brit, she thought with an ache in her heart. She stood looking on for a spell before changing the subject.

"Don't forget to make some lunch for Mama."

"How can I forget that? And how is your favorite grouch today?"

Nylah averted her eyes and wished that her sister wouldn't talk that way. Their mother had some problems that she hadn't worked out yet. That's all. It could happen to anybody. "You mean our mother."

Barbara Jean snorted. "Whatever."

"About the same. She acts like she hates us for helping. Says she want to go out by herself today."

"Yeah, right. That's a laugh." Barbara Jean stood up and took off her white lab coat, glad to be at home. "Looks like I might have to work a double shift tomorrow, and I need my rest. So don't be expecting me to be babysitting Mama all day. Might even have me a date tomorrow night. Depends on how I feel."

"Well, aren't you something else?" Amused, Nylah raised a curious brow. "Why are you planning to be going somewhere with a sick child to look after?"

"She'll be alright by nightfall. You'll see."

Barbara Jean took up her blue insulated bag and looked over at Nylah as if to be asking: 'will there be anything else?'

"Oh well," Nylah perked. "I'm outta here."

Listening for the front door to close and then for Nylah's car to start up and pull off, Barbara Jean went to the large living room window and gazed out to confirm that the coast was clear. She watched Nylah's trusty black Nissan back out and stop at the end of the oil stained driveway before easing away from the house. Hurrying back to the bedroom, she sat her blue insulated bag on the bed, ignoring the months of collected dirt and grime along the nylon exterior as she opened it up. The two wide shoulder straps even had a series of tatters from too much daily use, but she figured a few more good months could still be squeezed out.

To Barbara Jean, the invention of the insulated bag was a

God-send, really. It was more a part of her daily ensemble than her hospital uniform. She bit down lightly on her lower lip as a smile emerged. Underneath her sliced apple and nicely wrapped bologna sandwich, her concealing obstacles, she carefully reached inside the coldness and lifted out the two tubes of fresh blood and held them up. The dark, rich-toned samples felt like raw power in her hands, right at her fingertip. A small moan slipped from a wheezing Brittany as she lay sleeping.

For a moment Barbara Jean's body tensed up as she focused her attention on her sick child, watching the rise and fall of her tiny, brown chest. Sometimes, when the mood slipped over her like damp cloth, it felt like Brittany's illness was a curse. It was some kind of earthly punishment that she was destined to endure. A muscle in her jaw twitched as her eyes glazed over. Perhaps it was the cruel price she had to pay for having a child by another woman's husband. Sins of the mother passed down a generation. Whatever it was, it was the worst thing that could have happened to her child, her precious baby. Barbara Jean felt so desperate at times that she'd be more than willing to give up one of her own lungs if it would cure Brittany. No child should have to suffer so much. But she still had her hope.

Standing at the brown compact refrigerator in her room, Barbara Jean kept her mood light and airy as she pulled the door open and moved a few items around to make room for her newest collection. If the hospital where she worked only knew, she chuckled mildly as she closed the compact refrigerator door back up. She didn't want to think about what would happen if her secret was ever discovered. Right or wrong, she knew that taking blood samples from her job would not be taken too lightly. Would the hospital go so far as to fire her or press charges? Would she have to go to court and have a trial? Perhaps do some time like some low life criminal.

Shaking the thoughts from her mind Barbara Jean slipped her achy feet out of her white leather Easy Spirits, straightened up, and looked back over at Brittany.

"Don't worry, sweetheart," she cooed lightly in a tone used more for babies, "Mama will fix it."

On her way out, she reached over and felt Brittany's forehead to assure herself that the child wasn't feverish. Umph. She did feel a little warmer than usual, so she pulled some of the bed covers away from her. Humming to herself some nameless tune she'd heard earlier on her way home, Barbara Jean left the bedroom enroute to the kitchen to put a kettle of water to boil. By the time Brittany was up from her short nap, she figured she'd have some more soothing herbal tea waiting.

Chapter Three

Women. For the life of him Lovell would never understand them. The sad part was he knew that he was inclined to devote his entire life to loving them, even his mother. Though he had never known his real mother, had never glimpsed her face even on a photograph, he didn't hold it against her that she had given him up. Like a pair of tired, old shoes that no longer fit, she'd given him away, but he held no grudge. It was all part of his global affection for all women. Sometimes though, even his love wasn't enough, especially when he found women as mysterious and complicated as the galaxy itself.

Clutching the steering wheel harder, Lovell pressed down on the car's accelerator and maneuvered the large vehicle straight ahead down Imperial Highway, the pace of his heart racing along with the traffic. Despite the heat, the breeze slapping at his face did little to soothe his agitation. Kicked out. Just like that. He couldn't believe it. Sometimes it felt like his whole life was a fast-moving ship, and he was the only passenger on board. All he wanted to do was throw out his anchor into the murky waters of life and be at a reasonable stand still—a safe and steady harbor. As faith would have it, it seemed as though his ship was always moving too fast through the murk.

Out of one relationship and right into another, that was

what it all amounted to. He knew what his problem was. He trusted and loved women too easily, loved everything there was to love about them: the way they walked, the way they smelled after hot and steamy sex, the way they laughed at some senseless joke, and even the way they sometimes teased and pleased, then sometimes dogged you out in the end. The dogging out part he could do without. It was a disheartening reality and he knew it. Women would probably be the death of him, but he still couldn't help it. He loved women.

In a way, at least to him, women were like the beautiful flowers he enjoyed growing. The true power was in his heart and his hands. He planted and nourished them with his love and kindness. He spoiled and cared for them until they bloomed into full color and beauty, until they died out, replaced by new flowers the next spring. His relationship with Rita had simply died out.

At the risk of taking his eyes off the road for a few seconds, he looked down at the blood on the side of his shirt and grimaced, then looked over at the large box in the front seat, and wished he had someone who could listen.

"Rita's new man. What a laugh."

Lovell mentally chastised himself for not handling the matter differently, but in what way? How could he have channeled the incident away from violence? If there was such an answer, it eluded him. Powering down the car's window, he narrowed his eyes as he tried to think, challenging his mind to come up with something. Something like where he would he go from here. He needed a place where he could stay until he could do better, and buy him some time. The car was sailing up Imperial Highway heading east to no particular destination. He looked at the gas indicator. Half full. Thank God he'd had the foresight to use Rita's charge card to fill up his tank and get some extra cash out from the ATM two days earlier. He knew that his meager funds wouldn't last long, but he had all of eighty dollars in his wallet. Maybe somewhere at the back of his mind he'd seen it coming, but the realization of it had been glazed over by denial.

Rita's firing him. Fired! That's right, he thought with a tinge of indignance. Being somebody's man, in a way, was almost like a full time job itself. You clocked in with your constant presence. You clocked out with departure.

Reaching over to turn the car radio on, he relaxed his shoulders and exhaled a weary breath as he settled back along the seat. The sound of mellow jazz joined the oppressive heat in the car, and the afternoon sun held no mercy. Lovell couldn't decide which was worse, the heat in the car pressing to get out, or more heat threatening to get in. Disgusted, he powered the window back down and took a deep breath. Rita would be sorry. He knew that much. Maybe not today or the next, but in due time, she'd be sorry.

His hand tried to relax on the wheel as a foul taste was trying to take over in his mouth, the bitter taste of acid tried to inch its way back into his throat as the sticky-ickyness against his side was becoming more and more noticeable. Oddly, he had no pain. Just mild bleeding. And even that seemed very minimum from what he'd endured. A nice cool, soapy shower. He'd do anything for a cool shower about now, which made Rita's words come to mind about Yolanda. Before Rita had been Yolanda. Lovell allowed his mind to backtrack, but the deep and intricate details of what had really gone wrong with that relationship eluded him, but only for the moment. Yolanda with the hour-glass figure, a behind as big and promising as any sister he knew. So Miss Yolanda was still calling Rita's house asking for me. Small wonder.

"Wonder what's up with Yolie?" Yolie had been the pet name he'd given her at the beginning of their relationship. He recalled that he hadn't seen or spoken with the woman in what?. . . nine. . .ten? Maybe eleven months since the night she'd thrown all his nice clothes out into the middle of the street. "Maybe I need to find out."

Without a second thought, Lovell turned the car around at the next intersection and headed west. Yolanda lived in Hawthorne off LaBrea and Artesia Boulevard. He remembered that her apartment building sat directly across from the rear parking lot of a small community hospital overlooking Pleasant Park. Now there lived memories. Pleasant Park. A couple of times in the past, he and Yolanda had taken her Hibachi over to the park and spread a blanket down on the cool grass. Steaks and hot links had sizzled through many a summer days while they had talked, kissed and sipped on cherry wine. He remembered too well. During the two and a half years he'd lived with Yolanda, there had been a few good times, but certainly not enough to overshadow the bad times. Too jealous for his taste. Lovell thought of jealous women the same way some folks thought of drinking and driving—a potentially dangerous combination.

It was still hot when he got to Yolanda's place. Lovell sat in his car rehearsing his lines and going over the right moves and facial expressions. He knew that his antics meant a whole lot of nothing. But at the same time, his rap had to be just right. The most he could hope for was that the woman even wanted to talk to him.

Women, he mused again. Sometimes they went through phases where they wanted a good man like him in their life, and then they grew to a point of not wanting a man at all. Despite his lack of gainful employment, he still considered himself part of the "good" group.

True enough, getting some boring job wasn't in his immediate plans. It just wasn't his true forte—his calling in life. But all the same, he considered himself a good catch by most standards. Darn right, he thought proudly. He was as good as they came. He always respected his woman. Always. None of them in the past, not even one female soul, could say that he had ever hit or verbally berated her in front of another person. If fact, didn't he go out of his way to avoid violence or any form of loud confrontation with a female? Hell yes! What high strung macho man, black, red, or white, would do something like that? And I'm a good cook, he added to his mental list, a good listener, and I can keep a house and a yard cleaner than any woman I know.

"Heck. When it comes to pampering a woman, I am the king."

He let his thoughts slip back to just last week when Rita had come home from her tedious job, and he had had scented bubble bath waiting for her arrival. Following that, he had lavished a sensual body massage all over her. And he was very good at it too, always starting with the shoulders and working down to the feet. That was the real trick - a woman's feet. It was his belief that all the love, kindness, and desire in any female could be rubbed, massaged, and worked right out of her feet. It was a ritual art that most modern day men didn't know about or simply didn't want to perform. He didn't have that problem though.

Despite the torturing heat of the day, Lovell knew that the nights in California could be tricky and turn suddenly frigid. His car was certainly spacious enough, wide and roomy back seats with plenty of comfortable leg room, but heck, he couldn't sleep in a car all night. It was too dangerous, so that move was out.

His eyes felt tight and hot as he stared straight ahead, his jaw set in firm resolution. "I'm going home with somebody tonight if it's the last thing I do. Old and wrinkled or young and ugly, I'm going home with somebody." Besides, he chuckled lightly and felt silly, didn't old wrinkled ladies need love too?

Sitting outside Yolanda's apartment, Lovell felt like a hundred butterflies had been set loose inside his stomach. Why am I so nervous? What is it' He couldn't figure it out. It wasn't like he was meeting the woman for the very first time, but every time he felt like his courage was up enough, his mind played fleeting visions of their last haphazard night together. Scenes ran through his head like old film footage pulled out from somebody's dusty attic. Suspicion and jealousy had been the perpetrator that day.

It was a saddening thought chock full of reality, but sometimes it was as if his good looks were a curse. Women he met seemed to hold the belief that he could never be content with just one woman in his life. As a result, he was always trying to prove his innocence, always having to explain his whereabouts for great lengths of time, and always having to put up with questions of loyalty within the relationship. He was a good looking man sure enough, but it was a hard-core rule of his own self-worth, he never dated more than one woman at at time. Of course, it always proved to be difficult to get a woman to believe that much about him, but still, it was a standing fact. He believed in loyalty and fidelity in a relationship.

"C'mon, man," he told himself in the hot car. "Just do it."

Lovell sat for a little while longer trying to steady his nerves. The car radio was turned to a station he often listened to. The station played one oldie-but-goodie after another. One of his favorites flowed in and out of his awareness, but he was too wrapped up in what to say to Yolanda to pay attention.

Pulling down the visor's mirror, he mulled over his reflection. His hair still looked good, his mustache was still thin and black and precisioned off nicely. Once, a few months back, a young lady had approached him and told him that he looked a lot like the actor Mario Van Peebles, except for the eyes.

"Umph. Mario wished he did have pretty green eyes like mine." He checked his teeth, still nice and white.

"Damn, you one good looking man!" Looking around to see if any eyes were watching, he mocked a kiss to his reflection. "You devil, you." It wasn't his fault that he was so good looking.

"Man, stop tripping and wasting time."

Pushing the mirror back in place, he sat back straight along the seat and clenched his fist, then lifted his right hand to study his nails. Yolanda had once told him that he had pretty hands. The hands of a man that would never know hard work. His hands were large and smooth with a soothing brownness that could be compared to lightly roasted peanuts. Even his pedicure was still holding up after two weeks, but he could tell through the dark leather sandals he wore, that he was about due for another one. Maybe when he got settled in somewhere. Settled, he mused lightly. When would he ever be settled?

Switching off the ignition, Lovell pulled out the keys and got his light jacket and eased from the car and headed for Yolanda's apartment door. Given a choice, he preferred living in a house to living in an apartment. Apartment dwelling was too impersonal. But sometimes, just like the old saying, beggars can't be too choosy. It's now or never. The worst that could happen was the woman opened her door to see that it was him and slammed it back in his face. Lovell chalked it up as life being one big chance you had to take.

He got to apartment number three and stood for a moment before knocking with quick repetition. Waiting gave him time to slip his jacket on to conceal a bloody white shirt.

From just beyond the brown painted door, Yolanda's mildly accented voice called out, "Justa minute."

Soon the door was opening to a crack and Yolanda was sticking her dark haired head out and gazing at him as if he was Santa Claus arriving with early Christmas gifts. "Lovell?"

"What's up?" How corny, he thought, but couldn't think of anything else to say. "What's it been like?"

"Lovell Joyner."

"Baby, it's me. Live and in the flesh. By the way, you forgot to ask who it was before you opened your door, Miss Lady. Told you about that."

Yolanda's eyes lit up like new Christmas lights. "I don't believe this. Lovell, wow, man. It's really you."

Relieved, he grinned and stepped back to give her a better view. "Believe it, girl. It's me."

Guardedly, Yolanda held the door half cracked as she stood in the doorway, halfway out. "What brings you 'round this way?"

"You. I came to see you. Can I come in?"

For a second or two she appeared to be considering his request, then opened the door wider. "Sure, but just for a little while. Jesse went to go take his mama to the market, but he'll be back soon."

Jesse? Who the hell was Jesse? Lovell stepped inside already feeling out of place. Maybe it was the way she tossed out the name 'Jesse' like he should automatically know who Jesse was.

"I didn't catch you at a bad time, did I?"

"No. It's okay." Sleepily, she scratched her head. "Just resting before Jesse gets back."

"Jesse? That your man?" He stood in back of her while she closed the door.

"Yeah," she said thinly. "That's him." Yolanda peeped out from the curtain as if to be looking for something.

Lovell quickly scanned the room. The place still looked the same. Old and dark furniture and a couch and love seat camouflaged with old-looking throw covers. No sign of fresh flowers or a living plant anywhere. Too bad, he mused. A window-installed air conditioner threw out a low hum in the cooled room, which explained how she could stand being closed up with so much heat outside conspiring to get in. Poodle, her beloved black and white mixed-breed cat, did a slow stroll from the room as if his sudden presence wasn't appreciated. Lovell snorted over its departure. He'd never liked the cat to begin with.

When Yolanda turned back around, he caught a better look at her. She was still good looking with healthy glow to her olive-hued skin and those same thin, sweet kissable pink lips more prone to pout than smile. He still loved the way her dark eyes always had a deep and mischievous gleam to them. Her hair was in a teased pony tail perched high on a small head. No doubt about it, the girl still looked the same. A little rounder in the face, and whoa...a whole lot rounder in the stomach. With that red smock type blouse she was wearing over denim pants he had almost missed it. A sunken feeling invaded his stomach as he reached out and patted her expanded waistline.

"Say what now. And what do we have here?"

"Yeah, yeah." Pushing his hand lightly away, Yolanda brushed past him going to the couch. "What it look like?"

"A little grouchy too."

"Forget you, Lovell."

"And it looks like you have too." He beamed a smile.

Yolanda rolled her eyes in a pretense of annoyance before gesturing to a seat along side of her. "Park it, Lovell. But you can't stay long 'cause Jesse could pop back up and I don't wanna have to hear his mouth."

Through the gap in his jacket, Yolanda noticed his blood-stained side and softened her tone as she struggled back up to have a closer inspection. "You're bleeding. Oh my God. What happened?"

"Nothing really. It's probably stopped by now." She examined him much the same way a concerned mother might examine her child. In a way, it made him feel a little better—the fact that somebody cared. "It's alright. Some big fool stuck me with a broken bottle. Don't sweat it. It's nothing serious."

Ignoring his words, Yolanda lifted up the side of his jacket and shirt to scrutinize the two wounds. One looked a good three inches across but not too deep. Dried blood had already encrusted around it. The other wound looked more serious, like a deep puncture that was trying to close up. She pressed down lightly on it.

"Does it hurt?"

"Not really. It feels funny tho. Kinda itchy feeling."

"Here," she said sympathetically, "let me go get some alcohol to put on it. I think I have some bandages 'round here somewhere. But if I were you, Lovell, I'd get to a doctor. You never know about an open wound." She left the room, leaving him standing with his jacket and shirt hiked up.

Moving over in front of the air conditioner, Lovell allowed the cool air to blow along his side and mid section. The forced breeze felt good along his skin. "I don't mean to be causing you no problems," he called out to her. "I mean, I didn't know you were pregnant and living with somebody. My old lady told me that you were still calling for me at her house. That's why I dropped by to see what was up." He took his jacket off, tossed it to the sofa and moved away from the air back to where she'd left him standing.

Yolanda strolled back into the room with a few first aide supplies. "Yeah, man. I did call a few times 'bout some mail that came for you, but that chick...what's her name...?"

"Rita."

"Yeah, right. That Rita of yours always cursed me out and hung up on me. I figured she wouldn't bother telling you that I called no way, so I stopped."

Lovell looked puzzled. "What about my mail?"

"Hold still," Yolanda chided, trying to clean up his side with some cotton balls soaked in rubbing alcohol. "I kept it for a while, but Jesse threw it out. It didn't look like anything important, mostly junk mail."

"I believe that's illegal." Junk mail or not, Lovell didn't

appreciate having his personal things tossed out.

"I know, I know, but that's the way Jesse is. Now, hold still."

"You saying that you didn't miss me at all? Or maybe you wanted to tell me about the baby." He looked away at a picture of smiling cats on the wall. "Is it mine?"

"Does it sting?"

"What?"

"The alcohol, dummy. Does it sting?"

"No, it doesn't, and don't change the subject."

"Lovell, I swear. You're the only person I know that can use rubbing alcohol and not feel it. Man, you're weird. And no, I haven't had time to miss you."

"Is the baby mine?"

Yolanda sucked air through her teeth. "Man, please. Don't even flatter yourself. We haven't been together in almost a year and I'm six months along. Do the math."

Shifting the bulk of his weight from one leg to the other, Lovell frowned trying to remember. "Has it really been a year?"

"You sure you're not in pain?"

"What?" He was till trying to count off from the last time they'd been intimate to determine if she was lying. The thought of possibly becoming a father brought a smile to his face, but he knew that she wasn't lying. Eleven months had past since the last time he'd seen her, and she couldn't possibly be expecting a child by him.

"Your cuts, what else? Pay attention. Do they hurt?"

"Woman, I told you no. They just itch like mad. Dang. I could sure use a shower so I can change clothes."

Yolanda made a funny face. "Well, don't go thinking that you can get butt naked in here 'cause Jesse could come home any minute. I got enough emotional baggage with him as it is."

"I understand." Though he said the words, he didn't feel

it.

After Yolanda cleaned and patched up both wounds with gauze and tape, she turned to him with a concerned look on her face. "You really should see a doctor. One of those cuts feels funny to me, kind of hard underneath like something might be in it. Could be glass."

Snatching his bloody shirt down, Lovell snorted, "And do I look like I have Medi-Cal to you?" He couldn't help feeling annoyed that his plans of reuniting with Yolanda weren't going too well. "No way I'm going to one of those county operated facilities where it takes two days for a doctor to see you. I don't even wanna hear that."

"Well, suit yourself. Me, myself, I'd be too afraid of getting infected with that flesh-eating virus or worse. You heard about that, haven't you?" Yolanda picked up the bottle of alcohol from the badly scarred wooden coffee table and put the cap back on it. "You could try Park One Memorial across the street there. I hear it's privately owned, but occasionally they take in a few charity cases. They'll help you."

"Is that right?" Lovell made a mocking sweep of his hand. "Just stroll in and announce that I'm a charity case, please help me."

"You can do it, or don't do it." She was putting cotton balls back into a plastic bag. "I'm telling you, Lovell, they'll help you. I've been there twice with Jesse before he finally got some medical benefits on his job. I don't know how they work it, but they send you a bill eventually. If you can pay, you pay. If you can't, they get reimbursed some kinda way. Probably from the County."

The idea sounded easy enough, but there was something still about her suggestion that didn't feel right to him.

"Maybe if you go with me." He knew he shouldn't be asking such a thing with her condition and all. But the idea of just walking into a strange medical facility alone was a little intimidating.

Halting what she was doing, Yolanda looked into his face. "Man, are you crazy? My old man will be back any minute now."

"So. It's not like I'm asking you to go on a date. Miss lady, come go with me. You can be my moral support. Have a heart."

"Lovell...I don't know. My Jesse is a crazy, jealous man."

"So am I, but not when it comes to a friend helping another friend. Just do it for old times' sake, girl. Do it for a friend. You are allowed to have friends, aren't you?" Lovell knew that last remark would get her. If she was still like the spicy Yolanda he used to live with, a man telling her what to do, and when to do it, just didn't sit too well.

"Lovell, don't start."

"Okay, I'm sorry. Just do it for an old friend. C'mon, sweet thang. Do it for me. I'd do the same for you."

"Really, Lovell? You'd do the same thing for me?" She caught his eyes and stared mildly into them but quickly caught herself and copped a new attitude.

"Girl, you know I would." Lovell rubbed her shoulders gently. The tightness in her muscles trying to relax could be felt just beneath his fingertips. "You're sure it's not my baby you're carrying?"

"For the second time, it's not your child, so shut up." The spell was broken. "Let me slip on some shoes, and I'll walk over to the hospital with you. We can go to the clinic part, but understand this before we go: I cannot stay with you. Jesse will be wondering where the heck I am, and he's the type who'll come looking. The man don't play."

"Wow. Jesse sounds like a baby mother-scooter." Why some women chose to be with big ape type men that cowered them into acting the way they wanted a woman to act would always be a mystery to him. "I better watch myself."

"Joke if you wanna, but yes, you'd better believe it."

Looking suddenly contemplative, Lovell asked, "Think I should move my car? It's out front and full of my stuff."

"Heck yeah, fool!" Yolanda placed a sassy hand to her hip and added, "you want Jesse to kick both our behinds? Don't think the man don't know what kinda car you drive."

"He does?" Lovell raised a brow and felt flattered, but didn't know why.

"Yes, he does. Okay? Let's go and do this. You being here is making me nervous." Yolanda hurried into the room and came back with some slip-on white sandals on her slightly swollen feet. She moved around him and snatched open the front door. "C'mon, mister friend," she ranted with an impish smile. "Let's go and get it over with."

Chapter Four

The expansive parking lot of Park One Memorial was more than half full. Standing at Lovell's car with the afternoon heat beating down on her olive skin, Yolanda waited patiently while Lovell searched and found a clean dark blue knit shirt from one of several boxes inside his vehicle. He gazed over in her direction trying to figure out what had really gone wrong in their relationship, besides the obvious fact of her being too jealous.

"This is really special. I mean, you taking the time to go to the clinic with me. You know how I feel about hospitals."

"I just think that cut feels like something serious could be wrong, that's all." Smiling, Yolanda leaned against the car as she watched two young girls riding swiftly by on bikes. "And how would you know 'bout hospitals, Lovell? You used to claim you never get sick. Remember?"

"I don't," Lovell confirmed, looking sheepish. He loved her smile.

Yolanda turned around in time to see his shirtless, masculine chest full of thick hair. That same exotic black forest she used to love to run her fingers through at night. The way she remembered it, just playing with the curly black strands on his chest had been almost as exciting as making love itself. The two open gashes to his flesh made her turn her gaze away.

Noticing her, Lovell grinned and asked, "What's wrong?"

"Nothing," she shook her head fervently. "Just my sensitive stomach. Wish I could be like you, never getting sick. They say that's a sign of having good genes. Heart disease runs in Jesse's family. It makes me worry for our baby."

Pulling a clean knit shirt down over his chest, Lovell looked over at her again. "But you're young and strong. I'm sure the two of you will have a bunch of healthy babies."

"God, I hope so. But still I worry." Rubbing her swollen stomach in circular motions, Yolanda could feel the subtle kicks of her baby. "Too bad he won't have your good genes."

"You'll be fine." He could tell that she still liked him. He knew that look when he saw it. It was the look of passion held captive. Look at her, he mused fondly. Miss lady trying her best to play it off. "Hope you're right. Maybe I'll live to be a hundred."

"Don't worry," Yolanda said pertly, "You probably will."

He admired her eyes, warm and genuine. She had "smiley" eyes, as long as you didn't make her mad. "I never really stopped thinking about you."

"Man, don't even start." Yolanda made a smacking sound with her mouth.

"I'm telling the truth."

"Well, nothing wrong with a little truth. But you can save all that for the hospital people, Lovell, 'cause I don't wanna hear it."

He came up closer to her with the intention of giving her a mild hug, holding his arms out for her, but then thought better of it. "You saying you didn't miss me?"

Shifting her weight from her left to her right side, Yolanda drew in a good whiff of air. She could see boyish devilment dancing in his eyes. Those same green eyes had once been the sun and the moon in her life. Her whole existence had once been wrapped up in him. His words and his touch had been like the life jacket that had kept her afloat in a sea of dreams.

At least until she realized that green eyes and unlimited love-making didn't pay the rent. "C'mon, Lovell. Let's go so I can hurry up and get back home."

"Well, did you miss me or not?"

"I'm serious, Lovell. I'll just leave and go home now. I don't have time for this."

"Well, don't hate me because I still care."

"I'm not playing, Lovell."

"Okay, okay. Let's go."

Turning around, Lovell closed up the box containing his clothes and shut and locked his car door. It seemed like the more he tried not to think about his dispassion for medical facilities, the worse he felt as they got closer to the outpatient clinic entrance. What was it about hospitals that gave him the creeps? Whatever it was, it had to be something deep within his psyche. He'd never been hospitalized before, or even had to see a doctor, except for that one time his foster mother had taken him to see a dentist. But even that one time had been uneventful. No drilling had taken place because he had no cavities. In fact, the way he recalled it, the pink-faced white-haired dentist had called his foster mother into the room and explained to her that his teeth were too perfect. No plague build up; no cavities; no chipped or crooked teeth. Only a mouth full of perfect teeth.

Park One Memorial boasted two levels, and from what he could see, didn't look so huge and scary-looking afterall. Lovell immediately took a liking to the way the Japanese Boxwood hedges neatly wrapped around the side and front facade of the building, and above it, not too high or out of con-trol, grew bougainvillea with its dazzling orange and dark pink petals soaking up the abundance of sunlight. It was a beauti-ful contrast, but did little to douse his uneasiness. He grabbed Yolanda's hand for moral support only to feel a tinge of hurt when she snatched it out from his.

"And don't be holding my hand. Somebody might see us, and I do live 'round here. Remember?"

"Why not?" he asked teasingly.

She made a face. "All I need is for some fool to go back and tell Jesse they saw my pregnant butt holding hands with another man. Man, you better get real."

Lovell looked suddenly serious. "If you hadn't been so jealous, we'd still be together and you'd be carrying my child and wouldn't have to be so worried about Jesse."

"In your dreams, Lovell." Shocked, Yolanda gave him an I-can't believe-you-said-that look. His words only helped to speed up her walking pace. "Jesse is a good, hard-working man, and I know he'll make a good father. Man, you can be so crazy. So, don't give me no drama. Save it for the clerk."

"The what?"

"The clerk, Lovell. The clerk." She rolled her eyes at him.

Together they walked inside the outpatient clinic. The sudden change in climate jolted his alertness. Soothing cool air circulated through the entire room. The place looked okay. A few people were scattered here and there. No masked men with monster needles jumped out from hiding to whisk him away to obscurity. Lovell relaxed a bit. At least the place looked clean and professional. Right away he liked the decor of misty blue carpeting, off white wallpaper with light blue butterflies covering its entirety, and the scattering of real and artificial plants. The place gave off a cozy feel. More like somebody's living room instead of a hospital.

"Not bad," Lovell complimented with approval as they walked up to the in-take clerk, a fat and brown-skinned woman in rounded glasses with too much make-up on and dry-looking red hair trying to stay pinned back from her pinched face. Lovell noticed her name tag pinned over her ample bosom pushing bravely up from her white rayon blouse, Bernice Myers. He could tell that Bernice was a middle-age woman still desperately trying to hold on to her failing youth. If the wearing of a wedding ring was a true sign of marriage, Bernice Myers boldly had two sets of wedding rings on each hand as if one husband alone could never be enough for her. Lovell felt like laughing, but didn't want to seem the odd ball.

At their approach Bernice looked up and asked, "May I help you?"

"Yeah," Lovell quipped, and then paused to compose himself. "...ah, yes. I would like to see a doctor, please."

The way Bernice Myers was looking at him, some kind of hungry look, Lovell felt certain the woman was trying to flirt with him on the sly. A smugness came over him as he smiled. He didn't know why, but sometimes he just had that effect on some women.

"Your name, please."

"Lovell Joyner. That's Lovell with two L's."

"What's the nature of your problem?" Bernice used short and plump fingers to push her glasses up on her wide nose as she waited to key his response into a computer.

"I've been stabbed...well, actually cut, along my side."

"With a knife?"

"No," he sighed, already tired of her probe. Knife, glass or box cutter, what was the difference? He held these words. "With some glass."

"Have you been here before?"

"No."

"Insurance?"

"Say what now?"

"Do you have any insurance?"

Lovell shook his head. "No. I'm afraid that I don't." Shooting side glances to Yolanda, he wanted to just say, 'let's go', seeing as how it was her suggestion for him to seek medical attention at Park One to begin with. But one look over at Yolanda and he could see that her full blown attention was focused on a young mother standing behind them with a new infant wrapped and tucked in a carry-seat. Lovell turned his attention back to Bernice.

"And who is your employer?" Refusing to smile, Bernice waited for his reply.

"Nobody right now." Lovell forced himself not to tell the woman never mind. He felt like her point-blank questioning was nothing but a big spoon all in his Kool-aid.

"Excuse me." Bernice tilted her head down and had to push her glasses back up after peering over the top.

"I said I don't work right now."

"You don't work?"

Those three words coming from Bernice's full and too-red lips sounded like something dirty or unheard of. Annoyed, Yolanda spoke up.

"That's right. The man here don't have a job right now. So what's the problem?"

Becoming snooty, Bernice nodded her head allowing her glasses to slide back down her wide nose as she squinted over the top again.

"Well, Ma'am, personally I don't have a problem with the man not working. However, this is not the County General. Here, we do require some means of payment, be it medical insurance, credit card or cash money."

"So," Lovell said quietly, taking it all in with stride, "can I see a doctor or what?" Say no, woman. Just say no. Quietly, he wanted the woman to reject him so that it would at least look like he tried. Frankly, he could care less. Wasn't like he was dying or in great pain or anything. A couple of gashes, a little bleeding, big deal. A little bleeding never hurt nobody.

Spicy when necessary, Yolanda wasn't going for it. Bernice could tell that she had a growing problem on her hands by the way the pregnant woman was moving her face in closer. Yolanda challenged her with her eyes.

"Lady, that's bull. I've been here a couple of times myself, and I didn't have no insurance, credit card or no money. So, if you don't know what to do, maybe you should call somebody that does."

"Excuse me," Bernice tried again, her eyes in a bold blinkless stare down with Yolanda. "But it's like I said, this is not the free County General. If you need the address of a State run facility, I'll be more than happy to give it to you."

"Call the manager," Yolanda snapped. She fixed her jaw to firm and folded her arms as best she could over her expanded stomach. "Call 'im, we don't wanna talk to you, lady. Just call somebody else."

Bernice squirmed slightly in her chair. "Excuse me, but I don't have to call nobody 'cept hospital security. I work here and I know hospital procedures. We request proof of insurance, a valid credit card, or cash money."

Ready to give up, Lovell sighed and pulled at Yolanda's arm. Last thing he needed was another scene getting out of hand. "Girl, let's raise up outta here."

"Hell no," Yolanda insisted, keeping her eyes glued to Bernice. "This foolish woman act like she own the place. We want the manager or head doctor or whoever. Call somebody 'cause we're not leaving and right is right."   More words passed between the two females, but Lovell's ears turned immune to it.

Right is right?   Lovell looked away wondering what Yolanda had meant by that statement. Still, it made him feel special to hear her standing up for him. He gazed back over at Yolanda. Just look at her, he mused. Looking all mean and sassy standing there as big as two cows turned sideways. It was too much and made him feel lightheaded. The thought of two women verbally having it out over him. Imagine that.

Lovell's gaze ran along to Bernice's hand and found the two sets of wedding rings on her fingers. He started to ask her just how many husbands did she actually did have, but then another white uniform-dressed woman was coming over to the counter and looking authoritative as she craned her neck trying to see what the commotion was about. The woman was carrying an open shoe box with a tiny white fuzzy head bobbing up and down.

-❀ ❀-

Barely back from her late lunch break, Nylah Richardson could still taste the grilled onions that had been on her cheeseburger. Spotting the unrest at the admitting desk the second she'd stepped into the clinic entrance, Nylah couldn't trust her ears or her eyes. It appeared that the new clerk, Bernice Myers, was at it again for the third time that day. Good grief. The woman was forever giving new patients a hard time. That part probably wouldn't be so bad in itself, Nylah thought, if only the woman wouldn't go so far as to have quarrelsome word-for-word arguments with people. Lord, she sighed, the third time today.

Nylah made her way over to the counter. Normally during her busy schedule, she didn't have the time or the energy to be bothered with such trivial matters, but she knew that Edna Sanders, the Duty Nurse in charge of Bernice Myers, was out for the day. Being the good friends that they were, it only felt right that she should intervene to keep things somewhat in order until Edna returned to work. And when girlfriend did return, Nylah planned on giving her a thorough report on the new clerk. Bernice Myers was proving to be too difficult, and needed to recognize that Park One Memorial was way too white, too small, and too privately owned to have her kind fanning the flames of litigation by turning away patients after unnecessary confrontations.

Stepping up to the desk, Nylah put on her most professional expression. "Miss Myers, what seems to be the problem here?" She kept her voice as calm and smooth as possible, but what she wanted to say was: Bernice, let's identify and solve this problem before one of the hospital's overseers slithers from under a rock and takes notice. *Honestly,* she mused, *where in the world did the hospital personnel department find these people?* Bernice couldn't possibly be past her probationary period of employment, and already she's a problem.

"The woman don't know her job," Yolanda raved loud and boldly, gesturing over to a smug looking Bernice. "Talking 'bout my friend here can't see a doctor 'cause he don't have no insurance or no money. That's crap and I know it!"

"Bernice?"

Nylah looked wearily over at Bernice who drew in all the breath she could before spilling out her own lengthy version. "Well," she began, plainly taking her time. "Mr. Joyner here has no employment, no insurance, and no credit card. Nor does he have cash to pay for service. I was simply trying to explain to these...these nice people that this is not the free clinic."

Lovell snapped to attention. "Woman, how you know if I have a credit card or not? You just assumed that I didn't."

Knowing that he actually didn't have one, Lovell felt a tad uneasy at trying to lighten the issue. He was half leaning on the counter looking remotely concerned, then started noticing the nurse who'd come over to help them. On the sly, he scanned her nametag: Nylah Richardson. Nylah. What kind of name was that? he wondered. Definitely different. A nice ring to it. Probably pronounced Nie-lah. He noticed her hands. No wedding rings on either one. That was a good sign. She had nice hands, slim and dainty fingers for a woman not so small. Well-manicured nails, unpolished. He liked that in a woman. Her left wrist had some kind of bandage on it, but she definitely wore no rings.

Lovell stole a glance down at her legs. Not bad there

either. Nothing like a woman with big and shapely legs, even if she did have on those God-awful, nurse-looking white shoes. He drew himself closer for a good whiff of her. Hospital soap, expensive perfume, a little too floral, grilled onions, and strawberry soda. Probably in her early thirties he figured. No kids; no husband; maybe a distant boyfriend or two. No. Too cocky to think that such a nice looking woman had no boyfriend at all. Boyfriend or not, he could tell that Miss Nylah was a woman that was deprived. He watched her every little gesture, from the way she stood so perfectly straight like a stiff, invisible rod held her up, down to her manner of talking. She pronounced each word with effortless clarity, making good eye-to-eye contact. Clearly, she was not a woman easily intimidated. He could tell that much. Yet she was still a woman deprived. It was something about her eyes, and the subtle stiff and fidgety movements of her body. Her lips were thin and sensuous and yet, she had a warmface, but definitely a female that took no mess. He knew her type.

Lovell and Yolanda both stepped aside and allowed Nylah to do the talking to the in-take clerk. His silence gave him more time to sum Nylah up more. His mind danced with delicious thoughts of Miss Nylah. The woman probably wore only satin bikini cut panties under her take-no-mess uniform look.

Nylah cleared her throat. ". . .and let me remind you, again, Miss Myers. Your job here is to take down all the necessary information and refer the patient to the billing department if necessary."

Definitely a woman that takes no mess, Lovell thought, intrigued by her mannerism. Watching her talk that talk, it was hard to take his eyes off of her. Clearly, she was a woman who could be bossy, but in a sweet and mellow I-mean-business kind of way. He admired that.

When Nylah got through with that snooty acting Bernice, Lovell was given some forms to fill out. Mostly a bunch of questions that he had to check no for, and then he was escort-ed to an exam room by Nylah herself.

"Remove all of your clothing and put this gown on, open at the back, please."

"Will this take long?" Lovell wanted to know before undressing. He supposed that he should be happy just to have a place to park himself and rest his tired soul for a while, but Yolanda had said that she would wait for him.

"It shouldn't," Nylah said in response as she changed the thin paper on the exam table.

Not that he was expecting the same luxurious accommo-dations as the Beverly Hills Hilton, but the spartan exam room was way too cold for anybody to be taking their clothes off. The room was painted light blue with fairly new-looking dark-er blue vertical blinds at the singular window, which was too small for his liking. Typical medical instruments sat atop a wall-anchored, formica-topped table. Just beneath it rested a thickly cushioned round stool equipped with wheels. Again, Lovell could feel nervousness trying to creep up on him.

"Before I undress, let me go tell my friend that I won't be long. She'll be waiting for me."

Mildly amused by his request, Nylah looked up and nod-ded. She was too mentally exhausted to protest. "Sure, Mr. Joyner. But come right back. The doctor will be here soon."

"Right back then." Suddenly giddy, Lovell felt like giv-ing the woman a quick peck on the cheek to show his gratitude for all she'd done for him. He never would have gotten past the in-take clerk if it hadn't been for her. Maybe later.

With the intention of thanking Yolanda again for moral support, Lovell hurried back through the wide hallway leading to the clinic waiting area. When he entered the room, his eyes scanning over at the in-take desk and then on to take in the rest of the waiting room area, Yolanda, his good friend, was nowhere to be found.

Chapter Five

"Barbara Jean! Barbara Jean!"

Of all the times for her throat to be acting up, Mama Jo braced herself as she yelled to the end of her lungs and hated every second she was missing of the Simpson trial. In order to faithfully keep up with her daytime soap stories, the trial had to be recorded on a daily basis to be viewed in the evening. 'That poor O.J.', she thought as she shook her rag-covered head and studied his expressionless face on her television screen.

"Look plain bored to me. Poor thing. Just had to go and get yo'self in a world of trouble behind some white thighs. Didn't you? Just couldn't leave them white women alone, could you? A damn shame."

"Barbara Jean!"

She didn't know what it was, but it felt as if all the moisture had just taken up and completely moved out of her throat. At one spell her throat had felt fine, and then the next thing she knew it as hot and dry as the Sierra Desert. To make matters worse, her water jug was completely empty. Silly woman-child of hers was probably somewhere sleeping while she was about to die of thirst.

Carefully smoothing out her dingy white cotton gown, she got up from her bed,   and walked to the security door, and tried the knob. Locked. Still locked.

"Barbara Jean! You people gon' drive me to drink, I swear. I need some water in here!" Mumbling lowly under her breath, she went back over to her rumpled bed and eased back down. Collected heat of the day swirled around the room taking her thoughts along with it.

She'd done the I'll-be-a-good-mama role, but things were trying to get out of control. It felt like she could pass out and shrivel up as she closed her eyes for a spell and opened them. On her screen Judge Ito was calling another side-bar for the Simpson trial attorneys. Mama Jo snorted, "Hmph!, probably ain't talking bout nothing 'cept what salad bar they going to for lunch. Who they fooling?"

Soon she heard the key in the security door lock and looked up to see Barbara Jean ambling in followed by a sleepy looking Brittany with no slippers on her tiny feet. Barbara Jean was dressed in a pair of gray cotton knit shorts that she usually slept in with an oversized matching tee-shirt. With her strawberry-covered shortie pajamas on, Brittany went over to her grandmother and climbed up on the bed beside her looking tired and listless. Mama Jo rubbed the top of her grandchild's woolly head playfully.

"Chile, what's wrong with you? You too young to be looking half dead." She slid her hand away.

"Ganny, I don't feel good."

"What's wrong with this chile, Barbara Jean?"

Barbara Jean didn't like the tone of her mother's voice, the way her words had rushed out too fast and too close together. It sounded to her like her mother was about to complain. "Can't you tell she don't feel good?"

Looking halfway sympathetic, Mama Jo reached over and felt Brittany's forehead. "Is that right? Seems to me that you said that yesterday and the day before. What's wrong with the chile now?"

Annoyed, Barbara Jean folded her arms in front of her

and sucked air through her teeth. "You know what's wrong with her."

"How should I know when I'm locked up in this stank room all day with no water. What a woman gotta do to get a drink of water 'round here?"

"You act like it's my fault you gotta be up in this room." Fixing her face to carelessness, Barbara Jean walked over to the insulated water jug and picked it up with one hand while trying to rub sleep from her eyes with her other. "And it smells in here 'cause you need to have this old carpet taken up. Probably got mildew and mold underneath it. I don't know why you don't just take it up and fix the place up some."

"Umph. I don't see you putting up some money to help fix up nothin' 'cept for the room you and Brittany sleep in. It might be my house, Barbara Jean, but you and Nylah live here too." She paused to catch her breath. "And this house is too damn quiet for one thing. Wasn't for my Simpson trials I'd go completely crazy." Pointing to the television set she confirmed, That's my man there, O.J."

"Yeah, I know." Barbara Jean stopped and glanced over unconcerned at the television and covered a yawn.

"Why you gotta say it like that? You act like he's guilty."

Barbara Jean wanted to laugh. If her mother only knew how she really felt. "Mama, to tell you the truth, whether he did it or he didn't do it, he'll always be guilty to 'them.' He shoulda been with his own kind in the first place."

"Maybe so, but it's still too quiet in this house."

"That's 'cause I was sleeping." Leaving the room for a minute or so, Barbara Jean came back with the jug filled with chilled water and sat it down on the floor next to her mother's bed. "Brit was taking a nap too. Her asthma been trying to act up, but I gave her some herbal tea to stop her wheezing."

Her mother's expression looked pinched. "Good for you, Barbara Jean, but I want outta here today."

"Not now, Mama. Maybe when Nylah comes home. I'm too tired."

Brittany laid her little head against Mama Jo's thin brown arm. "Me too, Ganny, I'm tired too."

"That's granny, not ganny. And chile, you too young to know what tired is."

Making her annoyance obvious, Barbara Jean walked over and pulled Brittany up from the bed. "Mama, stop picking on her and don't talk to her like that. I said she don't feel good."

"Oh hush up, Barbara Jean. You keep telling the chile she sick all the time, and that's what she'll start believing. Ain't nothin' wrong with this girl."

Barbara Jean rolled her eyes. "Whatever. C'mon, Brit."

Mama Jo eased up from her bed with her hands on her hips. "Don't you 'whatever' me." She could still remember a time when children respected their parents and went out of their way to please. Barbara Jean was far from being a child, but Mama Jo never gave up hope. She still expected a certain amount of respect and recognition in her own house.

Being pulled from the room, Brittany yawned and looked perplexed down at her feet as if trying to figure out why they felt so funny along the old and dirty carpet in her grandmother's room. "Ganny, you fuss too much."

"I fuss too much? Well, you ain't nothin'. Girl, you better get up on out of here with yo' lazy mama."

"Don't worry," Barbara Jean said, "we're going. We need our sleep."

"Sleep, sleep and more sleep. That's all we do in this house is sleep, Barbara Jean. I want outta this room today, and I'm not playing."

Barbara Jean uttered a weary sigh. "When Nylah comes home. I'm going back to bed."

"Hell," her mother shot back bitterly. "That's all I hear. Wait 'til Nylah comes home. And when she comes, it's wait 'til

Barbara gets home. All I know is I wanna go out and I'm going."

Brittany stood quiet and motionless by her mother at the open door, both watching Mama Jo go to the room's small closet and ramble for something clean to put on. Black wire hangers and a few thick tubular ones hung like multicolored Christmas ornaments along the closet's wooden rack, but nothing was hung up waiting to be worn. Barbara Jean shook her head at the sight. All her mother's clothes, it appeared to her, were retired to a blissful heap along the clutter of the closet floor.

"Hell," Mama Jo snorted in her customary tone of defiance. "Y'all think I have to take this mess. You can't keep me locked up in here forever." She pulled out some light beige cotton pants and examined them. Grease and dirt stained the front. Flinging the pants back down in the heap, she put her whole body into bending over to ramble some more; her too small behind wiggled in the air, barely discernible through her thin gown. Her short-cropped black hair was covered with a black scarf, which only helped to give her the appearance of an old sun dried woman absorbed in the art of picking cotton. Brittany couldn't help but giggle at her.

Lord, thought Barbara Jean as she watched her mother's antics for a spell, tired. Just plain tired. "Mama, you can't go out now and you know it."

"And you can't keep me here either."

"It's not my fault, Mama. No guilt trips today, please."

"Barbara Jean, all I know is I'm going out! Today!"

Sleep weary, Barbara Jean stood watching for a spell longer, then turned and quietly left the room, pulling Brittany by the hand behind her. At the sound of the security door banging shut Mama Jo jumped back startled. For a few seconds her eyes flashed frantic before she ran over to it.

"No! You open this door, Barbara Jean! Now!"

"Look, Mama, it's like I said. I gotta get some sleep or I'll be too tired to work tonight."

Barbara Jean stood briefly on the opposite side watching her mother mash her face into the door's mesh giving her a surreal, distorted look that was almost comical. Her mother knew that look. Like it had to feel so wrong trying to save her mother from her own self. But what else could they do?

"You can't keep me caged up in here forever, Barbara Jean. No sirree. I'm not some common criminal to be punished."

Wearily Barbara Jean sighed. "Mama, nobody's punishing you."

"Let me out then."

"If anybody should be feeling like they being punished, it's me and Nylah."

"Then let me out."

"You will go out when Nylah gets home."

Her eyes pleaded. "I'll be good, I promise."

"You said that last time, Mama." Barbara Jean nodded and scratched her head thinking about the last time she'd trusted her mother to go to the store alone, only to find the woman a week later sleeping in a dilapidated crack house on the far side of town. Luck had been on their side that time. Luck and too many sleepless nights. Only with the help of a ten dollar-bribe tip from another druggie were they able to locate their mother at all. "I worked hard last night and I'm tired. Good or not so good, I can't take you out right now. Can't be dealing with no foolishness right now. Not like last time."

Averting her eyes to the dirty carpet, Mama Jo snorted, "Last time I had money, but not this time. No money, no trouble." Pathetic, she looked back up through the black steel mesh. "Just for a spell."

"No, Mama. I said not now. Not 'til Nylah comes home. No tricks today. I haven't forgotten."

Defeated, Mama Jo let her thin shoulders sag along with her spirit. It was in her heart, the truth of what her daughters were trying to accomplish, keeping her locked away, a good thing trying to protect what little was left of her self. She knew that much. But still her resentment, like water under a frozen lake, ran deep. Didn't feel right though. It felt too much like she had just as much right to destroy her own life as anyone else did. "No right at all, you and Nylah, keeping me cooped up in this house like this."

"Blame it on love, Mama. Love makes folks do funny things."

Mama Jo shot her a hateful look. "You unlock this door!"

"I'm going back to bed now."

"Damn you, Barbara Jean! I'll beat the black off... You just wait...think I'm playing with y'all." She shook the metal door, rattled it, hopped back and kicked it, then tried throwing her meager body up against it. Nothing budged. Exhausted, she stepped back and silently watched Barbara Jean turn and amble back through the dimly lit hallway with a slightly wheezing Brittany right on her heel. "Well. . .what about somethin' to eat then? Is that too much to ask?"

Immune to her mother's antics Barbara Jean called back, "In a minute, Mama. Let me put Brittany back down for her nap and I'll heat up that spaghetti from yesterday, or I'll make you a sandwich."

She went back to the bedroom that she often shared with Brittany and helped her back into bed. Her body craving sleep, Barbara Jean sat along the side of the bed and pulled the top sheet over Brittany and then put her ear down to her small chest, listening. It sounded like most of Brittany's wheezing had stopped. She was relieved and thankful for that. But just for good measures, she made a mental note to make some more herbal tea later.

Smiling innocently up at her mother, Brittany suddenly

looked serious. Her eyes, by shape and color, were identical to her mother's, like large brown almonds. "Mama, when will ganny be okay again?"

Barbara Jean straightened the covers at her chest. "Brit, the word is granny. Not 'ganny'. And I really wish I knew."

"I like calling her ganny better."

"It's better to say the right word, right?"

"Ganny still gotta disease, huh Mama?"

"Looks that way, baby. But you really need to get back to that nap right now."

"When I grow up, I'm never gonna catch cocaine. Never, ever."

How cute, Barbara Jean thought, and kissed her forehead. She couldn't help wondering how much truth was in her young daughter's words. "I hope not, Baby. I really hope not. Maybe by the time you're all grown up they'll have a cure for cocaine addiction. Who knows? Maybe they'll find a way to completely destroy coca plants."

Brittany's eyes brightened. "What's a coca plant, Mama?"

"The plant that cocaine is made from."

"It's a disease too?" Her eyes were genuinely curious.

"No, baby. It's a plant."

Brittany looked confused and Barbara Jean realized that it was pointless to be having such a conversation with a five year old. Plenty of parents didn't take the time to talk to their children about drugs, which to her, only added to the problem. Barbara Jean knew that wouldn't be the case with her child. She planned to talk, watch, monitor, even snoop into Brittany's life for as long as necessary. Whatever it took. Besides, who was she fooling? Cocaine and the widespread abuse of it would probably be around until the end of the world. Even if scientists could find a way to totally wipe out the growing of the coca plant, wouldn't there just be another new designer drug to take its place?

The more she thought about it, for the life of her, Barbara
Jean couldn't figure it
out. What would make a woman of her mother's age and
social status go from healthy, outgoing, all the way down to a
lying, cheating and stealing for a hit-on-the-pipe kind of
woman? What could have been so bad? It made her heart feel
as heavy as bricks just to think about it.

Her mother had once been a beautiful black woman who
owned two nice luxury cars and several small homes, living in
the very one that she maintained; a strong woman taking care
of her own family and business after her husband was killed in
a car crash six years back. There was a time when her mother
had cherished her two daughters, loved and feared God, and
went to church every Sunday, sometimes even singing in the
choir. She was a woman who had lived and loved life with a
passion that was strong and well steeped in family values.
Gone. All gone up in smoke, except for the house they now
lived in.

To Barbara Jean, it was like the real Jodie Mae Richardson
went somewhere to a party with some new friends one night,
and forgot to come back home. Sometimes, it felt like this
woman living in the same house with them really wasn't the
same person that had spanked and chastised them when they
did wrong. She wasn't the same woman who had pressed
sweet fragrant oil into their hair before church service on
Sunday morning while searing wisdom into their young minds
at the same time. She wasn't the same woman that had nur-
tured them into adulthood at all, but some kind of misplaced
clone of their mother—someone too painful to even look at
lately. The woman even talked and smelled different. Of
course with her medical background, Barbara Jean knew that
smelling different sometimes resulted from other chemicals
and hormones reacting to a foreign substance in the body.
Barbara Jean still missed the woman that had been their real

mother. One thing for sure, it was a constant drain on her mind and spirit to keep her own mother protected from a drug. It was even harder, a deep rooted torture to see her mother out on the streets dying a little each day just to live with the pipe.

"Mama, why you crying?"

Goodness, thought Barbara Jean as she wiped tears from her eyes. She hadn't realized she'd let herself slip so deep into thinking about Mama Jo's ordeal. If only she had the power to change all the bad things happening in the world, her mother's addiction to crack would be the first thing on her list. Well, maybe the second thing. Making Brit well with healthy lungs would be the first.

"Oh yeah, mama's sandwich."

"You feel better now?" Brittany asked, the brown in her young eyes deeper with concern.

"Yeah. I'm okay. And as for you little lady, you get back to that nap while I go make granny a snack."

"Okay, Mama."

"Good girl." She kissed Brittany's forehead again, got up from the bed and left the room.

In the kitchen, Barbara Jean slid open old dingy looking curtains to let some sunlight into the room but soon regretted doing so. The room was horrible. It was too dark in corners and cluttered with dusty shelf bric-a-brac and old decaying newspapers that her mother insisted on saving. The walls were an odd combination of dingy white and gray. They could stand a good paint job, but every time she and Nylah made plans to spruce the place up some, something else always popped up in the form of more bills—Brittany's illness, or Mama Jo running off somewhere to do heaven-knows-what. It was always something. A few times they'd even speculated about hiring somebody, but neither she nor Nylah seemed willing to give up money from their salary or savings to renovate the place. The place being a dump was why she never brought her dates to her mother's house.

Going to her mother's refrigerator, Barbara Jean opened it and stood for a few seconds, allowing the coldness to caress her face before she removed a few items that were half concealing her second secret cache. All the way at the back of the box, right behind the head of lettuce wrapped carefully in cellophane, she removed the cup that held the three vials of blood. Removing one of the vials she held it up in the room light checking for freshness. Only a day or so had passed. She never kept vials in the kitchen box for long for fear of Nylah discovering her supply. Smiling, it all looked good. Closing the refrigerator, she took the three vials from the cup and went to the rear door of the house leading out to the patio where she kept all of her special plants. Opening the door, she stepped outside.

Under the patio were numerous pots of varying shapes, color and size. A few pieces of old patio furniture sat like abandoned relics from a happier past, weather-worn and covered with months of microscopic dirt and dust. She shook her head each time she came out, just at the sight of it all. Hardly anyone came out onto the patio anymore. Not with the yard in such a disaster with tall dying grass badly in need of mowing, thirst-dying trees and shrubs, and sun baked-flowers quietly withering about the fenced-in yard.

In the past, on more occasions than she cared to remember, her mother had talked about paying a gardener to come in and clean the place up, get the lawn back to green, and maybe start up a new flower garden to add some charm to the yard. Perhaps more quality family time would have followed with grilling meat and sharing of chilled watermelon outside on a hot summer day. Where had the family closeness gone? Yep, she chuckled as she looked around. A gardener to come in maybe twice a month would be nice. But so far, it amounted to talk. No one ever came out to the patio, which made it a perfect isolated spot.

Barbara Jean kept all her wonderful plants here. About ten pots sat on one side of the covered patio around the square wooden poles that had once been white. Neglected, chipping paint curled and peeled itself in muted protest along each of the two poles supporting the patio canopy. But it was nothing for her to be concerned about. Ten more potted plants were equally placed around the opposite pole directly across. Her eyes glazed over. It was her own little experiment. Her own little cohesive collection.

Of course to some folks, her collection of blood might seem odd, perhaps even bizarre. Sometimes she found herself wondering if she were ever asked the question of why she stole and collected blood specimens from the hospital and carried out clandestine experiments with those same specimens, a clue to her answer would run as deep as the Pacific Ocean itself. It was a question she simply did not have a clear answer for. The reason why was as vague and ambiguous as the answer of why wives expected total fidelity from husbands incapable of giving it.

All the plants on the left side, her philodendrons, day lilies, voodoo lilies and pygmy palms were taller and healthier looking than her plants on the right side. She went to each side and took a long calculated look. Pleased with her findings, she moved back over to the pots on the left side and took her finger and scratched small deep circles around the moist base of each plant before uncapping each vial of red one at a time. The first time she had experimented with the red liquid had been a curious attempt to revive a dying pet parakeet. After making a remarkable recovery, the bird remained healthy until the day it flew out a window after someone left its cage door open. That was when she discovered that all blood wasn't the same. There was the good stuff and the bad stuff, and just to make sure that she experimented only with the good stuff, she tested each batch for bacteria contamination and HIV.

The afternoon air was light and crisp around her with a smell of something good cooking in somebody's kitchen. She recalled hearing something on the news earlier that the temperatures might soar into the nineties for the day. But so far, it wasn't too bad under the patio.

The smell of something cooking reminded her that she still had a snack to prepare for her mother. Sniffing at the air brought a smile to her face. It smelled like old Mrs. Parker next door was simmering some of her famous ham hocks and turnipgreens on the stove. Too bad the old woman had had a falling out with her mother a few months back and stopped speaking to everybody else living in the house. Barbara Jean could still recall the many days her own feet had sat under her neighbor's kitchen table while she was chowing down on some turnip greens and hot water cornbread followed by peach cobbler or a slice of of Mrs. Parker's friendship cake. Mrs. Parker, as far as Barbara Jean felt, was God's personal cook sent down from heaven, even though she never did give up the secret recipe for her friendship cake.

Humming softly to herself, she squatted down and poured some of the crimson liquid, thick and slow into each finger-created circle. Swiftly she covered each back over with more moist dirt before standing back up and gazing down at her experiment on human blood. It was all so utterly amazing, so unbelievable, that sometimes the sight of it almost took her breath away.

"Barbara Jean! Barbara Jean, where the heck are you?!

Cringing at the loud timbre of her mother's voice screeching through the house, Barbara Jean tensed every muscle in her body, squeezed her eyes shut, and clutched the empty vials tight enough to pop each one in the palm of her hand. She hated it when her mother screamed out her name like some lunatic.

"Crazy old woman. Now what?" Probably screaming for something to eat. She opened her eyes slowly and relaxed her back. Hating to leave her project so soon, she took a deep breath to steady herself, calm her nerves.

"Make me sick sometimes." Her mother's shrill voice reeling her in, Barbara Jean turned and quickened her step as she headed back into the house to see about something to eat for her mother.

Chapter Six

Lovell's dry lips parted as he eased one eye open and then the other one. Of all the places that he could be, he was mildly surprised to find himself still in a hospital gown, in a hospital bed, and in a room. It took a few minutes for his vision to clear, but when it did, his mind was a complete blank.

His head felt odd, like someone had over-filled it with a gallon of ice cold water and neglected to let the pressure out. Rubbing the top of his head, he wondered briefly if a headache felt this way, considering that he'd never experienced one in his entire life.

He looked around to see that he was alone. Two additional beds in the room loomed cold and empty. He was all alone in this strange and isolated room, which wasn't big or unusual. It looked like a typical hospital room very much like the ones he'd seen plenty of times on various television shows. Two doors rested along a wall. One, he supposed, was a closet and the other was probably a small restroom. A wooden framed beige vinyl chair sat off to one side beneath the window. A full length mirror framed the closed restroom door. No pictures hung on the wall, only the same wallpaper he'd seen when he'd first entered the clinic, light blue butterflies on an off-white background. Metal railing was pushed down at each side of the massive bed.

Good Lord, he thought as he gave the bed a good scrutiny. With all these control buttons and gadgets, it looks more like the inside panel of a 747. He noticed that a copper-looking water pitcher, complete with its own matching cup, sat waiting on a small square table next to his bed; then he noticed that an IV drip had been hooked up to his arm, its clear tubing hanging like clear and limp spaghetti from a pole.

"What the heck. . ." An intravenous drip? Why would he need a drip to stitch up a few cuts? he puzzled. He felt so disoriented.

Lovell threw back the thin covers on the bed and lifted his gown up. Underneath he wore no clothes, and on his left side was somebody's medical handy work; a large white surgical patch was taped to his skin. He felt it, prodded every inch of it with his finger, and pondered what kind of designer medication he'd been given, because he couldn't recall exactly what had happened after he had been admitted.

Going over it step by step in his mind, his thoughts seemed fuzzy. It was just yesterday, wasn't it? He remembered coming to the hospital with his friend, Yolanda, and being put in a small exam room by a nurse. He even remembered the name on her tag. Nylah. Right. Nylah something; Richards, Richmond or something like that. The nurse had left him to wait for the doctor to come in to examine him, and then...then, after the doctor...

He forced himself to think. The doctor had been nice enough, a little rushed and somewhat curt when he spoke. He was a short and pink man with thin, dark hair, too many teeth in his mouth, and eyes way too large for a man of his size. He remembered. The doctor had informed him that a small piece of glass had nicked his intestine, which would have to be repaired. Let's see, he probed, prompting his mind to hurry up with the information. But somehow, it wasn't coming fast enough.

Reaching for the buzzer, Lovell pushed his finger into it frantically to summon a doctor or a nurse, anybody that could shed some light on his condition. His throat was hot and tight, and the room was too cold, not to mention all the questions that were gathering themselves up in an disorderly manner in his head. He was being a tad too suspicious, but something didn't seem right, and he needed answers.

Right away a nurse came in dressed in her neat white uniform with her arms in front of her holding a small black tray with a paper pill cup containing two tiny red pills. Lovell felt silly making haste to throw the thin sheet back over his naked behind, as if the woman hadn't already seen every inch of him by now. Thankfully the knowing smile on the nurse's face told him that she understood.

Her face looked radiant and vaguely familiar.   Lovell checked out her name tag to be sure.   Nylah Richardson. Thank God for a familiar face. He felt some of his tension roll away. She had a pleasant, easy disposition that tried to relax him. In fact, if it hadn't been for her, he wouldn't have been admitted to Park One to begin with. He felt the glow of gratitude sweep over him. Pulling himself up to a sitting position, Lovell watched her for a second or two.

"Well, good morning, Mr. Joyner. Good to see you're awake."

"Morning to you too." He watched her like a cat watching a bird.

Nylah picked up the pill cup and extended it to him, obviously wanting for him to take the pills. Probably something to ward off infection, he figured. After he took the cup, she took up the pitcher and poured him some fresh water.

Lovell stared into the clear liquid for a brief spell, then without protest popped the two tiny red pills into his mouth. He made a face as the ice cold water rushed down his throat. His eyes shut and opened as he pursed his lips. It was almost as if his body was going through some kind of adjustment on its own. There was a tingling feeling somewhere in his stomach, and then an odd queasiness. Sniffing, he reached the empty cup out to her.

Taking the cup from his hand and placing the tray down, Nylah smiled before lowering her eyes, taking his temperature and then his blood pressure. He waited patiently for her to offer up some information about why he was still in the hospital for something so minor as a couple of cuts along his side, but when silence stretched too long between them, he couldn't take it anymore.

"So, what's up now? How long have I been here?" Lovell asked when his mouth was clear of the thermometer. "Did they find some glass in me or what?" Somehow it felt like he had just been admitted to the hospital earlier that day, but the way his head was feeling and his body so out of sync, he couldn't be sure.

"Not now, please."

A quick silence with her finger hushed his words while Nylah inflated the pressure cuff to the max, which was too tight for his comfort. Lovell held his tongue and squirmed on the bed like a child that had better things to be doing and wished that she'd hurry up and finish. Not that he had any particular place to go, but even so, staying any longer than he had to in a hospital room was more than he could stand.

"Guess you're not much of a talker, huh?"

"Only when I have something to say," Nylah said in response.

"Is that right?" Lovell kept angling his face up and down, trying to get her to look him in the eye, but she seemed too caught up in her duties to notice.

"Are you in any pain?" Nylah asked, the tone of her voice professional, but ringing with concern. She walked around to his chart and wrote a few words and numbers down.

"Say what now?" He'd heard the question the first time but liked the sound of her voice being interested in something about him. Even with sense enough to know that her inquiry was only part of her job, it still made him feel good when a woman acted like she cared.

"Pain. I asked if you were in any pain."

"Guess not. At least not while I'm looking at you."

"Don't you know for sure?" Nylah gave him a sly smile before looking away.

Lovell took in a deep breath. The corners of his nostrils flared as he inhaled deeply to take in the essence of her. Baby powder freshness emanated from some secret place on her body. He could smell her. It was a smell like wild honey-suckle and Ivory soap—like a mixture of sweet exotic flowers and rich earth mixed with everything good in the world. She wore no strong perfume, and he was glad for it. She had a wholesome smell. Once, when he was young, he made the mistake of telling a female friend about his super sensitive sense of smell—how he could smell the fresh of rain weeks before its arrival. How he could smell buried seeds about to burst up through the nourishing earth, and new life hidden deep within the petal-pink folds of a mother's womb. Ultimately, which had been a big mistake, how he could smell when a woman's monthly cycle came around, even from across a room. Big mistake. Silly girl had called him a freak, and never spoke to him again after that. But he had learned. He could still smell every inch of a woman's body, the good smells all mingled in with the bad. Lovell saw his extraordinary sense of smell as a good thing, and a bad thing. It was a curse as much as a gift, and something that he could never tell another living soul about.

"Well? Are you? If so I can have doctor prescribe something stronger for you." She put his chart away and moved back over to his bedside and motioned for him to lie back along the bed.

It wasn't easy, but Lovell forced himself to relax. "Nah. No pain, but my head feels kinda funny. Like it's too heavy for my neck. And it's so cold in this room. You could freeze a brother into a popsicle in a place like this."

"Probably the anesthesia. Some people are sensitive to it. As for this room being cold, hospitals are supposed to be cold. Helps to control germs. Let me have a look and change your bandage."

For no reason he stiffened at her request, noticing the bandage on her hand, but she pulled out a pair of latex surgical gloves from her pocket and slid them on easily, which, oddly enough, was a relief to him.

"Just lay back and relax," Nylah said soothingly. "You're in good hands."

"Is that right? Well, that's nice to know." Taking in a deep breath and closing his eyes, Lovell could feel more tension rolling away from him like the waves in an ocean. For the moment, he let his thoughts slip away and forgot all about all the questions that had been ready to ambush her with the second she stepped into the room; he forgot about the coldness running a path of goose bumps up the length of his spine. For the moment, he forgot about his lack of a place to live. He liked this woman...this Nylah person. He liked the subtle definition of her nose, not too sharp and not too flat or wide. When she smiled, he could see a hint of dimples at each cheek. The delicate sweep of her neck was perfect, not too long, and definitely not like some short women who had necks that appeared to be sitting directly on their shoulders. Beautiful almond shaped brown eyes. There was something bewitching in those eyes of hers that he wanted to know more about. And those lips. If only he could just have a sample of what lips like hers would taste like. Like the kiss of heaven, perhaps. He definitely was in good hands.

"Looks like we're out of clean dressing. Let me go get some more. Won't take but twenty seconds. Don't move now."

Lovell half heard her. His mind sailed away with private thoughts. The off-white blinds were open at the window, and as he pressed his head back along the firm pillow and gazed passively out at the new day, he could see the neatly trimmed bougainvillea, their orange and lovely pink petals praising in the pristine sunlight. A few quarreling brown sparrows shot past his view and took perch on a nearby branch for their dueling. Rowdy ghetto birds, he grinned. Amused, he watched them until they tired and both took to the sky.

Even with all the cozy thoughts of Nylah rambling around in his head, he couldn't dismiss his own situation. Nothing had changed much. He was still homeless, yet he felt so peaceful. The sun was up and bright, another hot one, he could tell. And when he was released to go home, he wondered exactly where that would be—a bus station, a laundromat, or a dirty freeway underpass perhaps? Or maybe he would have to join the army of homeless victims bravely sleeping at a public park or just plain out on the cold streets, but so be it. He refused to let his situation get him down.

Could it be the medication that he'd just taken causing him to feel so in tune to his own existence, so peaceful, and unburdened. Here he was, after all, a man with no mother or father to ask for help. The last set of foster parents he'd lived with had taken up stakes and moved back south leaving him no pretend-family as well. No sisters or brothers to lend him a dollar or two for something to eat, or offer him a roof over his head for a few days. Nobody he could call that would care. But these thoughts flowed like easy water through his mind, and he felt so good and free about it all, so relaxed.

"You should be pretty hungry after sleeping for two whole days."

"Say what? I'm sorry, I didn't hear you." Lovell stiffened

and then pulled himself up again. Smiling amiably, Nylah was back at the side of his bed, quiet as a mouse, and he hadn't even heard her enter back into the room.

"Don't move," Nylah ordered softly as she carefully proceeded to pull back his bandage, taking her time not to disrupt the few healing stitches holding his smooth brown flesh together, and risk more bleeding, not to mention possible infection. She was silent during her observation, but Lovell could tell by her facial expression that something was up.

"Well, I'll be darn," she said speculatively.

"What?"

"Amazing."

"What is it?"

Paying little attention to her remarks, Lovell's mind went back to musing over the part about him being asleep for two days. Those four words kept circulating around in his head like lost foreigners to a new country. What did she mean by asleep for two days? "No way," he shook his head.

"You have to hold still," Nylah chided.

Looking totally confused Lovell asked, "Today is Sunday, right?"

"This is incredible," Nylah ventured. Her face was positioned closer to his exposed side than he wanted it to be, and it was something about the way she was pinching up her face while looking that bothered him. "I wouldn't believe it if I didn't see it with..." She went silent and moved back, adjusting her eyes, but the view was the same. ". . .my own eyes . . ."

"I wanna know what day it is," Lovell persisted with lined up questions in his head getting restless and ready to jump right out. At least she was pleasant to look at, not drop dead beautiful, but attractive in an average kind of way. He wondered if she'd ever been married. A quick confirming look to her hand showed no signs of wedding rings. Of course he knew that one couldn't always go by that.

"Maybe I should go get the doctor and have him come take a look."

"Or maybe you should just tell me what's wrong...what is it?"

"Nothing to concern yourself with, Mr. Joyner."

"Then why you need a doctor? Is the wound infected or something?"

"I'll have doctor come talk to you."

"I wanna know what day it is? Is it too much to ask what day it is?" Trying to get uppity with her, Lovell ignored her look of muted shock and pulled the crisp white sheet back over his body in a gesture that read that the show was over. "Is it Sunday or what?"

"Hold on justa minute, Mr. Joyner."

"Can't you just tell me?"

"Mr. Joyner, please."

Nylah placed a hand to her mouth as if to hold more words at bay. Her eyes grew large and skeptic as she regarded him for a few seconds in silence before she could take rein over her professionalism.

"Just relax. Let's not get all excited," Nylah cooed as she taped his bandage back along his skin.

Too many years in the medical field reminded her that anything was possible when it came to the human body, and why should Mr. Joyner be an exception? Heck, she mused, just a couple of years back she recalled a man admitted to Park One Memorial with two penises. One penis halfway severed because the man had attempted to remove it himself with a dull kitchen knife because he was tired of being looked upon as a freak. A few months back, the hospital had experienced its first infant born without a brain. It didn't take long for the media to get wind of the doomed child's birth. She still recalled how hard the young couple had taken it when their baby died after six whole days of non-stop media publicity.

And what about the woman who gave birth to twins three months apart? Bottom line was, the freakish, the strange, and the unusual happens in hospitals all the time. It took weeks for the talk and morbid jokes about the man with the two penises to die down.

Moving back over to his chart, Nylah briskly snatched it up and jotted down some more findings. She didn't want to overlook or leave out any pertinent details. Lovell stared on with mounting impatience.

Nylah always felt like she had to stay on top of things when it came to her patient observations. The doctor in charge of Lovell's case was a young, white zealot by the name of Kinsley who always burst into a room like a bad wind and acted like his main purpose in life was to give all nurses on the planet earth a hard time about every little nit-pickish thing he could find. None of the nurses at Park One Memorial liked him, and Nylah was no exception. In her opinion, Dr. Kinsley was a rude, over-educated pompous fool making good money that he probably was too snobbish and uptight to really enjoy. It took all her strength and a few silent prayers before the start of her shift just to be able to work with the man on a daily basis.

She was still writing furiously on his chart as Lovell stared at her with a quizzical expression on his face. Tension in the room was thick and slippery as slime. As hard as he tried, Lovell couldn't gauge her demeanor or what it could possibly mean. The fact that she still hadn't bothered to answer his simple question was enough to make him want to take up the buzzer and ring for another nurse. It seemed to him that if a hospital patient asked, they had the right to know about their medical condition. She was attractive and all, but who did she think she was anyway? He gave her a quick head-to-toe scan.

"Miss nurse, are you going to tell me what's up or what?" he asked for the final time. "The suspense is killing me."

Nylah's hand felt crampy from writing too hard and fast. She stopped long enough to grin over at him. "Nothing. Everything's fine, and today is Tuesday."

"Tuesday?"

"That's correct, Mr. Joyner. Tuesday."

"Tuesday?" he repeated. The word was almost like an echo in his head. A tight knot rose in his throat. "No way. I just came in Saturday."

"That's right," Nylah agreed. "You came in on Saturday with an Hispanic female." She kept writing, stopping only briefly to look back over at Lovell and wish that the man would stop staring at her with his mouth half open.

"But...If I just came in yesterday, which was Saturday, how can it be Tuesday?" His look was serious. "Maybe you looked at your calendar wrong this morning, Miss nurse."

"I doubt that, Mr. Joyner. And please call me Miss Richardson."

"Oh," he said, mocking a face of snobbery. "Do excuse me, Miss Richardson." He was finally getting her full attention.

Nylah had to admit to herself that the man was better looking than the other patients on her schedule. And those green eyes alone were enough to die for. Oh yeah, she smiled inwardly, Mr. Joyner was quite a looker and he probably knew it. He was definitely a feast for the eyes. When she looked at him, she saw a whole lot of things; she saw a handsome man that many women would probably fall prey to. She saw a man who was well trained in using his looks to get his way with women—not to mention that he carried himself with a cocky air of confidence. He probably stayed in the mirror admiring himself more than she did. But Lord have mercy, he is one handsome devil. She reminded herself that a good looking man was usually a prelude to a relationship of nothing but trouble.

Nylah allowed her mind to slip quickly back to when she

was dating Glen, another too handsome man who had delusions that his main purpose in life was to wine, dine, and seduce as many females as he possibly could before his time was up on the planet. Talks of marriage had been regular. More so, to pacify her need to be his wife, so Glen had thought. Glen had even gone so far as to buy her an expensive engagement ring, which she had worn proudly for months like some sparkling flamboyant 2-carat badge of defeat. That ring, another shiny piece of stone, had said a lot. That she had courageously fought the battle of dating and love, and she had won. She had found that one man, and he had chosen her. That was what that ring on her finger had said to all eyes that saw it.

Not one soul, not even her own mother, knew about the beautiful white dress hidden in a locked trunk in her bedroom closet. The pearl and lace affair that had been specifically made for her to wear on her special day in the spotlight. The day she would have become Mrs. Glen Turner. Nylah still remembered the day she had picked it up from the seamstress, and how she had left the dress in the trunk of her car, all neatly laid out and bagged up. She remembered how she had clandestinely brought it into the house to hide away in her closet at the strike of midnight when everyone else in the house was asleep. Waiting for Glen. Waiting for the date to be set. But that day never came.

Glen had avoided setting a date for their wedding the way some folks avoided nagging bill collectors. She couldn't possibly count how many caring friends had actually tried to pull her coat tail about Glen and warn her before she actually settled too deep into a marriage bed of lies and deceit. She would never forget how she'd thrown the ring in his face the same night she'd showed up at his apartment to cook a surprise dinner and found him in bed kissing another female. Served me right for using that darn spare key, her mind screamed.

She had sense enough to know that the truth always hurt when it slams you in the face. Seeing Glen with that other woman had been like a bullet train through her heart. She knew then that it wouldn't be the last time, even if they were married. There would always be one woman too many somewhere in the shadows of their life. Nylah knew that a lot of wives simply turned their heads, looked the other way, and held their wounded tongues and accepted the philandering ways of their husbands as if it were all part of the marriage vows that read 'To love, honor and cheat'.

Even her own mother, in her better days, had been reckless enough to advise her that, "True, a man might give a little of his loving away every now and then, but one thing for sure, he can't give it all away." But Nylah couldn't see herself buying into such nonsense. To her, what was the point of even getting married just to share? No, sir. The way she remembered it, the only thing that Glen had truly loved was his own handsome self and the slew of willing females that had flocked to be with him like bees to honey. Of course that was all behind her now. She had the daily caring of her mother to take up the void of not having a man in her life—not being in love or having someone to return that love.

Hmph. Good looking alright. Nothing but a bunch of heartache and pain. And hadn't she been burnt enough times to know the difference between a good man and just another pretty face?

"Excuse me, but I still don't get it," Lovell interrupted her thoughts. "How the heck could it be Tuesday when I just came in yesterday?"

Nylah turned her gaze away and rolled her eyes. For someone that had taken the medication she'd given him, he sure was talkative.

Lovell looked around the small room feeling confused. He was the only patient occupying the room, but suddenly it felt too cramped, and felt as if there wasn't enough fresh air circulating. "I'm getting a bad feeling here."

"Mr. Joyner," Nylah finally said in her most soothing voice, a voice usually reserved for her elderly patients and small children, "you've had minor surgery to remove embedded glass along your left side. The doctor also had to repair a small laceration to your lower intestine. Nothing too serious, and I'm sure you'll live. However, you were given anesthesia and you slept for two days. Your IV was just removed this morning and you're doing just fine." She placed his chart back in its rack at the end of the bed.

"My IV? Why would I need an IV for two whole days?"

"Stop worrying. You're doing fine."

"I can go home today then?"

"I'm not sure 'bout that part, but the doctor will be in to see you around one o'clock. I'm sure that you can ask him then." Moving swiftly back over to his bed, she took up his pillow, fluffed it before positioning it back under his head. He couldn't see the point of her doing so. Nothing was wrong with his pillow to begin with, but maybe it was all part of good nursing.

"I'm sure," she went on as she carried out a slew of duties about the room, "when the doctor comes in to see you, you'll have all your questions answered."

"But everything is okay, right?"

"Everything is fine."

Still not satisfied with her answer, Lovell asked, "There's no reason to stay longer, right? I mean, I'm really okay." At the back of his mind he imagined a riot of possible things going wrong with a simple procedure to remove some glass embedded in his flesh: a slip of the surgeon's hand and a slice clean across his belly; a surgical sponge accidentally left inside of his body; a dirty scalpel used and major infection; a procedure done on the wrong side. The possibilities were endless.

"I'm not trying to be funny, Miss lady...I mean, Miss Richardson. I just don't want no problems."

Nylah only nodded. "Like I said, Mr. Joyner, the doctor will be here around one o'clock today, and you can direct all your concerns to him at that time. But it seems to me that you're doing fine."

"And what doctor would that be?"

"Kinsley. Dr. Kinsley." She wanted to tell him that the man was a wonderful and overly caring human being, and a great asset to the medical profession. But that would be lying.

"Why can't you tell me yourself?"

He searched her eyes, almond shaped, brown, and some-what elusive. She was lying or holding back on something. Always check the windows to the soul. There was something about her eyes; Lovell could see it. Plenty of times he'd seen that same look in the eyes of a woman—his woman. How he had missed the truth in his former girlfriend's eyes, Miss Rita, was still a mystery.

"Because, Mr. Joyner," she paused, "nurses aren't doctors, and doctors get paid to diagnose and consult with patients to share their findings. You wouldn't want me to get in trouble, would you?" Another pause. "Now," she stopped and smiled graciously at him. "Does that answer your question?"

"Not really," Lovell replied and looked away at the wall. Uneasiness began to surge through him again like new blood dueling with his urge to jump up, find his clothes, and flee from the room. So what if he didn't have the faintest idea where to go, as long as he was as far away from the hospital as possible.

He didn't care what anybody said, there was something she wasn't telling him. "You wouldn't fake a brother out, would you?" Lovell searched her face again, her eyes. Then she was saying something.

"Mr. Joyner, I'll order you some breakfast. I know you

must be starving by now."

His eyes brightened. Got that right, he thought. But before he could verbally respond to her summation, she'd put away his chart, moved back to the side of his bed to fluff his pillow again in an effort to smooth out his uneasiness.

"You take such good care of a man. I bet your husband don't let you get too far from his sight. He's one lucky man."

"Mr. Joyner," she said ever so smoothly as she fluffed the sides of his pillow. "If that's your round-about way of asking if I'm married, I'm not. That's why I told you my name was Miss not Mrs."

"You're right."

While raising up from his pillow his head brushed lightly against her full breasts. It was the lightest touch of skin to material that was over with as fast as it had started. But all the same, it excited something in him. Her firm softness against his face along with the tangled smells of her body caused a stirring in his groin, and before his better judgment could catch up with the rest of his senses, he shot his lips up and kissed her cheek. A quick peck on the side of her startled face. It was more than a kiss of gratitude. He wanted to feel the full bloom of his lips pressed against hers, but knew that such a stunt could be risky. What if she slapped his face?

Nylah froze over him, looking down into his eyes. For a moment her expression looked. . .well. . .a bit stunned. Quickly, she recovered. "Mr. Joyner, please. . ."

"Just my way of saying thanks." Lovell regarded her with a wide, silly grin.

"Just doing my job, Mr. Joyner. No need to thank me." Must be the medication, Nylah mused as she crossed the room to adjust his window drapes to block out too much sunlight. Several times in the past a patient or two had kissed her before she could protest. Usually older men or young boys operating under the power of having a crush on her. She did her best to steer clear from patients that couldn't control their affections while under pain medication. Not that she had anything against a patient showing their gratitude for all the things a nurse had to do, but it wouldn't look appropriate if another nurse or one of the hospital's bigheads popped into the room and witnessed such a sight. Fraternizing with patients in anyway deemed unprofessional was greatly frowned upon at Park One Memorial.

"I'll have some food sent to you."

Lovell wanted to tell her no, and not to leave. At least not yet. He wanted to gaze at her for a while longer. He wanted to feel her radiating aura, like sweetened light, or just the good feeling of being around her. Too many of the women of his past lacked a certain kind of class—a certain deep inner strength wrapped in a softened core. But not this woman. Not Nylah.

Lovell smiled to himself. It was all so refreshing the way he was feeling about a woman he hardly knew—refreshing and a little scary. He was just about to ask her to stay longer and talk to him, but too late. Nylah's back was to him and fading out. Already she was on her way out of the room with her funny-shaped white shoes making tiny squishy sounds on the beige tiled floor.

The second the door closed, Lovell sprinted out of bed but had to stop short and stand still. His head felt like it was an oversized top spinning around on his neck. He held his breath, then released it slowly. The room went blurry, but after a few seconds his eyes slipped back into focus and he felt his balance catch.

Taking another deep breath, he leaned against a wall and steadied himself before slowly making his way over to the foot of the bed and grabbing up his chart from the rack. Not one thing could he make out clearly. Words he couldn't understand, cryptic medical jargon, were scrawled across the page.

And he thought his handwriting was bad. He placed the chart back, moved to the full-length mirror, and lifted his gown to expose his left side.

The room felt cold, his hands even colder and almost numb as he lifted up the cotton gown and snatched off the bandage, running his hand along the cool flesh where the bandage had been. He held his breath expecting to see a total horror, somebody's botched up surgery job, or worse. But to his amazement, there was no gash, no ruptured skin, nor surgically repaired wound to see. There was no scar, only skin as smooth and perfect as the day he'd arrived into the world.

Chapter Seven

The brilliant white beams of light were his hope. The rise of the cavalry and rescue. The beams filled his soul to the brim with a radiance. At one end of his existence, they danced around inside of him like all the happiness and love that had once been his. Like pure magic, they bounced around to one corner of his head, then over to another, filling him with an awe and wonder driven by innocence he hadn't felt since childhood.

Lovell slowly opened his heavy eyelids and tried to focus. People were in his room. Their mingled smells and tangled spirits gave off an odd combination of antiseptic, expensive colognes, and musk. Their outlines were like swollen shapes of blue that were becoming increasingly clear. Lovell counted four, and he could tell by the sound of each exchanging voice, gruff and swift, almost surly, that they were men. Two tall ones, one of average height, about his own stature, and one even shorter. The four men, all white, and from what he could make out, were gazing expectantly at him from where they stood. Two of the men were dressed in dark suits that seemed more fitting for the executive suite of a major corporation instead of a small privately owned hospital. The tallest and the shortest of the four were clad in white, the same puritan garb he'd expect to see on a doctor. One of the men, the shortest, was forcing his right eyelid up and shining one of the small beams of light into it .

He could make their faces out clearer. They smiled down at him, but to him, even in the sparse lighting, their smiling lips told another story and looked oddly sinister like thin snakes moving fretfully slow across each pretentious face. When they spoke, their voices were like hushed whispers meant only for certain ears. He caught bits and pieces of their conversation...something about family. Someone was saying something about family, and that his papers claimed that he had none, and then something about blood. Somebody, though he was too sleepy and disoriented to be accurate, somebody wanted blood. Something about his blood.

Lovell could hear them clearly enough, but for some odd reason their words lacked full meaning and swirled up and all around him. The ceiling light was off in the small room, and suddenly he wondered who were these men discussing him in their clandestine whispers at his bedside like some mysterious plot unfolding in the dark of his hospital room.

"This is the young man," an unfamiliar voice said.

"What?..what's going on?" The voice didn't even sound like his voice asking the question.

"Good evening, Mr. Joyner, I'm Dr. Kinsley, and these are three of the hospital's board members, Dr. Franklin, Dr. Kent, and Dr. Shilling. There's nothing to be alarmed about, we're just doing late rounds."

In a voice that was low and raspy one man said pointedly, ". . .get him to sign. As long as we have a signature."

"Looks like he's really out of it right now," Dr. Franklin offered.

"Who cares," countered Dr. Shilling, the shorter of the four. "Get him to sign. That way we cover our asses."

"Hand me a pen," Dr. Kinsley snapped.

At one point a pen was shoved into his hand. A clipboard

was held up, and unsuccessfully Lovell tried to pull his own hand out and away from the grip of another that was guiding his over the clipboard.

Lovell tried to protest, but not strong enough. "Wait a minute. . .I. . ."

"Sign here, Mr. Joyner," Dr. Kinsley instructed him. "We'll take care of everything."

"Nothing to worry about, Mr. Joyner," insisted Dr. Shilling, smiling a smile that Lovell couldn't see in the semi-darkness. "Just standard hospital forms to run some more testing on you."

As hard as it was, Lovell tried to see from which face the last voice had come, then tried to raise himself up more to a sitting position. But with the bright pen light directly in his already blurred vision, his efforts were futile. A large, splayed hand gently pushed him back down onto the pillow, and he could feel more hands touching him—a feeling like a thousand small snakes sliding all over his skin.

The sudden coldness to his body signaled that his bed covers, two thin sheets and one thin blanket, had been pulled back, and the spot where his wound had been was being exposed and prodded, and closely examined.

Dr. Shilling's raspy voice inquired, "He came in when?"

"Saturday afternoon," replied Dr. Kinsley.

"Unbelievable." Dr. Shilling shook his head at the spot where the beam was trained on Lovell's side.

"Who knows about this?", Dr. Franklin queried in a quick, pompous tone that sounded too rushed.

". . .water. Can I have some water?" It took a while for Lovell to realize that it was his own voice asking. His mouth felt as dry as the desert. God, he wished that they would keep that dang light out of his eyes, blocking out his view, covering up their eyes. He needed to see their eyes. Lovell heard himself speak something else, but his words, small and muffled, made little sense to him. ". . .nurse, the nurse ...call her please."

Another male voice answered, "A nurse, maybe a lab tech who ran the test even on the HIV virus. A cure could be closer than we think. But we have a tight lid on it. Definitely no media. Last thing we need right now."

Lovell felt like all his thoughts and emotions were spinning around out of control in one giant pool. Why couldn't he think straight? Something was wrong with his speech, and even his lips, for some strange reason unbeknownst to him, were dry and hot and wouldn't cooperate. His words didn't feel right in his own mouth. He wanted to know who these people were; he wanted to scream for them to get out of his room and leave him alone so that he could sleep, but his mind seemed filled with tangled sentences, and webbed words were trapped inside his mouth.

There was more talk about his miracle blood and testing. Lovell tried to catch every single word uttered, but some of them flew clean over his head and scurried away like small, frightened animals seeking shelter. He kept hearing whispers. What were they saying now? He cocked his head, and perked his ears trying to listen.

It was all too much. Lovell closed his eyes tight and let himself slip away, back down into the darkness for a moment. When he opened his eyes again, the men were gone. They had been there one minute, and were gone the next like a bad dream. But he was feeling a flowing carelessness and total peace—his mind was the ocean; his thoughts were the waves languishing back and forth with the rhythm of the tides. Had he dreamt it all? Had he really dreamt about four aliens probing him, talking in hushed tones at his bedside, and getting him to sign something that he had not been allowed to read? Had he really? All he wanted to do was sleep. Just to close his eyes and be allowed to float far, far away on the soothing waves.

Chapter Eight

"Mr. Joyner. Mr. Joyner, wake up. C'mon now. You gotta wake up."

The heaviness and sleep took its time slipping away from his tight eyes, but groggily Lovell opened them and tried to think once again, of where he was. Nothing looked familiar, and wherever he was, it was a cold place—a place where rest and relaxation were literally impossible. He could feel a rise of small goose bumps come up on his skin. He heard the voice again. A woman's voice, sweet and low, and a different smell. The mild, but equally distinct aroma of vanilla. Someone smelling like pure vanilla was in his room.

Thanks to the small light over his bed, the room wasn't completely shrouded in darkness like it had been earlier. He could see the woman's face, a black woman with a look of true concern, right in front of him. Gawking. She was standing with a haunch to her posture over his bed, her insistent hands felt warm on the skin of his arm as she shook him. Her face was so close to his that he could smell the coppery zing of her breath mixed with mint. He felt a kiss, light as feather, on his forehead. "Wake up now."

"What?" Craning his neck, Lovell looked around for the others but there were none. He was half expecting to see the same four men, like mysterious aliens from another planet, prodding and examining him. But this time there were no men. All he wanted was sleep, but here was this woman, a new face at his bedside, shaking him, trying to rouse him from sleep. "I said what?"

"You have to wake up."

He couldn't pull his mind together fast enough to figure out who, what, or why. Here was this stranger in his room telling him that he had to wake up when his mind and body was craving more sleep.

Pulling himself up in bed, Lovell rubbed heavy eyes with the back of his hand and eyed her suspiciously.

"What the. . .what's going on?"

"We can't talk here. We have to go."

"Go?"

"Just trust me."

The woman had large luminous eyes that looked to be glowing, but he knew that it was the angle of the light in her face. Her hair, from what little he could see, was slicked back along her small head, giving her an innocent tomboyish look. She smiled at him for reassurance.

"C'mon now, we have to go. You can't stay here."

". . .say what?"

"You can't stay here I said. Your life could be in danger. We have to go now. C'mon, wrap this blanket 'round you. No time to get dressed."

". . .but, I. . .who are you? Lady, I don't know you. I'm not going no where. . ."

"Look, fool!. . .", the woman whispered harshly before catching herself. Her eyes softened and she stopped and blew out a thin breath to calm her voice. "Some men came to see you earlier tonight, right? They wanna detain you here so they can study your DNA, your blood. Do you hear me? Understand what I'm trying to tell you? Now, you can stay and end up a dead guinea pig, or you can try'n save yo'self by coming with me. We don't have a lotta time, Lovell."

"Woman, who you calling a fool? And how you know my name?" He stiffened, making it more difficult for her to help him up from the bed.

"No time to talk now. We have to go."

"I asked how do you know my name? You work here?"

Adjusting the blanket around his shoulders, the woman didn't look up. "Shoots. The whole hospital might know your silly name by now. Word gets around. No telling what kind of plans this place could have for you. That's why I'm helping you out."

"Help me?. . .woman, what makes you think I need help?"

"Oh you need some help alright. Trust me. So c'mon, let's go before somebody finds out I'm here. I could get fired behind this."

He tried to think of another protest, but not for long before she grabbed the back of his shoulders and eased him off the bed. Lovell could feel a whiff of cold air zip up his gowned rear, but the woman seemed too hurried for him to complain.

Fixing his mouth to ask her something, the woman came on with, "B'sides, this is the best time to be leaving. The night duty nurse is making check rounds and old Nurse Pruitt is in her sex den with the security guard, so let's go."

"Go where?" He couldn't concentrate, and if this was what hospitals were like, somebody disturbing your sleep all through the night, well he could just do without it. All the rushed movements she was assisting him with made his stomach feel queasy. "I wanna know where I'm going first." He tried sitting back down along the cool sheets, but that didn't stop her from pulling him back up. Lovell couldn't believe how incredibly strong she was.

"Any place but here. Away from this place." Agitated, she sucked air through her teeth and rolled her eyes. "Man, you ask too many questions."

"Lady, I don't even know you. Who the heck are you anyway?"

"Here," she hissed impatiently, leaving him to stand perilously on wobbly legs while she got his few clothes hanging in the small closet. "We have to hurry."

"Heck no...I don't know about this..." Lovell shook his head and felt the heaviness inside roll from one side to the other as if there were wheels inside his head. His legs felt like they wanted to collapse, and if it wasn't for the woman in his room messing with him, he could be getting his beauty rest. And she had kissed him! What kind of hospital was this anyway?

"Look, my name is Barbara and I work here. I could lose my job behind this, Lovell. That's why we have to leave now."

"Barbara?" He stood on wobbly legs and cocked his head reflectively. ". . .no, I don't know a Barbara."

"That's okay," Barbara Jean murmured. "You still have to leave."

Before he could protest she guided him to the door, opened it and peered out, then guided him down the long shiny hallway past the vacant nurses' station and right out into the night air. Weak and dizzy, Lovell had the sensation that he was going to pass out any second with each step he took. He felt so physically helpless, like he was allowing himself to be kidnapped but couldn't stop her, even if he really wanted to.

She guided him to a the hospital's parking lot with no more than ten or fifteen cars. The woman kept scanning her surroundings, making quick and suspicious looking gestures that wouldn't have fooled a group of five year olds if some had been standing around to notice. In a way their departure was one of stealth, and Lovell couldn't help feeling like he was playing out some part in a script. Like maybe he was one of two spies on a top secret mission. Across the way, the deserted park seemed filled with their enemies in pursuit.

Standing at a vehicle, shivering in the late night air, Lovell supposed that it was her car he was being helped into. It was some kind of small and brown foreign model with a bad dent on the front passenger's side. Once inside, he saw that the interior was cluttered with items, mostly toys for a small child and discarded fast food bags and wrappers.

The woman that called herself Barbara hastily threw his few items of shoes and clothing along the rear seat and cracked a window to give him some fresh air, which was a good thing because his stomach felt like a volcano trying to erupt. He put his hand on the door handle and jiggled it, which was useless. In no time, she was around on the driver's side mumbling something, sliding in next to him, and starting the engine that coughed and sputtered and sounded like it was on its last leg. Lovell's ears could detect that the car wasn't running properly on all four cylinders, probably from a lack of a recent tune-up, he surmised. Not that he was an expert on cars, but he did know a few things to get by on. He rested his heavy head back along the brown cloth seat while the car pulled away from the hospital, his eyes barely able to stay open in spite of the bumpy ride. She definitely needed a tune up, but some new shocks wouldn't hurt either.

"Tell me where we're going again."

"Don't worry. Just long as it's away from this place."

"Tell me anyway," Lovell invited. If he had to wait any longer he knew that he'd be asleep. His eyes felt so burdened.

"I know this all seems wild and crazy right now," Barbara offered as she rolled down the driver's side window, "but I'm trying to do a good thing here by helping you. Like I said, my name is Barbara, but most people call me Barb or Barbara Jean." Steering the car to the parking lot exit, she put on her right side blinker and looked both ways before pulling out onto the street. "You can call me what you want."

"Right now," Lovell said in response, "that wouldn't be a

nice thing."

"If you feel that way, call me Barbara."

The cool, welcome breeze coming in through the open window caressed their faces, and Lovell loved it. The night air always smelled clean and exotic to him. Plenty of folks did their best to play down praise to California air, but he loved it. In fact, he couldn't imagine himself living in any other state. Once, a few years back, he was staying in the city of Tacoma, Washington, with an army-enlisted female he'd met at a party. For the life of him, Lovell couldn't remember what the woman's name had been. He only remembered that the relationship had been more platonic—like brother and sister, and hadn't lasted more than two or three months. He still remembered how he couldn't wait to get away from the place and back to California. All that rain had kept him moody and depressed.

He raised his head up and looked over at her, then rested it back on the seat. He imagined that if this Barbara woman had wanted to hurt him, she certainly could have done so in the parking lot of the hospital instead of taking him on a joyride first. And what about that kiss back in the hospital room? There was no denying what he had felt. Somebody's warm lips had kissed him, and she had been the only one in the room at the time. He stole a quick glance over at her. What kind of woman goes around kissing on a complete stranger while they tried to sleep?

"Who did you say you were again?"

She kept her eyes on the road. "Call me Barbara Jean."

"This is weird."

"Look," she said quietly. "I love my job, but sometimes it's a crazy place to work. A lotta strange stuff be happening. I guess that's why I've always known that I would end up working at a hospital." Her voice was slow and mellow as if she were taking the time to share some new tidbit of her life to a long-time friend after work. "I work with blood, body waste, and other body fluids all day long. . ." she paused for a nervous chuckle, which seemed trite at most, ". . .well, all night long 'cause they got me on graveyard right now. I get to do the non-stat fluids, you know, non-emergency. Mostly the whenever-you-can-get-to-it stuff." She grinned at some unspoken thought. "Funny, the things that can come outta human bodies. I could tell you some stories that would make those ears of yours fold up in shock." She chanced looking over at him. "Ever seen blood cells under a high powered microscope?"

"No. . .guess not." He lifted his head again. Her question about blood drew horrid scenes of spilled guts and splattered brains to his mind. So much talk about blood in one day. Blood was the last thing he wanted to talk about. His stomach felt like it was turning over as bile rose up in his throat. Lovell didn't answer, couldn't answer. Instead, he let his head fall back along the seat. So Tired. He felt so tired, so spent of energy. A good, long sleep would do him good. Swallowing hard, his stomach finally settled back down.

Barbara Jean watched him in silence with concerned eyes before she went on. "That's how they found out about you, about your blood being special. In a way, I feel like it's all my fault. Guess I shoulda kept my findings and my big mouth shut, but you probably don't feel like hearing all of this right now, huh?"

"I'm sorry. . .I'm just so sleepy." Lovell stiffened his muscles temporarily and tried to pull himself up more in his seat and open his heavy eyes wider and pay attention.

"That's because you've been drugged. They gave you somethin' to keep you sleeping so that they could harvest all the blood they wanted."

"What. . .?"

"I said blood." Her tone was almost a shout. "They wanted your blood. Found out it was like no other blood they've tested. Imagine that, hmph. A black man's blood making rare antibodies. They even had you nicknamed around the hospital as 'Healing Man Number Two'."

"I don't get it...who wanted my blood?"

"Probably everybody at the hospital by now. Rumors have it that a similar patient like you surfaced about six years back. An old white man that had never seen a doctor in his entire life. Never been sick or nothing. No colds, no fevers, no mumps, measles. Nothing. He lived to be one hundred and twenty before his heart just gave out. One of the older nurses told me about 'im. What a trip, huh?"

"Lady,. . .look. . .I hope you're not taking me off somewhere to rob me. . .'cause if you are. . .the joke's on you."

Barbara Jean gave him a scrutinizing look. "Negro, paleeezz. I didn't hear no money jingling in those pockets. You act like you still don't believe what I'm saying."

"Special blood, huh? Yeah right."

"If you only knew."

"And why should I believe a wild story like that?" Lovell asked quietly. In all of his years of life, he'd known some pretty weird females to do some pretty strange things, but this...this was something new. It was almost like being kidnapped or should he call it 'man napped'?

"I could break down in a chat about molecules, DNA, antibodies, electrolytes, cell structures, and plasma if you like. But you wouldn't understand that either. Anyway," she sighed. "I was the one who personally drew your blood two days ago, right after your surgery. I did the testing on your pre-op blood work too. I know what I'm talking about. Only thing is, I shoulda kept my findings to myself. Made the mistake of playing show-and-tell to a co-worker who told another and so on."

"Is that right? And you expect me to believe such a story?" He turned his gaze out the window where a blur of scenery ran past his view. For the time of night they were out, not many people were out on the streets walking about. Looking up at the darkened midnight sky gave him a mild feeling of melancholy.

"Didn't you think that it was odd that you came to a hospital two days ago for a minor procedure and stayed so long? Honey, the procedure you had was out-patient stuff. Not a room and bed kind of thing. You shoulda seen them around that place. Everybody in their own little corner whispering about the patient in room 102."

Room 102? Lovell pondered. Wasn't that the room he had been in?

"Finally, a memo came down earlier today from the bigwigs that own and run the hospital that we weren't allowed to discuss any patient cases outside of the hospital. Talking 'bout your case in point. Like they have the power to control what comes outta folks' mouths." She shook her head at the thought of it. "But it was just a matter of time tho', and news about you woulda been nationwide on the eleven o'clock news or you would have been laying somewhere dead and bloodless."

"Wow, and I thought I was there because they liked my company."

"Oh, it's like that, huh?" Barbara Jean knew his remark was meant to be humorous, but she wasn't laughing. Great, she thought, just what I need, another arrogant black man. "Still don't believe me? Did you check out your surgery spot? Notice anything odd?"

His stomach wasn't feeling any better, probably from the rough ride of the car, but he didn't want to be the one to tell Barbara Jean that her car could probably stand some new spark plugs and some shocks.

"Yeah. I checked it out." He paused as if to reflect on her inquiry. "Big deal," he said finally, after the wave of nausea settled back down again. "I heal fast. I always have, even as a kid. Plenty people do. Nothing mysterious or so special about that. So, if you're really taking me off somewhere to rob or do me any bodily harm, I only have a few bucks, but not enough to be killing somebody and going to jail over. And if this is about some twisted revenge, you've got the wrong guy 'cause I try to treat everybody right. Don't like a lot of mess going on. So, whatever your real motive is, looks like you've wasted your time." No sense in mentioning the eighty bucks hidden in his wallet.

Barbara Jean laughed at his careless words. "You so crazy. You still don't get it. That's all right tho'. I know that it's those drugs they gave you talking."

"It's like I said, I don't have nothing to give you, or nothing for you to take, so don't be trying no hurting stuff."

"Man, why would I wanna hurt you? I hardly know you. B'sides, consider this, One-of-no-trust, I coulda smothered your behind while you were lying in your hospital bed trying to sleep off that medication they gave you. Happens more in a hospital than you wanna know about."

"Now that I believe," Lovell agreed. He went quiet trying to think of when was the last time he'd eaten and what that meal had consisted of. His stomach still didn't feel right.

"I hope I'm not talking too much."

Lovell tried to rest his eyes. "What on earth would make you think that?"

Barbara Jean focused on the road ahead. "It's just that... I feel like it's basically my fault that they found out about you. If I hadn't been messing around with a test that I had no business doing in the first place, all of this wouldn't be happening." She smiled over at him. "You shoulda went home the same day of surgery and you'd be somewhere sleeping in your own comfortable bed now or cuddled up somewhere with your girl-friend."

"My what? My girlfriend?" Even in his groggy state of

mind Lovell almost laughed out loud at her last summation. Little did she know that he had no girlfriend or bed to be sleeping comfortably in. With all the slow circulating confusion going on in his head, he wasn't sure if he had his own self. "If you say so. But if I was getting paid to be somebody's guinea pig, I could have handled it."

"So you think. The truth is, you know nothing about those people at the hospital or what they're capable of doing." Barbara Jean changed the subject. "Do you live close? I could take you to your own place." She cut her eyes sideways as a prompt for an answer.

"Say what. . .?"

"Your own place. You know, that place called home. Where do you live?"

". . .I. . .I don't know. . .I. . ."

With her eyes back on the road she shook her head slowly. "Man, you in worse shape than I thought. Lucky for you I was there for the rescue. I'm try'n to tell you those hospital folks had big plans for you. Might not be a good idea to go back to your place if you used your current address."

"This is all so hard to believe," commented Lovell dryly.

"Well, believe it cause harvesting blood properties could mean profit. But I'm talking big bucks for them, not big bucks for you."

Lovell had closed his eyes and ears for a moment catching her last few words. "Like I said, I don't have any money. None."

"Maybe so. No money," conceded Barbara Jean with another quick glance over at him. "But you have blood. Lots and lots of it, and that's all they really wanted, at least for starters."

"You some kinda nurse or somethin'?"

"Man, I told you I work in the lab. . .I do. . ." Her smile faltered as she considered the possibility that he still didn't believe a word she was saying.

Suddenly pitching his body forward Lovell cupped a quick hand over his mouth. "Pull over a minute."

"I'm trying to get you home to a bed."

"Woman! Pull over or I'll puke in your car."

"Okay, okay," snapped Barbara Jean. "Just hold on. Let me get to the curb."

He was holding it all back as much as he could. Seemed like it was taking the woman forever to come to a stop. Finally, to his relief, she took a sharp right at the next stop sign. Not bothering to come to a full stop, she steered the car to the curb. Sick to his stomach, Lovell opened the car door and allowed his head to hang clear and over while he did his business, which was mostly dry heaving. He couldn't remember the last time he'd really had a full meal. At last, when it felt like he wasn't going to purge up all of his insides, he wiped his mouth with the back of his hand and closed the car door. Drained, he let his head fall back along the cloth seat.

"Sorry. Didn't mean to holler at you."

"No hard feelings." Barbara Jean felt another small tinge of joy for being able to help out. "Looks like they gave you too much medication, but don't worry," she said with an air of total confidence. "You'll be okay once I get you home and in bed. You'll be just fine."

Chapter Nine

Soft scrambled eggs, buttered sweet grits, strawberry jam-kissed toast, thick sliced ham, and fresh perked coffee—a big home-style breakfast. It was the first thing that popped into Mama Jo's head the next morning, which was something kind of wild and unusual for her. For months on end, her bird-like appetite had gone slack in imagination, but this morning was different.

"Darn it," she muttered to herself and climbed from her bed with her bones squeaking like rusty springs on an old bed. "I could eat a whole cow this morning." She scanned her view around the room, and pondered what time it was. There was no clock in her bedroom, which certainly wasn't the fault of her two girls. Nylah herself had bought two of the darn things only for her to bang each one into tiny pieces against the wall. The tiniest sound, like the swift and muffled ticking of a clock, sometimes drove her crazy, as if there were tiny workmen inside her head hammering and tearing down a brick wall. Not having a clock didn't matter though. Living too many years with a military man had taught her how to tell the time of day by the position of the sunlight filtering in through the half open dingy white drapes.

After going through a series of stretches for her tired and aching bones, she stood at the side of the bed for a moment looking down at her large feet and thought fondly of Poppa James. Her long-dead husband had always teased her about her large feet, always saying silly things like: "The bigger the feet on a woman, the bigger the heart." And sometimes being too silly with, "Feet big enough to kick the biggest behind." Even though rarely she showed it lately, she missed him, like the fresh from air. Perhaps, she often mused, if her James hadn't died on her so suddenly, her life now wouldn't be such a shamble—wouldn't be so controlled by her two daughters who, God bless their hearts, really meant well, but somehow, had voted themselves as the keepers of her life. Dictators born from her own flesh. But what the heck, she mused, she was hungry for a big breakfast.

She found and slipped her feet into some dirty, over-sized slippers, then looked around for her robe, but couldn't find it among the heap of dirty clothes strewn about the floor. A few items of clothing were on the unmade bed, where they had slept fitfully along side of her like sated lovers. She searched through each piece before casting it haphazardly to the floor. Ham and grits. Each item was growing on her taste buds with each fleeting second. The yellow smell of rich, buttered grits filled her nostrils.

"Heck, I haven't had a hankering for some ham and eggs in. . ." she rubbed her rag-tied head trying to recall a memory long gone. Along the floor's clutter she spotted her old, trusted, black Bible, half hidden beneath a faded blue cotton blouse. Once, too many years ago, there had been a time when she carried the good book wherever she went, reading passages from tattered pages to those who would take the time to listen.

She got down on her knees and picked it up and opened it. Inside the cover page her name was written in thick bold letters: Jodie Mae Richardson. She flipped through a few pages of what had once been her beliefs. Now, the bold black writing looked like Greek from someone else's life, and words she no longer understood. How long now? Between the tattered pages she found some old photographs of herself and her husband, James. In the photos they were younger and happy, smiling as if all the happiness in the world had been given to them as an eternal wedding gift. How attractive she had been then, and James, a once-handsome prince. Why did those happy times have to go away? People had looked her straight in her eyes back then and called her Mrs. Jodie Mae Richardson, out of respect. Now, on the rare occasions that she went on outings with one of her daughters, she noticed that people turned their eyes away from hers. And no one called her Mrs. Jodie Mae Richardson any more.

She got up and placed the pictures back between the pages, then opened a drawer and tossed the good book inside and closed it. Nothing could get her mind off a good breakfast right now. Nothing.

Panning her gaze around the untidy room, she absently scratched herself through the thin pink cotton gown that hung too loose on her frame. True enough, she lived in a room of mess, but it was a mess that brought about a certain amount of comfort, a soothing bridge to familiarity.

"The hell with a robe! It's my house and I can walk around 'butt naked' with a pair of dirty drawers on my head if I wanna." She went to the closed door of her bedroom and turned the knob and paused while still thinking hard on ham and buttered grits. Maybe on this morning, she decided wistfully, she'd surprise Barbara Jean for a change and make breakfast for the family. Maybe even make some of those silver-dollar-sized pancakes that little Brittany was so fond of. Yes indeed. And what was it that chile called 'em? Pannycakes. That's it. She'd make her little grand baby some pannycakes along with some ham and grits, and some eggs. The works. The whole idea gathered itself up inside her like a small hurricane of excitement.

Smiling to herself, she opened her bedroom door and felt her spirits sink to the bottom of her calloused feet. The darn barred door! She'd forgotten about it. How could she have forgotten about the security door? She tried the knob. Locked. Definitely locked. She hated the thing so much that if she had the power or just half the strength she needed, she'd wrestle that darn door from its hinges and snatch it completely from the frame. "Dang silly girls make me sick!"

"Barbara Jean! Barbara Jean, you get on out here!" Rattling the steel door, Mama Jo gathered up all her inner strength to pound on the thing, which wasn't much strength for her size, then tried screaming to the top of her voice again. "Barbara Jean!"

"Lord have mercy. The same ole thing day in and day out. Locked up in this room. But not today. No way." Getting ready to scream out again, she halted all her antics at the sound of one of the bedroom doors slowly being opened.

"It's about time!" she snapped loudly. "Come open this door now!" She was upset to the point that she had to turn away from the door to keep her daughter from seeing the fire in her eyes. It seemed to her that it was taking forever to hear the key in the lock. What part of her duress didn't that silly Barbara Jean understand? Steam felt like it was about to blow from her ears as she turned back around and pressed her angered face into the cool steel just for her eyes to grow wide and serious at the sight of a strange man stepping out into the hallway. The man was young. In fact, she saw that he was handsome even as he scratched his head like some small child awakened prematurely from a long afternoon nap.

"Well, I'll be... some fool up in my house..." Probably some new boyfriend of Barbara Jean's, she figured. Even odder, the stranger was wearing some kind of light blue hospital gown that he sought slyly to close at the back with one hand. His other hand couldn't seem to stop scratching at his head, giving him the appearance of being disoriented.

She stared him down. "..I'll be darned."

Pressing her face into the door harder, Mama Jo kept her eyes glued on him. Perhaps the man had overslept after a wild night. And how many times did she have to tell those girls of hers about bringing those nasty men to her house? How many? Well...maybe not so much Nylah, but with Barbara Jean it was getting to be at least once a month. What the heck did they think her house was, a brothel?

Narrowing her eyes, she watched the man slowly stroll over to her door, still scratching his head and looking groggy. He stopped short in front of her and cocked his head as he looked, his eyes like light green marbles barely focusing.

"Who're you?" She didn't give him a chance to answer. ". . .and what the heck you doing in my house? Where's my daughter and grand baby?"

". . .whoa. . .say what now?" Lovell looked as confused as she was.

"Who the heck are you?"

"Lovell. My name's Lovell." He stopped scratching his head and studied the white steel door before him. "Umph. Never seen one of these on the inside of a house before. What a trip."

"You Barbara Jean's boyfriend or Nylah's? I'ma kill them girls of mine for letting a stranger in my house." Mama Jo knew that if she ever had to chose between the sensible daughter and the gullible daughter, the culprit had to be that brain-damaged Barbara Jean. The girl would trust the devil himself if he smiled at her the right way. "You know Nylah or Barbara Jean?"

Nylah. The name pulled at Lovell's memory, sounding too familiar but not enough to draw out information. He did recall something about somebody named Barbara Jean from last night. Or was it the night before? Barbara Jean was the one that had driven him from the hospital the other day, or was it just last night?

"Well? Nylah's boyfriend or Barbara Jean's? Which is it?"

"I'm nobody's boyfriend, and that's for real." He touched the door, moved both his hands along the width of it, then tried the knob only to find that it was locked.

"You a burglar or what?" She couldn't take her eyes off of him, not even for a second to blink.

Now that was funny and Lovell had to grin. "Say what now? Lady, do I look like a burglar to you?"

Mama Jo narrowed her eyes to slits. What he looked like to her was a handsome young stud too full of himself, but she wasn't telling. "Who says you gotta be ugly just to steal? B'sides," she commented like a pro on the subject. "Can't judge a book by its look."

"Got that right." He held the look of a person trying to figure out why a tiny, frail-looking woman was behind locked steel. ". . .still, I'm no burglar."

"Where's my daughter then? What have you done to my kids? And who the heck let you in this house? I'ma kill that darn Barbara Jean." She looked around him as if he suddenly didn't matter and screamed to the top of her lungs. "Barbara! Barbara Jean!"

Risking his hospital gown opening up again to expose his derriere, Lovell covered his ears with his hands. "Lady, please, you don't have to do all that. Stop screaming, please. You giving me a headache." He took his hands down and regarded her eye to eye through the metal. "And why you behind this door anyway? What's up with that? You some kind of crazy woman or somethin'?"

"I need to go to the bathroom." She stiffened and eyed him more suspiciously. "Can't hold it no longer, get the key."

Lovell's expression crumbled to askance. "The key?"

"Yeah, the key," Mama Jo pointed her thin brown finger to

the hallway table where the small lamp perpetually glowed. A devilish smile found its way to her face. "Look there, right under the lamp. Just lift it up."

Grinning, Lovell shook his head. "Nah. I don't think so. Not so quick. Not 'til you tell me why you behind this door in the first place. You the one could be some kind of mass murderer."

"Oh, that's funny. Just get the key before I pee on this floor! It's not your bizzness, but I'm behind this door 'cause of burglars and my two crazy daughters know how afraid I am to be alone in this house. Now get the key!"

It almost made sense to him. Clutching the back of his hospital gown, he moved over to the lamp, lifted it up, and got the key, which was exactly where she said it would be. He opened the door and stood back some to give her room to sprint through the narrow path down to one of the rooms along the hallway that he guessed to be the restroom.

Ambling back to the bedroom from which he'd emerged, Lovell patted his hair into place while he searched around for something more appropriate to put on. The old lady seemed harmless enough, but he couldn't be walking around in some hospital gown opened at the back for his cheeks to hang out. All he found was some light cotton hospital pants that matched his gown, and the way they were laid out so carefully along the foot of the twin sized bed seemed to suggest that it was meant for him to find them. Hurriedly, he slid into the pants and went back out in time to see the old woman coming out of the restroom and drying her hands along her sides.

Stopping in her tracks and frowning, Mama Jo looked up at him with a new puzzled expression. "What did you say your name was?"

"Lovell. Lovell Joyner." Pulling at the draw strings on his pants, he looked away from her at his surroundings. Nothing looked familiar to him. He looked back at her with quiet expectance. "What about you?"

"I didn't say." Suddenly sassy, Mama Jo brushed passed him and headed towards the kitchen with him slowly following behind like a shy puppy. "But I guess you can call me Jodie, or Miss Jodie. My girls call me Mama or Mama Jo most of the time." Once in the shabby kitchen, she sniffed the air before filling a filter with fresh coffee. "Well, anyway, I don't know why you're in my house Mr. Lovie. . ."

"That's Lovell."

She put a hand on her hip. "Do you have a cigarette on you, Layvell?"

"Afraid not. And that's Lovell with two l's."

"Layvell. . .Leevell, same difference. Don't interrupt me."

"Yes, Ma'am." Suddenly it was almost like he was standing in front of his old teacher, Mrs. Putney, being reprimanded. Back in those days, if there had been a contest for the meanest teacher, the sassiest, the tell-it-like-it-is teacher, Mrs. Putney would have won on all accounts. But she had been a warm, caring teacher at the same time. Lovell stayed close to the entrance, just in case the woman before him had some kind of serious mental problem.

". . .like I was saying, I don't know why you're here in my house, but if you some kind of burglar, you've made a bad choice. This place is a dump, and we dirt poor on top of it. Like they say, 'We so broke we can't pay attention'. Well, hmph, that's us."

Lovell looked around the room and had to mentally agree with her on the part about the room being a dump. Even bright sunlight couldn't bring cheer to this room, he thought. The place was a mess with too much clutter sucking up space. And the walls looked thick and burdened with yester-year's grease and grime that even new paint could get sucked up in it. Dusty curtains hung cafe-style at a wide window that could stand some cleaning. And fresh flowers. Lovell cringed at the thought. It would be an insult to nature itself to place fresh cut flowers in such a neglected room. He smacked his dry lips and kept silent. As if reading his mind, Mama Jo went over, reached up and scooted each side of the curtains back some to allow more light in.

"Now. Which one of my daughters you say you know?"

"I'm a friend of your daughter, Barbara. Matter of fact, I wish I knew where she was right now."

"A friend of Barbara's, huh?"

"Yes, Ma'am."

"It figures. That woman-chile of mine would trust Satan himself." She paused to consider her own words. "Well, you might as well have a seat, and I'll make us some breakfast, seeing as how that silly Barbara Jean has ran off somewhere and deserted us. The nerve of her." She moved over to a cabinet and knelt down to find her good cast iron skillet. Lovell, seeing clean through her thin gown, turned his head away to keep from looking. "Got any kids, Mr. Leevell?"

"That's Lovell, with an 'o'. I'm afraid not."

Scratching at her leg, Mama Jo turned and regarded him for a brief spell. A notion came; a notion went. "Leevell, Lovell, it's all the same. It don't matter what a person calls you, as long as they call you in time for some good eating. Hope you like grits and eggs. Have a seat."

"Yes, Ma'am." Lovell's face lit up with a feeling like a deprived kid being offered a new toy on Christmas morning. "Oh yeah, that's me alright." Eagerly, he took a seat at the table, a once nicely finished wooden piece with a few pot burns and some scratches on the top. He mused that some top grain sandpaper and some wood stain could fix that easily.

"Hope you like some good eating like me." Mama Jo smiled over at him, feeling some strange new camaraderie with this new face.

"I know that's right. Nothin' like some good eating."

While Mama Jo fumbled around in the cupboards and refrigerator, he made more mental notes of his tired-looking surroundings and shook his head mildly: an old, well-worn tiled floor with some of the tiles turning up at the corners; old newspapers stacked almost to the ceiling; two, not one, but two ancient-looking vacuum cleaners in one corner of the room; wooden cabinets so heavily cloaked in years of paint that it would probably take a small demolition crew to make them right again.

The counter top itself was a yellow pathway of broken and chipped square tiles that he hadn't seen in a kitchen for years. Just old and outdated. Even the stove where Mama Jo's slippered feet stood was antique looking, but it did look reasonably clean. It wasn't the kind of place that he could truly enjoy living in. But for a hot spell, if he had to, he could deal with it.

"I'm stuffed," Lovell said later, smiling as he leaned back in his chair and patted his stomach. He was full and he was pleased, at least for the time being. She was a comical sight to watch around the kitchen, but Mama Jo knew how to hook up a breakfast. Unfortunately, though, her timing was a little too off for him. All the same, it was the best overly-cooked scrambled eggs, slightly burnt white toast, buttered stiff grits, dried out pieces of ham, and watery black coffee he'd had in a long while. But Lovell knew he couldn't really complain. Just to be eating something at all was enough to be thankful for.

They had just finished off their meal when the front door opened and shut. In strolled Barbara Jean looking sheepish with a bunch of shopping bags. Surprised at seeing Lovell up and out of the bedroom, she was even more surprised to see her mother perched at the table nursing a mug of coffee.

Barbara Jean sat her bags and purse on the counter and smoothed down the light blue short sleeved jacket to her matching shorts. Out of habit, she ran her hands along her head to confirm that her gel was still holding everything back before mumbling her greeting. "Good morning everybody."

Lovell spoke back quietly, at the same time looking over to Mama Jo, trying to read her expression. It didn't look to him like she was too pleased the way she shifted restlessly in her seat and sealed her lips tighter.

"You not speaking, mama?" Barbara Jean looked from one to the other, but her attention was soon snagged by an energetic Brittany who bounced into the room with a pink, plastic water gun in her hand and the look of a child about to whine for something else.

"Can I put water in it now, mama? Please, mama, can I?"

Mama Jo looked up at her daughter, then nonchalantly down at her spoiled grandchild and wondered when Barbara Jean would have a problem with her being out of her usually locked room. She couldn't wait for her to say something. Anything. She had a few spicy complaints of her own to voice about finding a stranger in her house, but Barbara Jean surprised her by not bringing the subject up at all.

Noticing Lovell for the first time, Brittany let the matter of her water gun fall to the side, while she curiously looked him over. Lovell gave her a quick wink and a sly grin, making it hard for the child not to smile back.

"Mama, who's that man?" She pointed her empty gun at him. "What's his name?"

"His name is Mr. Joyner and he's a friend."

At Barbara Jean's words, Mama Jo rolled her eyes and sipped more of her watered down coffee. The lukewarm beverage was another bitter taste in her mouth.

The matter of Lovell quickly forgotten, Brittany whined again. "Can I put some water in my gun, mama? Please. . ."

"In a minute, baby. Let mama catch her breath first."

Making faces, Brittany wasn't giving up that easy. ". . .but I can do it myself, pleasssseeeee. I know how to do it."

"Not right now, Brittany. You go and take your jacket off, hang it up, and wash your hands. I'll fix you a snack." Barbara Jean had dressed her in all pink, complete with a riot of pink berets scattered about her multi-ponytailed head. Brittany could tell by her mother's expression that she meant business. Reluctantly, she trudged from the room.

Barbara Jean avoided the glare of her mother's eyes because it was obvious to her that the woman wasn't happy. Probably somethin' to do with Lovell being here, she mused. She gave a quick look over to Lovell, who was not staring over at her as if trying to remember something important. Ignoring Mama Jo's sour face, Barbara Jean kept her attention on Lovell. "I picked you up some underwear, tee-shirts, a pair of pants, and a couple of shirts for right now. I hope they fit. If you wanna take a shower, you'll find what you need in the rest-room. You know, soap, deodorant, toothpaste, and stuff. Oh, and here's a new toothbrush."

She walked over and handed him a large, white department store bag. "You probably know where the restroom is by now."

Grateful, Lovell got up from the table. "Thanks. I could stand a shower and a fresh mouth." Anxious, but suave as usual, he left the room to go freshen up, at the same time glad to be moving away from the tension in the room.

Waiting for a storm of ugliness, Barbara Jean strolled over to her kettle and turned the fire on under it, determined to make herself some calming herbal tea. She didn't care what nobody said, Chamomile tea was the best thing for frazzled nerves.

"And just where the hell have you been, Barbara Jean?" Mama Jo's words cut like sharp ice, but not too loud. "And what kinda mess you trying to pull now?"

"I went out to buy a few things for a friend, Mama, but now I'm back."

"Yeah, after leaving me alone with this man. I swear,

Barbara Jean, sometimes you have the judgment of a head of lettuce." room. "It's not a good idea to leave your chile, but it's okay to leave your mother alone with a stranger?"

"Mama, stop over-reacting." Opening up a tea bag and placing it in a cup, Barbara Jean chuckled mildly to herself. Mama being afraid. How interesting the thought was Her mother was such a rough-to-the-core tyrant at times that it seemed unfeasible for her to hold fear for anything.

"What I wanna know is why you would go off and leave 'im here?"

"Oh, Mama, he's no complete stranger. I've been seeing Lovell for weeks now." She turned the fire up higher under her kettle, hating every second of having to lie to her own mother. "I just haven't told anybody about 'im, that's all."

"Then how come you didn't stay at his place? And why you have to go out and buy 'im some new clothes? This one don't have a job either?"

"Oh, Mama, stop bugging. The man got kicked outta his apartment and lost his job all in the same day. He's looking for a new place, and I'm just trying to help 'im out. Don't worry about it. He won't be here long."

"I know that's right. I just don't understand why it is that you have to be the one that picks up every stray puppy that crosses your path. This ain't no hotel or boarding house, Barbara Jean. This is my home, and it's already too many folks living here for me. The last thing I need is another face to look at in the morning."

Barbara Jean tried to humor her. "You know you don't mean that."

"The heck I don't. And you need to try asking if it's okay before you do stuff like move another person into my house."

"I know, I know. I said he won't be here long, Mama. I promise. Just a few days. Give a brother a break. He won't stay long."

Mama Jo snorted into her empty coffee cup. "You got that right, especially when your sister, Nylah, hears about this. She'll have a cow."

Heading out of the kitchen to go check on Brittany, Barbara Jean made a face. "Mama, she can have two cows if she wants to. Don't worry about it," she threw carelessly over her shoulders. "I can handle Nylah."

Chapter Ten

"Barbara Jean, girl...you must be outta your mind."

Nylah could care less who heard her harsh rush of words. Her sister, far from being the sensible one of the family, had done plenty of crazy things throughout their lives, but this...this thing with bringing this man to her mother's house was the cake and the icing too. "Girl, you must be crazy."

They were out on the patio, away from prying ears. After having a snack, Barbara Jean had put Brittany down for a short nap while Mama Jo had sauntered back to her room and closed her own door leaving her two daughters to hash out the problem at hand. The problem being Lovell.

The evening sun had given up its daily fight and was on its way down against a yellow and red backdrop. Normally asleep herself this time of day, Barbara Jean was perky as ever and dressed in a purple and pink silk lounge dress that swept at her feet. Stooping down to water her collection of plants, she allowed Nylah's brashness to bounce off her back with her own careless silence.

"Look, I don't know what he told you, but he can't stay here." Nylah's tone was calmer, but it took a great effort. It was always so unnerving to her, so downright irritating, when her younger sister flat out ignored her. She could feel a storm of emotions coming on, a hurricane if she didn't win control over her feelings. Slowing her breath to calm herself, she waited a few seconds giving herself time to pick and choose her words, her tone, her attitude. True, she was upset, maybe beyond upset; she was enraged and somewhat baffled. With all the stories of seemingly good-hearted people doing horrible crimes against the innocent nowadays, it baffled her how her sister could be so gullible and so trusting.

"Look," Nylah said finally, pausing to take in a deep breath. The hot and rising pressure behind her eyes was the start of a bad headache. "I don't know what this man has told you, but you had no right to take him from the hospital. And in case you don't know, there are people looking for him."

Barbara Jean pulled a dead leaf from her ficus and tossed it aside with casual indifference. "He's a grown man, Nylah. I didn't have to take him from the hospital, he walked out."

"You're lying, Barbara Jean, and you know it. The man was medicated."

Standing up to face her sister, Barbara Jean stared at her with accusing eyes. "So you knew about the hospital's plans, didn't you? That's why they kept him full of drugs, so they could do whatever they wanted to 'im, and you knew."

Shocked, Nylah let her mouth sag open and then closed it. She couldn't deny that part of what her sister was saying was true. Following doctor's strict orders, she herself had been the one administering the alleged medications. "I work there just like you. I don't own the place, Barbara Jean. The doctor gave orders for a drug to be given to a patient; I gave it to him. I wasn't the one to go jumping into hospital business like it was mine, just like it's none of yours."

"Well I guess I was just too stupid to sit idly by and let them people drain him dry and maybe even kill 'im for top grade body parts. Silly me." Turning her back on Nylah, she knelt down and went back to the watering and tending her plants. "Don't think that I don't know some of the secret activities going on in that hospital, Nylah. Like folks recovering nicely and suddenly dying so some body parts can be used for other folks with more money. I know, Nylah. I know."

Nylah rolled her eyes. She didn't want to admit it, but she too had heard a few rumors but refused to believe any of them. Besides, she consoled herself, rumors were rumors and she had no real proof of any illegal practices taking place at the hospital. "Barbara Jean, that's a bunch of bull. And even if it were true, it still wouldn't be none of our business."

"Then whose business is it?" she challenged boldly. "Tell me that."

Avoiding the question, Nylah looked around pensively for something else to focus on. Anything. She couldn't believe the condition of the yard. Everything looked so dry and dead that it reminded her of desert living. She made a mental note to look into the cost of getting a regular gardener. A few of their neighbors had someone that serviced their lawns every two weeks, and she could see no reason why they couldn't pool some money together for such a worthy cause. "Well," she threw in as an afterthought, "you can't go believing everything you hear."

Still in her nurse whites, her arms folded stubbornly in front of her, Nylah moved over for a closer look at Barbara Jean's precious little plants and wondered briefly why one side of her collection was withering and dying out, while her group on the opposite side screamed out with an abundance of life. What was that all about? She wanted to ask her, but the question, perched perilously on the tip of her tongue just didn't seem right with the issue at hand.

"Barbara Jean," she said calmly, more in control of her emotions, "I hope you know that you could loose your job behind this. This is serious business. It's almost like stealing hospital property." She rubbed her uncovered arms where the evening air was growing chilly along her skin. "All behind some man you don't even know."

"He's not a piece of property, Nylah. He's a person, a real human being. B'sides, who knows I had anything to do with Mr. Joyner leaving the hospital? Except for you, him, and I, no one knows. And my lips are sealed. Hmph, I don't supposed Lovell would tell a soul, so I guess that leaves you, big sis. Are you telling?"

Nylah swatted at a fly. The darn thing was being too bold and pesky and wouldn't leave her alone. "All I know is. . .," she eased out finally, after knocking the fly off her arm, ". . .he can't stay here. We have enough problems dealing with Mama running off every chance she gets. We don't need no more problems."

Standing back up, Barbara Jean brushed fragments of dust and potting soil from her hands. She gave Nylah the kind of look that implied that no matter what was said, nothing would change in her book. "Who says he's gonna be a problem? And if he was, it wouldn't be yours. Now would it?"

The hell with trying to be sensible. "You fool of a woman!" Nylah hissed with her small fists balled at each side. "You can't just invite some complete stranger to come live in our home! Don't you listen to the news enough to know that all kinds of crazy, twisted people are looking for easy prey like you? Use your head, Barbara Jean. You're not the only one living here. And in case you've forgotten, it's not your house to be making such a decision to begin with, not to mention Brittany. You do have a young child's safety to think about."

Mulling over her sister's last few words, Barbara Jean gave her a quiet look of composure before looking away. "I don't feel like arguing with you, Nylah." It was time to back down. One of them had to know when it was time to back down. Her sister, Nylah, was known to be a sweet and easy-going person until worked up to fits of anger. Barbara Jean had experienced that anger on too many occasions and still recalled the time that Nylah had hauled off and slapped her so hard in the face that it blurred her vision for a whole day. Two weeks of not speaking to one another had Nylah apologizing and promising never to do such a thing again. "Let's forgive and forget," Nylah had said. Hmph. Sure, she forgave her, but Barbara Jean knew that deep within her heart where bad memories took permanent residence, she would never forget. It taught her to be leery of crossing the line. "You're right," she said softly, hoping to quell at least some of Nylah's anger. "It is Mama's house, and she should have the final word about it."

Annoyed, Nylah put both hands on her hips and sighed. "Great. Like she's really in her right frame of mind to make rational decisions. Give me a break."

Barbara Jean arched her back straighter, dusted her hands again and went over to the push broom resting against the back of the house and started rearranging dust about the patio. Tiny billows of dust rose and hovered briefly like low hung clouds before settling. "Nylah, I'll talk to Mama about it. Okay? Just leave me alone for now."

"Not until you tell me what you plan to do about this man. I'm sure he has some family he can stay with."

"And what if he don't? It's really not your problem to solve, Nylah. Why you always have to be trying to handle everybody's business? Just leave me alone about it I said."

Nylah rolled her eyes to heaven. What in the world could have gotten into this woman, she wondered. It had been like coming home to a bunch of complete strangers with the four of them sitting around the kitchen table eating and chatting like old time friends. Barbara Jean sitting on the floor Indian style smiling and looking gooey-eyed up at Lovell. Even her mother was out of her room, laughing and talking like she was the star of her own show or some birthday girl at her own party. Even worse, her niece, little Brittany, had the nerve to be sitting in Lovell's lap. Nylah had felt like she had entered the wrong house entirely. She must have stood for a good five minutes, like some zombie in a trance, speechless and bewildered. The whole scene had been too surreal.

Stopping to wave away dust from her nose, Barbara Jean snorted, "Maybe you need to just mind your own business for a change."

"It's my business alright, and he can't stay."

Nylah took two steps forward with her hands still on her hips. "When a complete stranger is brought to live under the same roof as me, it becomes my business."

"Well, I disagree." Placing the push broom back along its resting place, Barbara Jean swiped her hands lightly along the silk of her attire and took a deep sigh. Heck, she thought. If only she had her own place she wouldn't have to worry about folks always jumping in her face trying to tell her how to live her life. 'Barbara Jean, you too young to be having and raising a baby by yourself'. 'Barbara Jean, you don't need to be spending all your money on somebody else's husband just so he'll love you back'. 'Barbara Jean this and Barbara Jean that'. She felt so sick and tired of it!

"Nylah, I'm not discussing this any further with you, okay."

"Fine!" shouted Nylah as she twirled around and stalked back into the house, kicking up a cloud of dust in her departure. "I'll just go and call the cops to have him removed from this house." As much as she really wanted to follow through with her threat, Nylah had sense enough to know that her threat was weak. For one thing, if she were to call the police, what would she say? 'Help police. Please come and remove this good looking guy from my mother's house because the rest of my family seems to be too smitten with him.'

At her departing threat, Barbara Jean could feel resentment welling up inside of her. She loved her sister. She honestly loved the woman, but sometimes, and this was proving to be one of those times, her sister wore her nerves down to the raw. It always had to be Nylah's way or no way. Even as kids growing up it had been the same thing. She still remembered the episode with the Easter dresses. She had to be around seven then. Two beautiful yellow, chiffon dresses cut and sewn from the same pattern. The only difference was size. Her sister, Nylah, had refused to go to Sunday service wearing the same identical dress that she had on. After several fling-down-to-the-floor tantrums, her mother had given in. Even after so many years, it was still painful to her that she had been the one made to change into another dress to wear to church. All part of Nylah's way or no way. Some kind of control thing. Her sister was some kind of control freak and always trying to control all the moves and plays of a person's life, as if it were some game of chess. If it wasn't her life, it was Mama Jo's or Brittany's life. It was always something.

Leaving her thriving project, Barbara Jean followed behind her. "I think you're forgetting one itsy, bitsy little fact before you go dialing 911 and getting yourself embarrassed, Sis. This house belongs to Mama. Mrs. Jodie Mae Richardson. That's what the deed says. Not Nylah Richardson. So go on, call 'em, Nylah. Call the cops."

Having picked up the kitchen wall phone, Nylah punched up a few numbers when a sad thought assaulted her senses. Mama Jo. No one had really asked her mother, even though she knew that the woman wasn't competent in matters dealing with her own life, it still rang true that the house that they shared belonged to her. She cradled the receiver and drew in a deep weary breath.

"And I know Mama won't be no big fool like you about this. Darn right, I'll ask her 'cause you don't know the first thing about this...Lovell person, except that nonsense about his blood being a rare type. And trust me, that ain't enough. I'm sorry, Barb, but somebody's gotta act like they have good sense in this house."

"Fine with me," Barbara Jean muttered. "Do what you have to do."

While in the kitchen, Barbara Jean put her trusty kettle on to boil. Perhaps a steaming cup of some herbal mint tea with some chamomile would help to sooth her frayed nerves, get her mind settled. Hmph. She wished that Nylah would settle down, have some tea, and chill out.

Restless and eager to settle the matter, Nylah padded softly through the dimly lit hallway to Mama Jo's room with Barbara Jean's words slapping at her backside. "Yeah, you go and ask her, Nylah. Let Mama decide if he can stay." Something had to be settled and it had to be settled today.

Nylah bit lightly on her lower lip feeling drained, both physically and spiritually. It was times like this that confirmed what she had always known, but chose to overlook. Three grown women had no business still living under the same roof. Everybody wanted to be the one to run the house but clearly lacked the good judgment to do so. How she had managed to survive thus far in the shadow of her mother and sister was still a mystery to her.

The security door leading to her mother's bedroom was still open. Nylah didn't bother to knock on her mother's closed door, instead she seized the door knob and swung up into the room with an air of authority. "Mama, this thing about...." She caught her breath looking around the unkempt surroundings. Everything still looked the same, just the way her mother liked it. The room was a mess, and their mother was gone.

"Great! Just great, Barbara Jean. She's not even here!"

Eating a folded bologna sandwich, Barbara Jean hurried through the hallway to investigate. "Not here? Where could she..."

"She's not here!" Nylah shouted, in case her sister was having a hearing problem too. "Mama's not here!"

Together they stood in the messy room with disbelief. Oddly, Nylah's hand rash began to itch like crazy. Just nerves, she told herself. She shot her attention to her younger sister. "Now what?"

"Let me go and ask Lovell if he seen Mama leave." Barbara Jean went and knocked on his closed bedroom door. She knocked again, still nothing. It seemed only natural to open up the door, but no one was there as well.

Standing behind her with her brown arms folded in an I-told-you-so message stretched taut across her face, Nylah shook her head. "I hope you're happy. No telling where she is." She dreaded to even think too hard on it. Her mother was good for getting lost, coming up with enough money to buy her drugs, and forgetting to return home. The last thing she needed right now was such an episode. That was the part that worried Nylah the most, her mother not showing back up to the house. The last time it had happened, Nylah had laid in her bed night after night agonizing over the possibility of her mother lying half-dead somewhere and no one doing anything to help her. To make matters worse, after she'd called the local hospitals, the local precincts, and the county morgue to inquire about any recent unidentified bodies, all she could do was wait. Wait and worry while her heart ached. Sometimes Nylah still had nightmares about it. "This is all your fault, Barbara Jean." She felt like crying.

"Oh put a dirty sock in it, Nylah. You can't keep her locked up for the rest of her life. She's a grown woman."

"Oh yeah, right. Well don't hate me for caring." Nylah hurried to her bedroom and got a light jacket to slip on, went to the front door, and paused before heading out. "I guess when she turns up dead in somebody's alley that'll be okay with you too. Maybe that's what you really want. She might be grown, Barbara Jean, but you need to realize that our mother is sick right now."

As if to punctuate her words, Nylah went out and stood looking down the street for any sign of Mama Jo. Lord, she thought disheartedly, didn't she have enough to deal with keeping that Barbara Jean from being fired from Park Memorial? Though she hadn't mentioned it yet to her sister, things were coming up missing, and more than once she'd overheard the mention of her own sister's name as a suspect. And it worried her. Add her mother's drug addiction and having to be constantly supervised like some wayward child, and it was more than anybody should have to suffer. "Lord, give me strength," she mumbled to herself. Now Barbara Jean wanted some stranger dragging his own misery into their private hell. When, she wondered, when would it all come to an end?

Nylah had a hand cupped over her eyes, looking. So engrossed that she hadn't even noticed that Barbara Jean had come up behind her until she spoke.

"Wherever they are, Brittany's with 'em. She wasn't in her bed like I thought."

"Heaven forbid," Nylah said under her breath. Now her sister looked a bit worried. Nylah felt like just slapping her, but her cold-hearted stare blinking 'your fault' on and off was enough for the moment. As much as she didn't want to believe that it was so, it was becoming more and more obvious to her that when it came to being totally concerned and loving of their mother, Barbara Jean's love ran shallow. Actually, her sister's love and concern was more like a cup. Some days that cup of devoted love and concern was filled to the top, running over the edge. And then there were other days that same cup came up half full, or ran perilously close to empty. Unfortunately, Nylah didn't see herself as having such options. As the oldest child, she felt that her own cup was expected to stay full. Perhaps, she thought from time to time, some children loved their mother harder than others. Unsavory as it was, Nylah kept trying to dismiss the bitter thought from her head. "Well, what now?"

Suddenly stricken with the reality of her child missing, Barbara Jean suggested that they take her car and go out searching, but they couldn't have been more relieved to learn that they didn't have to drive far. Three blocks over, coming from Mr. Charlie's local neighborhood store, they spotted the trio walking slowly like one small happy family.

"There they go," pointed Nylah, excited and equally relieved that it was nothing more than a quick trip to the store. Everybody looked okay. Mama Jo had a canned soda in one hand and a pack of cigarettes in the other while little Brittany, dressed in her purple sundress, busied herself with a nut-and-chocolate covered ice cream.

Trying to stay calm about the matter, Barbara Jean had a good mind to tell Mr. Lovell a thing or two about going off with her child without checking with her first. But she decided it would be best to wait until she drove everybody back to the house before saying anything.

Back in the drab living room, Mama Jo got to sit on her own outdated dark green sofa and smoke a cigarette after months of resisting temptation. "I know you girls are probably upset at me for taking a smoke after I quit," she said with a satisfied look on her face, "but I don't give a hoot." She puffed away and sipped happily on her cold, orange soda while Barbara Jean went back to making tea in the kitchen.

Playing with a stack of cards that Brittany had located in the house, Lovell shuffled the deck and prepared to deal the excited child a hand of Fish while Nylah slipped away from the pack to take her shower, hoping to steam and sooth away her frazzled nerves.

He had done something wrong. Lovell could feel it like thick smoke in the room, a sense of something forbidden, but he wasn't sure of what it was. He let his mind back-track events, trying to decide where he'd gone wrong. Mama Jo had knocked on his bedroom door and said: "Come walk down to the mom and pop store with me." Not really a question for him, but more like a subtle command, and he'd agreed. Then Brittany had emerged from her room and had casually announced that she was going too. Mama Jo had told the child okay. No problem there. Before the three had actually left the house, he'd pondered over where the two sisters were, but Mama Jo had acted eager to leave by announcing, "Let's go."

Now Nylah seemed upset with him, and from what he could decipher from Barbara Jean's expression, she didn't look too pleased either.

Sipping her soda, dragging on her new cigarette, Mama Jo seemed more alive than Barbara Jean could ever remember. From her place in the kitchen, she could hear her mother talking good sense and laughing at jokes, her own and some of Lovell's. Heck, the woman was throwing off more happiness than the bulb was throwing off light in the room. Even Lovell was full of energy for somebody just home from the hospital. Barbara Jean didn't know what it was, but somehow, it all seemed so pleasing.

Mama Jo stopped blowing perfect smoke rings into the air. "Barbara Jean," she said when she glimpsed her daughter coming back into the room with a tray of steaming mugs of herbal tea. "It's all settled."

"What's that, Mama?" Barbara Jean hoped her mother was just going through a brief spell with wanting to smoke cigarettes again. It was hard enough dealing with Brittany's asthma flare-ups without cigarette smoke being in the house. "What's settled?"

"About Lovell here." Mama Jo paused and looked fondly over at Lovell with a sparkle in her eye. "He can stay on for a while as my caretaker. Claims that he can bring this place around, and he even knows a little somethin' about garden-

138

ing." She gave a little smile and smacked her lips. "We'll give
'im a chance, see if he can bring this place up to par. And I
don't mean like a live-in boyfriend for you. I mean like a
handyman to get this place back in shape."

Barbara Jean blushed on the part about a live-in boyfriend.
The thought of Lovell as a boyfriend hadn't crossed her mind.
Well...not really. "You think you can tackle the job, Mr.
Lovell?"

"Hey," he gestured with his hands. "I'm the man." Lovell
smiled, and both women caught their breath for a second or
two. His smile was as mesmerizing as a perfect white beam of
hope.

"Sounds good to me, Mama." Barbara Jean set her tray
down and carefully passed him a mug. "We definitely need a
handyman 'round this place. But we can't pay you much
though. A small, weekly allowance maybe."

"I don't ask for much." Surveying his surroundings,
Lovell liked what he was hearing. At least he wouldn't have
to sleep in a park until he could find another suitable place.
Sure, the house wasn't much to look at for the moment, but he
knew a few things about painting and repairing stuff. Not only
that, but landscaping and gardening could turn out to be his
true forte. "We'll work it out."

Brittany beamed up at her mother with delight. "Mama,
can Mr. Lovell stay with us?"

"Girl, can't you hear good? Didn't you hear what we just
said?"

"Oh, goodie," Britany squealed. "I like Mr. Lovell. He's
a nice man."

"Yes, baby," Barbara Jean beamed. "He is."

"Well, it's settled then," Mama Jo confirmed. A new face
around her house was just what everybody needed, not to mention someone to spruce the place up a bit.

"It's all good then." Lovell patted the top of Brittany's

head lightly. "I just need to pick my car up from the parking lot at Park Memorial. That is... if it's still there."

Barbara Jean raised a brow. "Lovell, you didn't mention anything 'bout having a car."

"You didn't ask me."

"No problem," said Barbara Jean. Going for his car would be the perfect time to bring up the matter about Brittany. She didn't care who he was, the President of the United States or the Pope himself, she didn't want nobody just taking her child off without first consulting with her. She knew that she was being a bit overprotective when it came to her child, but that's just the way it was. "We can go for your car later tonight if you like."

"Sounds good to me," Lovell said in response. Such nice people, he thought. At least on the outside. Good people, he could tell. Already, he felt a certain amount of comfort, as if he'd known everyone for a long while.

The room was quiet for a spell; everyone was pleased with the discussion at hand. Suddenly, like a swift wind blown off its course, Nylah was standing at the living room entrance dressed in her red terry cloth bathrobe, her skin still moist from her shower as she glared from one face to the other. She didn't know what it was, but for some reason all four faces looked guilty.

"Well now," she said, softening her expression, trying to lighten up. "Looks like everything's all summed up and we have a new guest in the house. The hell with what I think, huh? Everybody sitting here looking all cozy with each other and Mama smoking after she went through so much to quit. And Brittany, sitting here sucking in second-hand smoke like it's going to help her asthma while playing cards with the stranger that her own mother dragged home."

Barbara Jean smirked behind her mug of tea but said nothing.

Brittany looked up at her with expectance. "Wanna play cards with us, Auntie Nylah?"

Mama Jo took another drag on her cigarette, and pinched her face. "Nylah, just make your point and be done with it."

"Oh I'm done with it, Mama. I'm done with all of y'all because I think the both of you have lost your mind."

"Aunt Nylah," piped Brittany with her hands full of cards, "I like Mr. Lovell. He's a nice man."

"Have some tea, Nylah. It'll help you relax." Unruffled by her sister's caustic remarks, Barbara Jean prepared to hand her a mug.

"Drop dead, Barbara Jean." Nylah turned her attention to her mother, "I hope you're happy now, Mama. I'll start looking for my own place as soon as possible." Shaking her head, Nylah turned and stalked back to her room and slammed her door.

Chapter Eleven

Two weeks later, with the early warmth of the Tuesday morning sun beating down on his bare back, Lovell had his hands deep in some planting soil when he heard noise coming out of the rear of the house—noise created by a whole lot of hoop-hollering and jumping around. He took his time arranging the last of the white and purple pansies in the neat little row he was working with. As he stood up and used the back of his hand to mop some sweat from his brow, Mama Jo came bursting from the rear door shrieking something about 'guilty'.

"Not guilty! I knew it, I knew it!"

"Say what?"

He stopped what he was doing, angled his head and watched her hop down the few steps with fuzzy gray bunny slippers on her feet; her thin white house dress barely concealed her fragile frame. October sunlight glistened off her too happy face. Along with the dingy white scarf tied around her head and the bunny slippers on her feet, it made for a comical sight. Lovell suppressed an urge to laugh.

"What's got into you, Miss Jodie?"

"Not guilty, that's what. They found my man not guilty."

"OJ, huh?" Duh?, he thought. Who else could the woman be talking about? He didn't know what the fascination was with the popular trial, but Mama Jo couldn't seem to get enough of it. Twice the woman had almost snapped his head off when he tried to ask her a question while the trial was on. From then on, he made it a point to leave her alone during her viewing times.

"That's right! Not guilty!" Mama Jo shouted at the top of her voice, then swirled around and did some little foot dance— more kicking up dust than anything. "For a minute I was getting kinda worried 'bout that man."

"Well, it's all good then." Lovell mopped sweat from his forehead again as he looked up at the sky and guessed it to be somewhere after ten a.m. He couldn't figure out what the big deal was. Whether the man was innocent or guilty had nothing to do with her or him one way or another. He could hear the muffled growling of his stomach, reminding him that he hadn't eaten yet.

Gazing at a still shuffling Mama Jo with curious eyes, Lovell wished that the woman would get happy enough to dance herself right back into the kitchen and get happy about fixing him some breakfast. "Hate to see what you woulda done if they had found the man guilty." Picking up a garden hoe from the ground, he leaned on the wooden pole and watched her for a spell longer, amused.

Mama Jo stopped dancing and smiled up like some sly city slicker about to make him privy to some juicy gossip. "'Shoulda seen the looks of some of those white faces when the verdict was pronounced. Lord, have mercy. Looked like they wanted to kill 'im."

"Who's that?" Lovell watched her expression crash to disbelief.

"OJ, silly! Who else?"

"Oh yeah. How could I forget." Truth be told, he could care less. To him, the whole Simpson trial had been too long, too media-hyped, and just another example of exploiting the crimes of famous black people, as if no other race committed horrendous crimes in America. For this reason alone, when the trial had all started, Lovell had made it a point to avoid it entirely. No television. No radio broadcasting. No listening in to private conversations while standing in line at a supermarket. And if anybody asked him anything about OJ, his only reply had been: "Sorry, but I really don't know the man."

Mama Jo's face was lit. "The best darn news I've had in months! My man is walking and no more talking. I feel so good, I feel like baking a cake."

"Sounds good to me. I'm partial to chocolate."

Peering out of the screen door leading to the patio, Barbara Jean stood in her yellow cotton flannel gown and scratched her head. "What's all the noise for back here? Brittany's still sleeping."

Mama Jo trained her attention on her. "They found my man not guilty. Them white folks are fit to be tied. Hot diggity." Her words ended with a devilish smile.

Barbara Jean stepped out onto the patio despite her attire. "For real, Mama?"

"That's right. He's a free man."

"That's nice to hear."

Turning his attention back to his work, Lovell sauntered over and leaned the hoe against the back of the house so that he could tackle the pile of wood that had been part of the old fencing that he'd taken down. He didn't want to talk about OJ or no other black man who could allow his life to be ruined by loving or lusting after some white woman, when there were plenty of black women waiting to be loved.

White women were okay, but he preferred a sistah any day. And the sister he was thinking about was Nylah. He had to find a way to get on her good side if it was the last thing he did. He wondered about her reaction to the flowers he'd sent to her job earlier that morning before tackling the yard work: a whole dozen of yellow long-stemmed roses to Park One Memorial, and to be signed for by Nylah and only Nylah. Though it had taken him a while to locate a floral shop open early, he hoped the flowers worked to put her in a better spirit. He had signed the card at the floral shop 'Your Admirer Always'. It bothered him that the two of them had gotten off on a bad start, which was certainly no fault of his. The cold reality of seeing her show up at the house he'd been brought to by Barbara Jean, only to learn that the two women were sisters. He was just as shocked at seeing her as she was at finding him at her house. Nylah had made it obvious to him that just his being there had freaked her out. Somehow, she hardly seemed like the same sweet, gentle nurse who had tended to his needs while he had laid in bed at the hospital. He knew that her staying away from the house and coming in late was just a ploy to avoid him as much as possible. Sending roses to her job was his way of showing her that he wasn't as bad as she had him pegged.

The new fencing turned out better than he anticipated. He surveyed his work with a feeling of pride. Red cedar flanked the entire rear yard, bringing out the casual beauty of his newly planted flowers. Not that he liked doing a lot of manual labor with his hands, but if need be, he could build a few things. He looked over at Barbara Jean for a few words of approval.

"He's a free man," Mama Jo announced again. "Free."

Barbara Jean studied Lovell's face for his reaction to the news. "...and what you think about it, Lovell?"

"Who me?" He pretended to scratch his head. "Frankly, I really don't know the man."

Shaking her head, Barbara Jean walked over and stood admiring the variety of flowers that Lovell had chosen—beautiful yellow and orange California poppies and low-growing pansies. Ignorant to the growing seasons of certain plants, she was both astonished and mildly curious as to how in the world he had gotten those starter plants to shoot up and flourish so quickly. Two weeks. It had only been two weeks that he'd planted them, and now they were fuller and spreading out like crazy. "Wow, Lovell. Looks like you have a green thumb or somethin'."

"So, you like what you see?"

"What...?" Even Mama Jo stopped her rattling about OJ for a few seconds and took notice. "That's real nice work. I just hope no riot breaks out behind this trial. Last thing we need is for some more misguided souls to go burning down our own communities like the last riot. Hurt more blacks than it did white folks. Just plain crazy it was." Mama Jo put her hands on her hips, looked around, and noticed that the yard was coming along just fine. "Umph. Starting to look like people actually live in this old house. Some real nice flowers you planted."

Barbara Jean bobbed her head. "For real, Lovell. You do know some gardening."

"Well," chirped Mama Jo as if to conclude her survey of the yard, "I'ma go get started on my OJ victory cake." With no one halting her departure, she turned and moseyed back into the house.

With her mother out of ear range, Barbara Jean made a face. " Yeah, yeah. The hell with OJ."

"Word up," Lovell agreed. "Why worry over other people's fate when you have your own to deal with?"

"For real. And when was the last time that man did somethin' positive for his own people?" Barbara Jean took a deep breath, looked over, and admired Lovell's bare chest. Normally, she liked her men with more meat on their bones, maybe a little more muscle definition. But what she was seeing wasn't bad at all. Matter of fact, she liked it. "You really got this yard looking nice, and that paint job you did last week on the kitchen is jammin', too. Even Mama likes it. I can tell 'cause she's back to cooking."

"Nothing wrong with that. How's Brit?"

Sighing half heartedly, Barbara Jean shook her head. "She's still wheezing a little, but she's sleeping. I gave her some herbal tea, but sometimes it takes a day or so to get her asthma under control. God, I hope my child outgrows that mess. It's like a curse I wouldn't wish on my worst enemy."

"I hate to hear that. Can't you have one of those doctors where you work to give her somethin' to help?" Lovell knew that he shouldn't be prying, but it just seemed odd to him that she didn't take the child to see a real medical doctor, seeing how she came in to contact with some every day on her job.

"Are you kidding?" Barbara Jean said in response with a face to match. "You can't trust half the drugs on the market nowadays. Nothing but pure poison for the body. If the good Lord wanted man to be constantly taking designer drugs made by man, he wouldn't have given us natural healing herbs. She'll be okay in a day or so."

"I hate to hear that. Such a sweet little girl. That's my little buddy. Anything I can do to help, just let me know." He hoped she could tell how sincere his offer was. After a couple of weeks, he'd grown pretty fond of Brittany.

How thoughtful, she mused. "You really doing a great job 'round this place, Lovell. I don't know what it is, but even my own mama seems different since you've been around. Have you noticed?"

"Not really. Different how?"

He started picking up old pieces of wood fencing and tossing it into a large trash can, trying to ignore the growl of hunger radiating from his stomach. To get an early start on the yard, he'd skipped breakfast. Now he was paying the price.

"I mean with me being new around here and all, how would I know?"

"Oh, I don't know. . .more energetic. . . happier. . .more at peace with herself." What Barbara Jean thought about saying was that her mother was more in charge of her drug addiction, and not so eager to slip away from the house. Since Lovell had been living at their house, not once did they have to go out searching for their mother. Not once. "I guess what I'm trying to say is that you've been more of a help than you realize."

Smiling proudly, Lovell kept up his pace picking up from the pile of discarded wood. "Wait 'til I get finished. It'll be like somethin' out of a garden magazine."

"You the man. Sounds good to me." Barbara Jean beamed with delight. "I'm really impressed. This place was such an eyesore that I was embarrassed to bring friends home. Now look at it." She took it all in; the neat patches of flowers, the budding tropical palms, a new fence, and patches of dark green grass rising up. "Just lovely. . ." she paused, then added, "I guess I'm awed by the magnitude of it. I still can't believe how fast everything is growing. It's amazing."

"I've been called that too," he grinned.

Barbara Jean tried to imagine if it were possible for seeds and starter plants to be super-charged by Lovell's mere handling. Maybe the man's touch was more special than she knew. The thought was wild, perhaps even too far-fetched, but who really knew?

"The fact that you can build a fence, too, still trips me out. You seem like a man of many talents. What can't you do?"

Lovell knew that if she kept it up, he'd be blushing. The words, 'work a nine-to-five job' jumped to mind, but he kept them to himself, pulled at his work gloves. "Oh, I know a little 'bout a lotta things. But not enough about everything. Used to live with a foster family where the father was a master carpenter. Mr. Peters. I swear, that man could build anything."

"Well, all I know is we did a good job on our fence." Proud that she had actually gotten with him to pull the old rotten wood fencing down, board after board, she had even helped with the digging of the anchoring post. Barbara Jean was sure of it, the smell of rich, nurturing earth was still seeping from her hands. She had helped. She'd done more than just supply a credit card, a financial means of making it all possible. She had actually helped.

Now the pile of wood had to be removed and carted away. This was the part that Lovell hated. No matter how much digging down into the soil he did, he never got tired of it. The smell of freshly turned over earth was like a healing salve to his raw soul, a mingling of the spirits. Cleaning up the mess behind himself was a different matter.

Picking up piece after piece of discarded wood and tossing them into the waiting trash, Lovell planned to haul the old wood to the spacious trunk of his car where he could later dispose of it.

Barbara Jean watched in silence, a warm sense of satisfaction radiating up from her feet to the top of her head. She kept her eyes glued to him as she watched his strong, brown back contour with lean muscle as he bent down, and his small, masculine waist twist on cue. She saw at the precise moment he stepped backwards, even felt the panic zip through her senses the second his foot made contact with the rusty nail.

"Watch it!" Barbara lunged forward to help but not in time for Lovell to shift his weight or stop his right foot from landing on sheer pain.

"What the...darn it!" Lightning shot through his right leg and settled somewhere in the center of his back. Angrily, Lovell tossed the rotted panel of wood he was holding to the ground and pulled at his foot to free it from its impalement. Rich, red blood was already seeping out from the bottom of his tennis shoe as his foot came up.

Hurrying to his side, Barbara Jean lent her shoulder for support while he hopped on one foot to a dusty patio chair and plopped down, his face contorted with pain.

"How stupid, stupid, stupid. . ."

"It's okay, I'll fix it." As soothing as she wanted her words to sound, Barbara Jean knew that such a long nail ripping up through muscles had to be painful. Lovell was clenching his teeth, trying to be strong and calm about it. "Looks like you're going to tear yourself up before you're old."

"Guess I should'a checked for nails. It was stupid of me."

"It'll be okay. Just relax."

Lovell eased back along the recline of the patio lounge chair while she went to work undoing his shoestring and wrestling his tennis shoe off. Barbara Jean noticed the small puncture at the top of his leather sneaker and felt a sympathetic chill race through her body. The nail had gone clean through his foot.

"You poor thing."

"Just stupid and careless, that's all."

"It's gonna be okay, stop babbling about it. Keep your sock on while I go find somethin' to sterilize the wound and bandage it." Barbara Jean went back into the house and it seemed it was taking her a short eternity to get back to him. Surprised that Mama Jo hadn't emerged from the house again to see what was going on, Lovell gathered his composure to stand up and go see what was taking Barbara Jean so long. Finally, she appeared at the door, calm and collected as ever, with some first aid supplies bundled in her arms.

"Were you going somewhere?" Her expression was nonplused.

"God, woman, what took you so long? I'm laying here bleeding to death while you're somewhere looking for heaven knows what. You act like you 'bout to perform major surgery or somethin'."

"Well I'm here now, so quit complaining."

"I hope you don't treat patients like this at work."

The first thing he noticed her placing around his foot was

a large black towel, then a shiny, stainless steel catch pan. The same kind he'd seen at the hospital.

"Such a kidder, you. Stop being so dramatic. I had to look in on Mama. You know I still have to keep an eye on her every now and then. Thank God she's sleeping."

"Good. Just let me bleed to death while you check." His words sounded serious, but she could tell by his mocking expression that he was only teasing with her.

"Oh, stop whining, sit back, and relax. I'll have you fixed up in no time."

"Guess I'm not used to seeing a lotta blood, especially my own. That fool stabbing me in the side with that broken bottle almost scared me to death. It wasn't so much the pain I felt. But the thought of blood coming outta me." He paused for an afterthought. "I really can't recall having a lot of injuries when I was growing up. Matter-of-fact, now that I'm thinking about it, I can't recall having any."

"You're kidding. No toothaches, no measles, no mumps, no sore throats?"

"None."

Smiling, Barbara Jean shook her head. "Now, ain't that a trip."

"Guess I'm getting a little careless in my old age."

"Don't worry," she offered. "You'll live. And just for the record, you still got plenty of good years left." Handling his foot with the gentleness of a mother handling her newborn infant, she got his bloodied white sock off and felt amazed at how much blood his wound was oozing. Barbara Jean felt a hot rush to her senses at the sight of so much red. It was so awesome, so exhilarating... Her hands felt like they wanted to tremble, and her breathing was starting to quicken. She paused and held her breath to keep from hyperventilating. "It's not as bad as it looks." A quiet shiver· zipped up her spine as she braced herself.

Wiping his foot with some alcohol-drenched cotton balls, she set his foot over in the steel basin and watched the crimson stream pool into its depth. The most wonderful sight in the world, the red river of life.

It was fascinating when she really thought about it, human blood. Barbara Jean had been only six years old when she first realized how important, how vital the liquid was, after seeing it gush out of her own beloved dog, Toby, as he lay bleeding in the street that hot summer day. The big car had kept going, leaving Toby to bleed out his life force. Desperate to save her beloved pet, Barbara Jean had tried in vain to scoop the redness up from the blackened street with her small hands—tried to pour it back into the gap at Toby's side. The sight of it had stayed vivid in her mind for years, a crimson reminder etched deep into her memory. If only she could have found some way to keep Toby's blood in, perhaps her precious pet would have lived. She understood from then on, that blood was the red gold of life itself.

Sure. She saw blood day in and day out on her job at Park One Memorial, but never tired of it. Never. It was still fascinating to her that blood came in a variety of shades of red. She'd seen blood thick like pudding, and some, oh yes, some as thin as red-tinted water.

Once, years ago, her mother had taken a belt to her young behind for cutting her own hand on purpose, just to play with it, just to smell and taste it, her own blood. Barbara Jean believed that there was no other taste like it, and there was something else, too—something that she could never tell another living soul. When she found herself looking at an abundance of the crimson, she often felt a tingling, wonderful glow in to her center. The feeling so close to sexual stimulation, that she felt sure that both feelings, though positively separate, were still one in the same. She felt it now.

"Excuse me...helloooo. Hey, you're squeezing my foot!"

Barbara Jean's eyes rolled back down to normal. Oh my God, she thought, what have I done? She was sitting on the patio, looking like an oversized child about to pat out a few mud pies, sitting Indian style; her rump was oddly familiar with the cold concrete, yet not feeling its coldness. Lovell's foot was still in the stainless steel basin with her hand tightly around it. When had she positioned herself that way. . .and why? "Oh my goodness, Lovell. I'm...I'm so sorry."

"Woman, you are hurting my foot, not helping it."

"I said I'm sorry."

"That don't stop it from hurting."

"Lovell, stop acting like a big baby."

"I wouldn't have to if you weren't sitting here like you're in a trance while you squeeze the life outta my foot! What the heck you try'n to do anyway, make tomato juice?"

Looking down to see what he was talking about, Barbara Jean saw that she was indeed holding his foot over the pan with vise-like tightness, using the same intensity as one would to squeeze juice from an orange with a bare hand. She released his foot, to his relief, and stared down at the collection of blood.

Lovell studied her eyes. "Thank you."

"You probably could stand a Tetanus shot, just to be on the safe side. Don't worry. Tonight I'll see what I can get from work."

Lovell didn't say anything, letting her rattle off while he mulled over why she had squeezed his already sore foot that way. He was beginning to wonder about her, if she was really stable.

Barbara Jean struggled up from her place along the concrete and brushed imaginary dust from her gown. "Be right back to put a bandage on that foot."

Right back? Now what? Irritated, Lovell sighed heavily, leaned back in his seat, and closed his eyes for a short spell, and forced himself not to focus on the pain. "Maybe I should just do it myself."

"Lovell, stop tripping. I said I'll be right back, God. I'm just going to dispose of this. Don't be so impatient." She headed into the house with the pan of blood, straight to the bedroom she shared with Brittany.

Standing over her still sleeping daughter, Barbara Jean could hear Brittany's struggled breathing as she entered the room. Under the thin pink blanket her child lay limp and fighting for every little bit of air her rebellious lungs could grasp.

"Don't worry, baby. Mama will make it all okay. Brittany slept on, unaware of her mother opening the small room-sized refrigerator door where she placed the pan of blood until she could get back to it.

Before hurrying back to Lovell, she stopped again at Brittany's bedside and felt her forehead for fever. Thank God, the child felt fine, just wheezing a little. "Just hold, on mama's little angel. Everything's gonna be okay." Quickly, she bent and kissed Brittany's forehead before sauntering out the room to go give some real medical attention to Lovell's foot.

Chapter Twelve

The apartment was perfect, well almost perfect, except for the carpet. Nylah stood in the vacant bedroom, pinching up her face as she shook her head. "Lord have mercy." To her, the nappy orange and brown rug qualified as a disgrace to the carpet industry. She could handle the monthly rent by herself. No problem with that. And it did help that utilities were included with the rent. But the carpet, how would she ever get used to such hideous sight?

The place was upstairs—one of six units. Thank goodness for that much. Anybody in their right mind knew that the larger the apartment complex, the more scandal to be dealt with. All the same, just to be able to escape the madness going on in her own life, she could deal with it. Nylah knew that what she really needed was some peace and quiet—a private place to come home to and lay her head.

The woman from the property management company led the way into the second bedroom. Nylah found the woman a bit overdressed in her lavender wool blend suit and white pumps. And judging from the woman's too thin, delicate white frame, she was either sickly or bulimic. Her dark hair was stretched back from her equally thin face. Nylah noticed that her small bony hand nervously clutched the clipboard of rental applications she held.

"I really like it." From the bedroom window, Nylah could see all the grandeur of Pacific Coast Highway headlights roaring by. The idea of living alone again was both thrilling and a little scary. "It's just what I'm looking for."

As if trying to read her thoughts, the woman turned and regarded her with blue pondering eyes. "Will it be just you or will you be sharing?"

Sharing? Hmph. Lady, please. "No. Just me. No boyfriend, no kids, no pets. Nobody." For a second her own words sounded so void that they saddened her. "Sometimes it's better that way tho'."

An odd look flit across the woman's face. "Of course."

"Is it a quiet neighborhood?" Nylah asked looking interested. Anything would be better than the neighborhood she'd grown up in.

"Oh yes. In fact, our company is very selective when screening our applicants. Not to sound discriminating, but we try to refill any vacancy with compatible tenants. You know, families with other families, and singles with other singles. In fact, this would be perfect for you." Her eyes lit up. "Nothing but singles live in this small unit."

"And now for the shocker," Nylah mocked. "How much?"

The lady had to consult her papers for a rental price list. "Oh, of course. . .let's see here. It rents for nine hundred, and we do ask for first and last, and a credit check fee of fifty dollars. We do check references."

"References?" Nylah said the word as if she'd never heard it before.

"Yes. We check references. That won't be a problem for you, will it?"

Problem? Heck no, Nylah mused. It just didn't make a whole lot of sense to her. What was the point of checking past records on apartment renting? Her philosophy was: as long as you can pay, you can stay. It was nothing to be proud about, but she knew it had to be told. "No, not really. It's just that I've been living at my parent's house for the last eleven years. The only reference I would have would be my mother, and she's not in her right frame of mind right now." She hated lying about her mother like the woman had some kind of serious mental handicap, but in a way it was partly true. Her mother wasn't thinking rational. If she were, why would she have allowed that...that man to be living in her house?

The woman held her tongue and smiled amiably. "Apartments have been rented to people with worse stories. Depending on the situation, sometimes we make exceptions."

Nylah felt like she needed to explain, "It's not that I couldn't get a place sooner, but I was taking care of my mom. She's been ill."

"Of course. Time to cut the old apron strings."

Ignoring the woman's last remark, Nylah's tone lifted. "But. . .this is just what I'm looking for: a nice location from the job—not too close, not too far. Looks like a clean place, too."

"Oh yes. We have an exterminator out once a month. No bugs"

Suddenly besieged by mathematics, Nylah tried to figure out the total move-in cost. "Nine hundred a month, huh?...and you say that's first and last?"

"Total move-in is two thousand and seventy."

"Wow, kinda expensive."

"It's what a nice apartment rents for," the woman said in a nice, but snooty way.

"Guess I've been living in a time warp." Nylah tried a small nervous laugh to lightened the air

"Have you been looking long?" The woman's question was too casual to sound like prying.

She didn't want to tell all her business, but did offer,

"Actually it's my second week." Truth was, she'd taken a few days off from work to look. "I've been all over the place looking too."

Nylah was sure that it was the two piece burgundy velour outfit she had on that was making her feel a bit too warm. Even her feet felt hot and tired in the confines of her white athletic shoes. After going to one apartment complex after another, she was disappointed to discover that some of the places she'd looked at, in her opinion, weren't fit to be rented out to alley dogs, let alone to humans. Now, with the evening sun calling it quits for the day, the idea of giving up her search played heavily on her mind.

As she stood in this place in south Long Beach with its move-in cost as ridiculous as a four dollar bill, and the hideous burnt orange carpet looking like something out of House Horrible, somehow, Nylah still felt like it was a place she could call home for a while. She could add a few things here and there, and mold the place into a cozy dwelling for herself. It was nothing spectacular or special, but it was a start at a new beginning. Anything to get away from her mother's house.

The living room was spacious enough with typical off-white walls throughout the place. A large picture window looked out beyond the walkway and banister and down to some well trimmed hedges. A typical kitchen for a two bedroom apartment, and the sink looked newly installed. The place came with a built-in range top, but now it meant she would have to buy a refrigerator, not to mention other furniture and household needs.

"Two thousand and seventy, huh?"

"That's correct."

Nylah shifted her weight on her right leg to ease some of her discomfort. It was dark outside, way after dinner time, and already she was tired of searching. She thought of her girlfriend at work who was known to move every three months.

How on earth the girl could swing it financially and emotionally was now a mystery to her. "I think this is the place for me." She gave the woman a big smile. "Just show me what I need to fill out."

❧ ☙

On the drive home, at least to the place where all her belongings were still being housed because her mother's place no longer felt like home to her with that dreadful man living there, Nylah found herself wondering if she was doing the right thing about planning to move out.

Never before had she considered leaving her mother's house after being a tenant for so long. Of course, she knew that she had been more than that. Her mother had always needed her, and she, with no one else in her own life to need or be needed by, was somehow needy of her mother. It was a mutual need that neither one had put into words, yet, it still existed.

At first, it had been her mother's loneliness after her father had died, then the crack cocaine. The drug had reared up in her mother's life like a prized fighter and challenged her mother. The fight was long and hard, and the drug had won. If it weren't for me, Nylah speculated, Mama would probably be a homeless hooker living and dying in the streets. She was the one who had kept her mother's financial situation intact and kept her mother tethered close to the homestead. She had done all that she could to keep her mother healthy and focused. Nylah wanted to believe that the old house normally ran smoothly because of her. After all, she was the one that saw that bills were paid on time, made sure that the cabinets and the refrigerator were always stocked with food. Sometimes she felt as if she ran the house, at least it used to be that way.

Things were different now that Barbara Jean had that man

in the house. Nylah hated to even say his name, and just the thought of him made her left eye go into a mild, uncontrollable twitch. Even her rash, still not healed, began to itch. And the nerve of him, sending her some yellow roses like she couldn't figure out who they were from. What was that corny signing?..'Your Admirer Always'. She shook her head, wondering what in the world could have been on Lovell's mind for him to send her some roses.

Keeping her eyes on the road, she reached her hand over and snatched off the bandage on her left wrist. Despite the use of every cortisone ointment and fungal cream she could find at the hospital's pharmacy, the dry, reddish scaliness persisted. The rash was still the same size but appeared more red and scaly than ever. Sometimes the urge to scratch was maddening. Hopefully, she thought, the new dermatologist she would be seeing in a week would have some clear-cut answers for her malady.

Nylah was sure of it, that man being in her mother's house was just another thing to grate on her nerves. She has just lived through the worst two weeks in her life, and she still couldn't figure out what it was about Lovell she hated the most, his cocky over-confidence, his joblessness, the way he rolled those green eyes along her body in subtle suggestions, or the fact that he was Barbara Jean's friend. Okay, okay, she thought, her emotions running deep and cold, so what if he's doing a good job around the place. The kitchen did look better with its new paint job. The house was always filled with fresh flowers from some local florist shop he'd discovered. And she had to admit, the fresh flowers did lend a heady mist of floral to the air. And her mother, she mused, how much happier around the house could the woman get?

As much as she hated to admit it, the man was quite a find in a domestic kind of way. Even though he was nowhere near her type, he could cook, and was a darn good one to boot. He kept himself well groomed and clean, picked up behind himself, kept a watchful eye on her mother, and was turning out to be quite pleasant to be around. Still, for no reason she could come up with, Nylah couldn't stand him.

But it was the end of a glorious day, and she didn't want to spoil it with bad thoughts. Not even bad ones about Lovell. She couldn't wait to get home to spring her news on her family about finding her own place. No more chasing behind her mother trying to see what was up. No more worrying about whether Barbara Jean would keep working long enough to pay her share of the household expenses. No more putting her two cents in and interfering with Brittany's health problems. No more. She knew the latter drove her sister crazy, but too bad. Sometimes she just couldn't help it. And definitely no more free-loading Lovell Joyner. "Wonder what he'll find to fix around the house when everything's all done?"

Nylah pushed it all from her mind.

Before going home, she stopped at a local supermarket and picked up a few staples: milk, bread, eggs, and a gallon of Brittany's favorite ice cream, which was also Blueberry Waffle Cone. Despite her own offish mood around the house lately, she didn't want her young niece to think that she was mad at her about something. It wasn't her fault her mama, Barbara Jean, was weak and gullible when it came to men.

She made it home a little after eight and found the house quiet. Out of a long-formed habit to look in on Mama Jo, Nylah set her bag of groceries down in the hallway, eased into her mother's room, and stood quietly over her mother's exposed sleeping form. Peace and serenity were etched across her mother's ebony face—a face that looked like it was plumping back up again. Plumping up and sleeping more—that was a good sign. Picking up a blanket, she draped it lovingly over the sleeping woman. She loved her mother so much. The idea of having to leave her felt like a slow, smothering hole clean through her heart. She eased back out the room.

On her way to the kitchen to put Brittany's ice cream in the freezer, Nylah froze in the entrance-way at the sight of Lovell sitting at the kitchen table reading an *Essence* magazine. She felt a small sigh rise up out of her on its own. The man had the nerve to be sitting at her mama's kitchen table with black sweat pants on and no shirt. A cup of something steaming hot sat in front of him. Right away, she noticed that he had a bandaged foot up in a chair. Lord have mercy, she sighed quietly to herself, now what's happened?

Not chancing a word lest it be unpleasant, Nylah straightened her posture and acknowledged him with a careless toss of her head as she went straight to the freezer to put Brittany's ice cream away. Lovell glanced up at her with equal nonchalance and then back to the article he was reading. A tall, slender wooden stick rested against his thigh.

Chuckling lightly to himself, Lovell decided to break the ice. "Did you have a nice day?" He didn't have to look up to know that she was frowning over at him. She was always frowning at him. He could feel it.

See. There he goes again. Trying to be Mr. Nice. Must be up to something. Nylah snorted in his direction. Two could play at that game.

"You could say that." She paused momentarily to smooth her hair back. I can be nice as as apple pie, she mused. "Where's Barbara Jean?"

"At work. And Brittany's at the babysitter's, and your mom's in her room sleeping."

"I see." Emptying her bag, Nylah walked over to the plastic trash can and tossed it in. The kitchen was so much nicer with its new coat of paint—white with yellow borders with pastel fruits. Her mother or Barbara Jean had taken the time to add a few trailing plants in decorative hangers from the ceiling, which gave an even cozier effect to the room. Lovell had done an excellent job, but she fought the urge to compliment him on his work.

"So, what's wrong with that foot of yours?" Silence was permeating the air like thin smoke.

Obviously absorbed in his reading, Lovell merely turned the page of his magazine. The gesture was simple, but well intended, and enough to scratch at her nerves.

"Forget it." Nylah breezed past him going to her room. She got as far as the door before she had to turn around and let him have it. "Actually, Mr. Lovell, this is perfect timing. Finally, we get to talk without everybody else being around to hear what's said."

Putting aside the periodical, Lovell raised a brow. "I take it you didn't like the roses I sent."

"This is not about roses."

"Let's have it then." The look on his face was a mixture of mild surprise and amusement. "What's up?"

"I know all about men like you. So-called men. You come a dime a dozen. Two dozen on a good day."

"So what's the real problem, Miss Nylah? Just say it."

"Leeching, Mr. Lovell. That's the problem. Leeching."

"You act like you know me."

"I know your kind, and that's enough."

With his foot still paining him, Lovell got up and half-limped towards her. Trying to put any of his weight on his assaulted foot only brought agony. "So you hate me, Miss Nylah? Is that it?"

"I hate men like you. And stop calling me Miss Nylah. We're not that different in age." She blinked and licked her suddenly-dry lips. It flashed in her mind that his coming upon her was some feeble attempt at male intimidation. Whatever it was, it wasn't going to work on her. She refused to be intimidated and stood firm in her spot as he drew closer. Good Lord, she braced. The man was right at her face. In the artificial kitchen light, she could almost see straight through those green eyes; she could smell his body scent, a mild concoction of male musk and aftershave cologne. Nothing offensive, but a warm, human smell.

"Is this supposed to scare me or something?"

"And why would I want to scare you, Miss Nylah?"

"I'm not sure. You tell me."   He was so close, so damn close. His breath was incredibly light and milky, like the breath of some of the infants she sometimes held in the neonatal ward on her job. It reminded her of smothered rose petals and new milk. I will not move, her mind chanted, I will not move.

Lovell looked long into her eyes. "...And to think, Miss Nylah, you were so nice to me at the hospital. I was thinking that you really liked me. Now look at you."

"I just know your type. I was doing my job, that's all. I get paid to be nice to all my patients."

"You knew my type while I was at the hospital too. You were nice to me then. What's changed? Do you have a man, Miss Nylah?"

"I asked you to stop calling me that." She wanted to step back away from him, but she wouldn't give him the satisfaction of thinking that his being so close and in her face had an effect on her. "And, that's none of your business, is it?"

"Guess that means no. No you don't have a man. It's okay, it's nothing to be ashamed of."

"Excuse me? I suppose you think I need one, right? Perhaps one just like you?" Nylah could feel anger well up inside her like a river on its way to overflowing. Who was this foolish man trying to read her like some open book? She wanted to say the right words to get the right point across—make it as plain to him as possible that. . .

With one swift movement, Lovell thrust his face closer to hers and licked the tip of her nose—not a hard brush of his tongue, but a warm and wet flick around the tip of her nose. Then it was over.

Nylah stood in shock, her mouth slightly open, her hand rubbing the spot where his tongue had been as she watched with disbelieving eyes as he turned smoothly and limped back to his bedroom.

Chapter Thirteen

"Ooh, child, you'll love living on your own. Ain't nothing like it. Shoots, the first time I moved away from my mama's house...that was...umm..."

Nylah did her best to focus on Gail's conversation, but honestly, the woman's incessant chatter was wearing her out. If she had to list all the things that Gail was good at, talking would be at the top of that list. She glanced up at the wall clock. It felt like the hours in her work shift were dragging by on purpose. Going over a patient chart, she stood at her station and allowed her friend's words to fly over her like air over water. In a way, she regretted that she had even brought up the subject of her moving. Rarely did she open up and discuss her personal life with her working peers.

Even though she was short by most standards, Gail Matthews was at least half an inch shorter. An average looking woman of thirty, she was pleasant enough with dark, friendly eyes and a perpetual happy expression on her walnut-hued face. Nylah had known the woman for the entire year and a half of Gail's employment at Park One Memorial, and in no way did she consider the woman a good, trustworthy friend. In fact, it was puzzling to her why she had even made Gail privy to the information about her moving. Gail was okay, sometimes. But on several occasions, Nylah had frowned on the woman's gossiping ways, not to mention her "hip-hop," cool way of talking that seemed out of place in a business-like atmosphere. Gail had an easy way of putting a down-home-sistah twang to every story she had to tell. The woman was full of stories about everybody else's life, and sometimes her own. One thing for sure, if there was something juicy going on at the hospital, Gail Matthews was certainly part of the clique that knew about it.

"Aren't you excited?"

"Not really." Nylah looked over at her and tried to smile. She was only going to say so much, and even with that she had to be careful, especially with Gail. "I guess I'm just worried about my mother. The thought of leaving her alone with my sister, Barbara, is more frightening than living by myself." Nylah wasn't crazy. She wouldn't mention a thing about Lovell moving into their home. Barbara Jean is so stupid, she thought, getting herself involved with Lovell. She was even more gullible if she thought that the hospital didn't have spies planted, trying to find out if anyone knew the whereabouts of one Mr. Lovell Joyner. Nylah saw the whole thing as one scandal that soon enough would blow up in Barbara Jean's face. Heck. Wasn't it just the other day in the hospital cafeteria that she overheard two of the hospital's new doctors discussing "the man with the rare blood"—some rumor that he was living in a halfway house uptown. Nylah had almost choked on her tuna salad sandwich, craning her neck trying to hear their low-volumed conversation.

That was another thing she was planning to bring to Barbara Jean's attention. People were still looking for Lovell. The other thing was the incident that happened just the other night when Lovell had the audacity to kiss her nose, well, if you could call it a kiss. She had to think about that one a minute. It was more like a lick instead of a kiss.

Nylah didn't think that her sister and Lovell were lovers,

but still she considered Lovell Barbara's Jean's man, or something close to it. As far as she was concerned, the man had no
justification in kissing her or licking her nose or any other part
of her body.

"If you need any help with moving," Gail offered happily,
"just let me know. My boyfriend has a truck and plenty of big,
strong friends. He's always looking to pick up a few extra
bucks."

How nice. "Thanks, Gail. How sweet of you to offer."
Trying to sound grateful, Nylah knew she couldn't dare trust
the woman to come to her mother's house and possibly see
Lovell. She felt like coming right out and asking Gail if she
knew anything more about the hospital trying to locate Lovell,
perhaps throw a little bait on the line. If anybody knew anything worth knowing, it would have to be Gail.

"I'm just glad that all that hype about the man with the
special blood finally blew over, aren't you?" Nylah picked up
another patient chart and proceeded to go over the doctors'
instructions for the day. She hoped that Gail could tell her
something new.

"Child, hush." They were the only two at the nurse's station at the time, but Gail eased over closer to her as if no other
ears were meant to hear what she was about to say. She looked
around to see if anyone was listening, then lowered her voice
to almost a whisper. "Girl, you won't believe this, but..." pausing to allow two scrub nurses to stroll by, then seeing that the
coast was clear, "...it seems that this rich man who owns part
of this hospital is on the waiting list for a kidney transplant..."

"Is that right?" Nylah made her tone serious.

"Rumors have it..." Gail went silent the moment a visitor
came to the station asking for directions to room 115. She
smiled professionally and pointed the way before going back
to her account. "...rumors have it that this same rich man is
offering a reward, or what you could call a finder's fee to any-

one who knows the whereabouts of. . .of. . .whatever his name was. . . You know. The man with the rare blood going on. Guess how much, girl?"

Nylah felt a sickening lurch in her stomach. "I don't know. . .twenty thousand maybe."

"Try fifty thousand dollars. Can you believe it? Child, I wish I knew where the man was myself. That's some real cash duckies, and this 'sistah would be gettin' paid. You hear me?"

"Fifty thousand dollars just for locating the man?" The sound of her own words made Nylah's head spin.

"That's just the finder's fee—more money for the kidney itself. Now, that's what I heard." Gail pulled a piece of gum from her uniform pocket, unwrapped it, and stuffed it into her mouth. "We're talking big bucks here." Remembering her manners, she pulled the half-empty pack of spearmint gum from her pocket and offered it in Nylah's direction.

"No thanks."

"I just wish I knew where Mister Man was."

It was too crazy to think about. "And what for?" Nylah confirmed. "Just for some blood?"

"Girlfriend, please. You mean just for a kidney. It seems Mister Rich-man wants a special kidney."

"That's sick," Nylah said lamely. She'd read the chart in her hands two times, and none of it held any comprehension for her. Nylah realized that it was only normal for a person having organ failure to want the healthiest replacement organ they could possibly obtain. Of course, that made sense. But the idea of taking an organ from a healthy, living, unwilling person didn't seem morally right to her.

"That's enough money for a nice Lexus," Gail was saying. "Maybe a nice 'Beemer'. Lord, I love those cars."

A terrible thought popped into Nylah's head. So, her sister had been right about that aspect of Lovell's stay at the hospital. The man's life would have been in danger, if not his life itself, then certainly his freedom. First, it would have been the harvesting of his blood antibodies. Eventually, they would have wanted more from him: a lung, a kidney, and maybe even his heart. Who knew? "Wow," Nylah said more to herself than to Gail, "just dissect a healthy person for some body parts, huh?"

Gail sighed with her own thoughts. "It happens more than you think. They even think they might have a lead."

"They who?" Nylah was beginning to get the feeling that she'd bit off more than she could chew by inquiring. "What kind of lead?"

Looking around to make sure that no one was paying any attention to their conversation, Gail moved over to pick up an inventory sheet and scrolled down the items. "The ones I refer to as "they" are the hospital's "fetch people." Spies. Don't think they don't have any 'cause it's how they weed out the bad staff. Especially doctors that self-medicate or pill-popping nurses who steal patient medication. They're looking for this man." Gail paused before adding, "A black man with rare blood is serious bizz." She paused for a few seconds as if she had to give some serious thought to her own words. "Like I said, they think they might have located him living on the streets. I heard that the man gave a phony address when he signed admission papers. They think he might be homeless."

Nylah couldn't help asking. "Why would they think that?"

"Well," Gail droned on as she pretended to be busy look-ing over some hospital supply requisitions. "...about three days after the man mysteriously left the hospital, some preg-nant Hispanic woman came in to check on 'im. Girl, they had that woman hemmed up in a small room shooting one question after another to her trying to find out where that man was liv-ing."

"What? When was this?" Nylah blew her nose to clear her

sinuses. Either her allergies were trying to kick up, or her head was beginning to feel heavy from all the information that Gail was putting in it. "Did they find out?" Glancing down at her watch, she noted that Barbara Jean's shift had begun. Maybe she should take a break, go down to have a little chat with her, and maybe try and talk some sense into her head. It looked like the best thing they could do was to put up the money to put Mr. Lovell on a train or a bus to the city of his choice—a one-way trip, of course. Her ears felt like they were heating up with all the news she was hearing. Gail was like a cup running over. It was unbelievable how much information the woman was holding.

"A few days ago. And I heard. . .," Gail added, pausing to look around on the sly, ". . .that the Hispanic woman told 'em that he might be homeless. Something about his current girl-friend throwing him out the same day he'd come to the hospi-tal. Claimed that she didn't know where he lived, and he prob-ably on the streets. What was that name . . .Lovee. . .Lover. . .no. . ."

"Lovell. Lovell Joyner."

"Yeah, girl, that's it. I don't know how I can forget a name like that with so much talk about 'im around this place." Against her better judgment, she popped her gum loud before realizing how unprofessional her behavior was. "Oops..sorry. And how come you remember his name so well?"

Nylah gave a mock look of disgust. "The man, Mr. Lovell Joyner, was on this floor, Gail, remember? I was his nurse."

"Oh yeah, and you let 'im get away?" Gail raised a brow jokingly. "I hear he was fine too. You didn't by any chance get to give 'im a sponge bath, did you?"

Rolling her eyes to heaven, Nylah sucked air threw her teeth and shook her head. "Girl, you are too much, you know that? You should hear yourself." She thought about what Gail had said about the possibility of Lovell being homeless. That explained why her sister had brought the man to her mother's house. But still it was no excuse. If her sister was so concerned for his safety, why didn't she put the man up in a hotel someplace? Nylah put the patient chart down. "Well, anyway, keep me posted if you hear anything else." She excused herself with the pretense of going to the restroom.

On her way out, Nylah went in the opposite direction and took the elevator down to the main floor where the labs were. Passing through the lobby, she could see through the main entrance door of the hospital that it was already dark outside; a slight Santa Ana breeze was swaying the branches of a tree in the distance. It was always so irritating when the time changed. Daylight saving time was a joke. The days seemed as though they dragged by at a snail's pace, and the darkness was always so impatient to claim the California sky. On this day, she'd agreed to do some overtime when two scheduled day nurses called in sick. Not only that, but by staying at work longer she would be able to catch Barbara Jean when her shift came on.

Nylah's first issue with Barbara Jean was the little incident Lovell pulled the other night. The incident with him up in her face and kissing her nose. Well, licking it. She had to chuckle to herself at that one. Telling her sister that the man licked her nose like a new puppy showing affection would sound a bit silly. Heck, the man kissed my nose and that was what it was—a kiss. But then again, after listening to Gail rant on about folks still looking for Lovell, she had plenty of topics to talk to Barbara Jean about without bringing the kiss up at all. So what if the man had lick-kissed her nose? Obviously, it had been his silly way of trying to intimidate her, and nothing more.

Park One Memorial being a hospital of only ninety-five hundred beds, Nylah knew that it wasn't one of the best facilities in the state, but it certainly wasn't one of the worst. Not only did the hospital boast a staff of some of the finest doctors statewide, but it was also a place growing in medical technology, and proudly housed four high-tech labs. Barbara Jean worked in Lab Two.

Nylah said a little prayer, hoping to find her sister in a good mood and willing to talk to her. Lately, they'd been at such odds with one another that it was a pure strain on the whole household. When she let herself think too long on the subject, it hurt her that she and her sister had grown so far apart. Sometimes, it felt as if their sibling love was divided by not one, but two oceans. She didn't know what it was, but it was becoming harder and harder to reach Barbara Jean with reasoning. The atmosphere around the house was almost to the point of being intolerable. For that reason, Nylah decided to stay out of everybody's way. She went to work, came home late, and stayed holed up in her bedroom. Mama Jo was doing more around the place, a little more cleaning, a little more cooking; she had to admit even if it was just to herself that Lovell was doing a good job keeping an eye on everything. No locking her mother up, and not once since the man had been living at the house had they experienced a serious disappearance that required them to go looking for their mother.

Entering Lab Two, Nylah stood at the entrance and scanned around the room and found a few lab techs busy with some blood samples. Some of the faces she recognized, but a couple of new ones caught her attention for a second or two. The room was typical for a hospital lab; it boasted ample lighting, expensive, high-powered microscopes, trays and trays of patient-labeled blood and urine. Petrie dishes and wooden stick swabs were scattered at various stations, giving the place the look of a lot of work going on.

Nylah just didn't get it. Of all the things her sister could have been at a hospital—a doctor, a nurse, perhaps even an admissions clerk—why pray tell, a lab technician? Just the idea of looking into the depths of somebody's bowel movement, sliced tissue samples, or playing dip-dip with other folk's urine day in and day out turned her stomach, not to mention all the other icky stuff that had to be examined closely.

Dressed in the typical lab whites and a surgical mask, there was Barbara Jean standing at a microscope, her hair covered with a light blue paper cap. Nylah walked over and stood quietly by her. When Barbara Jean finally looked up, sensing her presence, not only was she mildly surprised to see her big sister, but seemed equally delighted.

"Hey, girl." Barbara Jean greeted her. Her tone was pleasant. "I was just thinking about you. All good thoughts." She turned around to face Nylah, a kind of knowing smile along her face.

"Oh?" Keeping her expression light and neutral, Nylah didn't want to give off the wrong signals too soon. It was hard enough trying to determine her sister's demeanor. Smiles could be so deceiving.

"Yeah, Sis, I really was. Gotta little somethin' for you." Barbara Jean picked up the open jar next to her microscope. "This will take away that nasty rash on your hand."

Her interest aroused, Nylah asked, "What is it?"

"A new medicated cream I got from one of the new doctors. No Hydrocortisone, no steroids, and it works like a charm."

". . .Well. . . I don't know. I already have an appointment with a dermatologist."

"Squash that. This is the real deal." Giving Nylah no time to protest, Barbara Jean lifted up her hand and pulled the bandage off. The skin looked like brownish-red lizard skin to her. It was a bumpy mess. "You won't believe this cream, I'm telling you." She dipped two fingers into the pink tinted mixture and carefully smoothed the coolness onto Nylah's hand while Nylah held her breath for a second or two to focus on the mildly warm tingle along her skin and then a coolness along the back of her hand. "This stuff is the talk of the hospital. Somethin' the doctor blended up herself."

"Feels pretty soothing. Which doctor?"

"Never mind who. I'm telling you it really works."

"That's nice." Nylah watched and waited patiently for her younger sister to stop rubbing the cream in. Her sister had the most happy and peaceful look about her face, and in a way, she hated to spoil it with negative news about their houseguest. "Look, Barbara Jean, we need to talk."

"Is that why you're still here at work? You must be pulling some overtime or somethin'."

"Yeah," offered Nylah. "Something like that. Actually, I wanted to wait around to talk to you. It's hard to do it at the house nowadays."

Her happy expression crumbled like dry cheese. Barbara Jean didn't blink as she looked straight into her eyes. "I hope this isn't about you know who. We don't have to keep going there. Give it up, Nylah. Lovell is staying for a while."

"Even if people are looking for him? Even if his life could be in danger? Hell, Barbara Jean, you could be jeopardizing your own safety. I don't think you know what's going on around here."

"Nylah, keep your voice down," Barbara Jean hissed and looked around. "I'm not stupid. I know what's going on." She scanned around the room to see if anyone was listening. "I have ears too."

"The bottom line is, Lovell shouldn't be staying at Mama's house."

"Give it up, Nylah. It's not your problem to solve. No one is asking you for anything. So why make it your business?"

Folding her hands over her chest, Nylah looked resolved. Her foolish-minded sister was going to hear her out whether she liked it or not. "I hope you know that this whole thing could get messy."

"Don't you have some boxes you should be at home packing?"

"And you could get us all hurt behind this man. Don't you care about your own family?"

"Of course I care."

"Then darn it, act like it!"

"Nylah, I'm not listening no more."   Aggravatingly, Barbara Jean emphasized by shaking her head and putting both hands to her ears. "I don't wanna hear it."

"Barbara, please. Stop being so pig headed and listen. . ."

"No. I won't."

Nylah felt pushed to her limit. Even she wasn't really prepared for the words that jumped out of her mouth, ". . .he tried to kiss me!"

Not sure of what she had heard, Barbara Jean dropped her hands down and looked at her sister with ears willing and ready to listen. "He did what?"

"You heard me." Nylah pinched up her lips as she blew out air.

As if all noise and piped-in air about the room stopped circulating, the wall clock stopped ticking so loudly; bacteria stopped breeding in their petrie dishes. Those last three words skipped through Barbara Jean's head with spikes on the heels. "He kissed you?" The look on her face said it all—disappointment and disbelief.

Feeling silly, like she'd somehow been forced to stoop to Barbara Jean's level, Nylah threw her head up proudly. "That's right, he kissed me."

Inquiring ears were trying to listen in. Barbara Jean looked up and around, ready to verbally scold any eavesdroppers. The few other technicians working in the room only sniffed at the air, scratched their pondering heads, and focused back on their own work. The thick veins in her neck throbbed as she locked eyes with Nylah.

"You mean, you tried to kiss him, don't you?"

"Get real, Barbara Jean Richardson." That was a slap in the face. She sucked air through her teeth and felt her own boldness welling up. "He's not my type."

"Oh, yeah, right. Just tell me anything. Like you don't find him good looking, maybe even available."

"Big deal. That still don't make 'im my type."

"Of all the beautiful females Lovell could have, including myself, why would he try'n kiss you?"

Another slap. "Believe it if you want, but I know what happened." Nylah knew that her sister's words were meant to be insulting but she refused to claim it. "I was there. You weren't."

"Nylah, you're so funny. I mean, give me a break. I can't believe you'd stoop to lies on the man."

Nylah's expression turned to disgust when her sister started laughing. A few giggles at first and then staring at her with ridiculing eyes, then a loud heckling laugh rising from someplace deep within. The only thing that was missing from her antics was a pointing finger. And here she was standing there, doing her best to reason with the woman.

Too furious for words, Nylah felt like running from the room and all the ears who had heard. Maybe they all were laughing, mocking her. Barbara Jean had tears in her eyes as she laughed, and she laughed even harder as Nylah turned and headed from the lab.

Nylah felt like a fool even as she rushed down the corridor and stood at the elevator. The wait was torturous. The sound of her sister's laugh was a loud, taunting echo in her head.

Chapter Fourteen

"Lovell, I don't wanna hear it!"

"At least hear my side. . ."

"I said I don't wanna hear it."

With her face set like stone, Nylah rolled down her Nissan's driver's side window to allow the cool night air in. She couldn't believe how her day was ending. First came that humiliating scene at the hospital with Barbara Jean, who had the audacity to laugh in her face after hearing that Lovell had tried to kiss her. Now this. Her mother had taken Lovell's car, and now they were out looking for her.

"I'm sorry," lamented Lovell as he rubbed his hand along the side of his head and shook it. "But, I refuse to take the full blame. Your mom can be pretty tricky when she wants."

"That's no excuse. You gave your word that you'd keep a good eye on her." She was giving him no slack.

"And I kept my word, but she tricked me."

Somewhere in her stomach, Nylah could feel flutters like butterfly wings beating too fast along her insides. Her nerves were on edge, and the proof was beginning to manifest itself by way of a tension headache at the base of her skull. Just too much stress, she mused, which also made her think about her hand rash. Maybe the constant stress of trying to see after her mother was beginning to take its toll. As young as she was, sometimes it felt like her body was trying to fall apart on her. If it wasn't one thing, it was two. Lord have mercy, she sighed. "I knew it was all too good to be true. I knew it. If it's not your fault, Lovell, who then?"

On the sly, she released her right hand from the steering wheel and rubbed it along the top of her left hand, feeling for the rough texture of rashy skin that had been plaguing her for weeks. But to her surprise, the skin on her hand was soft and smooth. The cream that Barbara Jean had used, whatever it was, had worked. Her rash had finally cleared up. Nylah took in a deep, calculated breath and let it out slowly. With all the different medicated preparations she had tried, it had taken Barbara Jean all of a few hours to use something on her hand to clear it up. Just like that. Wow, she thought. Maybe when things got back to normal at the house, she'd ask her sister more about the product to get more information on its ingredients. Who knows, she ventured, maybe there is an investment possibility.

Normal. When would things ever be back to normal at her mother's house? Nylah pondered the possibility of it for a while. She doubted it, not with Lovell living under the same roof with her family. From the moment she had pulled her car into the driveway of her mother's house, the feeling was all wrong. The house had looked suspicious with every light on in the place. When she had first noticed that Lovell's white Cadillac Seville wasn't parked as usual in the pebbled driveway, she had gotten a sick feeling in the middle of her stomach. No car in the driveway. All lights on in the house. It hadn't looked good.

Of all the things she had expected find, and the possibilities were endless, Lovell locked in her mother's room certainly wasn't one of them. Great. Just Great. Hoping to get off her tired feet after working all day had to be put aside to search for her mother—just what she needed. Out the corner of her eye, she stole a quick peek over at Lovell to ensure that he felt as uncomfortable as she wanted him to feel. "When will it ever end?"

Lovell could feel the tension like thick, menacing smoke in the car. "Look, I said I'm really sorry. She tricked me, okay?"

"You obviously don't understand English well," Nylah said it with a hint of arrogance in her voice. "I really don't wanna hear how sorry you are."

"I just want you to believe that I'm sorry. I thought your mother liked me. I guess I thought wrong."

The traffic light flashed red. Nylah hit the brake so hard it jolted both of them. Lovell looked over at her like she'd lost her mind. "Woman!, what the heck is wrong with you?"

"This isn't about like or love, Mr. Lovell! This is about an illness! My mother has an illness right now. Why do you think we lock her in her room? Payback for spanking us when we were kids? Is that what you thought?"

"She tricked me, okay?!"

"Yeah, she tricked you alright, but you allowed yourself to be tricked. "

"How was I suppose to know she'd pull a stunt like this?" Lovell was silent for a spell before adding, "said something was wrong with her television set, so I went in to see what was up. I was just trying to help. I didn't even see her when she eased out the room and locked that security door on me. Damn!"

"Well, you were the one that claimed that you could keep an eye on her, so now you know."

"I felt so helpless locked in that room. I couldn't even get out from the bedroom window, and that's a safety hazard in case of a fire."

Nylah eased down on the gas, giving the car a smoother take off. "What?" She was listening but not really hearing what he was saying, while her mind tried to figure out what crack house to search first. Thanks to Lovell, her mother could be anywhere.

"I said I couldn't get out the room. The security bars at your mom's bedroom windows are the wrong kind. They should be swing-outs in case of an emergency, you know, like a fire."

She rolled her eyes to heaven. "And who died and made you an expert?" Usually a pleasant, easy-going person, Nylah knew that she was being downright witchy, but she couldn't help it. Lovell had a lot of nerve putting his two cents in her family pot.

"Look, woman," Lovell quipped, trying to sound more authorative. "Stop being so bull-headed and listen to me."

"Who you calling bull-headed?" she snapped. She felt like pulling her car to a stop and slapping his face. "You don't know me or my mother well enough to pass judgment."

"True enough, I don't know you or your mother well enough to be judging, but I do know that all that bitterness you're carrying around won't get you very far in life. A dried-up, bitter old lady is all you'll get to be. No, I don't know everything, but I do know enough to know that your mother wouldn't be able to get out that room if that house caught fire!"

"Lovell, what makes you think that I don't already know that?" The horrid scene played itself in Nylah's mind: the house ablaze, her mother frantically tearing at the steel window bars unable to free herself, burned to ashes. Would it mean that her mother would go straight from the fire to the fire? All drug addicts would surely burn in hell. Wasn't that God's plan? She shook such thoughts from her head.

"Look," he said, calmer. "I just think that you and your sister mean well, but you're going about this problem with your mom all wrong."

Nylah took a quick glance in his direction. "Oh you do,

huh?"

"Yes, I do. I mean, keeping her locked up in a room all day won't stop her from wanting drugs. She needs professional help."

"Great," snapped Nylah sarcastically. "Now my mother's illness is your business too. And you're an expert. Right?"

"I know enough to know that you can't keep her locked up forever, and that's a no-brainer. Your mom has to be the one who wants to beat her illness. There is no other way."

Biting lightly down on her lower lip, she held back a rush of angry words. "Let me ask you something, Mr. Know-so-much Lovell." She took a sharp right at Central Avenue and drove down to 111th street and took another right. "Have you ever been addicted?"

"Can't say that I have."

"Have you ever cared for a family member that's addicted?"

"No. I guess I haven't."

"Then excuse me for saying so, but until you have, I think you should hush up about it."

"Fine then." Lovell made a mock gesture of zipping up his lips.

"Thank you."

They drove in silence for a while. The run down tenements, better known as Nickerson Gardens Projects, loomed before them. Nylah remembered a time when the tenements had been low income, temporary housing for hard working, decent people. Now the place was best- known as an infested jungle of yesterday's trash, gang-banging youth, drug peddlers, die-hard alcoholics, welfare queens, and community prostitutes. Nylah saw the inhabitants as souls who have long given up on doing any better in life.

The air was mildly chilly, and the night hosted a full moon, creating the perfect hang-out atmosphere. A small group of tough-looking young black boys leaned against cars listening to blaring rap music and smoking heaven-knows-what, while a couple of guys demonstrated some dance steps to their peers. Even with the loud music and sporadic curse words that reached their ears, Nylah could tell by sight and sound that there was a genuine camaraderie among the group—an unspoken sense of unity.

An uncomfortable feeling settling within him, Lovell looked around and wished that they were someplace else. "Uh, why are we here?"

"Why do you think? We're looking for Mama."

"And you think she's somewhere 'round here?"

"Unfortunately, I suspect she might be here somewhere. These Projects used to be one of her main stomping grounds. A dope fiend could find anything up in here."

"I believe that," Lovell replied dryly.

Their vehicle was cruising at a slow pace, and it looked to Lovell that some folks didn't appreciate it one bit. A strange car cruising slowly through the 'hood' could only be asking for trouble.

"Nylah, I don't like this. I think we should go. Maybe check out someplace else."

"Do you see your car anywhere?"

"No, I don't, so let's go." Lovell noticed that some of the boys had stopped leaning and stood up to watch to their slow moving vehicle. "Let's go before somebody gets the wrong idea and thinks we're about to do a drive-by shooting."

"Sounds like you're scared, Mr. Lovell." She smiled over at him, enjoying every minute of his squirming. So Mr. Know-how-to-do-everything is not so perfect after all. How interesting, she smirked. The parking lot curved around in a circle. Nylah turned her car around and headed out the complex with a puzzled look on her face. "Maybe she went to Nasty Man's house."

"Nasty who?"

"A crack dealer over on Figueroa and Rosecrans." She sighed. "I found out about him when my mother first started doing that mess. Rumors have it that Nasty Man caters mainly to young girls while their bodies are still fresh and tight. Sex for drugs. Guess that's why they call him Nasty Man."

"That's too bad," Lovell commented. He hoped his voice sounded as sincere as he felt. "Look, if it means anything to you, I feel really bad about this. If I hadn't been so tired from yard work, I probably could have caught her before she locked that door on me."

"Too late for talk like that. But that's my mama. Always two thoughts ahead of the next person. Hard to believe that she used to be a beautiful, black woman in her younger days, huh?"

"That's the poison of the drug." Lovell pressed his back further into his seat. "Pure poison."

Nylah let her tone soften. "That's true. Just the right stuff to erase a lotta black dreams from a lotta black minds. Exactly what most white folks wanna see." She noticed that it was the first thing that they'd agreed on since she'd met him.

"I couldn't agree more." For some strange reason he was suddenly thirsty. "And listen to you. Next you'll be saying it's all the white man's fault that crack cocaine abuse is so widespread among minorities."

Cocking her head sideways, Nylah thought about his words a moment. "I certainly don't think it was no black man who discovered cocaine or brought it to the States. Do you?"

"No, it probably wasn't. But our race can't continue to blame another race for all their problems forever either."

"Maybe so, but you have to admit that most cocaine abuse is centered around blacks and Hispanics? Mostly blacks tho'. Just another form of slavery, that's all. Chemical slavery."

Taking a half piece of gum out of his dark silk shirt pocket, Lovell unwrapped it and stuffed it into his mouth. "Yeah, but, do you see anybody pulling a gun to anybody's head to make 'em smoke cocaine?" He felt a tinge of guilt for not having any gum left to offer to Nylah, but his mouth felt like a dry, dusty road. Furthermore, he didn't agree entirely with what she was implying about it not being blacks' fault that cocaine was so prevalent. "And how can anybody say that more blacks and Hispanics are addicted to crack cocaine than any other race?"

Rolling her eyes, Nylah breathed, "Oh please. Try working at a hospital where folks come in all hours of the day and night for over-doing their substance abuse. Not only that, read the papers, watch the news, and try listening to your friends who speak of such things, then do the math. Minorities are killing themselves softly with substance abuse."

"That's sad to know." Lovell shifted uncomfortably in his seat. Who was he trying to convince anyway? Somewhere inside of him, he knew Nylah's words weren't far from the truth. Ultimately, two of his past girlfriends had chosen cocaine over a relationship with him, and that was two too many.

"I guess genocide comes in many forms." Dang, thought Nylah. She hadn't meant to sound so cold-hearted and street-wise, but she couldn't help feeling that there was plenty of credence to her account. Who would have ever thought that drugs could find their way into her own mother's life? Certainly not her.

"I don't think I have one friend who don't have at least one family member suffering from a substance abuse problem. Not one, Lovell. All of our lives have somehow been permanently affected by this poison."

"You got that right." At the mention of family Lovell felt a sadness slip easily over him, but didn't give in to it. Dysfunctional or not, at least she did have a real family. A true blood line. "I think it's just the times we're living in."

Nylah's hand tightened on the steering wheel, and her eyes misted over with thoughts of her mother. Sometimes it felt so hopeless. "Maybe too many of our sisters and brothers are trying to find the easy way out of life by hiding behind drugs, which sometimes forces other people to pay their way through living and they suffer as well."

"I hear you," Lovell added quietly, "but let's change the subject."

If you think my last remark was aimed at a leech like you... Nylah mused as she kept her eyes on the road... you're right! "Sure. You'll probably tell me it's none of my business, Lovell, but exactly where did you stay before you came to live with us?"

"Is it important for you to know?" Lovell looked out the passenger side window at the night scenery blurring past him.

"Is it a secret?" She could care less, if she was being bold with her prying. He had entered their home, became part of their family, and soaked up some of their family secrets like a sponge that soaks up water. She had a right to know. Hell yes she did. "Well?" she prompted.

Lovell grinned widely and shook his head. "You could say that I had an old lady on the east side of town."

"An old lady?" Just like she expected. No real respect for females.

"A girlfriend. A main squeeze. My woman."

"Did you work then?"

Cool and calm as always, Lovell let a small sigh escape his lips as he straightened up in his seat and cut his eyes sideways at her. "Does it make a difference?"

"It makes a difference to me. It's bad enough that the structure of a strong, black family is slowly slipping into oblivion, but it's men like you that help perpetuate its destruction." She let out a few nervous chuckles before adding: "You're what the girls at work call a BMK."

Lovell raised an eyebrow. "Say what?"

"A BMK. You know what that is, right?"

Tired of her game, he thought about not answering at all, but no. He'd play along. "A BMK? No. Can't say that I do know. Could it be a 'bold manly king'? Maybe a 'bad man knocking'?"

"Oh, that's real funny, Lovell. But no. A BMK is a 'Black Man Kept'. Sorry black men who live out their lives preying on affection-starved females. Females who'll pay to have a man to lay with and pretend that he belongs exclusively to her."

"Oh, so now I'm the cause of the fall of all black men? Now, I'm really sorry."

"Don't be cute, Lovell. I think you know what I'm talking about. Men who prey on women to support them are the weakened link of any relationship."

Lovell felt his temper trying to rise. "And I guess that's why you don't have a man in your life right now. And I guess I should be sorry for that too."

Nylah snorted. "If having my own man means having to finance his life while I work every day and he lounges at home, I guess I don't need one."

"Thank God all women don't share your opinion."

"Obviously," she snapped, biting back more words.

"Look, I feel like I've been earning my keep around your mama's house. It's not a day go by I haven't tackled some job, except for that time I stepped on that rusty nail and had to keep off my foot for one day. But, I was back at it the next day."

"Don't sound so upset about it." She softened her tone, realizing that there was a lot of truth in what he was saying. The man probably never had a real nine-to-five job in his entire life, but he did keep pretty busy around her mother's house.

"So, Miss Lady, you can see it anyway you wanna see it,

but I've been earning my keep. Just one day off for my foot, so I got your 'BMK' alright. Never worked so darn hard in my whole life."

That much was true about him being off his foot for one day, Nylah silently agreed. How could she forget the big deal Barbara Jean kept making over the fact that Lovell's foot was completely healed the following day with no trace of a nail having pierced clean through it. "Yeah, yeah," she mocked in a frivolous tone. "For now you have things to do around the place, and then what?"

"Stop the car!"

"What?"

"I said stop the car!"

"Lovell, this is my car and you don't. . ."

"Woman, if you don't stop this car right now, I'll stop it for you!"

At the next corner, Nylah swooped to the right and put the car in park. She looked around the seemingly deserted street just in case he got out of control and tried to strangle all the life from her body. She knew he was upset, but from the tone of his voice he sounded like he was furious. Good, she thought smugly, his true color was finally bleeding through. The truth always hurts.

Lovell undid his seat belt and twisted around to get into her face. "I guess I'm just full of apologies then because I'm sorry that you don't like me no matter how nice I try to be to you. I'm sorry that you find my way of life so offensive, and I'm really sorry that you can't understand why some women would be willing to pay just to have some of what I got." He snatched her hand away from the steering wheel and brutally forced it down on his swollen member.

Nylah wasn't shocked that he was furious with her, but that he had an erection! Appalled, she tried to jerk her hand away from the smooth, warm stiffness. "Lovell, stop it! How dare you...!"

"No!" he cut her off. "How dare you! Allow me to show you what it can feel like. You don't know me that well enough to judge me, so feel me!"

In the small, cramped space he moved upon her so fast, she didn't have time for a good protest. "Lovell, no! Stop this right. . ."

His face was right at hers as he pressed his lips onto hers, sending his warm, slippery tongue into her mouth.

Nylah kept trying to ease back, turn her face away, and come up for air, but her lips were being held hostage. And she couldn't say no. Her mouth wanted to say one thing, but her body had turned completely against her, against her will, against all resistance.

He was gently rubbing her velour suit with slow whispered grace at the spot so warm between her legs, a rhythm in tune with her inner spirit. Her body seemed to rise up slightly on its own free will, her pelvis gyrating in slow sensuous moves. Now her hand needed no assistance with rubbing his shaft—the length of it, the hardness of it. His manhood was pulsating under her very touch, beckoning.

Nylah felt so sure of it. She was up under a spell, some kind of voodoo or witchcraft or something. She couldn't explain how he had done it, but somehow, Lovell had worked some kind of voodoo-man magic on her. Thoughts of locating her mother slipped away from her mind like anxious water from a slanted green leaf as his kiss melted into hers.

"Nylah, I can't help how I feel about you." He kissed her again, harder, pulling her as close as possible within the confines of the car. "I felt it the first time I laid eyes on you, that day at the hospital."

". . .but, what about Barbara?"

"What about her?" He kissed a spot along her neck, close to her ear. She could feel his breath teasing at her earlobe, sending small shivers through her body. His breath along her neck was so hot. "Let's go home and talk about it."

"Mama. . ." Nylah managed, when her lips were free again. "What about Mama?" His lips felt like soft marshmallows against hers.

"Don't worry. Your mama's a big girl. She'll be alright for now."

Chapter Fifteen

The tall white police officer, one of L.A.'s finest, took one last look at Mama Jo before heading for his waiting vehicle. "Lady, you're one lucky woman."

"Thank you, officer. Thanks for bringing her home." Nylah and Mama Jo both stood patiently at the front door, waiting for his exit. Finally, the officer nodded his slightly balding head in Mama Jo's direction and stepped lightly onto the porch. Sighing with relief, Nylah closed and locked the door behind him.

"Thank God you're safe, Mama. You had us worried half to death." She gave her mother a light hug, a few pats on the back. "Thank goodness, thank goodness," she kept muttering under her breath.

"Nylah, you worry too much."

At her mother's words, Nylah pulled away feeling a tinge of hurt. "Only because I care, Mama. That's all."

It was six-thirty a.m. Already the early morning air was filling with life and movement. Nylah had been up and dressed in her uniform for over an hour, making her usual preparations to go to work, trying not to let the worries of her mother's disappearance seep into her bones. Normally, when her mother was out on one of her extended excursions, she would have called in sick to work to keep up a vigil and organize a two-woman search party. But after listening to Lovell, Nylah knew that he was right. Her mother was a grown woman, and it was high time that her mother started taking some responsibility for her own life.

"Don't worry so much," Lovell had assured her after their steamy kissing session in her car. "Time will bring her back home." He had been right. Lord knows it hadn't been easy for her, but Nylah had forced herself to wait it out. Not soon enough, but the storm was finally over. Her mother was back at home. Having to draw the line somewhere, Nylah realized she couldn't move away from her mother's house if she always felt somehow responsible for the woman.

Appearing like a small and rumpled child, Mama Jo gave her daughter a sad, painful look as she clutched the top of her assaulted satin top, now dirty and torn in several places, and made her way over to the sofa. Nylah watched as she flopped down on it. It was obvious to her that the night had been brutal. Her mother's clothes were dusty and tattered; three buttons were missing off the new satin blouse. Nylah felt so disappointed. It all chipped in for a look of total dishevel, like her mother had somehow been caught in the middle of a fight with a pack of wild dogs. It looked like the wild dogs had won.

Mama Jo's tattered look was one thing, but what concerned Nylah the most was the contusion along the left side of her mother's forehead. The broken skin, bluing nicely around the edges, slowly oozed blood that kept heading for her eye.

Nylah stood over her, feeling a mountain of emotions, each one threatening to tumble down into an extreme reaction: anger, happiness, contempt, disgust, and then a sudden rush of compassion. She's safe now. The words floated around Nylah's head like cumulus clouds. At least her mother was safe at home.

"Here, Mama, let me get something for that nasty looking bump on your head." Hurrying to the restroom, Nylah came back with some hydrogen peroxide, a few cotton balls, and a large bandage and eased down beside her.

"Now don't go fussing over me." Ignoring her buttonless blouse, Mama Jo let her fragile hands go limp in her lap, eased her head back along the worn out sofa, closed her eyes, and thought of how good it felt to be back at home while Nylah doctored on her forehead. "I'm so sorry, Nylah."

Tiny specks of dust fairies and lint danced wingless in the stream of yellow morning sunlight from the window just beyond Mama Jo's eyes. Tiredness vibrated down the length of her back and settled somewhere in the swollen brownness of her feet—swollen from too much running. "I guess sometimes the world is like a jungle. And last night I was in the middle of that jungle." She took a long, tired breath. "Last night I heard the cries of the beast himself. That same white beast caught up with me last night. And when there wasn't anymore, me. I went looking for the beast." Mama Jo went silent to think about how dangerous her night had actually been. "That's when those young thugs spotted the money on me. All that money. Gone. Nylah, I've never been so afraid in my entire life." The same emptiness of her hands she felt inside.

Mama Jo brought her head up suddenly and looked into the eyes of her daughter. For a few fleeing seconds she couldn't say one word. Just looking into the depth of Nylah's eyes confirmed the love and gave credence to the concern for her—a love so rich and strong that her own shame forced her look away. "You hate me, don't you?"

A tug at her heartstrings, Nylah smiled warmly. Already her eyes were trying to get misty. "I could never hate you, Mama."

"You having to look after me this way. . .this is all wrong, all of it. My life, and your life, revolving around mine and all the misery I've cause. All wrong." She sniffed, keeping her face turned away, gazing down at the floor. "You have to hate me. And I deserve it."

"Mama, I love you. We all love you. We just want you to get better, that's all we want. And I think you want it too."

". . .I do want it, I really want it. But. . .I just can't. . ." She let her voice trail off.

An inner voice kept telling Nylah not to cry, not to give in to the sentiment for risk of ruining her mascara. She had an early shift to start, but her mother, slouched back along the sofa with the room's sunlight glowing along her bruised face looked so pitiful, so beaten down by life. She wanted to be the tower of strength that her mother could always lean on, but she couldn't keep the tears from her eyes as she reached over and slid her arms around her. They held each other in silence. Her mother's body felt almost weightless, like padded bones.

"I'm gonna beat this thing, Nylah. Honest I will."

"I know, Mama. I know you will."

"Each day I open my eyes; it's like a ghost hovering over me. I keep telling myself no. No, not this time. But it just stays with me, that ghost. I can't get away from it. . ."

"I know, Mama. I wish it were something more I could do." She patted her mother's back softly, wishing that by doing so she could pat more strength into the woman.

"I'm sorry, Nylah. I wanna be better." Crying softly, Mama Jo rested her head on Nylah's shoulder.

"I know you do." As much as Nylah wanted to believe her mother's heart-felt words, she'd heard them so many times before. Somewhere at the back of her mind, those same broken promises were temporarily stored away like dusty computerized information ready to be retrieved along with the same voice of empathy, inner pleads, more understanding, and more tears. There was never enough tears to say how sorry her mother was after each of her excursions. Never.

Nylah kept petting the delicate curve of her mother's back as if she were an infant needing to be burped, when a new thought popped into her head—Lovell's car. If a police officer had found her mother wandering around disoriented on the opposite side of town, where then was Lovell's car?

"Mama?" Nylah arched her own back and pulled away and made the woman look her straight in the eyes. "Mama, where's the car?"

Mama Jo stopped whimpering and sat up straight. Furrowing her brows, her apple-red eyes looked more alert. She sniffed twice.

"What car?"

"Lovell's car, Mama. Remember? You took his car last night. Where is it?"

Confused, her facial expression was a brown puzzle. "Lovell's car?"

"Try'n remember, Mama. You took his car last night, where did you leave it? Did you leave it in the Projects?"

Looking down at the floor, she allowed her eyes to scan around the carpet as if doing so could unclog memory. The car. What had she done with it? "Let's see. . .," she said tentatively, using tiny words, like a child stalling for time. "after they chased me. . .I. . ."

"Chased you? Oh my God, Mama. Who chased you?"

"I don't know. . .some guys, some young thugs. They wanted the money."

Oh for heavens sake, thought Nylah. If it wasn't one thing it was two. "Money? Mama, what money?" She couldn't imagine what money her mother could possibly be referring to. Each month after her father's Social Security check was automatically deposited into the bank, Nylah herself made sure that her mother never received more that fifteen or twenty dollars in cash at a time—a meager allowance for minor necessities. Sometimes, even that small amount seemed like too much. After doing all her mother's bill paying and shopping, she couldn't imagine what other minor necessities her mother really needed money for.

"Did you get a good look at the boys?"

"You mean like from the back of my head while I was running?"

"Okay, okay, Mama, never mind. At least you're safe now. That's what's important."

"Darn thugs," she muttered, more to herself than Nylah. "Took all the money and knocked me upside my head with some kinda stick. It's a miracle I managed to break away. I was running for my life. I don't know where I left that man's car." She knew it was a stupid thing she'd done, but she wasn't completely stupid. No way was she telling Nylah about the amazing wad of money she'd found in Barbara Jean's small refrigerator, hiding behind vials of blood. That wad of money, when she had time to unroll it and really look at it, had the smell of power. It had consisted mostly of one hundred dollars bills, all crisp and new in a neat green roll of happiness. No. She shook her head, tired of answering questions. She didn't know where the car was. "Somewhere in the projects, I guess. That's where I had to run from. Ran so hard I mighta ran right past it, running for my life."

Nylah dropped her head and looked away. "Mama, no." It was too much for her to even imagine. Thank the good Lord above that her mother had even made it home at all. Still, it was unbelievable the things people did to innocent folks just for money.

Wearily, Mama Jo looked up and asked quietly, "Where is he? Where's Lovell? Might as well break the bad news to 'im now and get it over with. If he wants to kill me, I'll just have to understand. Where is he?"

"Sleeping. Where else?"

Nylah felt a warm glow come over her at the mention of Lovell's name. Lawdhavemercyjesus, what a night it had been. She couldn't remember the last time she'd enjoyed kissing so much. It had been so exhilarating. If kissing was a contest, Lovell could win first prize. The goodness of it, she couldn't get it out of her mind. If sinful thoughts could kill on the spot, she mused, she'd be one happily dead woman along the floor. But a tinge of guilt came along with those same good feelings. Nylah couldn't help feeling that if she and Lovell had continued their search for her mother last night, instead of rushing back to the house to be the sole contestants in a kiss-athon, her mother probably wouldn't have been robbed and beaten. What had she been thinking to let it get so far?

Even though neither of them had taken their clothes off, Nylah still felt strongly that last night shouldn't have happened. It had been great while it had lasted, but she couldn't get away from the feeling that she had done something wrong. She had betrayed her sister's trust by allowing herself to be halfway seduced by Lovell. Almost seduced by the same man that a mere two days ago she had felt she hated. Delicious scenes of Lovell sucking sweetly on her bottom lip while she had deliriously fondled every part of him that was available, kept repeating itself in her mind like an old classic movie that couldn't be destroyed.

Lovell had been so gentle, and his hot kisses on her face and neck had excited small fires all over her, in every spot that he'd kissed or touched. Places she had forgotten about. Perhaps that was why it had all happened. It had been way too long since she'd allowed a man to make her feel that way, like a young, desirable woman. Nylah was sure that going too long without loving had made her weak for a spell, but not weak enough to shed her clothes and sleep with the man. The way she saw it, Lovell had simply caught her at a vulnerable time and taken advantage of that weakness.

But it was okay. Nylah felt like she was back in control, and it wouldn't happen again. That much she felt sure of. She just had to get it through her head that Lovell was Barbara

Jean's man, and things were bad enough around the house between her and her younger sister without interference of a man's betrayal.

"Guess I messed up big time this go 'round," Mama Jo sighed.

"Well," Nylah said as she stood up and smoothed down her uniform. ". . .don't worry about telling Lovell right now, Mama. I'll call back to the house and talk to 'im later. Then we'll have to see what we can do about finding his car or replacing it. For now, I gotta get to work."

"I'm sorry, Nylah. You do so much for me, and I keep letting you down. I'm sorry."

"We'll talk about it later, Mama." To lock her mother in her room again, or not to lock her mother in her room. It was a question Nylah didn't really want to think about. "Mama, did you get enough of what you were looking for?"

"I think so."

"Can we get past this episode and get on with living?" Nylah questioned, fearful of the answer and at the same time needing to know. Each time, the fight to kick the habit was like starting from scratch all over again. "Well, can we, Mama?"

"I think so," Mama Jo replied easily, sounding too weary for a long conversation. "Matter of fact, I'm sure of it."

"I'm glad then." Nylah helped her up from the sofa.

"Guess you can lock me back in my cage now. Looks like I've done enough damage for now." Mama Jo turned and headed for the quiet sanctum of her room, dragging her tired, worn-out spirit behind her. "Folks like me deserve to be punished."

"No you don't, Mama."

"Yes, I do."

Nylah nodded towards her. "You can go to your room now if you want to. You say you want to be better and this time...this time I truly believe you. We won't be locking that door. From now on, it's up to you, Mama."

To punctuate her words, Nylah walked into the next room, got her purse and keys from the kitchen table, and walked briskly to the living room door and opened it. She paused for a moment, allowing the morning warmth to sneak past her through the open door as she considered if she was doing the right thing, then held her head up high as she walked out the door.

Chapter Sixteen

Nylah's skin glowed like a well-oiled walnut shell in the flickering candle light. Her firm breasts offered full dark chocolate nipples with tiny beads of sweat at each tip. Her hips were wide, but well proportioned for her height. As if on a floating cloud she glided toward him, her smile was radiant—a gesture that heaved and pushed at his anticipation as their bodies touched and slid perfectly into a blissful lock.

With his eyes still closed and utilizing one hand, Lovell slowly massaged the warm mass of flesh between his legs, pressing his buttocks deeper into the firmness of the bed. Hmmm. He had just tightened his grip on his pillow, which had all the softness of a sweet and desirable woman meant to be loved, when the sound of his bedroom door being kicked open struck against his main nerve. Light flicked on instantly in the room. Opening his eyes, he sat up in bed, his mind in a gray fog, still blurry from the dream about Nylah. In the room that was temporarily being called his, with her face twisted and looking meaner than two junk-yard dogs, stood Barbara Jean still decked out in her hospital garb. Wearing long pink pajamas, Brittany stood beside her mother, and even she had the nerve to have her little hands on her hips, trying to look as sassy and intimidating as Barbara Jean.

Lovell wanted to laugh, but judging from the expression

on Barbara Jean's face, it would have been a bad idea. He'd seen her upset before, but this time, the woman looked mad enough to fight the devil himself. "Hey, what's. . .up?"

Rolling her eyes upwards, even with the red flashing like warning signs in their depth, Barbara Jean stepped in closer, cocked her head and kept her voice slow and premeditated. "Now, me, I'm a reasonable woman. And Lord knows I can understand and accept a whole lotta things in this cesspool of life. But somebody stealing from me isn't one of 'em. Now I don't know which one of the three grown folks living in this house took it, but I want it back. I want all of it, and I want it now." She stood looking down at the carpet that could stand another good cleaning. Over the past few weeks, Lovell had done a fantastic job of painting almost every room in the house except for the one he slept in. The wide window across from the doorway still needed new curtains, but to add to the room's unattractiveness, the single bed and twelve-inch television sitting on a heavily scarred mahogany stand gave his quarters a cold, unfinished appearance. "You know anything 'bout my money, Mama?"

Mama? What the heck. . .? Lovell clutched bed covers closer to his nakedness and leaned over his twin size bed. Curled up on the floor, right beside his bed, lay Mama Jo sporting a bandage on her forehead. Surprisingly, the woman had taken a couple of pillows and a thin, dingy blanket and crept into his room quiet as a mouse. What the heck is going on? What kind of family is this? He wondered how long had she been there.

"Whoa...what's up down there?"

Shining Lovell's question on, Barbara Jean looked from one to the other, waiting for her money or at least some kind of answer about it. Asking her mother about her head was a fleeting thought, but not as important as finding out about her money. It was all she wanted for the moment, and her expression said so.

Sitting up, Mama Jo ran her hands back along her slicked hair. For a second the room was dizzy, spinning out of control. "You see. That's what's wrong with this place. A person can't get no sleep in this house."

"My money," Barbara Jean insisted, trying her best to keep calm. Some where at the back of her mind a storm was brewing. She blinked back a dam of angry tears. "I just want my money back." Suspiciously, she looked over at Lovell, who seemed more concerned and puzzled over Mama Jo sleeping on the floor in his room than about her money. "Well?"

"What?" Lovell quipped, sitting up straight and scratching his head again, finally realizing the pressure in his bladder. "Can I please have some privacy to put some clothes on?"

"Who's stopping you?" Barbara Jean's tone was cold and flippant. She wasn't thinking about him. The fool that had enough gall to take her money was the fool that didn't know who they were messing with. "You think you got somethin' we haven't seen before?"

"Look," pleaded Lovell, feeling about the burst, "I'm not dressed; I need to get up to put on some clothes so I can go to the restroom."

"So," Barbara Jean said sarcastically. "get to it. Get up and handle your 'bizzness. All I want is my money back."

"Woman, will you let me put some clothes on?"

"Not 'til you tell me where my money is."

"Fine. I'll get up like this then...I'm not playing."

"Where's my money, Lovell? And Mama, what the heck you doing in this room?"

"My house ain't it? I can sleep in any room I damn well please." Unconcerned, Mama Jo fluffed one of her pillows and laid her head back down on the floor.

Barbara Jean allowed her spicy response to sail over her head. Brittany balled her fists to each side and yelled. "You better give my mama her money back now!"

"Hush up, Brittany, and let me handle this."

"Yes, Mommie."

"Consider yourself warned." Lovell leaped up from the bed naked as the day he'd come into the world. Careful not to step on Mama Jo, whose head rose from her pillow just in time to see his baby-smooth behind eclipse her vision. She pulled the blanket over her head. "Lawd have mercy. Ain't no shame in the world no more."

Realizing what she was seeing, Brittany screamed, then burst into a silly grin that propelled her past her mother and straight to her own room where she closed the door and giggled like crazy.

Nowhere near amused, Barbara Jean only shook her head. "That's real cute, Lovell. I thought you at least had on some underwear."

"I tried to warn you," he through back over his shoulder.

Barbara Jean grinned. "Next time have some respect for yourself."

Taking his time to find his robe hanging in the small cluttered closet, Lovell ignored her comment. He didn't own a lot in the way of worldly possessions to be proud of, but he was proud of the fact that he did have a nice body. True, he wasn't all buffed up in the arms and chest like the muscle men he saw lifting weights at the local gym. But still, his body still had it going on with tight definitions in just the right places. It wasn't his fault they wouldn't leave the room so he could get proper.

"Sometimes a man's gotta do what a man's gotta do." He could feel Barbara Jean's eyes watching like trained laser beams, taking it all in and no doubt storing juicy tidbits about his body away for future reference. He could feel it.

"If I wasn't so upset about my money, I could find your antics refreshing, maybe even pleasing, and something to act upon, especially with a nice-looking behind like yours. But right now, all I want is my money back." Barbara Jean waited for a confession from somebody, anybody. Even though she hadn't seduced him yet, the quick glimpse of his semi-rigid penis bouncing happily in front of him made a tingle radiate, run up her leg, and nestle somewhere in her special place, adding more to play on her mind at night. More than once, she'd lain in her empty bed at night and questioned herself, asking what was she waiting for? He was there, a single man. He was available. What was she waiting for? But the answer to her question never came to her before sleep did. "I don't have all day to be waiting for my money!"

"Woman, what money?" Lovell secured the black satin sash of his robe. The robe had been a gift from Barbara Jean, one of many items that he couldn't help feel a tinge of guilt for accepting. He didn't know what it was, but women were always buying and giving him things without him having to ask. In a way, he almost expected it.

Sometimes the gifts came before the romance, sometimes afterwards. Regardless, he made it a point of never asking a woman for anything. The idea was to always let the woman know his needs. After that, it was up to that woman, whoever it should be at the time, to see to it that his needs were met. Lovemaking, sometimes, but not always, was the reward, which usually came after days or weeks of gift giving. But somehow, for some reason still evasive to him, it wasn't turning out that way with Barbara Jean.

After all the things that she'd done and purchased for him, Barbara Jean still wasn't quite ready for his reward, and he wasn't ready for her to have it. Actually, he didn't see their relationship going in that direction at all. Not once had she given him the slightest inclination that she was ready, or her body willing. No suggestive touches to his body. No subtle eye messages. No words spoken. And it did take a lot of pressure off of him. Mostly, he thought of her more like a protective big sister, or more like a good friend that stemmed from early childhood. He liked her all right. She was generous, kind-hearted, easy going, and seemed to truly enjoy doing things for a man. But sexually, he hadn't felt that sparkle, that challenge, that overwhelming male urge to conquer her in bed. He just hadn't felt it. Seeing how Barbara Jean hadn't pushed the issue, he felt that there was no sense in him doing so. "Look," he said finally in a tone to be taken seriously. "Wish I could help you, but I don't know anything about your money."

"What about you, Mama? You know what happened to my money?"

Throwing the cover away from her head, Mama Jo sat up and sighed. "Your money. . ." she started, then paused in mid-thought as if to think of how to put it. After her dreadful night, she was too tired to care about anybody's money. Silently she stared down at the floor.

Slightly annoyed, Lovell brushed past Barbara Jean and went to the restroom. After emptying his bladder, he washed his hands and face, brushed his teeth, and headed into the kitchen to make some breakfast. God, he was hungry. He wished that Nylah had stayed home from work so he could prepare breakfast for her, his beautiful Nylah, instead of Barbara Jean and Mama Jo.

The unhappy camper, Barbara Jean appeared in the kitchen with her hands crossed at her chest. With a look of ready-to-do-battle, she watched Lovell get some coffee brewing in the newly decorated kitchen. "I'm still waiting..."

"So I see." Lovell got out some white bread, eggs, orange juice, and some wrapped slices of ham from the refrigerator. "Hey, look," he tried to reason, feeling Barbara Jean's stare on the back of his head. ". . .I might be a lotta things, but I'm no thief. I didn't take your money."

"Well, who then?" Barbara Jean leaned against the recently painted wall where sunlight was already a welcomed guest through parted thin cotton curtains. Nylah had found some paper-matted paintings of various flowers and strategically installed them along the walls, giving a homey look to the place. Fresh cut carnations, pink and red, peeked out from a clear crystal vase. It didn't look like the same room, but even after days passed, Barbara Jean could still smell traces of new paint in the air. "I trusted you, Lovell."

"Don't you think I know that?" He thought about telling her the news about Mama Jo locking him in her room and taking off with his car. But what good would that do? More bad news was the last thing the woman needed at the moment. "I don't steal."

"Then where's the money? All I wanna know is where's my money."

"You really think I took it, don't you?"

"Who else?"

Not wanting to just blurt out everything that had happened last night, he had to tell her something. Lovell could see the hurt, way past the annoyance splayed across her accusing face. She had done so much for him, given so much of herself, and now she stood accusing him of taking more from her than he was entitled to, or more than she wanted him to have.

"It's like I said, I'm no thief. You got some money missing from your room, I suggest you talk to your mother."

She stood motionless for a good while, glaring at him while he went through the rudiments of preparing breakfast. Soon after that Mama Jo, dressed in the same dusty, tattered clothes and still sleepy from her wild night out, ambled silently into the room, glad to see somebody making coffee.

"Three thousand dollars just don't get up and walk away by itself!"

"Chile, stop your hollering in this house." Mama Jo got

her favorite orange ceramic mug from the sink, rinsed it out, and went over to the coffee maker, removed the glass pot and stuck her mug up under the strong-smelling, dark flow. "No need to do all that screaming and hollering, so just stop it."

"When I get my money back, Mama. And why you dressed like that?"

"Never mind. You just stop all that foolish hollering. Won't solve nothin'."

After pouring cream and spooning sugar in her coffee, Mama Jo eased herself over to the table and sat down. Her joints creaked and ached like she'd done two bouts with a younger Muhammad Ali. She stirred her coffee with her head down. "You probably don't care, but I got robbed last night."

"What?" Barbara Jean perked up and paid attention. A glint of sympathy surfaced in her eyes as she let her arms slide down from her chest to her sides. ". . .Mama, no. How?"

"Say what now?" Lovell cut the fire off under his ham sizzling low in a black cast iron skillet. He had been asleep when Mama Jo got in. The part about her being robbed was news to him. "Robbed?" He got four plates down and proceeded to prepare them, keeping his ears tuned in.

"I said, I got robbed last night. Somethin' wrong with your ears?"

"That's awful." Lovell sat a plate of ham and lightly scrambled eggs and toast down in front of Mama Jo. That explained her tore-up look and the bandaged lump on her forehead.

"Mama, when was this?" Looking concerned, Barbara Jean went to the table and took a seat too. Lovell placed a plate of food in front of her as well, then got a plate for Brittany and himself. After dispensing forks, he pulled out a chair and sat down.

Barbara Jean picked up her fork and leaned slightly forward, looking at her mother. "Are you saying that someone broke into this house and robbed you?" She took a small nibble of perfectly scrambled eggs.

"No, I'm saying that I went out."

"You left the house with Lovell?"

"No," replied Mama Jo reluctantly. She kept her guilty eyes on her plate. "I left the house with Lovell's car and I got robbed."

"Are you saying that Lovell gave you some money or what?" Barbara Jean couldn't lift her fork, couldn't eat another bite until she heard the whole story. She was hearing what her mother was saying loud and clear, but it just didn't make sense. Lovell could have given her mother some of the money that she'd given him as an allowance. "Mama, stop playing head games!"

"And you stop shouting in my house! What. . .what I'm try'n to say is I found the stash of money in your room. Right in that. . .that little ice box of yours, and I took it and I went out. Now. It's said."

Lovell kept his head down and focused on his meal. For a hot second, he thought about taking his plate up and going to his room to give the two women some privacy. But, no, he needed to hear what had happened for himself, straight from Mama Jo's mouth. He needed to know about his car.

"You did what?" Her appetite suddenly gone, Barbara Jean dropped her fork. The loud clink of metal against stoneware echoed in the room. She knew the rest of the story well. It hadn't been the first time her mother had stolen money from her to purchase drugs. What would make her think that anything had changed? She studied the bandage on her mother's head. "All of it?"

"Barbara Jean," she tried pleading. "I'm sorry. I made a mistake. . .some thugs, youngins really. . .they chased me. . .I ran as fast as I could. . .I tried to. . ." She let her words trail off.

"That's cold blooded," Lovell offered, who still hadn't

heard the part about his car yet. He was too busy shoveling scrambled eggs and ham in his mouth.

"The police brought me home this morning. You can ask Nylah."

"All my money is gone?" Barbara Jean couldn't believe her ears.

"The police?" Lovell stopped his chewing. Now it hit him. "Wait a second. What about my car?"

Gazing up pathetically, Mama Jo couldn't bear to look into his eyes either. "Guess Nylah didn't call back to the house and tell you about your car yet, huh?" Placing her fork down, she stared at her food. "I was so afraid I ran off and left it."

Lovell gave her an incredulous look. "You left a ninety-two Cadillac in the Projects?"

Something snapped in Mama Jo. "Didn't I say I had to run for my life?! Them boys coulda killed my black behind. And I think that's what they was trying to do. . .hitting me with that stick like that!"

Barbara Jean shot up from her seat, knocking over her chair. The room was spinning, trying to make her knees go weak. "Crazy old woman! You gave away a car that didn't belong to you and my three-thousand dollars thinking about your own selfish self! They shoulda killed your butt, Mama. They should have!" She bumped her chair backwards and hurried out of the room.

"Hey. . .hold up now." Lovell was just about to tell Barbara Jean that she didn't mean what she had said about wishing her own mother had died. But before he could get the words out, Barbara Jean was like a strong wind that had reared up suddenly and blown away.

Chapter Seventeen

"This is nice."

Reclined on his back, his head resting in the open palms of his hands, Lovell looked up at the erratic sky and wished that the weather would make up its mind. One minute it seemed as though it was going to be a warm and glorious Saturday morning, the next, windswept clouds moved lazily across the blue canvas, temporarily blocking out the sunlight as if to hold its soothing warmth as a hostage. A few birds perched in the branches of the flowering cherry tree they'd chosen to picnic under.

There was something about the sunshine that he loved almost as much as he loved beautiful flowers. The sun was the sky's personal healing sphere, the catalyst of all living and growing things. Sometimes, it felt to him as though radiant sunlight was the lifeline that fed his spiritual being. Food for the soul.

"I hope you like fried chicken." Barbara Jean commented eagerly.

"Are you kidding? What fool don't?" Turning over on his side with an elbow propped against his head, Lovell watched Barbara Jean patiently spread out a thin yellow blanket with brown teddy bear faces printed all over it and take the time to smooth each of the four edges down evenly along the grass as if each green blade itself had to cooperate in making the blanket lie flat and perfect with the earth.

"Brittany's favorite blanket," Barbara Jean offered with a wide smile. "You wouldn't believe how long my child has had this old blanket, not to mention everything it's gone through."

"No kidding?" Returning a smile, Lovell enjoyed hearing cute stories about Brittany. Brittany was his buddy, his forever-happy little friend that always made sure that he didn't miss out on any desserts after dinner or some new discovery in her life. The child was the kind of spirited little girl that he would love to have some day. He smiled, relaxed, and let Barbara Jean rattle on.

"Went to visit some friends out in San Diego once. Almost three hours of driving. Brit musta been about two at the time, and Lord-have-mercy, I made the mistake of leaving Mama Blankie in San Diego. Man, that child cried half the way home, hooping and hollering to the top of her voice like some crazed lunatic. You know, I had to turn my old car around and pray that we made it back to San Diego in that old clunker of mine. Had to pray even harder that we made it back home. That girl, she can't sleep at night without it. Ain't that right, Brittany?"

Too busy flying her bubbles through the air, Brittany squealed with delight as she ran from one end of the picnic area and back again. Lovell leaned over to thump a brown scouter ant from their spread while Barbara Jean busied herself unpacking food and various items she'd brought along for their day out.

"Brittany, you be careful, and don't go too far."

"Stop worrying, she's fine. I got my eyes on her." Lovell sat up and watched her play, trying to figure out how Barbara Jean had the time and patience to fix the girl's hair up the way she often did. Brittany's hair was a collection of long, thin black braids with crystal-like balls at each top and end. When the sun peeked between the clouds and caught one of the balls at the right angle, a prism of colors danced at the top of her perfectly rounded head. Her white romper with rainbow trimming, complete with little matching rainbow sneakers, was quite dazzling. "She's such a happy little soul, and so well behaved."

"Why thank you, Lovell. I do my best with her."

"I can see that."

Lovell had to give it to her, Brittany was one lucky little girl. A mother like Barbara Jean could only be a plus in any child's life. During the month he'd known them, not once had he witnessed the child dirty, hungry, or neglected of love or attention. If he was looking for a wife, and someday he imagined that he would, he could see himself selecting a woman with strong paternal traits just like Barbara Jean to be the mother of his children. She wasn't knock-down beautiful or what you could call a "fly" girl, but in no way could he tag her as homely or ugly either. She didn't fit into the category of thin, but he couldn't exactly call her fat. Healthy-looking was more like it. Pleasingly plump, but still shapely and sexy. She was kind, decent, and kept herself neat and clean. Nice nails and pedicures. The works. No doubt about it, she definitely possessed a takecharge kind of personality when it came to social and business matters, which to him, explained why she and Nylah were always bumping heads.

Nylah and Barbara. Lovell saw them as two of a kind, both strong willed and stubborn, which only proved that too many females in one house trying to be the boss always brought on a slew of control problems. In his book, Barbara Jean was alright. Of course, he could do without her bossy nature at times. Deep down inside, he knew she didn't mean no harm when she bossed him around in her playful, but serious way. She told him what to do, when to do it, and usually topped it off with instructions on how to do it. For instance, the picnic that they were now on had been Barbara Jean's idea.

Initially, Lovell had planned on finishing up his painting project for the day, and calling Nylah at work to see if she wanted to take in a movie later in the evening. But things didn't work out that way. Nylah had taken off from work early, claiming that she needed a 'mental health' day to work out at the gym and later go shopping for new clothes. To his surprise, Barbara Jean had gotten up early to drop Mama Jo off at the local beauty shop for a makeover treatment to include her hair, a facial, and her nails. He'd gone in to take his shower and shave; he came out to find Barbara Jean bustling around in the kitchen frying up chicken parts and packing away food items into a large wicker basket, ranting something about, "We're going on a picnic, Lovell. Get dressed." Just like that. We're going, get dressed. No 'would you care to join me on a picnic?' politeness. No 'are you free today?' inquiry. Just get dressed.

Lovell had thought seriously about protesting, but after she told him how she'd taken the time to make him a strawberry-topped cheese cake the night before, how could he have possibly said no without seeming ungrateful and hurting her feelings?

So here he was. Cerritos Regional Park, his baby-oiled body supine on the crisp white bed sheet alongside of Brit's 'Mama Blankie', listening to the mellow flow of jazz on the boom box tuned in to 94.7, the Wave. Barbara Jean had assured him that it would be hot out and had even suggested, no, had actually told him to wear short pants. Two weeks earlier, she'd bought him two silk short sets, one dark gray and the other navy blue.

Lovell felt slightly ashamed to think about it, the fact that the pants to his dark gray set were probably ruined for good after that hot and heavy kissing session with Nylah the other night. During his arousal he had unwittingly stained his nice silk pants. So far, the pants were folded up under his bed until he could try a good hand washing to remove the stain.

Today, but only because Barbara Jean had insisted, he'd worn his navy blue set. Lovell smiled with a truly devilish thought. That slick Barbara Jean. Girlfriend was trying her best to be sly about it, but already he'd caught her eyes roaming over his lap area on more than one occasion and lingering before finding another place to rest. Lovell fought off an urge to ask her what was it she kept looking at, but didn't want to embarrass the woman. Conforming to the heat of the day, he'd left the top buttons of his shirt undone, which allowed his thick, dark chest hair the leisure of peeking out and over the V of silken material.

A deep warmth radiated through him at his own confirmation. Women loved the feel of a man's skin under the delicate caress of silk. To him, no other material measured up. Heck. They all loved it. He knew this because he, too, loved the feel of his own skin under silk. Consequently, he owned a fair share of expensive silk garments. Whenever he wore the luxurious fabric along his bottom half, he frequently found himself, accidentally of course, running his own hand along the length of his thigh, slowly savoring the faintest touch gliding along his flesh. Usually he did this more times during the course of a day, maybe even more times than he chose to speak of, but considered it all good and healthy.

"That's a good thing you did for your mom, treating her to a makeover."

"I know," Barbara Jean grinned slyly. "Good for her, and good for me. Heck, If I hadn't found somethin' to keep her busy for a few hours, she'd be at this picnic with us for sure."

Lovell chuckled at her candidness. "Sounds like a hidden motive."

"You could say that. And she needed it. I'm still shocked that she agreed to go to the beauty shop. I've been trying to take her for years now. It's about time."

"It's all good then. Nothing like a beautiful Saturday and some good food."

Now Barbara Jean brushed a brave picnic ant from her hairless leg. "I brought along all your favorites, Lovell."

"No kidding?" Lovell pondered how the woman knew what his favorites were, seeing as how she'd never even asked him.

"Oh yeah. Got some cheese cake, sweet potato pie, cantaloupe, fried chicken, garden salad, homemade potato salad and potato chips." Barbara Jean reached over and smoothed down the loose material of her white Rayon culottes. With her big, shapely brown legs stretched out straight along the sheet, she wiggled her pedicured toes in her white sling sandals and looked totally at peace with the world.

"Sounds too good," Lovell said in response to her culinary list. It was so nice to see her in a good mood again after that ordeal last week with Mama Jo and her money. Three upset women with an attitude problem in the same house was more than he could deal with.

"Even got some white wine." She pulled out an ice bucket. "Nothing too fancy, but enough for a buzz."

"Say what now, some wine too? Barbara Jean you're somethin' else. You 'bout to make a man feel special."

"Got that right," she grinned like a shy schoolgirl, then straightened her face. "I don't know. I just thought that maybe you might wanna do somethin' different for a change. You know, anything to get outta that house. Lord knows I needed to get away before I ended up hurting somebody for taking my money like that. But let's not talk about bad stuff." She uncapped the chilled wine and pulled out two Styrofoam cups, poured, and passed him one.

"And when did you have time to make potato salad?" Studying her face, waiting for an answer, Lovell could see the subtle resemblance to Nylah in the same walnut shell complexion, the same dark brown eyes shaped like large almonds, and the small well-defined lips that were meant to be kissed. Both sisters had the same kind of warm, perfect smile that shied away from being pretentious. Of the two, he would have to say that Barbara Jean was slightly heavier in frame, maybe even a tad shorter than her older sister, but certainly not by much. Barbara Jean was also the fashion hog and the perfume freak of the two. Today her smell was an exotic combination of coconut and warm vanilla bean. Delicious and heavenly, the scent made him think of something sweet to eat as it wrapped all around him like new skin.

Barbara Jean grinned from ear to ear and lightly patted her hair to assure its style. Today she had it up in a ponytail with large black, firm curls cascading from her head.

"Whipped up some potatoes last night while everybody else was sleeping. Had to do something to keep my mind off Mama and my money. I still can't believe the nerve of that old woman going in my room and taking my money like that. I need to buy me a big safe. That'll stop her roaming hands."

"Hey, but still," he licked his lips, suddenly dry. "That's your mom and you have to get over it."

"Don't care whose mama she is. It don't give her the right to be taking my money."

"But all is forgiven, right?" Lovell took a careful sip of his wine and bit down lightly on his bottom lip. He resisted the urge to tell her that the more she kept bringing the subject up, the more she kept reminding him that his own car was still missing, stolen, or even worse, probably stripped down and parted out by now. Even after Barbara Jean had driven him back to the Projects to search for his Caddy the next day, the vehicle was no where to be found. It had hurt him to his heart too. The car hadn't been worth a lot money-wise, but its sentimental value was still high and irreplaceable to him. Giving the information to the police department hadn't helped much either. His car had been a gift from an older sugar-mama a few years back. "I think she feels bad enough about it. People make mistakes. Stuff happens."

"Mistake my foot," Barbara Jean snorted with vengeance in her voice. "Good thing you're taking it so lightly about your car, but I'm not down with that. I swear, Lovell, if she wasn't my mother I would have snatched all the black from her bony little butt and . . ."

"Hey! cool it. Let it pass. Thought we came out here to chill out and have a good time? You know, take in the sun, admire the beauty of life around us."

Barbara Jean's shoulders heaved up and down with the deep breath she took. "Sorry. You're right," she agreed, feeling a bit silly for getting so carried away. "I forgive mama for what she did. Really, I do." She went silent a spell before adding, "Actually, there's something I wanna talk to you about. Something I need."

Hey, hey now, Lovell thought, feeling flattered that the time had finally come for the asking of the reward. Get straight to the point. He liked that in a woman. After spending her money to wine, dine, and dress him, a woman had a right to be expecting something in return. But now after all that had happened with Nylah, it didn't seem quite right, and stepping on folks' toes only led to more hurt feelings. But somehow, he would let her down easy. It wasn't like he could put it off forever. He had to tell her about Nylah and him. He had strong feelings for her sister, and he couldn't help it. No matter how bad it sounded, he had to tell her.

Zooming over like a whirlwind, Brittany wanted to know if she could go play on the swings. She put the remainder of her blue plastic jar of bubbles away and jumped up and down, her braids bouncing like limp, black snakes. "Pleezze, Mama, pleezze."

Shielding her eyes from the giant peek of sunlight,

Barbara Jean had to stand back up to see how far a distance away the swings and slides were from their spot. "Okay, okay, Brittany, calm down. You can go, but don't wander off any further. I can keep an eye on you from here. And remember what I told you. No talking to strangers. You go on now." Excited, Brittany skipped away on the same rush of air she'd come in on. Easing back down on the crisp sheet, Barbara Jean turned her attention back to Lovell. She loved his eyes in the sunlight. They looked so much like emeralds on fire. He had to be a heartbreaker. How many women had he hurt? and why hadn't he been snatched up in marriage? These were the thoughts bumping around in her head.

"You like kids, Lovell?"

"Say what now?" He shot her an inquisitive look. "Do I like kids?" His long, dark lashes fluttered. A sly smile half mooned his face. Oh no, he thought. Not another female who believes that having a man's baby is the lock and key for keeping him.

"Do you?"

"Sure. I love 'em."

"What about sick kids?" Her expression was light.

"What?"

"Do you ever think about sick kids?"

"Well. . .not really. Why do you ask?" He sipped from his cup.

"I see sick children all the time."

"Guess it comes with the territory of working at a hospital."

"You got that right. Sometimes you get to wishing you can do more to help."

Barbara Jean skipped the small talk and jumped to a serious matter. "What I mean is. . ." She paused searching for the right words, the right tone. ". . .do you care enough about kids to help a sick child?"

Lovell could feel his body slowly tense up as he searched her eyes trying to understand where she was coming from and then tried to figure out where such a conversation was going.

"Sure I would. I'll help anybody if I can." He looked away at some lovey-dovey teenagers strolling by, giggling as they walked hand in hand, then aimed his attention back to Barbara Jean. "Why?"

"Her name is. . .well, it's really not important about her name. She's only seven years old. She's a patient at the hospital, and she's dying from leukemia."

His own eyes grew cloudy with concern. "A little girl?"

"The doctors think that she can be saved with the right bone marrow transfusion. The problem is they haven't found a suitable donor yet."

Laying himself back down on his back with his cup of wine resting on his stomach, Lovell took in a deep breath, looked up at the cloud-speckled sky, and let his mind go blank. A large, yellow butterfly fluttered lazily by, so far up, but yet so close; he felt like he could just reach his hand up and gently pull it from the air. And then what would he do? It wasn't in him to intentionally hurt a fly. He thought about the sick child in a hospital bed and tried to imagine her fear and pain.

"You should see her, Lovell. The cutest little thing with copper-red hair, freckles, the biggest blue-green eyes, and a smile that could melt down a mountain of snow. But she's dying."

"That's awful."

"For real," She sighed. "Sometimes doctors can only do so much. I see her almost every day at work when I have to draw her blood. I know I shouldn't be getting so involved, but I just can't help it. She's just a child." Barbara Jean went quiet for a quick spell as if contemplating a solution. "Sometimes I creep into her room at night just to hold her little hand. She looks so innocent, so weak. Just like an angel right here on earth."

"What's her name?" He could almost imagine the red haired child lying listless in a hospital bed.

"Why you wanna know her name? You know I'm not suppose to be discussing a patient's case with anybody."

"Barbara, what's her name. Give me a sense of knowing her. Tell me her name."

"Amy. Amy Kirpatrick. I believe her parents are poor Irish immigrants. God. I don't know what I would do if it were my child dying in some hospital and I couldn't do a thing to help her."'

"And you think I can help her?"

"Lovell, I know you can help her. Not with bone marrow, but with. . ."

Were the birds chirping louder in the trees or was it just his imagination? Lovell thought hard about what she was asking. Granted, it was a wild idea and not exactly your every day request. To him, it had to be one born of sheer desperation. It melted his heart that she could be so concerned about the health of somebody else's child when her own child was so prone to illness. Still, it was a wild idea that kicked itself around in his head, rattled around in his conscious. He didn't quite know how to respond. It was all so new to him—this thing about his blood. No matter how much he thought about it, tried to sort it out, it just didn't make sense to him.

Lovell realized that he had been asked for many things throughout his life: love and respect, loyalty and honesty, and devotion and companionship. But he'd never been asked to give up something so vital, something so personal and so much a part of him like his blood, his life force. How was he supposed to feel?

"Would I have to come to the hospital? You know I don't like hospitals."

"Lovell, don't be silly. I can hook it up right at the house.

It's just a matter of keeping it chilled until I get it to the hospital. Wouldn't take more than ten, maybe fifteen minutes of your time. It's what I do everyday, remember? No big deal."

"It's a big deal to me."

"Sorry. Didn't mean it like that."

"And you say it'll save the child's life?"

"Lovell, the good Lord always blesses those that help others."

Lovell regarded her seriously. "And this will be the first time and the last time, right?"

"For real, Lovell. I won't have to ask you again, ever."

"It's settled then. I'll do it." He propped himself up on his elbow. "Is there anything else you want to ask me for?" A devilish look glinted in his eyes.

She couldn't look too long off into his eyes. Barbara Jean almost felt hypnotized and had to look away. Goodness. He was so darn sexy and good looking. So cocky and sure of himself with the way he talked and the way he handled himself—like no matter what you said to him, he took it in and analyzed it, and stayed calm as he gave his reply or opinion. With that cocky, sexy look playing in his eyes. She felt sure of it; she could sit on the cool grass beside him this very way for the rest of her life. Bracing herself, Barbara Jean looked back over at him as bold as she wanted. This time she didn't flinch or avoid his stare.

"Oh, don't worry. I can think of a few other things too."

"Is that right?" Lovell knew his words were flirtatious, playing up to hers. He didn't see any harm in it if it made her happy. A little innocent flirting never hurt anyone. Women loved it.

"Lovell, you might not know it yet, but I plan to make you mine. My main man. Oh yeah. You'll see." She paused to give him a coyish school girl look, a flutter of her lashes before a wink. ". . .a girl like me like to work it slow and easy. Guess that's just the way I am."

Speechless, Lovell looked away. As much as he loved conversing and exchanging conversation with an attractive woman, for the first time in a long while, he couldn't think of what to say.

Chapter Eighteen

The call about her apartment being ready to move in came a few days later on Tuesday while Nylah was still at work. After talking low into the phone at the nurse's station to keep that nosy Gail Matthews from hearing all her business, Nylah hung up the receiver, feeling a rush of joy and excitement. She felt like jumping up and down. She was now standing at freedom's threshold. Finally, she would be able to move into her own space, have her privacy, and run her own house. No matter how handsome Lovell Joyner might be, no strange man from out of the clear blue would be moving into her domain.

Suddenly she was besieged with a myriad of things to do: utilities needed to be turned on in her name, an address change needed to be put in with the postal service, and new furniture needed to be picked out and bought along with a bunch of odds and ends.

Nylah was sure that a cleaning crew had been through the entire apartment, which was one of the reasons it had taken so long before she could move in. A few minor repairs had to be taken care of, and even though she'd requested to have some new carpet installed, she knew that she couldn't be too demanding. Finally, the place was clean and ready, but still she felt the need to gather some Pine Sol and Lysol to do her own cleaning and sanitizing. She needed a small truck to move her few things from her mother's house: towels, a bed, linen, and cleaning products. Lord have mercy, she thought, the list is endless.

"Be right back," she told her co-worker, Gail, who'd been slyly watching her expression in a silent effort to get Nylah to tell her what was up.

"You alright?" Gail asked, eying her suspiciously.

"Sure. Just a little headache." Nylah knew the woman had plenty of work to do to keep her tied up for hours, but was too busy trying to get in her business to focus. In a small way, she felt guilty telling her a little lie. Gail really considered her a friend—one that she could share all sorts of tidbits of her personal life. Unfortunately, Nylah didn't feel the same way. Her head felt fine. The problem was, she just didn't feel like being at work when she had so many things to take care of.

Going to Mary Ellen's office, her supervisor, Nylah went through a long drawn out rhetoric that her mother was sick and she needed to take a few days off to tend to the woman. In her powder puff blue office and sitting behind her beautiful cherry wood desk, Mary Ellen was a thin, blue-eyed, red-haired, frail-looking woman that Nylah had always admired. Over the years, they had grown to love and respect one another beyond the realm of working together. A few times in the past, Nylah had helped the woman out of many tight situations from staff shortage by pulling double shifts.

Mary Ellen owed her big time. Nylah still recalled the numerous occasions a so-called happily married Mary Ellen had to be covered for while she broke in some new resident doctor in the privacy of a locked hospital room. A couple of times, Mary Ellen had even sent her on a couple of personal errands and fixed her time card so that she got overtime for complying. Out of a long-steeped respect, Nylah never judged the woman on infidelity or pried beyond what her older supervisor was willing to tell her. It was Mary Ellen who had taken the time to really listen to her following the breakup with Glen after two long years. The woman had even given her a week off with pay. She could never judge Mary Ellen. The two women were more than just good friends at a working level, but to Nylah, sometimes it felt like they were partners in crime. Crimes of the heart.

It was short notice to ask to take off, but Nylah knew that Mary Ellen wouldn't give her any hassles; not after all the favors she'd done for the woman. Deep down inside, Nylah was thinking, 'She'd better not'.

"Don't worry about it." Mary Ellen looked like she truly understood. "You need a week, take a week. Take two if you need it. I can call in a few people."

"Thanks, Mary Ellen."

"No problem. You just get that mother of yours back to good health."

"You know I will." Nylah smiled in relief. "I'll call you in a few days."

"Sure."

Like a bird ready to spread its wings for the first time, Nylah hurried and finished up her patient charts before punching out for the day, getting her things, and leaving.

Outside, the noon sun was a giant glowing ball of inspiration in a clear blue sky as she went to her car. It was a beautiful day. Not too hot, but just right. This was one of the things that she loved about California—the endless days of glorious weather always afforded the perfect time for a long drive or a shopping spree.

Again, the idea of actually leaving her mother's house saddened her for a spell, but the feeling soon passed. Who would have ever thought that she would be moving out from her mother's house for the very reason she had? In the past, when she had mused over the time she would move away from her mother, Nylah had felt certain that it would be for the comforts of marriage. She had wasted many of her younger years waiting for her dashing knight to ride into her life and sweep her off her feet, and take her away to a place where she would be loved and cherished for the rest of her life, but it never happened. She had been so foolish to think that Glen was that dashing knight. And now, not exactly old, but not exactly a 'spring chicken', she'd given up on the idea of someday finding Mr. Right. Just to be happy and healthy would have to do. She certainly didn't want to settle for less than what she wanted in a man. Regardless of what anyone else thought or said, she refused to let her life be tainted by men who only wanted her for a roof over their head and a warm body to hold onto at night. If her mother and sister wanted to keep living in the same house with some man they knew very little about, fine and dandy! But she wouldn't have to put up with it.

She got into her car and headed home. No more having to look in Lovell's face for her. No more trying to avoid him since that night. Lovell. She thought back to the night that she had given in and allowed him to kiss her. She'd been kissed many times in the past, but for some reason she couldn't interpret, Lovell's kiss had moved her like no other man's kiss had. It had been as if his lips, pressed like soft and fragrant rose petals against hers, knew her soul on a long-standing, personal basis. Her body had quivered, tensed, and then liquefied right in his arms. Those strong, gentle arms had made her feel so needy, so wonderfully whole. If she hadn't stopped him that night, even as intoxicating and woozy as her head had felt, they would have. . .

"Steady, girl. Steady." She wouldn't have to put up with the possibility of something like that happening again. Not now that she was moving out.

The first thing on her agenda was to hurry home and change into some street clothes. The plain white uniforms that the hospital overseers insisted all nurses wear were way outdated, but every time the nursing staff got together as a united group and tried to protest about it, they were promptly reminded that they'd signed a standard hospital dress code contract when they took the job—a code which gave the hospital the right to say what their staff of nurses could and could not wear to the job. After all the years of wearing the same style of starched white uniform dress, Nylah still wasn't used to it.

Half an hour later, she pulled her white Ford Escort slowly into the empty driveway and cut the engine off. She sat for a moment, pondering the scene of no cars in the driveway, then reminded herself that, oh yeah, thanks to her mother, Lovell didn't have a car anymore, and Barbara Jean was probably out somewhere shopping for something new to bring home to Lovell.

She chuckled lightly to herself. Barbara Jean and her shopping—her favorite past time. Her baby sister loved shopping as much as eating and breathing. If she wasn't somewhere at somebody's Mall buying up cute little outfits for Brittany or herself, she was somewhere buying something for a man. The lucky man at the time just happened to be Lovell.

The man's name running through her mind brought back the memory of the night of steamy kisses. She was proud of herself because she had been strong that night, not giving in to her weakened flesh. Almost. Lovell might have kissed her a few times in the past, but she was back in control, and in no way would she allow it to happen again. That much she knew for sure.

Nylah climbed out of the car and went to the door and let herself in, moving slowly through the hallway calling out.

"Mama? Lovell? Anybody home?" She couldn't wait to announce her good news of having a move-out date.

"Anybody here?" The place was too quiet. Just to be sure she knocked on Lovell's door before opening it only to find the room empty of the man she didn't feel like seeing to begin with. Probably out for a walk or something. Who cares, she mused, maybe Barbara Jean took him out on another picnic like the one on Saturday. Previously, she had found it amusing to hear from her young niece that the three had shared a fun day at the park, and how Mama Jo had looked so 'boodeefoe' when they picked her up from the hair salon. With Lovell being at the house, Barbara Jean was spending more quality time with their mother, and Nylah saw it as a good thing—something to be happy about. She checked in her mother's room, sticking her head through the open door and taking in the usual disarray. "What a mess." Even her mother was gone.

For a second or two, she stood and mulled it over if she should be concerned with her mother's absence or not. But once in the kitchen, she found her sister's small note assuring her that their mother was off shopping with her.

"Good," Nylah chirped. "Some peace at last." She was glad for that.

It looked like she had the whole house to herself for a change. She cherished such moments, though they came few and far. Usually somebody was always at her mother's house. The thought of Lovell having tagged along with them was an added bonus. She slipped out of her uniform into a robe and some slippers.

In the bathroom Nylah turned the water on in the tub, pouring some of her favorite bath liquid into the pooling water. Right away, the tantalizing scent of coconut floated up to her nose. Nylah liked the way the milk based formula made her skin feel so supple and smooth. That old ashiness stayed away from her body for days when she used her scented bubble bath on a regular basis. Sometimes, she had to hide her bubble bath from Brittany, who liked bubbles during bath time. She smiled on the inside thinking of Brittany. Her niece was such a character at times, but still, she wouldn't trade her for anything.

Nylah stood at the bathroom entrance and looked around.

Decisions, decisions. A shower would have been quicker, but Lovell had tried to install a new massage shower head, because Barbara Jean had insisted on it, and the shower hadn't worked right since. Tisk, tisk, she thought, taking some small pleasure in the knowledge. The man isn't so wonderfully perfect after all. Lovell claimed that he was still working on it between his many other on-going projects around the house, but so far, the showerhead still didn't work right. When turned on, more water squirted out from joints and seams than from the showerhead itself, which only proved to her that anyone that claimed to be good with their hands around a house simply wasn't. She shook her head. Too bad Barbara Jean was still too blind to see it.

Unwrapping herself from her royal blue satin robe, letting it slide to the floor, Nylah timidly stuck her right foot into the water to test it, then, feeling assured, slowly climbed into the tub and let her body slink deep down into the luxurious, exotic water. She lathered up her pink nylon sponge and washed under her arms, along her chest and between her thighs before leaning her head back along the cool white enamel, glad that she'd taken the time to pin her hair up and secure a terry wrap around her head. The gentle lapping of lukewarm water against her skin was heavenly as she laid her head back along the cool blue tile, closed her eyes, and allowed the scented bubbles to get acquainted with her skin. Now this was living.

The temperature of the water was just right to sooth her into a long nap. She could always go shopping tomorrow. The apartment could wait; the new utilities could wait. All these things were circulating in her resting head when she heard his voice.

"May I join you?"

Startled, Nylah popped her eyes open to see Lovell closing the bathroom door behind him. Quiet as a church mouse during Sunday service, she hadn't even heard him stirring in the house, let alone enter into the room. Dressed in a red tank top with red and blue nylon shorts, Nylah thought he looked more like a mischievous schoolboy standing at the door, his back pushing up against it as he smiled down at her. It was obvious that his eyes were trying to penetrate beyond the scented bubbles.

"Where'd you come from?"

"Out back in the yard. Thought I heard a car pull up." He paused to consider the scene. "Looks like somebody's playing hooky from work."

"If you don't mind, Lovell, I'd rather be alone." She didn't care if her tone reeked annoyance or not. He had some nerve. Just because they had one night of passionate kissing didn't give him the right to think that he could just barge in on her privacy any time he pleased. One night of kissing had been enough, and even that one time had been one time too many.

As much as she tried not to think about what had happened between them that night, for the life of her she couldn't figure out why Lovell didn't understand that he was Barbara Jean's man. Barbara Jean's man! And it was high time he started acting like it. Or was it that he was so bold and full of himself that he thought he could be with the both of them? As far as she was concerned, what they had almost done by allowing passion to take control that night while her mother was out somewhere being robbed had been wrong. And in no way, none, was it happening again, at least not in this life. Whatever she did, she had to be clear and firm about it.

"I want you to leave."

Lovell regarded her with a smirkish smile. "You didn't answer my question."

"Look, Lovell, I'm not in the mood to play games."

"I asked if I could join you."

"No. No you can't. I'm a big girl, and I can wash myself. Thank you and please leave now."

"You shouldn't be that way."

"Lovell, I'm not playing with you. I want you to leave."

"And what if I don't?"

Indifference in his gait, Lovell walked over and sat at the tub's edge, his back facing the faucet. He leaned over and dipped his hand into the water, then tasted the bubbles, licking the scented white suds from his fingers in one slow sensuous move as if they were flavored snowflakes.

"Lovell, just go!"

"I wanna stay and wash your back. Looks like we both want something."

"My back don't need washing."

A few chuckles. "Everybody's back needs a good washing."

"I think you should leave."

"Why? Am I making you nervous? No one is here to hear you."

"Look, just leave, okay."

"Not until you let me wash something, maybe your hair."

"Lovell, stop being childish."

"Childish?" He waited for her response. The expression on her face was clearly annoyance. If she had a shoe, anything, she'd probably throw it at him. "Is this childish?"

Nylah's eyes grew big as he stood up and snatched off his tank, then slowly peeled down his shorts, stepped out of them and into the suds. She tried to protest by not looking directly at his body, but little good it did. His semi-rigid manhood waved briefly before her eyes. Without an ounce of shame, Lovell was in the water with her, the flesh of his behind sliding softly down onto her feet, which she promptly snatched from under him.

"Lovell, I don't believe you!"

"Believe it."

Nylah thought about standing up and getting out, but

before the thought completely jelled in her mind, Lovell had one of her feet clutched firmly in his hand, slowly and tenderly soaping it up, massaging the top and bottom of it. A tug of war was going on, inside and outside of her; she wanted to jerk her foot away and kick him with it. She wanted to scream at him but couldn't get the sound out. 'My voice', her mind panicked, what's wrong with my voice!' Tension and anxiety slowly rolled off her like water from a duck's wing. His touch on her foot felt so titillating, so right, so soothing. Could he really see her eyes glazing over?

Nylah closed her eyes and felt so relaxed, like she could actually slip down to the tub's bottom and breathe the water and bubbles and not be harmed. How could she have known that so much pleasure could be in her foot?

Lovell finished her left foot and took up her right, soaping it up and massaging it like a trained expert. He massaged at the heel of her foot working up to the ball. His full hand bent her toes back in unison before massaging them straight before taking on each appendage separately.

Nylah slunk down into the water, peering sheepishly over the top of bubbles. She closed her eyes again as she experienced a jolt to her nervous system at the feel of something warm and tight clamping down on her toe. I should stop him. Easing one eye open to peek, and Lord have mercy, no he didn't! Ohmygod! The man had her big toe in his mouth, working his way over it with his long, thick, moist tongue, applying soft licks around her toes, between them. A small moan and a tiny shiver rocked her as the feel of her own juices being sucked right out of her soared. Never, never in her life, had she felt such a feeling.

Lovell was like a junkie out of control, running his tongue in and out the spaces of her toes, taking her to plateaus of arousal she'd never been. Slowly he released her foot, stood, and pulled her slippery brown body up and close to his. She

could glimpse his penis, like a long thick brown finger pointing at her thighs as his body pressed hers against the tiled wall.
He kissed her, sliding his tongue into her mouth as his warm,
wet fingers found her thick, black jungle of pubic hair and gently massaged the tingling area between her thighs. She put one
foot up on the edge of the tub, allowing him easier access to
the place he wasn't suppose to touch. His finger slid easily
into her moistness, teasing up and down the warm slippery
pink, then up to her swollen bulb where it repeated slow gentle circles.

Unable to wait any longer, Lovell guided himself into her
wetness and maneuvered a few long strokes before climbing
out the tub and pulling her with him. Handling her like fine,
delicate china, he took his time as he laid her down on the thick
bathroom rug half covered with her satin robe.

Nylah tensed, then allowed herself to relax. Heaven on
earth was on its way, and she didn't want to miss any part of it
as Lovell slid down into her. Her eyes rolled back, both lids
closed as each thrust they made brought heaven closer and
closer, like floating up a hill on a cloud of pleasure. Higher
and higher, their bodies rocking in perfect harmony and groov-
ing to a rhythm of their own. Heaven was just around the
bend. As if holding on for dear life itself, she clutched his back
tightly and felt the power of muscles working like fine tuned
machinery beneath her touch.

She licked her lips and opened her mouth about to moan
Lovell's name when suddenly the bathroom door burst open
with a force of whooshing air. In a flash, ice cold water rained
down on their hot, entangled bodies. The cold shock halted all
lovemaking and feelings of pending pleasure with it. In a flash
they were gone.

Water was in Nylah's eyes, forcing her to turn her head to
keep it from running down into her nostrils. A few trickles still
found their way down the wrong path of her throat, making her

arms reach out and push Lovell up a bit so that she could cough and clear her airways.

"Barbara!"

"What the hell!" Lovell almost lost his balance trying to scramble to the side of her but kept his back to his attacker. He dared himself to look, but he already had a good idea of who would be crazy enough to do something so bold.

With her back still to the floor, Nylah had to look up. Sitting straighter and reaching for her robe, she felt the spread of embarrassment as she looked up at Barbara Jean. But even worse, her feeling of shame was nothing compared to the hatred she could see. Hatred burning like the flames of hell in her sister's eyes.

Chapter Nineteen

"Woman, are you crazy?! I don't believe this!"

"Good!" Barbara Jean screeched to the top of her voice. "Maybe you should try harder!"

Lovell was still crouched along the beige-tiled bathroom floor, crouched in a puddle of splashed madness. Mildly aware of his manhood, like a once-new tire after doing battle with a nail, it was slowly shriveling up.

A wet coldness seeped quickly to his core. Lovell turned his face slightly away with a fire in his eyes that Barbara Jean would never see. He could barely contain his anger. Right when he was getting his second wind, feeling like. . .like he was almost to the end of some long-awaited journey—a feeling that was so deep, so consuming that he could have actually been falling down into a bottomless pit of pleasure.

Hastily, Nylah stood up and put her robe back on. Her eyes watched Barbara Jean's every move, trying to read her thoughts, and anticipate her sister's next action in case things turned violent. If ever again in life, peace would be a long time coming. Nylah wondered what words could she possibly say to ease the tension.

Pulling down a large bath towel from the wall rack, Lovell stood and quickly fashioned it around his waist and brushed past Barbara Jean on his way out. Not one word crossing her lips, Barbara Jean stood like the solid keeper of the gate, the red plastic bucket still clutched in her hand, hanging at her side like an empty ammunition bin.

Tired from walking around one used car dealership after another, Mama Jo wanted no part of a bad scene. Tight lipped and shaking her head at the thought of her girls feuding over a man, she'd gone into her bedroom and quietly closed her door. At the thought of possible trouble, Brittany had been sent to her room to watch cartoons.

Nylah turned her head and looked off at no particular thing along the bathroom wall, then bold and brazen, looked back into her sister's face. Her shoulders slumped at the thought of how unpredictable life could be at times. If only she had followed her first intentions to go shopping, she wouldn't be in such a predicament. What had started off as a good day for her was now spoiled beyond repair as she stared at her younger sibling. Barbara Jean looked so nice too, all dressed in her fancy white tee-shirt-type ensemble trimmed in gold. Large gold earrings dangled like shiny new bracelets at each side of her head. She sported gold sandals on newly pedicured feet. Today her sister's hair was up in a long dark brown ponytail that made Nylah muse briefly if it was a weave. Had to be. She couldn't recall her sister's hair being that long before. The girl was dressed so nice, getting ready to act so ugly.

Noticing that Barbara Jean's eyes hadn't blinked once, Nylah just didn't know what to say. But, she felt that she should say something. Anything to try to salvage any possible thread of a family bond.

"Barbara. . .look. . .I know how bad this looks. . ." She wanted to touch her, but when she reached out, the slightest touch to Barbara Jean's arm, her sister cringed as if her fingers were hot prods and pulled away from her.

"I...I mean we...we didn't mean anything. We weren't trying to hurt nobody. . ., I mean. . .it just happened, that's all."

Her fist balled tight at each side, magenta pink lips glued by resentment, Barbara Jean turned and walked away. Nylah tightened the sash of her robe and followed her outside to the back of the house, hoping that the woman wasn't mad enough to actually take a swing at her, at least not over some man.

Stepping out onto the patio, Barbara Jean paced restless up one end of the newly patched concrete where all her wonderful pots of foliage were still lined up in neat little rows before she dropped down on her knees and began tending to her plants, oblivious to her white outfit. Clutching her robe tight against her body, Nylah watched her silently pick off dead leaves and twigs and toss them aside with careless ease.

The evening air held a clean but strong, woody smell to it. Probably old man Morris across the street burning his fireplace. That man was the only person Nylah knew that burned his fireplace on a nightly basis in the summer as well as the winter months. Odd it was. But it kept the surrounding neighborhood air constantly permeated with a homey, burnt-mystic sandalwood scent that was almost cozy and nostalgic at times.

Nylah ducked with quick reflexes as a large brown butterfly braved itself across their path and flitted close around her head before moving on to higher air. She swatted a few times at it but missed. That butterfly felt like it was only one of many fluttering around in her stomach. Feeling uneasy, she watched it with mild interest before tying the sash of her robe even tighter around her body, stalling for time. Her skin was still wet and tingly, but thank God, she thought, the evening air was still a bit warm. Maybe it was just her imagination, but she thought she also detected the heavenly scent of jasmine mixed with the warm and inviting scent of somebody's apple cobbler.

Back to the matter at hand, Nylah sighed long and deep. And what a foolish move she'd made. She and Lovell both. As if things hadn't been bad enough around her mother's house, now this. What could she possibly have been thinking of to allow herself to become so weak? A slow indifference creeped up her back as she folded her hands across her chest and shook her head. None of this would have happened, she couldn't help thinking, none of it, if I'd just gone straight to the Mall as planned. Words of defense were lined up like soldiers along her tongue. She wanted her younger sister to understand that no man, no matter how special she thought he was, no man walking God's great earth, was worth the destruction of love and trust between two sisters. No man!

"Barbara Jean, listen to me...just listen. I know how this all must look to you. Like Lovell and I went behind your back trying to play some head game on you or something, but it's not like that."

Her mouth sealed, Barbara Jean ambled up and went from one luscious green plant to another, bending over to examine each foliage to give her hands something to do. Nylah saw her sister's antics as a ploy to harness her anger.

"Barb, we didn't mean to, it just happened."

Ignoring her words, Barbara Jean fetched her trusty aluminum water can and methodically began watering one potted plant at a time like a woman in a trance.

"Well?!" Nylah brayed, stomping her foot. "Say something dammit!"

Turning around slowly, Barbara Jean angled her head and fixed hard eyes on her like brown rocks burning over in two quiet flames. "How many times?"

"What?"

"How many times?"

"Barb, what's the point in..."

"I said I wanna know how many times you've been with 'im?! How many?"

Nylah thought about lying, but what good it would it do? Once, twice, heck, it felt like a hundred times and twice on

Sundays. Her body had felt like she'd been with him forever.
One soul living as two. It seemed like an odd question to be
asking, but who was she to be judging?

"Twice. Only twice."

"Twice." Barbara Jean made the word sound so. . .so
nasty. "In this house?"

"What?"

"Both times in this house?"

"Yes, but the first time was...well, just kissing, that's all.
And I really didn't enjoy. . ." Oh hell. Who was she fooling?
A streak of hot excitement raced through Nylah's body just
thinking about Lovell's arms around her. Lying about it was
futile. She had enjoyed every last minute of it. Entirely too
much time had passed since she'd truly been intimate with a
man. Too many nights of empty dreams, lonely arms, and seeing after a sick mother day in and day out hadn't helped her
love life one bit.

Nylah let her mind dip briefly back into the past. Two
whole years had passed since her last serious relationship with
Glen. Even that one had been short and sweet. When she really thought back on it, she had been the one dealt the short end
of the stick. The one so full of love and hope, so full of can't-
live-without Glen feelings, until the day the truth slammed her
in the face. It had taken a while for her to realize that Glen had
wanted to settle down and marry her as much as he wanted to
have his two legs amputated. The truth was, she was the one
giving ninety percent to the relationship while Glen was content to give only ten. And sometimes, the way she remembered it, even that ten percent was late coming.

After Glen, of course, there had been a handful of scattered one-time dates that led to no where, not even to a call
back or a second date. Mostly because she had never been the
type to just sleep with every man she dated just for the privi-
lege of being able to say that she did have a man. Nylah felt

like she hadn't missed much by being overly selective and too picky about who to date. But Lovell. Lord have mercy, she thought with a delicious inside smile. She didn't know what kind of magic he was using on her. But she felt like he had spilled liquid fragrance out from a bottle, and she had splashed herself all around in its essence. In his arms she was out of control. The man had cast some kind of wonderful but wicked spell on her. He had to! In a way, it was frightening to think that the man could have such an effect on her when she knew that she wasn't willing to give in, but yet found herself doing so against better judgment.

". . .and I won't forget this time, Nylah. You can count on it."

"Barbara Jean, I said I'm sorry. . ."

"You know, Nylah," her sister said in a quiet, peaceful tone usually reserved for Brittany, except her cold staring eyes weren't smiling like they did for her child, "ever since we were little girls, you were always jealous of me."

"Jealous?" Nylah rolled her eyes and resisted an urge to laugh. "Barb, you can't be serious. Me? Jealous?"

"Yeah, jealous. Kinda like you couldn't stand the idea of me having something, anything that you didn't have first. All through our childhood."

"That's not true, and you know. . ."

"No!" Barbara Jean interjected, slicing her words off with the sharpness of her tone. "You hush up and listen! You wanted me to talk, and now I'm talking so you need to shut up and listen." She paused to stare her sister straight in the eyes.

A cold shiver ran up Nylah's back. "I had no idea you felt that way."

"You have to have something to say or do with everything! The way I dress, where to find a job, how to care for my child, how to deal with Mama, who I should date and who I shouldn't date. Everything! You always have to have your say about it."

"Barb, that's not true."

Barbara Jean frowned and lowered her voice to an even tone. "Oh it's true all right. You just can't see it 'cause you're the one that's doing it."

Lowering her head, Nylah looked at the patio cement. Some of the small cracks in the concrete, resulting from earthquakes over the years, had been recently repaired by Lovell. Fixed. Made whole again for the time being. Almost like herself. Lordy, lordy, what couldn't that man do? She looked down at her odd-feeling feet. For the first time since she'd stepped outside with Barbara Jean, she realized that she was barefooted. Her feet, the same two feet that Lovell had so lovingly washed and massaged into total submission with his mouth, were not only dirty again, but half numb as they rested on the cold, dusty pavement.

"Finally," Barbara Jean said, her voice an octave higher, jolting Nylah from reverie, ". . .finally I find a decent single man that might be perfect for me. Not perfect for you because you were too busy pretending that you didn't like the man, that you couldn't stand the sight of 'im. But he could have been perfect for me. Maybe even make a good father for Brittany, and you couldn't wait to mess that up too, could you?"

"Barbara, I didn't try to mess up anything. . .we didn't plan for this. It just happened. Actually, I really didn't think you and Lovell were a couple." In a way, her sister's summation of their sisterly relationship was a bit amusing. Frankly, she had no idea that Barbara Jean even felt that way. How could she possibly feel like she was jealous of her and out to sabotage her happiness?

"Maybe I was waiting," Barbara Jean snorted, "waiting 'til we could be friends first before I just laid down and slept with 'im. All smart women know you should be friends before lovers except for you, Nylah. You'll sleep with anybody."

That last remark cut deep, but Nylah let it bounce and slide off. Besides, she knew it wasn't true. They were only words meant to hurt her. "I still say it's not all my fault. I know you can't see it now, but it's not."

"Nylah, it's never your fault!"

"I didn't want him here in the first place!"

"So, it's my fault then?"

"Hell yeah it's your fault! You never should have brought 'im to this house to begin with. You had no right, so don't try'n blame all this on me."

"No excuse, Nylah! If you had been the one to bring him to this house, I wouldn't have slept with 'im!"

"And I'm not you!"

Getting in her face, Barbara Jean retorted with, "So, I suppose if I was to bring a pile of drugs into this house and keep it here, it's just a matter of time before you'd be a drug addict? Is that how it goes, Nylah? Why can't you just let me have something that's all mine for once!"

"Barb, you act like the man is some kind of possession of yours."

"In a way, maybe he is!"

"Nonsense! You should hear yourself. You sound like some crazy woman. Lovell don't belong to you just like he don't belong to me. Get it through your head!"

"Just for once. . ." Barbara Jean broke down crying. ". . .I wish you would just stay outta my life. . .just for once."

"Fine!"

Point taken. With the evening gathering in around them, Nylah's heart softened; she wanted to hold her sister and comfort her. Wanted to, but backed away. Painful as it was, it was more than obvious that her words and hugs wouldn't do any good. Even if she were to just grab her baby sister in her arms and hold her, just long enough to make her understand that she was having a hard time understanding how the whole thing with Lovell had happened herself. Not once, but twice she'd fallen under his spell. Perhaps, she thought...perhaps she was bewitched or something. But what more could she possibly say to make it right? And what good would it do? No amount of forgiveness could right the problem for the moment. None.

Turning and heading slowly back to the house, Nylah halted in her tracks at the harsh sound of her sister's voice aimed at her back.

"I hope it was the best loving you've ever had, Nylah, 'cause it'll definitely be the most expensive. You can count on it."

"Yeah, yeah." Wondering what the heck Barbara Jean meant by that last remark, Nylah gathered up her composure and retightened the sash around her robe as she took the few short steps two at a time and hurried into the house to get dressed for her trip to the Mall.

She had an apartment waiting to be furnished. Her own place of sanctum. Thank the good man above, she had a place that she couldn't wait to get to.

Chapter Twenty

The scene was much better with his eyes closed. Beautiful. Visions of Nylah were ethereal, a surrealistic, brown Nubian princess floating around inside his head like a dancing ghost. Visions of her nakedness, soft and round, beckoned to his senses, tingled mildly at his groin, and cried out for his warmth, his touch.

Her body was facing his, nipples large, dark, and inviting perched like sun dried raisins on silken mocha slopes of flesh. She let her breath catch, swooned, a soft meow kind of sound more like a kitten's first purr, then moved closer to him. The feeling of their embrace was like a million small currents of electricity charging through his body.

The sensation was too much—a feeling that could truly overwhelm, melt him down into a helpless quivering heap, and then consume him. Nylah. Her name brushed light as a goose feather across his waiting lips.

Lovell stretched with leisure, opened his eyes slowly, and wondered if he was in love. Really in love. It had to be love. What other feeling could possibly render him so weak, and yet so full of life? He felt like all his senses were on fire. His mind and his body felt exhausted and energized. Even with empty pockets, he felt like a million bucks. The world belonged to him and him alone. There was nothing that he couldn't do. Nothing.

Attired in long black sweat pants with no shirt on, he was in the privacy of his room, on the top of the covers of his bed, gazing up at the ceiling while listening to his small table top radio. The provocative sound of Brandy's 'My Friend' played low in the background. The sensuous rhythm of the sound radiated through him, rocked and swayed his senses into a blissful mellow as a delicate Santa Ana breeze found its way to his space, and did its best to get his attention by swaying the new white vertical blinds at his open window. A full, pale blue-grey moon, nature's giant all-seeing eye, illuminated shadows about his room; tree branches like long thin fingers swayed in the night air; a single leaf breaking free from its tether slowly tumbled to the cooled earth; seeking night birds zipped expertly through the darkness past his window on some mission that he would never know. His breathing was even, and all seemed so right with the world for the moment.

Lovell allowed all his awareness to gather itself and seep down deep into every muscle in his body as he thought about love. What is this mysterious thing called love? Was it something that could be defined as the constant thought of another person? The need to feel that special someone against or near you at any given time of day or night. Love. Or was it only something sexual? As simple as the deep-rooted craving to feel your own body entwined with your lover's every second, every minute or every hour.

Had he really fallen in love with Nylah, or was it all part of some cheap thrill played out by the forces of nature? Lust had been the bait, pleasure the prize. But how did true love work itself into the picture, and more importantly, how could he be sure?

"Nylah, sweet Nylah." Just the sugary sing-song sound of her name, he loved it.

Love or lust? What confused him the most was the frightening similarity to the two, like one and the same. Was he really in love or was he just in lust? True enough, he'd known plenty of women in the past that he'd felt a similar feeling for, like their lives were destined to be entwined forever. Sometimes that feeling had lasted for days or weeks, but this...this feeling for Nylah was somehow different. When he was with her, up close to her, the very air that she inhaled into her lungs was his air—together, one and the same. He couldn't imagine what his life would be now without her in it. He didn't even want to think about it. No other woman had come half as close to what he was feeling for Nylah. No denying it, she was under his skin big time.

Against a myriad of emotions, Lovell closed his eyes again in an effort to think of where else he could possibly move to. The thought of continuing to live in the same house with Barbara Jean and Nylah both was a dubious one at most. Of course, he had no way to be sure of it, but he felt strongly that Mama Jo was probably at her limit and upset with him for disrupting her household and disappointed with him for causing a problem between her two daughters. After a month and a half, his welcome seemed already worn out. And Barbara Jean. He didn't really want to think of her. Barbara Jean had done so much to help him out, but now she probably hated his guts.

He still didn't know how Nylah felt. Nylah, he chuckled mildly. Now she was one hard cookie to crack. She was a smooth operator when it came to her feelings: hot like day one minute, cold like night the next. It was impossible to tell with her. Earlier that day, as his lips had sought and found hers during their peak on that cold tiled floor, for a second or two, as fleeting as they had been, he was sure he had felt something. He had felt something moving up and out of her, her true spiritual essence rising up to fuse with his. They had been two souls blending into one. She had stopped fighting her feelings and given him her all, unashamed, holding nothing back. But only for a split moment before the feeling had halted, and then faded away, her inner spirit seemed to suddenly remember something of more importance. But he had felt it, and nothing could take that experience away. It was a feeling now etched forever in his heart.

So engrossed in his reverie of Nylah, the tiny knocks to his door, barely taps actually, went unheard. Detecting a change of air in the room, Lovell opened his eyes in time to see Barbara Jean ease her head in, then the rest of her frame. She reached across, clicked the light switch on, and stood looking down at him with the oddest expression, perhaps the way a mother might look upon an unruly child to chart her next step in discipline.

Lovell's eyes sought out her hands to make sure that she had no weapon of any sort. Barbara Jean was dressed in some kind of long nylon lounger of brown and white African print; her hair was cocooned in a silken brown scarf fashioned atop her head in what he considered the 'Badu look.' Standing flush against the door as if some intruder was due any second to burst in behind her, she let her eyes meet his in a brief stare down.

The look on her face, the expression, what was it? loathing? hatred? understanding? Was he guilty enough to need her forgiveness? Darn it. He couldn't read her. Besides, his mind thundered, what did he really have to feel guilty about? He was a single man with desires, unfettered. It wasn't like they were married or they were even lovers. If she thought of them as a couple, no one had told him anything about it. Not one soul.

To get a better look at her, Lovell angled his head, pulled himself into a sitting position, and rested his upper body against the oaken headboard. His throat felt tight and hot, and despite the room's cool temperature, nervous sweat was sliding down his back. The silence was more than he could stand. Looking to her hands, he saw that one hand was balled up as if to be holding something. Lovell wondered what that something was—a tiny knife, a small gun perhaps?

Barbara Jean tried a brave little smile. "Lovell, we need to talk."

"Sure." By the peaceful tone of her voice, she didn't sound too upset by the earlier scene in the bathroom with Nylah. But a woman, and he should know, was as unpredictable as the weather. There was always the possibility of the calm before the storm.

Lovell still recalled the time he'd made the mistake of staying out all night gambling when he had lived with another girlfriend. The moment he'd walked through the door with the new sun high in the morning sky, the woman had a piping-hot breakfast waiting for him and scented bubble bath water. She even served him while wearing the sexiest babydoll gown he could imagine—royal blue lace on red-hot insanity. No sooner had he forked a mouthful of perfect eggs into his mouth, the woman had charged him like a mad bull with a large kitchen knife in one hand and a small pot of hot water in the other. If it hadn't been for his reflexes, he didn't know what would have happened. She would have messed up his pretty-boy face too. He couldn't have lived with that—not with burns to his face. Oh yeah, he knew all too well about the niceness of a scorned female .

"Mind if I sit on the bed?" Barbara Jean waited patiently for his reply.

"No. . .I mean. . . sure, park it." Gripping his composure he patted a spot and moved himself over a bit at the same time. "So what's up?"

"I know you think I'm mad at you." Barbara Jean aimed her bottom carefully along the edge of the bed, then looked at her hand that was holding a single key in her open palm. "And

I am. Maybe I'm just jealous 'cause it wasn't me." She smacked her lips. "I don't know. But anyway, this is yours." She held the shiny key up before handing it over to him.

"Say what? What's this?" His face lit up and for a second or two he thought that his car, his Cadillac, had finally been found. But that couldn't be possible. For one thing, the key looked nothing like the key to his Caddy. Lovell took it from her hand and looked it over. "A key to your car?"

"Don't be silly. It's a key to your own car."

"What?" What was he hearing? "You bought me a car?"

Smiling, Barbara Jean nodded. "Sorry it's not another Caddy, but I got what I could for the money I had with me. Paid cash too. No car note."

"Woman, are you saying you bought me a car?"

"It's not a new car, Lovell, but I felt so bad about Mama losing your car that way. She had no bizzness doing that."

Growing happier by the moment, Lovell exclaimed, "I can't believe you bought me a car."

"I know. But that's where Mama and I were all day earlier. Car hunting. I was so excited with my news that I rushed home just to surprise you and. . ." She let her words trail off before adding, ". . .but I guess the surprise was on me." Barbara Jean stopped smiling and looked serious. ". . .and what a surprise it was."

His smile dropped away as well. Lovell lowered his head. Suddenly he didn't feel so happy. "Look, I'm really sorry about. . ."

"Don't be. I mean, it's not even that serious and you're a free man. You have a right to choose. And that choice wasn't me. That's all."

"Hey look, it wasn't like that. . ."

"Lovell, I said I understand."

"No, I'm serious. What happened with Nylah and I just happened. Wasn't a matter of choice. It wasn't planned." Of course he thought callously, perhaps even a bit too cocky for the moment, love never is.

"Lovell," she sighed with a few loving pats to his leg. "I said I understand."

"I just don't wanna cause no conflicts between sisters, that's all. Matter of fact, that's why I've been thinking. . ."

"Thinking? Thinking about what, Lovell?" She angled her body around for a more personal view.

"Thinking that maybe it's time to move on. I mean. . .I got some friends up in Seattle I could probably go stay with until I can get on my feet. Think that car you bought will make it to Seattle?"

"Lovell, you know you lying. You don't have no friends in Seattle." Reaching over, she gently caressed his face. He was such a beautiful man, such strong facial features. "I said I'm not mad at what you and Nylah did. Maybe you made a mistake, that's all. People make mistakes." Looking into the depth of his eyes, she searched for something, a gleam of hope, anything, something she well knew wouldn't be there. He didn't love her. He would never love her. "I know you don't really want to leave here. At least not yet."

"Woman, you don't know that."

"I know more than you think I know." She paused and took time to clear her throat. "Just like I know you don't have no friends in Seattle, Washington."

Lovell fingered the key in his hand. The metal felt as cold as ice. She was right. Who was he trying to fool with lies? "Guess I'll have to find a real job then. Get some money flowing so I can get my own place."

Barbara Jean smiled at the thought of that one. "You have a job right here. This is a job. You're mama's caretaker, and you're our handyman." Nervous chuckles punctuated her words. "That's like having two jobs. Believe me, I know."

"I'm serious though. It's time to head out." Gently, he

moved her hand away from his face. Nothing could be more annoying to him than a hand playing in his face. He sniffed and looked away. His nose picked up faint traces of cigarette smoke somewhere in the house. Someone was either in the process of smoking in the house, or had smoked a cigarette earlier. He sniffed again. The offending aroma wasn't coming from Barbara Jean who, oddly, smelled like fresh honey, a thick but sweet delicate scent was coming from underneath her clothes. Looking away, it was yet another interesting thing for him to ponder. Lovell forced his mind to think about what kind of car Barbara Jean had bought. Anything to keep from dwelling on what part of her body she had used honey on, or even worse, why?

"Well I'm not ready for you to leave yet. So give it up."

"Where's everybody?" he asked gingerly. Lovell knew it was a weak attempt to change the mood.

"Mama and Brit are asleep in front of the television. I know 'cause I checked. Nylah still hasn't come back since she left earlier today. Probably somewhere seeing about her new apartment."

"So she's really gonna move out, huh?" Depressing as the thought was, Lovell sure hoped it wasn't all because of him.

"Looks that way. Maybe it's for the best." Barbara Jean looked out the open window.

Her words made him feel even worse, but he couldn't really comment on it. "So, what kind did you get?"

"Huh?" Seemingly lost in her own thoughts, Barbara Jean's eyes met his again.

"The car. What kind of car did you buy?"

"You'll see when you feel like going outside. It's not brand new, and it's nothin' too fancy. Actually, that's not the only reason I'm here."

Lovell braced himself. "I'm listening." This had to be it. She'd done so much to help him, gave so much of her time, had spent her own money, and now it was time. Time for him to pay up. What could she possibly want from him? An apology? A promise of undying love? A plain old romp-in-the-sheets, perhaps? He hoped the latter wasn't the case.

"Remember that little girl I told you about?"

"The one with leukemia?"

"Yeah, her," Barbara Jean replied.

"Amy. Yeah, I remember."

"Remember what you told me?"

"I remember that too."

"Well time is running out for little Amy."

Suddenly skeptical, Lovell lowered and shook his head. Considering everything that had happened, the idea of allowing her to stick a needle in his arm was the last thing he wanted to think about. "Look, I know what I said. . .but, I don't know. Somehow the timing is all wrong right now."

"For who, Lovell? For you or for little Amy?"

"For all of us."

"And what's changed, Lovell? Tell me what's so different now?"

"You know, with you being upset and all. . .I don't know."

Mocking shock, Barbara Jean queried with, "What? Now you don't trust me? Is that it? You think I might do something to hurt you?"

"Woman, no. No way. Don't be silly. Of course I trust you." He hated it. Hated lying straight in her face. Lovell felt he was turning into a real jerk—the kind of man he never wanted to be. The kind that fed a woman one lie after another. He felt awful. "Guess I'm the kinda guy that always keep my word. Okay, if you still wanna do it, let's just do it and get it over with."

Thrilled, Barbara Jean hopped up from the bed with the agility of a young cougar going after prey. "I'll go get my things. Won't take long."

In two minutes flat, she was back in his room and drawing blood. Fascinated, Lovell watched with quiet wonder as she filled eight small clear vials with the thick fluid and set each one over in a stainless steel bowl. The fact that her procedure was painless and swifter than he'd anticipated made him feel foolish for being fearful and untrusting to begin with.

"There," said Barbara Jean happily as she removed the faded yellow rubber tubing from his arm. "Now was that so bad?"

"Piece of cake," Lovell said. He allowed himself to relax as he reveled in the thought of doing something good to help somebody.

"And you're the perfect patient, Lovell."

"That's me alright." He gave her a thumbs up.

Barbara Jean gathered up her black lacquered tray of paraphernalia and stood up, smiling sincerely from ear to ear. Her eyes, if only for the moment, held such a fondness that Lovell felt taken aback with her pleasant attitude and mentally scolded himself for not having faith in her to begin with and not believing her to be a woman of true understanding. Oh yeah, he mused. In his book Miss Barbara Jean was still alright.

"Before you go," Lovell said, studying her face for something more, a slippage of truth. "Tell me something." He wanted to know, but it felt more like he needed to know.

"Sure."

"What's in all of this for you?"

"How do you mean?" Barbara Jean asked. She looked truly puzzled.

He gestured to her tray. "You're doing that for some little sick girl named Amy, but I wanna know what's in it for you. Better yet, Miss Barbara, what can I do for you? Tell me, how can I repay you for everything you've done for me?"

"Let me think about it, and I'll let you know."

Lovell gave her a suggestive smile, an innocent flirtation.

The woman deserved that much. "Guess I'll be waiting then. I don't want us to end up like enemies."

"Lovell," she said so sweetly, "you so silly. You don't have to be worrying 'bout that. We'll always be friends. Always."

"I'm glad to hear that. You had me worried for a minute."

"Well don't be," she said in response with a big smile. "Now put a shirt and some shoes on and go take a look at your car while I go put this away and check on Brittany." She gave him a cute wink. "Later, I'll make us a snack to help get your strength back." Having said that, she quietly closed the door behind her.

Chapter Twenty-One

Smiling ear to ear, Barbara Jean clutched her tray of goodies in her hand and moved stealthily back through the short, narrow hallway to her bedroom. With a push of her hip, she eased the door open and slipped in. Once inside, she could hear the muffled sounds of voices coming from her mother's television set, which was probably still playing to a sleeping woman. Good, she thought. The last thing she wanted to do was wake her mother.

Behind her bedroom door was a feeling of total privacy and sanctum. A temporary safe harbor from prying ears and invading eyes. A modest-sized oscillating fan did its best to blow a whirl of cool air through the room while her own small television set played.

The room's air was saturated with the scent of freshly cut pink and red roses, compliments of Lovell, whose backyard garden spilled over with an abundance of beautiful flowers including delicate red, pink, and yellow roses. For the short amount of time that Lovell had been living at their house, it didn't seem earthly possible for such a lush amount of growth in a garden. And if someone had told her of such an occurrence, she would be hard pressed to believe it. But the evidence was plain and clear from her window view. In a way it was nice, really. The man simply had the power of growing hands. There wasn't a room in the entire house that didn't sport a vase of fresh-cut roses. Sometimes, Barbara Jean felt like she was living in the middle of a fragrant garden without having to plow around in the soil. But it was certainly nothing that she could complain about.

In her bed, sweet youth of innocence, sprawled across it on her back and clad in a breezy white cotton tee-shirt and matching underwear, Brittany lay sleeping with the raspy sound of air wheezing in and out of her lungs. Barbara Jean went over and stood in the middle of the room, her ears, like radars, trained on the breathing sounds of her sleeping child. Just hearing her child having to breathe in such a manner tugged at her heart and made her eyes mist up. It just wasn't fair. So many healthy children ran around in the world. Why not her child? Though she tried hard not to think it too often, maybe God was still punishing her for allowing herself to become pregnant by another woman's husband. Maybe that was the reason why her child had to keep suffering. Her daughter had her good days and her bad days. Lately, she was counting more bad days than good ones. Sometimes, weeks went by without episode. Her child seemed as healthy and normal as any other child. And then slowly it came on, her asthma, sneaking back around like some thief in the night. It had to be part of her punishment.

Her mind slipped back into time as she thought about her daughter's father, and how wonderful things had been in the beginning. Not all that handsome, but Shelby had treated her well. Still, Brittany had never even seen the man. In fact, her child didn't have a clue to who Mr. Shelby J. Jefferson was, and probably never would. She had no previous pictures to show her child, and no cute, whimsical father stories to hold up his memory. It made her resentful that she also had no financial help from the man, nor did he keep in touch from time to time. She had nothing except a beautiful child that she loved with all her heart—a sickly child with challenged lungs that she would do anything in her power to heal. A stab of fresh anger shot through her. That damn Shelby Jefferson! How could she have been so stupid to trust a man like that? For a moment, Barbara Jean felt dizzy. A hard lump seemed to come into her throat and drop down into the pit of her stomach every time the man's name ran across her mind.

Though it had been years, painfully, she still remembered how Shelby had spun his web of deceit. Shelby Jefferson had pulled her in blind, yet, so willingly, into his sticky lair by staring deeply into her eyes and professing his undying love for her. The man had convinced her that it was only a matter of time before he could get his business in order to leave his wife of twelve years, and they could finally be together like a real family. Only, it hadn't worked out that way.

It still tugged painfully at her heart that five months into her pregnancy, after she'd finally gotten over her shame and had summoned up enough courage to tell Shelby that she was carrying his child, the man and his wife moved to Texas. Just like that, two weeks and three days after she'd told him the news about their love child.

Some undying love that had been. Barbara Jean drew back the tears that threatened to invade her eyes. Sometimes, it still hurt like a new wound. A little more salt was poured into it each time her mind dredged it up. Now, even after all the years that had passed, she still got the feeling that it all had been some kind of conspiracy. And somehow, Shelby's wife had been in on that same conspiracy to ruin her life with an out-of-wedlock child—a child that could never be perfect. She hadn't seen nor heard from Shelby Jefferson since, but in no way could she let his absence interfere with her love for her Brittany. Never, she thought.

Men were sometimes like buses in the big city - one leaving and another one, like clockwork, on its way shortly. Too many times had she been the fool when it came to trusting her feelings. It all seem to turn out the same, with her being the one on the losing end. But Lovell. . .Lovell would have been different. She could have helped him get over that last breakup in no time.

Lovell had opened up enough to tell her all about his previous girlfriend, Rita. Miss Rita had sounded more like just another pitiful 'strawberry' girl that didn't know a good man from a stick in the mud. Barbara Jean didn't exactly know why, but it was something she just felt. Lovell would have been a perfect choice for her, if Nylah hadn't interfered and gotten in the middle of her pending happiness. What could have been hers was now Nylah's, and the thought of it felt like another burning spear jammed through her heart—another big let-down. "It's just not fair!"

"Well, screw you, Lovell! Screw the both of you!"

Punishment. All of it. Her baby's battle with asthma and her own bad luck with finding a decent and caring man that wanted her and her alone was just God's way of punishing her. Just like all the diseases on the face of the earth, the way she saw it, just God's way of punishing folks for present and past life sins.

Balancing her tray and bending over Brittany, Barbara Jean felt her child's forehead but couldn't detect any rise in body temperature. "Thank goodness." She thought about throwing some cover over her precious baby, but considering the warmness of the room, the girl was probably better off without it.

Walking over and placing her tray down on the desk, she opened the small refrigerator and placed the bowl containing the blood vials inside, then lifted one of the vials up to her fascinated eyes. The force of life itself vibrated in her hand—red gold. Funny, she thought, Lovell had no idea how much money he could be making with his own blood. The man didn't have a clue. But it really didn't matter because she had all the connections she needed.

She moved back over to Brittany and stood over her still holding up the warm vial of red and feeling the surging power harnessed behind the thin presence of glass.

Brittany, as if sensing her mother's towering presence, stirred and opened one eye, then slowly the other. Her breath was coming in short quick wheezing gasps as if each draw of her lungs had to fight hard to extract the precious oxygen from the air. Obviously uncomfortable, she lay listless as a thrown-away brown ragdoll looking up at her mother. Her young eyes were weak brown pools. Barbara Jean felt like she could just breakdown and cry.

"You see this, Brit? Do you see it?"

Barbara Jean paused to give Brittany time enough to answer, but knowing all along that her daughter needed every ounce of air for breathing, not for talking.

"It's life, sweetheart. It's hope. It's even money. Wanna know how much Mommie can get from just this one vial alone, huh? Wanna know?"

Brittany moaned and fretted a bit, then went quiet but kept watching her mother. Microscopic beads of sweat dotted her forehead like tiny, crystal bumps. Her eyes held a lost and glazed look.

"Hundreds of dollars. It's that special, sweetheart. Maybe a good thousand right here."

She sat on the side of Brittany's bed, careful not to sit on the girl's small limbs.

"I know you don't wanna hear about us one day leaving this place. I know. But when we leave California, we'll be needing some money to be leaving out in style. Lots and lots of money. Won't be long from now either. Just you and me."

Looking sad, the child silently watched her mother's expression.

"You be still now." Removing the vial's rubber stopper, Barbara Jean lifted up Brittany's tee-shirt and aimed a few dime sized drops of the warm, crimson liquid onto the child's tiny chest, then used her bare hand to rub it in; her hand worked in a slow, methodic rhythm. Mesmerized, the rich smell of warm copper reached her nose. She never grew tired of it, the sometimes intoxicating sweet metallic aroma of life. The mere smell of it gave her purpose and another chance to dream. The tips of her fingers where they pressed lightly on her daughter's chest felt oddly tingly, like low currents of electricity sparking and skipping through each tiny skin cell. She'd felt that same feeling before when she'd massaged the priceless fluid into Brit's chest for the very first time, just like she was massaging in some store-bought menthol Vaporub. "Now," she hummed sweetly, "doesn't that feel good?"

Nodding her head, Brittany inhaled deeply, her small chest rising and falling like ocean waves.

"Now, let Mommie get you a warm towel to help that good stuff seep into those pores. Be right back."

In the small adjacent restroom, Barbara Jean turned on the gold-plated faucet and stood over the rose pink porcelain bowl, waiting for the water to warm up. Boy, oh boy, she thought, catching a quick glimpse of herself in the medicine cabinet mirror. Her own face looked slightly puffy and dark circles were beginning to form under her eyes. Too many nights had been spent staying up and trying to think of what to do about Lovell.

What to do, what to do. It had nothing to do with morals, but everything to do with chance. Morals were long covered by the blanket of chance and opportunity. Barbara couldn't get the main questions out of her mind. They kept running through her head like a computerized sign: Was it really so wrong to take one of a man's kidneys, sell it, and send him on his way just to finance her own new life? Was it? Heck, it wasn't like the man couldn't live with one kidney. Or should she keep Lovell around to ensure a steady flow of money to be made off the liquid gold cruising freely through his very veins?

Keeping Lovell around would lend her more time to hope for the best, that eventually he would fall deeply in love with her and need her the way all growing plants needed the embrace of the earth and the warm caress of the sun. He could grow to love her with time. Sure he could.

"Aren't I lovable?" She smiled at her reflection. It sure was funny how life turned out sometimes. When opportunity knocked, you just had to be brave enough to open the door or you might miss it. She had to remind herself that in a normal span of life, without years of college behind her, where on earth would a woman like herself get her hands on a large lump sum of money at one time? "Where?" she asked herself. The State lottery, perhaps? Some inheritance left by a long lost relative? A major law suit of some type?

"No way," she shook her head. Barbara Jean knew beyond a shadow of doubt that it was simply unachievable. The sudden acquisition of a large lump sum of money was something that could never be obtained from working day in and day out for somebody else. Lovell was the only answer to all her prayers. The man didn't know it, but he was really turning out to be "Mr. Opportunity" knocking right at her door. A door that she was ready to open.

Barbara Jean pulled out a side drawer of the vanity, reached into its depths and lifted out her brand new flip cellular phone. It was a fancy little gadget with a slew of features and something that she had never imagined that she could afford. Punching in the numbers, she waited for the familiar voice to answer, which it did after three rings. Without proper salutation, "It's me," she breathed into the line. "Got some more of what you want. Red and fresh out. I can deliver tonight. No check like last time. I need cash."

She studied her newly manicured nails as she listened. The dark pink of 'Cherries In The Snow' was one of her favorites. There had been a time when she had had to wait for her money to be right before splurging on manicures and pedicures, but not lately. The polish was so brilliant with gloss, so fresh and shiny, that she could almost see a tiny reflection of her smiling face, poised and pleased in each nail.

"Oh yeah. About that other thing we discussed," she said clearly into her phone. "I've changed my mind. We can do it. You get a set up and bring it here, and I'll make sure you have a sterilized environment. Don't worry 'bout a thing. I know exactly what to do by now. Oh, that'll be cash money up front. Let's say, uhmm. . .two weeks from today?" She paused and nodded her head. "Two weeks it is. We can do this. I know we can."

One hundred and fifty thousand dollars! Yes! She did a little hop and a half spin while standing. Special or not, who would have ever thought it? That someone would be willing to spend big money for one measly body part? Barbara Jean punched off her phone, folded it, and placed it back in the drawer, thinking of all the things she could do with that kind of money. Things like quit her job at the hospital and move away, or buy a brand new car—cash up front. She could drive away to her new life. Maybe she could move to Florida or Washington DC—or anywhere just to start all over. Just me and Brittany.

Besides, she thought with an air of defiance. What was here to keep her in California where her life held only the smoldering embers of what could have been passion? Instead, her life revolved around going to work, coming home, trying hard to stay in Nylah's good graces, and seeing after their mother. And nothing more.

Her mother. She took her hands and massaged her temples at the thought of her mother. That was another thing.

Barbara Jean knew with all her heart that she held a love for her mother that was as deep as any daughter's love could go. But the truth was, her mother had a right to do what she wanted with her own life: straighten herself up, or continue to wallow in the murk of substance abuse. How could she possibly throw a life preserver to a drowning woman who didn't want to be saved? Could she herself split the waters of the great sea? No. Could she tell the stars in the sky to stop shining at night? No. Whatever the case, she decided firmly, she couldn't see giving her whole life to what she had now, which wasn't much. And now that sister Nylah was moving out, the daily monitoring of her mother would surely fall entirely on her. No way!

"I don't think so. This sistah got her own plans."

The bold reflection in the mirror stared back.

Steam was coming from the running water collecting in the sink. Swiftly, Barbara Jean cut on some cold water and adjusted the temperature before taking a thick black handtowel from the bottom of the cabinet and drenching it. The heat had to be just right, not too hot for Brittany's skin. After wringing out the excess water, she brought the hot towel over to Brittany and sat back on the bed.

"Here, sweetie. Here's Mommie."

She peered down at her ailing child and smiled. Was it so wrong to want all the good things in life? A nice, new car; a new house and nice clothes for me and Brittany. How could it be so wrong?

"See, baby, Mommie's back and it didn't take too long."

She smoothed back the soft wisps of Brittany's hair. The golden, downy strands along her edges never seemed to act right without a dab of Murray's and a good brushing. All the while, she kept listening to the flow of her child's breathing. Already the girl looked as if she was beginning to feel better. She could see mischief gathering like a welcomed summer breeze in Brittany's eyes.

"Mommie loves you so much. I'd do anything if I thought it could make you better."

"Can I have some ice cream, Mommie?"

"Sure, baby. Right after we do this, okay?"

"Okay."

Gently, Barbara Jean placed the heated towel down on Brittany's small, heaving chest and smiled with a deep-rooted glow that could only come from a mother's love. Not a gasp nor a wheeze to be heard. Amazing, she thought, as she listened to each perfect breath her child took in as smooth and free as a clear stream.

"Mr. Lovell, you're simply amazing."

Chapter Twenty-Two

"Now, what else can I do?"

Nylah must have asked herself that same question three times that day as she folded and unfolded the edges of her newly purchased TV guide. Even with the television on, the sheer loneliness of her new place felt like it wanted to engulf her.

It was Wednesday, the middle of the week, and she'd taken some vacation time to finish up a few loose ends for her new apartment. Not that there were a lot of loose ends to take care of with no real furniture around, but with so much free time on her hands, she didn't know what to do with herself. The moving of her clothes and a few smaller items was done. All the cleaning was done. All the brooding and stewing over whether Lovell was going to leave her mother's house or not was done. Finished.

No more Barbara, and no more Lovell. "The man can live at mama's forever if he wants to." She felt silly talking to herself, but the truth of it was that with so much free time, she was bored. She'd been in her new place two weeks after the incident with Lovell in the bathroom, and the availability of the apartment couldn't have come at a better time. With her mother constantly moody around the house and Barbara Jean not talking to her, it was obvious that it was time to leave, and her own space was just what she needed.

The first two nights had been the hardest. Sleeping in an unfamiliar place had the equivalence of taking up roots and moving to a foreign country all by herself. Nylah knew that it had to be mostly her imagination, but the walls in her new apartment made strange and funny sounds in the middle of the night. And the floor, even with the ugly carpet strategically covered up with new throw rugs, creaked without being walked on. Sleep was a stranger. It took her forever to fall asleep, and those nights seemed to stretch on forever like a highway leading to nowhere.

Trying to avoid any further confrontations with Barbara Jean, she'd made it a point of staying away from her mother's house entirely, which amounted to taking only her clothes and a small television set with her. Working it out in her head, she planned to wait until the bad feelings settled down with her sister. After that, she'd see about having the rest of her things moved over, and maybe even plan a few family get togethers at her place. As painful as it was to think about, it didn't seem possible that her family could ever be close again the way a real family should be, especially she and Barbara Jean. That much she would truly miss. But she wasn't angry with her sister and found herself looking forward to the day that they could sit down and talk things out like two level headed and mature females. At least she was willing to try.

Nylah missed so much that it was hard to pinpoint what she missed the most. She missed sleeping in her own bed with her own familiar scent pressed deep into the woven fabric of bed linen; she missed the deep purple satin comforter set she'd bought on sale at Strouds. She missed her large, fluffy down-filled pillows that had cost a small fortune when she really couldn't afford it. But darn it! She had deserved it. She missed all of her trinkets and small items that had been left behind until she could figure out how to go about moving everything at one time without paying another small fortune.

For the time being, it was back to basics, especially since the furniture place where she'd found the perfect dinette set, sofa, and love seat two days earlier couldn't be scheduled for delivery for another two days. Stuck on being picky, she had scouted around in one furniture store after another for days looking for the right furniture that would catch her fancy.

Nylah had had to settle for her television set, her black cordless phone with her new number that no one knew, her new cookware set, and plenty of dishes, cups and utensils. Just enough items to exist in minimum comfort, but her sleeping accommodations still left much to be desired.

Browsing around in Montgomery Wards one day, she'd found the cutest thing for her apartment—a black cloth-covered flip chair. Somebody's clever, useful idea of a three-piece attached chair that flipped down into a foam bed. With the right pillows and blankets, it wasn't too bad to sleep on, but still she missed her own bed terribly. She missed her little niece, Brittany, and most of all her mother. Missing her mother surprised her the most, as if she had been tethered for too long and finally set free against her will.

Two weeks of not calling to even talk to her mother, just to check on things was like a slow-burning torture. True enough, the woman was loud, ungrateful, and cantankerous most of the time, but God, she still missed her.

Nylah kept telling herself over and over again that her mother would be just fine without her living at the house. And she believed it to a certain degree. But somehow, that little nagging voice hiding somewhere inside of her kept trying to make her think otherwise. Would Lovell really keep a good eye on her? Would Barbara Jean really make sure that bills got paid on time? What if Mama Jo ran off somewhere and no one misses her for days or weeks or even cared. What if this and what if that. Several times she'd thought about calling the house, just to check on things, but didn't want to give into it. 'Darn it!'

"I have to be strong. That's all, be strong."

She hated herself for not having more control over her feelings. She wouldn't give in so soon. Didn't the people at her mother's house see how much she missed not being at her true home? Maybe later, she told herself, she'd break down and make that call, and perhaps shoot the breeze a little with her mother. Maybe with her finally out of the way, Barbara Jean and Lovell could get their relationship started, and who knows, maybe even marriage was in the plan. It still wasn't too late for something good to come out of the whole situation.

Kicked back in her pink cotton shorts and matching tee shirt, Nylah flung the TV guide aside and let her mind roam free as she lifted her cold glass of lemonade that rested on a stack of books she'd found at a local library and took a sip. The stacked books made an excellent substitute for a compact coffee table. Amazing, she mused, what one can do with so very little. The thick aroma of food was in the air making her hungry. She had a whole chicken boiling on the stove and after a quick look at her watch decided it was time to get up and check on it.

It was a little after seven in the evening. The sun's heat was slowly slipping away like fog, and she was feeling lazy from lying around and doing nothing. While skinning the chicken she was planning to cut into pieces to make into a nice big salad, she entertained the thought of giving Lovell a quick call to see if he could possibly help her move the rest of her things from her mother's house by the weekend. She kept thinking about asking him, but then at the same time, felt a little leery about the idea of letting him know where she'd moved. All she needed was for him to come sniffing around her new place and trying to lure her into another passionate encounter. She couldn't afford to allow that to happen. What had happened between them, as far as she was concerned, was some kind of freakish weakness of nature—a break in the dam. Something that was never meant to be. Nylah didn't know how Lovell felt about it, but to her the one night of passion was nothing more than two people caught up in the rapture of pure human magnetism. Nothing more. Nothing less.

Strangely enough, when she thought of Lovell, she couldn't help but feel a warmness like liquid sunshine pour from her head all the way down to her toes. And a smile, though a tiny one, did find its way to her lips. Nylah pondered if the beginning of true love felt that way, or just the aftermath of good loving? A lot of folks made the mistake of confusing the two. Whatever the case was, she wouldn't tell Lovell where she lived. Absolutely not. She wasn't ready to reveal her location yet. She thought with an air of cockiness, if I let the man know where I live, wouldn't I be setting myself up for him? She could just imagine him popping up at her place any time he darn well felt like it.

No, she shook her head. Heck no. She would go pick up her own things. Even if it meant bringing her things over a little at a time or hiring a moving company. Anyway, just getting used to her own space, it was way too soon to let anyone know where she resided. She'd just have to get used to the loneliness and learn to bask in her own privacy.

After lying around for another fifteen minutes, Nylah got up to see about her chicken again. In her kitchen, she took up a small paring knife and pierced the skinless meat in various places before placing the clear top back on the large pot and turning the fire off below. Nagging thoughts of her mother crept back into her mind. By now she figured Barbara Jean should have taken Brittany to the baby-sitter, and should be on her way to work, which would be the perfect time for her to call and check on her mother. Two weeks of not knowing if she was okay or not was eating her up.

Going to the phone, Nylah picked up the receiver and dialed the same seven digits that had been her mother's phone number since she was a small child, and Lord, she mused, that was ages ago. She chuckled at the thought of a few years back when a prank caller wouldn't stop calling the house and breathing loud and heavy over the line, and how she had tried desperately to get her mother to change her phone number, but no such luck.

"It's the same number your father used to call me at," her mother had insisted each time the subject had come up. "No sense changing it now that he's dead." The reason for her mother's stern refusal seemed even more foolish now, as if the dead could actually call up the living. But the same number remained. Nylah allowed it to ring four times before starting to agonize over what was taking her mother or Lovell so long to answer. Six rings, seven, then eight.

"What in the world. . ."

Agitated, she hung up and went back to her chicken, removing the still hot meat from its broth and using a fork to pull the tender and steamy pieces easily apart, but she couldn't concentrate, thinking about her mother. She wondered if everything was okay at the house. What if her mother had run off and Lovell was out somewhere trying to find her? How would he know where to look?

"Darn it!" she yelled.

What was the point of having her own place if she couldn't stop worrying about her mother's welfare from across town? There was no point in worrying about Brittany because she had Barbara Jean. Nylah knew beyond a doubt that her sister would fight a demon from the far corners of Hell itself before she let anything happen to Brittany. And there was no point worrying about Lovell; he, too, had Barbara Jean, the mother of all mothers. But who would really be there for her mother?

"Shoots!" and then, "Later for this."

Almost flinging steaming chicken chunks back into the pot, Nylah slammed the top back on it and made sure that the fire was off underneath. Zipping into the bedroom, she got her keys and purse from the closet. Just to make sure, she tried her mother's number again before she left out. Still no answer. Nylah didn't know what it was, but something just didn't feel right. It wasn't like her mother at all not to answer her phone, and the likelihood of her being off somewhere again with Barbara Jean was remote.

Though her sister had done her best to convince her mother that all was forgiven with the stolen money and the matter of losing Lovell's car, Nylah didn't believe it one bit. She knew Barbara like the back of her own hand. Her sister was good at smiling and pretending that all was fine and dandy, but Nylah knew better. A lot of things could be said about her sister, but being one to forgive and forget wasn't one of them.

From the Long Beach freeway, it took all of twenty-five minutes to get to her mother's house. Nylah pulled into the driveway right behind the shiny blue 1989 Jetta that Barbara Jean had given Lovell as a replacement for his Cadillac. What a joke that was. A big difference size-wise, but having some wheels had to be better than having no wheels at all. Barbara Jean's car and a fairly new white Chevy panel van she'd never seen before were also parked in the driveway. Turning her engine off, Nylah got out and quietly closed her car door.

The front of the house was dark except for a porch light. How odd. Usually the light from her mother's bedroom window, which was the closest room to the front of the house, could always be spotted from the driveway.

At the front door she used her key, which slid easily into the lock but didn't turn the tumblers. "Well I'll be . . ."

Somebody had changed the front door lock. The back door. Refusing to be outdone, Nylah hurried around to the side gate and quietly let herself in. The night air felt good along her sleeveless skin. The sound of barking dogs in the distance made her stop and listen hard before continuing up the few steps to the rear door. She stuck her key in the lock and turned it. Praise the Lord, it clicked. Her key worked fine. Who else but Barbara Jean would have thought to have the front door lock changed so soon on her? Too bad she'd forgotten that the same key was cut to open both the front and the rear door.

Inside, the smell of the place was the first thing she noticed. It was nothing near to the familiar smells of her mother's house that she was so used to. Standing up straight, she inhaled a good whiff and detected a smell like Lysol and some other kind of disinfectant. Nylah knew that smell too well. It was a smell very much like the one she experienced every day on her job.

She moved silently through the kitchen's darkness, careful not to bump into anything or cause anything to fall and make a racket. The house was so quiet, like a mausoleum—a quietness that made the fine hairs on the back of her neck bristle. No television voices filtered through the house; no sounds of music from Lovell's bedside radio escaped into the hallways. Now that was strange. Did a night ever pass by without that man listening to some mellow music?

She moved stealthily through the hallway. All doors leading into the bedrooms were closed, not a sound. A strange feeling was taking root somewhere in the pit of her stomach, a churning feeling. Nylah thought that the sensation had to be similar to what a cat might feel as it crept up on its prey.

Where was all the life in this house? The sight of Barbara Jean's car out front was a good indication that she hadn't gone to work. And on such occasions, she always kept Brittany with her. But where was her young niece who should be playing house somewhere with her slew of artificial babies? Where was her mother that should be somewhere in the house watching her favorite television program? And Lovell, where was he? Wasn't he supposed to be the care giver? The watcher?

Words screamed in her head. It's too darn quiet!

The thought of calling out for her mother crossed her mind but was soon ruled out by her better judgment. Now a new fear leaped into her mind: what if she had stumbled in on a home invasion robbery in progress? It wasn't a secret that the neighborhood was being overtaken by the likes of thugs and gang bangers who didn't give a hoot about a woman being too old or a child being too young to rob or kill. What if her mother and Lovell were tied up and hurt somewhere looking down the barrel of a gun? What if. . .

She could hear the loud wail of an ambulance from a distance. Nylah stopped and placed her hand over her heart. She could almost hear each beat echo in her head, and if the organ beat any faster, she'd be the one needing the paramedics. She slowed her breathing trying to calm herself.

"Girl, you have been watching way too many late night movies," she whispered to herself. "Get a grip."

As Nylah slowly made her way to her mother's room, she couldn't resist the urge to take a small peek into Lovell's room to see if he was sleeping. She halted at the closed door and thought, should I knock? She still felt a simmering resentment over Lovell intruding on her bath a couple of weeks back, barging in on her like he didn't have the common sense he was born with. The heck with knocking. Seizing the doorknob, she swung up into the room.

"Oh my God, No!"

"Nylah! Don't come any closer!" Barbara Jean's voice was loud and muffled "You'll contaminate the area. Just stay where you are."

"Oh no. . ."

Nylah lost her breath for a good ten seconds at the sight before her. The room looked like a hospital surgical room. A newly purchased air-conditioning unit propped in the window and covered with gauze, droned on low key to keep the room cold. Barbara Jean and some other female were decked out in surgical blues, complete with sterilized gloves and surgical masks.

The other female had the kind of large, sneaky-looking blue eyes that a person didn't forget too easily. Nylah didn't know her name but recognized her as one of the hospital's new, white female interns from urology. She was sure of it. The woman had been at Park One Memorial a good three months and had a bad reputation of being loud and obnoxious. And how in the world did Barbara Jean get hooked up with the likes of her? The whole scenario was giving Nylah the creeps. She could actually feel the fine hairs running up her back standing up straight like stiff, prickly needles. When she finally found her voice, she had to restrain herself from screaming.

"Barbara, what the hell's going on here?"

The woman jumped in with, "She can't be here." Her eyes shifted from one side to the other, then looked askance at Barbara Jean while her steady hand was still holding a surgical scalpel about to lengthen the one inch incision to Lovell's back. "Just get her outta here!"

"Nylah, just leave!" Sounding like she was giving an order to Brittany. Barbara Jean added in a softer tone, "You'll contaminate the area. Leave now!"

Disbelief was still playing along her face. Nylah stood there numb and stiff, feeling like some innocent intruder catching perpetrators red handed in stealing, even worse, a possible murder. Her timing was incredible. Horrified, she moved in closer for a better look.

"I'm not leaving 'til I find out what's going on here."

"What does it look like, Nylah?" Barbara Jean sneered, snatching the mask down from her face. "You have no business being here. You don't live here anymore, so just go."

The more her sister talked, the more Nylah saw red. "Like hell I will! You have obviously lost your mind." She could see the IV drip that Lovell was hooked up to, and a monitor. Nylah pointed over at the instruments. This is too much! "I don't believe you could do something like this!"

"Believe it," Barbara Jean hissed and looked at her accomplice, who didn't seem to know if they should wait, proceed, or call the whole thing off.

Her accomplice didn't look too pleased. "Thought you said that she wouldn't be here? Looks like we have a problem."

"Darn right you have a problem!" Nylah shouted back. She couldn't recall ever being so upset, and she wasn't backing off. Not this time.

Barbara Jean frowned and snapped, "She's not suppose to be here, and she's leaving."

"That's what you think." Nylah moved over, looked at the heart monitor and then looked down at Lovell. Poor guy. The man was lying face down on the bed, which had been raised higher with two more mattresses piled on. Lovell was out cold with his eyes taped shut. Hospital draping lay everywhere. His intended surgical spot had been swabbed and was oozing a tiny stream of blood where the scalpel had started before her interruption.

"Oh my God, his kidney! You were going to take his kidney? And then what? Just sew the man back up and drive 'im somewhere and toss him out the car like spoiled meat?"

"Nylah, just leave. This doesn't concern you."

"Oh, it concerns me alright."

"It does not!" Barbara Jean shouted across the room at her. "Get out now!"

"How could you stoop so low, Barb?"

The accomplice shook her covered head. "I can't handle this." She pulled off her own mask with an air of the whole thing being off. "I don't think we can do this now."

"You darn right you can't," Nylah sneered boldly. She saw the woman's red face up close for the first time that night. High cheekbones, full lips, and skin dotted with pockmarks. It was a face that she would never forget. "And I want you out of my mother's house right now!"

"I don't think so," said Barbara Jean, daring Nylah with her eyes.

"No problem for me." Hastily, the woman began to wipe off and wrap up instruments with the careful ease of an artist putting away her precious tools.

"No! The only person leaving here is you, Nylah!"

Another thought assailed Nylah's senses. "Mama? Where's. . .where's mama?" Staring in Barbara Jean's face for an answer, she swirled and rushed from the room calling out for her mother. "Mama!"

Nylah knew that over the years her baby sister had talked her mother into a lot of foolish things that hadn't panned out the way they had thought it would. Some of those things had been good, and some not so good. Some had been only fool-ish, but a few others had been down right wrong. But no way, no way could she see her mother agreeing to something like this. Her mother loved Lovell like he was the son that she had never had.

"Try touching him while I'm outta the room," Nylah called back, "and I'll call the police and have you both arrest-ed!"

With her heart racing ahead of her, Nylah went to go check on her mother, leaving the two women bickering in quick, raspy whispers in the wake of her departure.

Her mother's security door was unlocked; the wooden door beyond that closed. She opened the door and found the room completely dark. She flipped on the light. Not only was her mother in the room, but Brittany was lying at the opposite end of the bed. With a shock, she saw that her mother's bedroom was neat and orderly for a change. A place for everything and everything in its place. Must be because Brittany's in here too, she figured.

Hurrying over and stooping, Nylah tried to wake her mother, shaking the woman furiously to no avail. A coffee mug with a trace of tea in the bottom was still in Mama Jo's hand. Another empty mug lay upside down on the carpet. Probably Brit's mug. Her mother and her niece had obviously been given something to make them sleep. She checked the condition of her mother's pupils and then her pulse.

Her mother's heart rate sounded okay. Nylah checked her young niece as well, detecting that her pulse was a little fast but not fast enough to be alarming. Nylah let out a sigh of relief, but still it made her mad as hell. Wonder what medication they used, she pondered, knowing whatever it had been, it had come from hospital supply, which was another illegal matter to add to the growing list.

"Imagine that." Brittany was knocked out cold. Now that was hard to believe, the fact that Barbara Jean had given her own precious child something to make her slip into a deep sleep. Will wonders ever cease? she mused. Even when the child had severe attacks of asthma, her sister constantly refused to give man-made drugs to the child.

"Foolish woman."

Nylah stood up straight and assessed the situation. She had to keep a straight head, but she had three people drugged to worry about; she had a complete stranger, an expert in the medical field, in her mother's house ready to cut a man open and take his organ, and a crazy sister that was probably furious enough with her to do heavens knows what. Now what? Should she call the police first or try to manually put Barbara Jean and her companion out of her mother's house? Whatever it was, she had to do something quick.

"Oh my God! Oh my God, no...!"

Screaming to the top of her voice, Nylah willed panic into her voice and ran like the devil himself was in hot pursuit behind her. She ran back to the room she'd left the two women bickering with a frantic look on her face.

"Something's wrong with Brit! I think she's stopped breathing!"

A disgusted Barbara Jean and her doctor friend were in the process of cleaning up and clearing away instruments and equipment for departure. At Nylah's words, Barbara Jean jerked up in alarm. "What?!"

"Call 911 now, dammit!"

"What about Brit?!" Barbara Jean flung a surgical instrument aside and raced from the room with her doctor friend right behind her. "Brittany!"

"Barb, I couldn't feel her pulse! Oh my God!"

The two women sprinted past Nylah like a strong wind, pinning Nylah tight against the doorframe in their exit. Nylah felt bad for lying about her niece's condition as she raced behind them and stood at the doorway. But it was the only thing that she could think of to do.

"Brittany!" Barbara Jean screamed, panic trembling in her voice. "Oh no. . .God no!" Once in her mother's room, Barbara Jean plopped down on the edge of the bed, snatched her child up, and shook her, trying to rouse her. "Brittany!"

"Let me take a look at her," offered her doctor friend. Seeing her panic and absorbing the urgency of the moment, she tried to get Barbara Jean away from the child, which was almost impossible. "How much did you give her? Here, step back now and let me have a look."

"I. . .I can't think," Barbara stammered ". . .but I didn't give her much, I measured just like you told me to. . .I did what you told me!"

"How much?!" the woman screamed at her. "How

much?!"

"I can't remember. I knew I shouldn't have. . .I knew I shouldn't have. . .I knew. . .Brittany. . ."

Rocking and cradling Brittany to her bosom, Barbara Jean kept calling out the child's name softly, the two women, so caught up in the moment, were completely unaware that Nylah was locking the steel security door behind them.

Chapter Twenty-Three

The sweetly exotic mixture of nutmeg and cinnamon hung in the air like a thin, delicate cloud over Lovell's sleeping form. Cocooned in light sleep, even with his eyes closed, his nostrils stirred and flared to take in every bit of the tantalizing fragrance twirling in the air, sucking it in deeper until his lungs felt sweetened with the aroma and about to burst. Somehow the smell, like a sinuous twine, mixed and wrapped itself around the vision unfolding in his head. Visions of Nylah and him.

Running along the edge of the beach, they were two lone souls under a gray mist of sky. The music of lapping waves was crashing against a deserted shore. Nylah wore white. Some sort of long, shear free-flowing dress down to her ankles that were lightly coated with moist, white sand, and he wore dark blue nylon trunks. He was taking in her strong, brown legs pumping in the mid-evening breeze. The print of her full breasts straining at the tie-string bodice was visible as she ran towards him. Right into his waiting arms. He wrapped himself around her; her smell wafted up like rose petals and heady musk as he closed his eyes and pursed his hungry lips waiting for her lips to find his.

When he opened his eyes again, ready to feel all she had to offer, ready to accept her love, he was looking into the eyes of a crazed woman. Instead of Nylah, it was Barbara Jean enclosed in his arms. She held an empty vial up to his face, thrusting the oblong shaped glass at him. Her eyes more red than apples, and wild: beast-like eyes. Along each side of her mouth, a fine stream trickled down. The mouth opened; the words tumbling out awkwardly: "More blood, please. I need more."

Lovell woke with a start, his heart pumping way too fast inside his chest. Rubbing the top of his head, he lifted up on his elbow and scanned his immediate surroundings. Even with his vision slightly blurry, nothing looked familiar. That much he could tell. And he was lying close to the floor on some kind of thick pad or mattress covered with a burgundy satin sheet. A large, fluffy pillow was under his head. His head. His head felt water logged and too heavy for his body—just like it had felt that last day in the hospital. Only this place was no hospital. It was somebody's dwelling. Somebody's living space.

"Hello!" he called out. Thin and weak, it hardly seemed like his own voice.

Two warm blankets were piled on top of him. The room was large and empty. For the life of him, he didn't know where he was, but seeing Barbara Jean in his head that way, her mouth dripping blood, it had to a dream. A bad dream. But then there was something else. . .the smell of rich, buttery cinnamon that seemed so real, just like the sight of Nylah walking out from the kitchen area with a tall glass of something to drink in her hand. Her gait was so smooth and effortless that she could have been floating. Walking or floating, she was a vision; she looked so calm and peaceful. At least she was smiling at him. Her eyes and her lips.

Nylah came and stood over him for a few seconds, as if to give him enough time to fully acknowledge her presence. She was so beautiful to him—a Nubian princess at his side as she knelt down in her denim jump suit and balanced her body on folded legs.

"Here," she offered softly. "Drink this."

"What is it?"

"Juice, silly. What else?"

Momentarily he saw the glass she held out, and then he saw two glasses extending from two hands.

". . .oooh, whoa. . .my eyes. . ."

He pinched gently at the top of the bridge of his nose, lightly stretching the skin over his eyes to the center of his face.

". . .a little blurry."

"Probably from the anesthesia they gave you. Don't worry," she added   mildly. "It'll go away."

"Anesthesia? Who gave me anesthesia?"

Ignoring his query for the moment, Nylah looked concerned. "You'll be alright once we get some fluids back into you."

Lovell took the glass, silently grateful for something to sooth his parched throat. It felt like somebody had aimed a blow dryer down his throat and turned it on full blast. The sweet, cold juice really hit the spot. "Thanks."

"You're welcome."

"Where are we?"

"My place," Nylah quipped happily. "Well, sort of."

"Your place?" Lovell felt like a big gap of time was missing. He remembered bits and pieces of what had happened. He remembered how good Barbara Jean had been to him all that day. She had taken him shopping and bought him some new clothes and shoes, gave him some extra spending money, and promised to make a good dinner for him. He remembered some doctor friend of hers coming over that evening—some Caucasian woman from her job. But for the life of him, he couldn't think of the woman's name.

"Do you remember what happened?" Nylah noticed the

puzzled expression on his face.

"Yeah, I think so...at your mom's house. . ." He recalled how they had all sat around watching television, eating popcorn, and drinking the hot, spicy herbal tea and chatting about the simple life of childhood days. All of them: Barbara Jean, Mama Jo, and Barbara's friend from work. The almost attractive woman with the funny looking blue eyes reminded him of shifty people who couldn't be trusted. Even little Brittany had been drinking some of Barbara Jean's tea and trying to talk him into playing a game of cards with her. He remembered how nice it had been with everyone having a good time, sitting around sharing tidbits from their day, and telling short stories about life and growing up. It had felt so right, almost like being with a family of his own. He remembered that much. After that, his mind drew a complete blank.

"How long have I been here? How the heck did I get here?" He didn't remember driving or being driven over.

"This is your second day. You slept all day Thursday. As for getting you here...well," she grinned at him, "it wasn't easy. I didn't have any choice but to call my friend, Gail, to help get you here. She has a brother with a truck and he helped. Gail's not big on keeping secrets, but after I threatened to tell her husband about the little 'fling' she's having with Dr. Rimsey in Pediatrics, I think her lips are sealed for a while. You should be sore from being bumped and almost dropped twice."

"I feel weird...like I've been drugged or something."

"You have, but it's all over, Lovell."

"What?" Lovell looked at Nylah. His eyes seemed to ask the question before his mouth. "What's over? I'm not sure what you're..."

"The madness with Barbara Jean and what she was really trying to do to you."

His expression was blank as he rubbed the top of his head. "I'm not following you. The last thing I remember, we were all sitting around talking . . .drinking tea. Just chilling out and talking, you know. A few friends having a good time."

"And?"

"And that sister of yours. . ." He shook his head and instantly regretted it. The shaking only started a serious throbbing at the back of his skull. ". . .she can be down to the bone nice when she wants to."

"That's true. Be right back." Nylah got up and went into the kitchen, returning with a plate of fresh cinnamon rolls and thinly sliced cantaloupe lightly dusted with cinnamon. She loved fresh fruit. Her early morning trip to the market had provided a good assortment of bananas, nectarines, oranges, and melon. She sat the plate on a stack of books beside Lovell. While he ate, feeding himself slowly at first before devouring the offering like a man who'd been deprived of food for days, she contemplated how to tell him.

While Lovell stuffed his face, Nylah filled his ears with all the details of how Barbara Jean had created a sterilized set-up at her mother's house where she and her doctor friend had planned to take. . . It was hard to say the word, and the embarrassment of her own sister conspiring to do something so awful made it even harder to look into his eyes. But she had to tell him. She told all of it, no details left out of how she'd arrived at her mother's house just in time.

"Are you serious?"

"Guess you had a guardian angel watching over you. It's the only way I can explain me going over to mama's house Wednesday night. A guardian angel was looking out for you."

Lovell stopped his eating long enough to regard her with disbelief. "It's too unbelievable."

"You were probably given something in that tea to put you to sleep. For two people with the right connections to hospital drugs and equipment, it wouldn't be that hard to obtain the things they needed."

"One of my kidneys?"

"That's right."

"My kidney?" The words held an odd ring on his tongue. It seemed too bizarre a story to believe, even about Barbara. He had trusted his life to the woman, had held so much faith in her. "I can't believe that Barbara would do something like that."

"It's kinda spooky when I think about it. Something just wouldn't let me rest until I went to mama's house to check things out. Just a weird feeling I had."

"For real?" Lovell pushed the plate away. Suddenly, he had no desire for food. "Damn, and I trusted her. I really did." He went silent for a spell, reflecting on all the events unfolded to him. "But...if I was out cold, how'd you get me here?"

"Like I said, I didn't have a choice but to call for some help. So I called Gail, another nurse from work. Gail, her brother, and a friend helped carry you here. Believe me, it was the hardest thing to do to tell her about you being at mama's house, but I needed her help."

"Unbelievable. And I thought Barbara Jean was really a friend. . .someone. . ."

"Anyway," Nylah interjected slowly. "After we deposited you safely here at my place, I had to go back to give Barbara Jean the key to let herself outta mama's room. I left my car running outside, ran in and threw that key into the room, and ran out. Looks like that security door was still useful, after all. I hauled myself outta there so fast I was like a flash of light-ening." She laughed lightly at her own words. "You should have seen their faces. They were beyond mad."

"I really feel bad 'bout all of this," Lovell said, looking more serious despite her attempt to make light of the incident. "I'm the blame."

"It wasn't your fault."

"But everyone's okay, right?" Lovell asked. The food

had left a bland taste in his mouth, as tasteless as the details of what Barbara Jean had tried to do. He was still a bit confused. "What about your mother and Brit? Are they okay?"

"Everybody's fine," Nylah said in response. "But let's just say that little sister is a little pissed off right now. She and her doctor friend will have a hard time explaining about the money they no longer have in their possession."

"What money?"

"The money that would have been payment for the organ."

"So, let me get this straight. Are you saying your crazy sister was actually trying to kill me for money?"

"I doubt if she wanted to kill you," Nylah shook her head. "She was just trying to get her greedy hands on a large sum of money."

"But you can't live without kidneys, right?"

"Well," she chuckled and smiled at him, "you can live with one. People sell or give up a kidney to save somebody else's life all the time."

"Dang," Lovell said looking down at the carpet and then back up to Nylah. It was all so crazy, just the idea of it. "And that woman had me believing that she only wanted a little blood for some little girl named Amy."

Nylah raised a brow. "Amy? Who's that?"

"Amy. You know. . .the little girl at the hospital that has leukemia. Your sister claimed that I could give her a chance at a longer life by donating some blood."

"Well, I make it a point to know all the really sick kids at the hospital. And believe me, there's no such little girl named Amy with leukemia."

"But I donated blood."

"Yes, you probably did, but it probably went for Barbara Jean to get some money. That's what she was up to."

"Say what now? Man, I can't believe this."

"Trust me. You can believe it." Nylah clambered up from

her spot with the half-full plate and empty glass and went back into the kitchen. When she came back into the room, she had her purse strapped over her shoulder and stood looking down at him. More than anything she wanted to stay, but she knew that she couldn't. It was too risky, and still too dangerous. Dangerous for both, her and Lovell. Nylah knew too well that her sister could be ruthless when she wanted to be. "Just be glad it's all over."

"Now, wait a minute, woman. Where you going?" Wrapping a sheet around his nakedness, Lovell tucked and secured it like a white sarong. He struggled up, feeling slightly dizzy, freezing all movements for a few seconds until the dizziness went away, leaving him steady on his feet. It was like everybody was letting him down—every woman in the world. First that darn Rita, then Barbara Jean, and now. . .now Nylah, too. "Don't go."

"Lovell, I have to."

"But you saved me. That means I owe you my life."

She shook her head. "You owe me nothing. But I can't stay."

"Go where?" He asked. There had to be pleading in his eyes, but he didn't care anymore. He just didn't care.

"Home. I called back to check on Mama, and she and I had a long talk. I think she's finally ready to get well, but she needs my help. Barbara hasn't been around for a couple of days, and Mama's all alone. I have to go home, Lovell."

"I thought this was your home."

"It was, but I have to go back to Mama's house. I have to."

Lovell went over to her, pulled her closer into his warmth, and brushed his cheek against hers. Against each other their skin was like velvet. "Nylah, don't you see? This is perfect. Now we can be together."

"No, Lovell. We can't."

Strangely, she could feel a power radiating from just his

chest pressing against her breasts.

"Nylah, yes we can. I've missed you so much this past week that I thought I was going out of my mind with worry. I even called your job trying to get information of where you had moved to, but nobody would tell me anything. Something about anti-stalking laws. I even drove up to your job a few times and waited to see you coming or going. I've missed you so much. Haven't you missed me?" He wanted her to feel what he was feeling.

"I have thought about you. I can't lie about it." She nodded and gazed down at the carpet that was still as awful as the first time she'd seen it. She wouldn't be missing it, nor the odd little sounds the place made late at night. She sighed deeply. If only it all could have been different.

"If you care, you'll stay."

". . .I can't, Lovell."

"Sure you can. Just tell me what you want me to do, get a job? beg you? I'll do it, Nylah. Love should never make a person too proud. Let's give it a chance. Give us a chance." He pulled her chin up to meet her eyes. "I love you, and I know you feel something for me."

"No. I mean, yeah. I mean no. . .we can't." She felt so confused. This man that she had tried so hard not to like in the beginning, felt so affronted by his very existence, was now too deep inside of her. She couldn't deny it. She loved him too.

"Admit it, Nylah. You really do care about me." Lovell kissed the top of her head, his nostrils taking in the scent of her. She smelled so good, like cinnamon and honeysuckle. "You wouldn't have helped me if you didn't care."

"Yes I would have. It's what I've been trained to do. To help people."

"Nylah, that's not what I mean and you know it. I love you and you love me. Stop trying to deny your feelings."

Nylah felt like her heart was melting into small streams

and racing to the bottom of her feet. It was so hard to say what she really felt, how she, too, truly wished that it could all work out somehow. But she knew it couldn't. Lovell knew it as well. Even if they did give love a chance, it could never be right. Not as long as Barbara knew where to find him. All the love in the world couldn't change that. A single tear slid from her right eye.

"Nylah, tell me you care. I know you do." Gently he kissed her, his body feeling weak as vapors. He felt as if her mouth could draw in all of him. Spirit into spirit.

When Nylah broke her lips away from his, she thought her legs were about to give out. No man had ever made her feel this way before. None.

"Lovell, listen to me."

"Nylah, please. . .don't make me beg. . ."

"You have to listen to me."

"Okay. I'm listening."

"This is your place now. Yours. I got my few things in the car already. The lease on the place is paid up for an entire year. I took the money from Barbara Jean while she and her doctor friend were locked in mama's room. Quite a bit of money too. I doubt if they could report the money as being stolen without having to expose the whole sordid story of what they were planning to do." She paused to reflect a second or two. "In a way, I guess it gives true meaning to the phrase 'blood money'. Money that would have been made off of you. And it's still not too late to file a report with the police department. It's up to you."

"I couldn't do that, not to your mother. She's been so nice to me and all. I don't even care about the money, Nylah. Just us."

"Lovell..." She paused and examined her hands against his chest. They felt so cold and trembly. Nervousness always did that to her. "Sorry, but I couldn't get the car she bought you.

It's probably for the best. She would use it to track you down when you have it registered in your name. I left the rest of the money in the bathroom, in the vanity drawer. You should have some furniture coming in a day or so. Some real nice furniture because I happen to have good taste. And I already took some of the money to settle the bill on that. It's all yours and all paid for."

"Nylah, no. Why can't it be ours? Together."

"Because of my sister. That's why. Because of a lot of things that I can't go into right now." She paused and hung her head. "And maybe because of my mother too. I can think of a lotta reasons why. I know my sister, Lovell. She won't just give up and let it all go so easily. She can't know where you are. Ever. Don't you get it? She can never know."

"I don't see why we still can't be together. . ."

"Don't you see? Me coming back and forth here will only lead her back to you."

"Let her come. So what. And who says we have to live here in California? We can hit the road. Maybe head for the east coast, settle down in New York or someplace. Nylah, we can do it."

She shook her head. "No. I can't just leave mama like that. And my life and my job is here. I thought. . .I really thought I could leave everything behind by just moving a short distance away. I'm really all that my mother has. Don't you see it? Her life and mine are intertwined. I thought I could just leave and let her handle her own problems, but I can't, Lovell. I just can't."

Lovell tried to sound sympathetic. "But, when two people love each other, they make a way. Don't they?"

Nylah looked past him, then down at the floor. Why was he making it so complicated? She looked back into his trusting face. "Sometimes, Lovell, even love isn't enough."

"True enough, but it's a good start at trying, Nylah. . ."

"Lovell, just accept it."

"I can't. Not when I love you so much. Not when I'm ready to stop wasting my life away and settle down with one good woman. That's all it really takes. And you're that woman. I can feel it."

"Lovell, I love you too. That's why I'm doing this."

"You mean by running away from what could be us?"

"No. By giving you another chance at living your life without waiting for some woman to decide whether she'll give you a place to sleep and some food to eat for another day. You can't live your life through willing females forever."

"Woman, please. You got it all wrong."

"This is your new beginning. A good head start to a better life. You'd be a fool not to take it and make the most of it."

"Nylah, you're talking nonsense."

"Look at it this way. You have your own place to stay, money to live on until you find employment, and enough to buy yourself another car if you want."

"But I have to be alone? Is that how it goes?"

"Maybe for now, Lovell." She looked away.

"Can't we meet in a neutral place from time to time?"

"It's too risky. And another thing, Lovell," she paused and looked back into his eyes. "If I were you. . . this thing about your blood. . .well, I think I would keep that to myself."

"And why is that?"

"For the obvious reasons. You telling the wrong person could put your life in jeopardy. I wouldn't tell a soul, if I were you. Just to be on the safe side."

It felt like the last time she would be with him. He wrapped her in his arms again and kissed her hard on the lips.

Nylah tried to brace herself against his affection, but she could feel herself growing weaker as she let her purse slip from her shoulder onto the floor. She kissed him back with the same eagerness, the same intensity. With his moist tongue sliding against hers, she could taste traces of sweet cinnamon.

"One more night, then. That's all I ask is one more night."

"Lovell, no. . .we can't. . .," her lips were saying between warm kisses. Her body was saying something entirely different as she allowed him to pull her over and down to the satin-covered pad on the floor. She didn't resist as he slowly peeled off her clothes. Nylah didn't know what it was about him, but his kisses were like none she had ever experienced. Deliciously disturbing. Almost like some hypnotic drug seeping from his tongue into hers. She needed to stop him before things got too far out of hand, but she felt so helpless. Instead, she released him, allowing him to slowly undress her. Her eyes locked into his. Mesmerized.

Nylah felt like they were two souls shipwrecked on a deserted island. He was so tender the way he touched her, as tender as touching a newborn baby. His lips were as light as sunshine along her waiting breasts and stomach.

Nylah closed her eyes and allowed the warm glow to roll over her as he kissed softly every inch of her body. His lips felt so incredibly wonderful along her skin. She couldn't help feeling that what she was experiencing was so unique—that she would never again feel this way with another man as long as she lived. She had never purred like a satisfied kitten, but that soft, mellow sound was rising up like sweet mist from some secret place inside of her. Purring.

She went to heaven all over again the moment he entered her. Each gentle stroke he slowly maneuvered was the waves in the ocean, rocking back and forth to the rhythm of her body. For the rest of the day and through the night, she allowed herself to be loved and pleasured, taking time out to eat a little something, shower, and freshen up to start a new beginning.

She had grown to love him, and she couldn't deny it even if she wanted to. Nylah knew that it was a night that she would never forget as long as she lived. But at the same time, she knew it had to end.

By the next morning she was lying in his arms feeling safe, but knowing that the feeling couldn't last long. Early morning sunlight was already doing its best to cheer up the room.

"Lovell, I really have to go. I have a lot of things to do at the house, and Mama has finally agreed to go into a center for professional help. I told her over the phone that I would take her down to see and get a feel for the place before she checks in. I know she's ready this time. No more being locked behind a door. It might be a little hard at first, but things will be different."

"That's good to hear," Lovell replied, but he sure didn't feel it.

"I guess you coming across our paths hasn't been completely hopeless."

"And you and Barbara Jean?" He released her slightly, giving her room to breathe and talk freely.

Nylah took a few seconds to think about his inquiry. She had no clear answer. She could only to tell him that time would heal things between her and her younger sister. "I called the house yesterday to check on Mama and she sounded pretty good. Still nagging and complaining. It's nothing new. Sisters fight and sisters make up. But right now, she's not speaking to me she says. Not until I bring the money back. I'm sticking to the story that I gave the money to you for all the trouble you've been through. I could care less if she speaks to me after what she tried to do. Wrong is wrong. Speaking or not, we've gone through this before. Mama asked about you tho'. Says she wants you to come back if you feel like it. Even Brit got on the phone and asked about you."

"Really? My little buddy." He gave her a skeptical look. "I'll miss everybody too, even that crazy sister of yours. It's weird."

"Goodness. It's only been a couple of days, Lovell. You'll get over it. Mama wanted to know where I was hiding you out, but I kept to the same story even with her. I want her to believe that you took the money and left. Just booked up and headed out of town."

"Looks like everybody got what they wanted or deserved 'cept me."

"Maybe you shouldn't look at it like that."

"Oh, I see. But you know it's true, Nylah. You could stay if you really wanted to." He watched her struggle up from the floor and take up her clothes.

"If you know that, then you really don't know me after all."

❦ ❦

After showering and dressing, Nylah came back into the living room where Lovell was still sprawled along the floor looking up at the ceiling. She picked up her purse and looked at him. His face held a look of misery, but Nylah knew that there was nothing that she could really do about it. Why couldn't he understand that she didn't have a choice?

"Well," Nylah said with mock courage, forcing a brave smile as she headed toward the door. "Guess I better get going."

At first it didn't seem like he was going to even get up to kiss her goodbye, but finally, Lovell did pull himself up from the floor with a blanket around him and walked over to where she stood at the door. Nylah opened it.

"I wish you would change your mind. I really do." Lovell pulled her to him and lightly kissed her forehead. "I can't imagine not having you in my life now."

Standing in the sunlight that streamed through the open door, Nylah held her breath, momentarily caught up in his embrace. She managed to pull away to allow air to escape from her lungs. Warmth radiated clean through her and teased at her soul. Pulling away, Lovell's hand grazed one of her breasts and she almost whimpered.

She nodded, turning her face away from him. "Lovell, don't."

"No, you listen to me. This is the last time I'll say it, and you know it's true. When two people love one another, they make a way. It might not be the right way, or it might not be the easy way, but they do the best they can." He turned her face to his, gently. His eyes bored into hers in an effort to see the truth. "If you really love me, Nylah, you'll stay. And I promise that together we'll get through it. I'll deal with your sister or your mother. Whatever it takes. Just give us a chance is all I ask."

"Lovell. . ." She was about to say something in protest, but he placed a single finger to her lips.

"Now look into my eyes and tell me that you don't need me, Nylah, because I need you. And I'm not talking just to shack up with. What little I do have, I want to share it with you. I want you to be my wife."

She couldn't say a word at first. "Your wife?" A small sigh escaped her as tears threatened her eyes. No, she couldn't. Not now. But before she could think of something suitable to say he pulled her to him and pressed his lips to hers again to remind her that she couldn't possibly say no.

"And I promise that I will do everything in my power to be the best husband you could ever dream of. I'll pamper you like a queen. I'll get two jobs if that's what it takes."

Words were snagged in her throat. Her mind was foggy.

Well?" he prompt her, pulling away for her reply.

". . .well," said Nylah, her head slowly clearing. "I guess I have to say. . ."

He kissed her again, long and hard before pulling away

again. "Nylah Richardson, will you please do me the honor of becoming my wife?"

There was a sparkle in Nylah's eyes as bright as the one in her heart as she took one deep breath and exhaled. "Yes," she said, almost breathless. "And I do mean yes."

INDIGO ORDER FORM

Mail to:
Genesis Press, Inc.
315 3rd AVE N.
Columbus, MS 39701

Visit our website for latest
releases and other information
http://www.genesis-press.com

Name_____

Address_____

City/State _____Zip_____

Telephone_____

Qty	Author	Title	Price	Total
	Beverly Clark	A Love to Cherish	$15.95	
	Kayla Perrin	Again My Love	$10.95	
	Robin Hampton	Breeze	$10.95	
	Rochelle Alers	Careless Whispers	$ 8.95	
	Crystal Wilson Harris	Dark Embrace	$ 8.95	
	Chinelu Moore	Dark Storm Rising	$10.95	
	Rochelle Alers	Gentle Yearning	$10.95	
	Sinclair LeBeau	Glory of Love	$10.95	
	Donna Hill	Indiscretions	$ 8.95	
	Donna Hill	Interlude	$ 8.95	
	Mildred E. Riley	Love Always	$10.95	
	Gloria Greene	Love Unveiled	$10.95	
	Charlene A. Berry	Love's Deceptions	$10.95	
	Vicki Andrews	Midnight Peril	$10.95	
	Gwynne Forster	Naked Soul	$15.95	
	Mildred E. Riley	No Regrets	$15.95	
	Gay G. Gunn	Nowhere to Run	$10.95	
	T.T. Henderson	Passion	$10.95	
	Beverly Clark	Price of Love	$ 8.95	
	Gay G. Gunn	Pride and Joi	$15.95	
	Donna Hill	Quiet Storm	$10.95	
	Donna Hill	Rooms of the Heart	$ 8.95	
	Monica White	Shades of Desire	$ 8.95	
	Sinclair LeBeau	Somebody's Someone	$ 8.95	
	Mildred Y. Thomas	Truly Inseparable	$15.95	
	LaFlorya Gauthier	Whispers in the Sands	$10.95	
	Beverly Clark	Yesterday is Gone	$10.85	

Use this order form or call 1-888-INDIGO1-1 (1-888-463-4461)	Total for books _____ Shipping and Handling ($3 first book, $1 each additional book) Total Amount Enclosed _____ MS Residents add 7% sales tax